The Hummingbird Wizard

Meredith Blevins

FORGE®

A Tom Doherty Associates Book
New York

This is a work of fiction. All the characters and events portrayed in this book are either products of the author's imagination or are used fictitiously.

THE HUMMINGBIRD WIZARD

Copyright © 2003 by Marcia Meredith Blevins

Map by James Sinclair

A Tor Book
Published by Tom Doherty Associates, LLC
175 Fifth Avenue
New York, NY 10010

www.tor.com

Tor® is a registered trademark of Tom Doherty Associates, LLC.

ISBN 0-765-34683-4
EAN 976-0765-34683-4
Library of Congress Catalog Card Number: 2003046849

First edition: September 2003
First mass market edition: October 2004

Printed in the United States of America

0 9 8 7 6 5 4 3 2 1

Praise for *The Hummingbird Wizard*

"Rife with wonderful people who never say anything dull. . . . This atypical mystery deserves plenty of readers who like a little humor and romance mixed in with their murders."
—*Rocky Mountain News*

"A terrific debut mystery . . . a warm, witty novel of life, love, death and family that will stick with the reader long after they story ends." —*The Denver Post*

"In *The Hummingbird Wizard*, Meredith Blevins covers new literary ground . . . pulling it off with flair and grace and humor."
—Jonathan Kellerman

"Damn fine book! A terrific read of a truly intriguing, finely crafted mystery. With *The Hummingbird Wizard*, Meredith Blevins explores new territory in a new dimension other authors have feared to go." —Clive Cussler

"Meredith Blevins has a sorcerer's command of language, an ear for electric dialogue, and the economy of style that usually comes after many years of honing in the marketplace. From the opening line 'Jerry and I grew up before smog was invented.' to the vivid impressionism of her descriptions 'Autumn vineyards rolled up the hills in deep red lines behind my house,' she has run up the banner of a new master in the making."
—Loren D. Estleman, multiple Spur and Edgar Award winning author of *Retro*

"I had a splendid time with the unforgettable Szabos—particularly the unsinkable Madame Mina and the wizard himself, one of the sexiest heroes I've come across in a long while."
—Julie Smith, Edgar Award winning author of the Skip Langdon and Talba Wallis Series.

"Meredith Blevins has a great sense of humor and a fresh, new voice. Fun characters abound and the Gypsy background is wonderful."—Barbara D'Amato, Mary Higgins Clark Award— winning author of *Death of a Thousand Cuts*

Back one hundred generations ago there was no people but Gypsies. Everything walked and talked. Flowers visited each other, so did rocks. As time passed they all lost their legs. Trouble didn't. It still walks anywhere it wants. So do Gypsies.

—Madame Mina Szabo, as learned from her grandmother

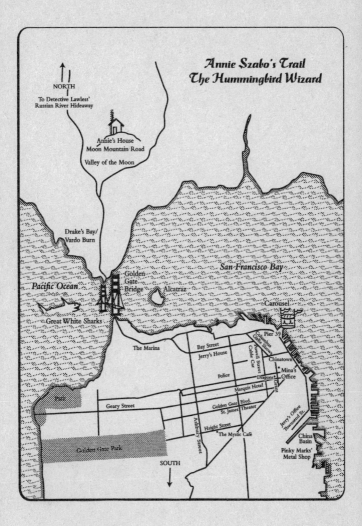

One

Jerry and I grew up before smog was invented. We both left Los Angeles when the hills disappeared and the ocean got tired of movie stars. Jerry'd been an occasional boyfriend and my oldest pal.

He met Capri at my wedding. I've always felt kind of guilty about that, but weddings are unpredictable events. Capri was drop-dead gorgeous, vulnerable, and crazy. Jerry was a prime candidate for a broken heart—they were a match made in heaven.

There were plenty of friends, lots of champagne at the wedding. Jerry juggled fruit and woodworking tools. He'd paid one dollar for a minister's license from the Universal Life Church and performed our ceremony. I don't remember the ceremony, I do remember Stevan's kiss. Madame Mina, Stevan's mother, brought her fortune-telling gear to our wedding. Trailing after her were a bunch of Gypsy dancers and guitarists.

When ministering was done and juggling got old, Jerry found Mina. She read his cards and studied his palm. Stevan and I propped each other up, peered over Jerry's shoulder, and marveled at his future. That's when trouble arrived. Capri breezed into our reception wearing a sequined bodysuit, legs up to here, and a killer smile.

She kissed Madame Mina on the cheek and said, "How's his love line, Mamo? He's kinda cute."

My new sister-in-law meant Jerry, and she sat down right next to him. Jerry wore the stunned expression of a shock therapy patient ready to go home. In her presence he'd lost fifty IQ points.

She put her feet on the edge of his folding chair, lit a cigarette and said to him, "Excuse the getup. I just got off work, and I was too pooped to change."

He looked at her outfit while pretending not to. "What do you do? I mean . . . for a living."

"I teach."

"Teach?"

"Circus School of Performing Arts. That trapeze bar is heavy like you wouldn't believe. Rub my shoulders, would you? They're killing me."

She zapped him again with her electric smile. Another 20 IQ points down the drain.

Capri twirled her car keys around one finger. The decorative plastic was shaped like a bird in flight. She turned to Mina. "Ready to go home?"

"No, either are you."

Madame Mina closed in on Jerry, and this time she meant business. The phony "You'll come into money and live to be an old man" stuff disappeared. She scrutinized both hands. She turned them over and traced the fine, barely visible crease at the base of each thumb. The future tumbled before her.

She looked at her daughter, held Jerry's hand, and pointed to the middle of his left palm. Mother and daughter argued in a foreign language, and it sounded pretty fierce.

When they got back to speaking English, Capri said to Mina, "You did it again. You skipped straight from page one to the end of a book that hasn't been written. I hate it when you do that."

"Big deal. What kind of mother would I be if you didn't hate me sometimes? I'm telling you, heartache for everyone when you get mixed up in love with a *gajo*."

"What happened to *Love comes in all kinds of packages*?"

"Some packages are wrapped in brown paper and go tick, tick, tick. Those you throw over a bad neighbor's fence."

Stevan gave his mother a look; Capri's expression mirrored his.

"Okay, okay. You two stop with the eyes."

Mina closed her eyes and ran her fingers over Jerry's head. She lingered over his left ear and repeated the procedure. Her face did a 180 turn in attitude, and her wrinkles relaxed.

She tossed her hands up and said, "What can you do? We're all crazy nuts. You two kids take a walk." Jerry's head was like a melon that had been pronounced ripe. It was a strange blessing.

Jerry and Capri disappeared into the shadows of our summer orchard. She turned and tossed Mina the car keys. When the full moon bounced off her sequins, Capri was a pulsing tower of light. Jerry had just fallen for the whole carnival.

Stevan held me and spun me around. We danced, but not for long. He got woozy and staggered off to stick his head under a hose. Things went downhill from there. Some Gypsy relative who'd come with Capri stepped in and asked me to dance.

He had dark curly hair and peach fuzz sideburns. I pegged him at fourteen years old. He'd had too much to drink, and he stared at my cleavage from a distance of two inches. He threw up down the front of my dress. I don't know why, but I laughed. My chest doesn't usually have that effect on men.

The kid looked pitiful, embarrassed. He stared at his feet, and they were a mess. I took his hand and led him to the hose, over to Stevan. The kid needed cleaning up, and so did I.

"Capri is trouble," he said. "She's born under a *prikaza* star. Tell your friend if he's smart, he'll steer clear."

There I stood with leftover wedding cake and champagne down my front listening to an adolescent's dire warnings. My new husband had his head under a hose, and Jerry was coming unglued beneath the apple trees. Into this sea Madame Mina sailed, wearing a necklace made from a sheriff's badge welded to a gold chain. I had married into a family of lunatics.

Mina wrestled with the boy's shirt as she tried to pull it over his head. "We're leaving," she said to me. "By the way, I hope you're paying cash to those dancers. They don't take checks." The boy's arms were hung up in the neckband.

"They wouldn't come unless we paid in advance," I said.

"New policy. That's good." Mina folded her arms across her chest. "Jerry and Capri, they're going to be an item," she said. "You'll stay away from Jerry now."

"I just married your son!"

"I know that. What I don't know is if it means anything to you people."

Stevan rolled out words, Romani, a wave of quiet storm. Mina's face went red, then white. She stood very still.

She smoothed the front of her skirt and raised her chin. "The message is clear. This family is ripped like an old sheet twisting on a clothesline. Why can't none of my kids stay away from *gaje*?"

The drunk boy, Jozef she called him, drove Mina home in a yellow Cadillac, no license plates, with his shirt dangling from one arm out the driver's window.

As for Stevan, it seems he was the one born under a *prikaza* star. We had two girls in three years, and we weren't even smart enough to be miserable. (Laughter is a powerful aphrodisiac, hence the kids.) When I was pregnant with child three, Stevan sailed off a cliff into the Pacific Ocean. No drugs or alcohol involved, just a French motorcycle and an exuberance around the curves that threw him over the edge. Sometimes joy rides a line precariously close to destruction.

Jerry and Capri stuck together several years after their hot and heavy beginning, had a son, and divorced. No more Capri? No such luck. More than a decade after we'd last spoken I came home to find a message from her on my answering machine.

Because time gets squishy, and things that once seemed important don't matter anymore, hearing Capri's voice was not a terrible thing. A strange thing, but not terrible.

Two

I pulled into my driveway, and the tires kicked back mud. The last leaves flattened beneath the soil under footprints and fallen branches. Autumn vineyards rolled up the hills in deep red lines behind my house. The air smelled fine and moist.

Under an explosion of junk mail, bills, and catalogs that littered my kitchen counter, the answering machine's light blinked twice. I pressed PLAY.

The first call was the one from Capri. "Hey, Annie! I bet you're surprised to hear from me, but who else could I call?"

"Anyone else," I said to the machine. Capri's voice hadn't changed much over the years, but her words were slurred, at least 86 proof. I think she was talking into the wrong end of the phone.

"You won't believe what he's done now." Capri ended her sentence with a whooshing sound. Probably blew a puff of cigarette smoke at me.

Rattle, rattle, volume up, she'd found the right end of the phone. "Jerry's in one sweet mess. I tell him—*You're gonna be eaten alive if you don't stay away from Pinky Marks!* Forget it—I'm a talking ghost. Please tell him to back off Pinky. Jerry listens to you." I don't know what gave her that idea.

One more puff of smoke from Capri. "And don't worry about

nothing from my end. I don't want trouble, just for Jerry to be okay. This means I didn't tell my mother I called you. Bye."

That much was good news. Mina and I had developed a non-relationship. I wanted it to continue.

The second call was from Jerry's law partner, Bill Wells. He said he was headed north, that he'd stop by and see me. I groaned out loud, not the good kind of groan. I'd tried Wells once, and it was more than enough. His good looks had sucked me in. It's confusing when defective people come in nice packages. Sometimes you can't believe the stupid things you've done—Bill was one of those things.

The phone rang again. Let it ring, I needed the ocean. I'd been tugged at by work, and by a growing stack of bills. Now I was being tugged by a past I wanted nothing to do with.

My answering machine picked up on the third ring. A bent voice asked, "Did you get my call? I forgot to leave my number." Capri stumbled through seven digits, an area code, and started all over in case I'd missed any.

Might as well get this over with. I called her back.

Her phone stopped ringing, but there was no answer. "Capri?"

Dead air met my voice, and then another voice, a woman, not Capri, heavy accent, cold sober, no kidding, no surprise. Madame Mina. Standing at the other end of her voice I couldn't think of a word to say. My vocal cords chickened out of the whole deal.

"Annie, I know that's you. Say something."

"You know it's me over the phone?"

"Sure, I smell your breath."

"What does my breath smell like over airwaves and metal wires?"

"Like bruised apples."

Nice.

"Also," she said, "I got a box with caller ID. That helps some."

I rubbed my forehead. "Listen, Capri called me. Twice. I'm calling her back."

"Good. She's resting pretty hard, but maybe you'll talk sometime."

Mina hung up. Capri was either drying out or soaking up at her mother's place. Now I was back on Mina's interior screen. She could smell me. At least with the help of caller ID.

Time to head for the ocean. Past time. I grabbed stacks of paperwork and bills. I tossed sweaters and jeans and one good dress into a suitcase. I made it to the car in one trip, opened the rear door, and jammed everything inside. My old Royal typewriter already sat on the passenger seat.

As I was about to leave, my daughter's root beer–colored truck bounced down the dirt road and ground to a stop in the orchard next to my car. The pickup bed had one metal sculpture in it, the one she'd been planning to sell. E. B. climbed out and leaned into my window. I love my daughter, but I was itchy to get going. I kept my engine running.

I said, "Buyer change his mind when he saw it?"

"Yeah. He wants eleven more just like him to stand in a circle in his courtyard—one for each month of the year. I'm sick of this project, but hey, the buyer's paying $20,000 a pop."

"If you weren't my kid, I'd consider that sum obscene. Since you are—congratulations. Bye, Honey."

She continued to lean into my open window. I cut the engine. She asked me what I was escaping from. I pleaded ignorance; she didn't buy it. She doesn't let me get away with anything. I copped to feeling claustrophobic and out of control and like I couldn't breathe. And that was just for starters.

"Oh. Is that all?"

"Ha-ha. By the way, Capri called me," I said. "You probably have messages from her, too."

"Yow. Capri called you?"

"Twice. She doesn't sound good. You see much of her?"

"Off and on. Grandma Mina treats her like she's mentally deficient, but that's where she usually hangs out. Capri's sweet, but very messed up. Life hasn't turned out the way she thought it would."

"Life rarely does."

E. B. cocked her head at the metal man under the tree, and pulled herself away from him. He was lying on his back, an expectant twenty-first-century Isaac Newton waiting for an apple to fall into his gaping mouth. He was compelling and grotesque at the same time, all seven feet of him.

My daughter's eyes, so dark and different than mine, looked right into me. "Grandma is nuts you know."

I pointed to her sculpture. "I know. And you take after her."

We laughed together, and it sort of blew the air right through us—blew Capri, Jerry, Mina, and the rest of them far away. Sometimes I need my kids in a way that's borderline too much. I hoped they didn't know it, and I was pretty sure they did.

I turned the engine over, but not before E. B. had gotten a load of my backseat. The chaos of papers and bills flowing over old coffee cups all the way to the floor mats was too much for her.

"Jesus, you're a slob." Then she really leaned in and got a close look. "Are all those bills?"

"Not all."

"Let me give you some money."

"I'm fine. I've got an interview with Cynthia Sloane on Tuesday that will take care of half the backseat." I pointed to the metal man and patted her head. "Don't worry about me. God knows what's inside a head that could create him."

"I've got to live inside here. You think it doesn't worry me?"

I shifted into first, she got the message and moved out of my window.

I leaned out and hollered over my shoulder to her, "I'm headed to Shelter Cove, then to Jerry's on Sunday."

She arched her eyebrows, and I roared off before she could put in her two cents about that one. I breathed deep—the highway would work its magic.

I drove to the ocean, to that place where no one could hear me but the sand when I walked upon it, where I could write and work, where I could read and sleep, where no one needed me except the shoreline to remark upon its incredible beauty.

Three

The Shelter Cove Inn sits on a steep cliff and faces the sea. If you stand on your tiptoes you can almost see Japan. The redwood stairs and siding are gray and old, cracked and splintered by the wind blowing off the ocean. Cypresses on either side of the stairs cling to the bluffs and are bent by the wind blowing off the sea.

The air was moist and pungent and smelled of salt. My skin felt alive, my bones felt loose.

I went to the front desk, and the third credit card they tried went through. I booked a small room for two nights, no television. I was holed up in a very romantic place with my old typewriter, a load of bills I'd promised myself to face, three articles to finish writing, and notes to make before interviewing Cynthia Sloane.

After Stevan died, when I needed to pull it together and do it quickly, I took stock of my assets. It wasn't a long process. I had bills, kids, no experience, and was too young for a decent job. As far as I could see I had one thing going for me. I was the daughter of Will Wilde, the Singin' Cowboy, the man who'd chased bad guys off the movie screens and clear across our lunch boxes. And, I was the kid who could shoot cans off a fence, toss a knife dead center into a post, and ride a horse bareback when she felt like showing off. I used Dad's name to wiggle my way into a few decent interviews.

I wrote for every publication from *The National Eye* to *Playboy*. These days I write for *The Eye* unless I need an exceptional paycheck. I prefer interviewing women with large wig collections to movie stars. Lots more real.

My room at the Shelter Cove was small, wood-paneled, had one desk with no drawers, and a double bed. I pushed the desk up to my bed. I set my typewriter on it and opened the sliding door onto a rare fogless day. I banged out stories on my old Royal, and breathed the heavy smell of salt and kelp.

I wrote until I was empty. One story about a dog who'd rescued the only cafe owner in a small Indiana town. He'd been proclaimed Citizen of the Year. The dog, that is. I deep-sixed a lead about Liz Stone's current affair with booze, bennies, and boys. Too tacky, and I liked Liz. I reviewed my Jail Babes notes. Nothing. I'd been asked to create an alien love story concerning the governor and an extraterrestrial named Lomax. Madame Governor was a snot. I was considering it.

I pulled the covers over my head and slept.

I woke up about 9 P.M., just in time to order up the last seafood chowder from the cafe downstairs.

I pushed the desk back against the wall, sat in the middle of the bed, and sorted bills. In the midst was a large envelope from Jerry's office postmarked the week before. Inside was a gray vinyl booklet. A note from Bill Wells was paper-clipped to the cover. *Here's Jerry's new will, not much different than the last. You're still the executrix. Try to keep track of this one. By the way, if you're in San Francisco, give me a call. I'm still a hot time.*

Someday I'd be old enough to forget my life, and that would include Bill.

I took the will and threw it under the bed. No good. I could feel it under there like a faint hum. I got up and tossed it into the closet. I didn't want to sleep on the possibility of death.

I was sick of the paper thing before I'd even started. I crawled into the sheets and phoned Jerry. Somewhere in the middle of all this life business—the coming and going, the working and planning—Jerry and I'd lost each other in some important ways. I wanted to find him again.

Jerry picked up on the first ring, like he was expecting someone to call. And the someone was not me. His hello was rushed.

"If this isn't a good time, I'll call back."

"Later's worse, Annie."

"You're out of breath. You okay?"

"Fine, just headed out the door."

"Big date?"

"Some loose ends to tie up at the office."

"At ten o'clock on Friday night?"

"My big date is with a walnut desk. Just work I've been putting off."

"Jerry, you sure about Sunday? It's been a long time for us."

"A long time, not an impossible time."

My one functional credit card could probably take a few more hits. "Maybe I should check into a hotel."

"We're beyond the I'm-checking-into-a-hotel game."

"True. I'm also beyond doing something that doesn't feel right."

"Everything that's happened between us has been right."

I couldn't argue with him about that, didn't want to, but there was one detail I needed to clear up.

"Capri called. She's worried about you and some guy named Pinky. I'm supposed to get you off the playground before he eats you up or beats you up. Something. She was pretty out of it. You know a guy named Pinky?"

"No, sounds like some circus person. She's been in bad shape lately."

"If you mean drunk, I understand. I also prefer drunk to sober with her family. Are you two getting involved again? I don't want to get caught in the middle, especially when it involves the Szabo clan."

"I'm involved with her, but not in the way you mean. Capri needs help, and I'm trying to get it for her."

"Okay. I'll believe you."

Jerry was still out of breath. I felt like I was talking on a cell phone with a bum connection.

"You really don't sound okay. I can come tonight if you need me."

"No," he answered too quickly. "Sunday. I'll have your favorite flowers waiting, and I've already bought us theater tickets."

"Can we break some rules, get out of line, even burn up the plans?"

No answer.

I wished this conversation had never happened. We were both in a weird space. Just end it fast.

I tried to sign off, but he wanted to make sure I still had a key to his place in case he was running errands when I arrived. This kind of pissed me off. On the one hand, I didn't want him waiting for me with bated breath, on the other hand, I wouldn't mind if someone waited for me with bated breath. On the other other hand I didn't want any complications.

I guess my irritation came across to him in the texture of its silence.

"Listen, Annie, we'll get out of line, break the rules, whatever. I'll remind you how to be loved, you'll remind me how to laugh. You're my anchor, always have been."

Uh-oh. I'd anchored my kids into a moderately sane form of adulthood, my mother into old age and beyond. I wasn't up for being an anchor anymore. Too heavy.

I told Jerry good-bye. He said he loved me. I said the same thing. It was true. He sounded distant, but I knew the distance had nothing to do with me. We hung up.

Our good-bye held a watery weight that was soft and rippled against my heart. It echoed across an eternal gorge. A mighty lonely way to say you love each other.

I laid my head on my shoulder and touched the side of my body, my stomach, and wanted someone's hand, not my own. I missed the smell of love. My legs longed to jump into exquisite buttes of night, and my skin craved new mischief.

I fell asleep wrapped in my own arms listening to the ocean pound the sand, then roll gently back to its source and dream.

> *I'm on a blanket beneath a tinker's moon. A dog barks, dinner sounds, conversations that curl up to the sky with campfire smoke. Not English. Guitars shoot their notes to the stars. Dark women dance up dust around the fire. Their wide satin skirts are a tease of red fabric flame that foams around their faces and touches the earth again. The night is warm, my body liquid purple.*
>
> *Jerry is lying next to me on the blanket. His arms wrap me in that safe place where a woman is loved by a man and her world expands, not contracts. He holds a rose, runs it along the edge of my ear, hands it to me. The flower is pale, grows deep red in the center. Going into that color feels like looking between a lover's legs. I close my eyes, inhale.*
>
> *When I open my eyes the moon is bigger than it's ever been. Jerry runs his palm along the small of my back. I face him. Jerry has turned into a gull, his wings arch across my chest, catching wet wind. I let him go. A guitar plays the same high note over and over, squeezing its notes to a screech. I try not to hear. I watch Jerry's wings, pure white and tipped with charcoal, fly away from me, soaring someplace high above a skyline that's colored like shattered opals. More screeching. I wake up. A ringing phone.*

The front desk. "This is your wake-up call."

"Must be someone else's. I didn't ask for one."

I hang up the phone and open the drapes. Hordes of hungry morning gulls circle a fisherman's boat.

Four

Dreaming of flight signifies a romance that should be watched.
It's hard to do in a dream, but keep both eyes open. Your heart
may be playing tricks on your head.

—*The Gypsy Guide to Dreams*
Zlato Milos, 1902

I drove south across the Golden Gate Bridge. Gathering fog
laced the struts and towers, towers supported by deep slate
water rippling green along its surface. A few sailboats blew toward
the harbor. One windsurfer stood alone. Four o'clock on a Sunday
afternoon, traffic going into the city was light. I wound through
the marina and pulled into Jerry's driveway.

A house in San Francisco is an immense luxury. These houses
more so. Victorians built on landfill, they look out over whitecaps
toward the Bridge. During the day the view is kites, dog walkers,
and Frisbees on Crissy Field. At night they face a cargo-ship light
show. The homes are the palest pastels, yellows that barely lick
butter. Jerry's was a Spanish-style house with roof tiles so old
they'd been shaped on the thighs of men who made them generations ago.

When I got out of my car, the back of my neck prickled. I
looked the street up and down. Ordinary disinterested pedestrians,
a few passing cars. I hadn't slept well last night, more strange
dreams, and had finally fallen asleep just before dawn. What sleep
I had wasn't enough to make up for the time I'd lost staring at
the moon and tossing in my sheets.

I climbed the stairs and knocked on Jerry's door. No answer
but the sound of barking dogs. Jerry didn't own *one* dog, but it

sounded like a pack of them was on the other side of his door. The extra key beneath the geranium planter was gone. I sorted through my key ring looking for Jerry's key. Madame Mina opened the door.

She motioned me inside with her hand. "Come in so the dogs will quiet down. It's the *Marla Trent Show*. These people talk about their lives like they belong to someone else. You wouldn't believe what they say, even about their husbands' private parts."

There was a bag of chips on the couch, two empty Diet Coke cans, and a bag of Oreos.

"Capri would never talk about Jerry like that, even though I guess they got kind of an open marriage."

"They haven't been married for a long time, Mina."

She swatted that piece of information away like a fly buzzing around her nose.

"We won't go into that. I wanted to see you personal. We've got to head off a future that don't look so hot."

"Sorry, my crystal ball's been on the blink a couple of years now."

She picked up the remote and turned off the television. "Drop the attitude, okay? Here's what matters—you got my grandkids, and Jerry feels like my flesh-and-blood son. Because of this I've decided to act nice with you. I'm even glad you're here! Imagine how desperate and worried I must be."

Sure signs of desperation all right. Maybe we could handle one neutral conversation planted in the present. I dropped the attitude.

"Tell me exactly what you're worried about."

Mina leaned into my face so close I could see every pore and line. "Someone is stealing Jerry's soul."

The old Jerry had soul and heart to spare. That was the Jerry who volunteered at the women's shelter dispensing free divorces and restraining orders, also the guy who smoothed things over for rebellious Gypsy kids who wanted to finish school. I don't know about matters of the soul, but I did know the old Jerry disappeared some time ago.

"Mina, no one's stolen Jerry's soul. He's lost it little by little, and we're partly responsible. We cheered him on when he learned to make mind-boggling sums of money, and we've taken advantage of him." I thought about the $5,000 I'd borrowed from him last year, and the measly payment he received from me every month.

"Losing your soul and having it stolen are two different matters," Mina said. "We won't get into that. The problem I'm having right now is this—I can't find the body that's wrapped around his soul. Not anywhere."

We were now moving into *National Eye* territory. I imagined Jerry rolled up like a burrito, his white body wrapped around the dark ingredients of his soul.

"I try to tune in, but all I get is black." She raised her eyes to the ceiling and cupped her hands in her lap. "This is turning me into a nervous wreck."

"Okay, let's calm down and figure this out. When was the last time you talked to him?"

"Pretty late Friday. He called from his office to say he had some papers, mine, did I want to come sign them and make things right. I said, *You crazy nuts or something? I got my nightgown on!* He said he'd come over to my place, and I told him to forget it."

"Friday night he told me he had loose ends to tie up at his office. I guess they were yours."

"Who knows? He never stops working, never stops with the big-deal ideas, even for me. Last month he talked about making Madame Mina's Mystic Café into a chain like McDonald's or something. He's fallen clear off the edge of nuts. I mean, there's only one of me to go around! Also, Jerry hooked up with that worm Pinky Marks. They've tried to get me involved with all kinds of stuff I don't understand. He even had us both meet at his office. Pinky, my sworn enemy!"

"Capri mentioned Pinky to me. Jerry said he'd never heard of him."

"Phooo. I wish I'd never heard of Pinky, but he's stuck to the bottom of my shoe like an old piece of gum. Jerry's known that sticky human scum almost as long as he's known me."

She zapped me good—full force.

"So," Mina said, "Jerry lied to you. Is this normal?"

"Lies aren't part of our relationship. At least they haven't been."

"See? Also he doesn't ask my advice about his business anymore. I tell him what he doesn't want to hear anyway. *Someone's got a scam going smells like week-old fish. Plus they're stealing from you left and right. And that Bill Wells partner of yours? He is a regular crook.* Does he listen to me?"

She spit on Jerry's plush carpet. "The world has gone crazy, and that's on good days."

"Mina, as soon as Jerry shows up I'll have him call you. He's burning the candle at both ends, and holding a blowtorch in the middle. His life needs to slow down. We'll work on him."

"Together. This time we're allies."

I decided to tread softly into the past.

"This means you no longer think I killed Stevan?"

"I never thought you killed my son!"

"I was just the random target of your spells, curses, and mailbox surprises."

She sighed. "I don't handle grief well. Also, I got a pretty lousy disposition in general."

I didn't say anything.

"You could at least argue with me."

I didn't say anything.

"Well, maybe I thought you killed Stevan a little, but it was nothing personal. I don't believe in Gypsies getting mixed up with *gaje* unless it involves money. The outcome's always bad. Look at my own family!

Of course one of the calamitous *gaje* she was talking about was me.

"Look," she said, "when I smelled you were coming I decided to put old matters in the past. Maybe you could do the same. At least for a little."

"Okay, we're on the same side, at least for a little. After that— we'll see how it goes."

From the far end of the house I heard a lapping sound. One dog, a poodle mix, was curled around my feet. Another was eating out of the trash can. To the slurping down the hall Mina yelled, "Bad boy. Out of the toilet!"

A massive dog with water dripping from his muzzle bounded into the living room and put his head in my lap.

"Katman is the only one of my eight dogs with that disgusting habit. I can't even put those blue tablets in my toilet because I'm afraid he'll drink the water and drop dead."

She started laughing, and her dogs started barking, laughing and barking, laughing and barking, like dry leaves whirled by a nasty wind.

Mina waved her hand in front of her face, pulled a hanky from a fold in her skirt, and mopped her eyes. "Enough. Sometimes when I'm real upset, I laugh. Go figure."

Better than experiencing her lousy disposition, that's what I figured.

She stood and arranged bright layers of fabric around her bulk. Watching her, I thought about the edgy feeling I'd had outside Jerry's house. Before I could mention it, Mina said, "Nah, that had nothing to do with Jerry. I was watching you from the window."

"I can't believe you still make me nervous."

"At least we know who has the upper hand around here. That's good."

She smiled and looked like she might bend down and kiss me. Instead, she patted me on the head like I was dog number nine.

"Jerry knows you're here, he's gonna show up. When he does, call me. We'll sit down and straighten out his life."

I was sure Jerry would appreciate that.

She whistled. Her dogs came running—eight mutts sat at her feet, waiting for a signal.

"Boy, if we could train our men this good, life would be smooth sailing all the way."

"Trained men are boring."

Mina threw back her head and laughed. "I got to agree with you."

She picked up a straw basket stitched with coconuts.

Mina touched my knee. "E. B. said you'd be here. She's turned out real good, hasn't she? Sometimes you can't figure out where your kids come from."

Score one for Madame Mina.

She put the house key under the geranium pot and lumbered down the stairs. A yellow Cadillac waited in front and took off when she climbed in. I didn't catch a glimpse of the driver, but the car was shining and sleek, with new tags still on the windows.

Five

$\mathcal{T}$he absence of Mina and her herd created a vacuum. Jerry's house was too quiet. I put my bag in the bedroom and turned the TV back on. I wanted the comfort of voices. I dialed Jerry's inside line at the office. No answer. I left a message on his machine.

I curled up on the couch and opened a book I'd been struggling with for a month. I still wasn't having any luck with it. It was recommended by several friends, it was a best-seller, full of angst, full of self-disclosure, sprinkled with hip humor, full of spiritual growth. Basically full of it. Maybe I wasn't mature enough for all that growth and awareness. I placed it on the teak table, deciding it could take up permanent residence in San Francisco.

I paced, thought about calling E. B., wanted to chew her out for disclosing my whereabouts to Mina. What I really wanted was to hear her voice and share my jitters until my brain flat-lined and went pink. Instead I ate the Oreos Mina left behind. I checked out the on-screen cable channel guide. Eight hundred forty-three television stations, and there didn't appear to be much more worth watching than when we lived in the black-and-white wasteland of channels two through thirteen.

Part of me circled around Jerry, then circled back again. Mina was so worried about him she had stooped to acting human with me. That was huge. I'd picked up her worry, and it was wringing my stomach into a wet knot.

Beneath the wet knot, I was ticked off. Most likely Jerry was fine and dandy, at least he would be until he came home and had me to deal with. This get-together had been his idea, and here I was cooling my heels inside his house, trying not to be mad, but it sure seemed like I had the right to be.

The phone rang. Probably Jerry calling with some lame excuse.

Before I could say hello, a man's voice said, "What's up?"

"Pardon me?"

"Is this Jerry's?"

"It is. Who's this?"

"Oh. I thought you were someone else. When he gets in, just tell him Joe called."

Joe hung up without saying good-bye.

I felt like numbing out. Food and sleep have become my drugs of choice. I went through the rest of them long ago, and these two are the only ones that haven't come close to killing me. I padded into the kitchen. The refrigerator was pathetic—clean and almost empty. I did score a container of Chunky Monkey ice cream buried behind frozen French bread. A half bottle of white wine sat in the refrigerator door.

Jerry still stocked every vitamin and herb tea known to man, enough to fill three cabinet shelves, plus a row of outdated prescription drugs. I made myself a strong pot of valerian tea. In half an hour, if I was lucky, the steeped root would knock me right out of the ballpark.

I dialed Jerry's office again, still no answer. I thought about driving over there, but discarded the idea as being too needy.

On the kitchen calendar was a circle around today's date with my name written in the middle. Two theater tickets were clipped to a magnet on the side of the refrigerator. Jerry had spared no expense. I'd seen *Phantom of the Opera* twice, but not without a pillar or some other cheap-seat obstruction. These were balcony seats, and they were for Tuesday night. Hopefully, we wouldn't be sick of each other by then. Hopefully, we'd run into each other by then.

There was a Welcome! note on the refrigerator. I tore it up.

I stuffed the wine under my arm, carried the ice-cream container with a spoon, the pot of valerian tea, and a large mug into Jerry's bedroom. I sat on the edge of his bed, then spilled my tea resting on the bedside table. I grabbed an old T-shirt of his and started wiping up the mess. The damage wasn't bad—the tea had spilled on boxes covered in shrink wrap.

The boxes weren't only new, they held some pretty interesting stuff. Heavy-duty handcuffs, wrist and ankle, BREAKAWAY the package read, a leather thong, some kind of rubbery thing that looked like a flyswatter with studs. Purple. There were also books, hot ones. One cover had a photo of two people doing something that defied basic anatomy. Looked like Jerry was getting bored with the garden-variety sex that comes without batteries and instructions.

The other bedside table was stacked three high with photo albums, books, and his journals. I opened an album and wandered through his memories. Capri and Jerry at the ocean. Capri on a tightrope. Baby pictures of their son. Mina and a strange man dressed in three layers of black in front of the Opera House. I poured myself another cup of tea. And there was Stevan and me, young and impossibly happy, sitting on our porch with a baby in each lap. A picture of Madame Mina's Mystic Café in the Haight. It was a decent-sized building, and the photo looked pretty new.

I behaved myself and didn't peek inside his journals. He'd kept one since we were kids. His first were written in crayon.

I picked up one of his books, *Genesis* by Eduardo Galeano. Creation myths. Nightbirds, Parrots, Time. One page was bookmarked, The Hummingbird:

Before the world was born he already existed. At dawn he greets the sun . . . He goes from flower to flower, quick and necessary like light itself.

Hummingbird brings messages from the gods, becomes a bolt of lightning to carry out their vengeance, blows prophecies in the ears of the soothsayers . . . As the sun, he flies to the moon, takes her by surprise in her chamber, and makes love to her. Before the world was born he already existed . . .

Very wonderful—a sacred ecstasy. Wrapped in the luxury of Jerry's Egyptian cotton sheets, the thick down comforter, the phantasmic oblivion of valerian tea, my bones relaxed to their center. Jerry's familiar scent made me feel safe and warm. Delicious. I upended the wine bottle, fluffed the king-size pillows, and abandoned unnamed fears. Jerry would be home any minute, and I would be glad to see him. I sank into his mattress and into reruns of *I Love Lucy* and *The Andy Griffith Show*. Somewhere between Little Ricky, Opie, and the Hummingbird I fell asleep.

I dream, and in my dream I am flying. My skin is made of light, my body feels as if it's held together by sound waves instead of bones. A man flies with me. He is wearing a cape, beaded and old. Feathers are sewn inside the red silk lining. His hair is a halo. He makes me ache in a way that's sad but good. I feel sexy. The kind of sexy that comes from being so in tune you want to be inside each other even though you already are.

My eyes are stuck with the glue of sleep. Jerry's lucky to have come home in the middle of my dream. In drowsy ecstasy he kisses the skin inside my thigh. He strokes my calves, he kisses my stomach, he sucks my breast into his mouth. I want to swim in sleep, devour sleep. No waking. No disturbing the fabric of my dream. My desire is stitched inside his cape. When we make love, it is sweet, strong. I whisper his name. I see an ancient lifetime in a Basque village. I don't let go of him. We move toward deeper sleep, and curl up like two moist spoons that have been lying in the same silver chest for generations. We fit that well.

Six

The trouble with resisting temptation is that it may never come
again. Love is the biggest temptation, but money nips close at
love's heels.

—Madame Mina Szabo, *The Gypsy Guide to Love*
Mystic Café Press, 2003

J woke up alone. Too bad. This morning I would have liked
to cuddle. I yawned and stretched my happy skin. I could
still remedy the anxiety of solitude with pleasure. That was a
relief. An awakening and a healing all at once. Just as I'd hopped
on the train of life evaluation, I heard rustling sounds coming
from the kitchen.

I arched my back, yawned again, and called to Jerry.

"Come in here and rescue me! I'm about to examine my life."

No response. I wanted to wrap him in my arms, feel my belly
next to his. Cabinet doors opened and closed, a chair scraped
against the kitchen floor. Breakfast sounds.

"Did you get those onion bagels I love? Jerry?" Still no answer.
Old houses are well built. There is real wood and plaster inside
the walls.

I put on Jerry's robe and walked down the hall to the kitchen.
Capri was sitting at the counter. She was crying and eating cornflakes floating in a clear liquid. Next to the bowl was a bottle of
tequila. The soggy flakes were halfway to her mouth, and she
dropped her spoon. It bounced off the Spanish tile into the sink.

"Jesus Christ," she said, "you almost scared the life out of me."

I pulled Jerry's robe around my chest. Body parts should be

fully covered when you're indignant. "What are you doing here?" I looked around. "Where did Jerry go?"

"How would I know? I believe in hell, heaven I'm not so sure about."

Try again. "When's he coming back?" I peered into the living room. "Your mother's not here, is she?"

She wiped her nose on her sleeve. "I told him Pinky was trouble, but he wouldn't listen. I guess he wouldn't hear nothing from you, either, and now Jerry's dead."

She looked me up and down. "I'm not even going to ask what you've been doing here." The tears rolled down her face, down her neck. She shook her head.

"Having an affair in a dead man's house, I hate to tell you, is the worst possible luck. Not to mention bad taste."

"No one's ever wiped their nose on their sleeve and lectured me about bad taste."

She kept crying. I'd never seen anyone cry and eat at the same time. "You're eating cornflakes in tequila, aren't you?"

"I've never liked milk. Strong bones? What does it matter? Nothing matters anymore."

"Stop crying. Jerry is not dead."

She didn't listen. I tried again. "He is not dead. We spent the night together."

The crying got louder.

I said, "Look, he told me you weren't getting back together. He shouldn't have put either of us in this position. I could kill that guy."

This woman really liked to cry. I handed her a Kleenex and pushed the bottle closer. "Either stop crying or pour more Cuervo on your flakes."

"Annie, listen to me. Jerry is all the way dead."

Some people love drama, and you can't talk them down. I spoke to her as if I were a very patient preschool teacher.

"Capri, I've known Jerry Baumann since the beginning of

time. Believe me, we spent the night together. That's not a very good omen if you're mending a divorce, but it's better than having him dead."

She put her hand on my shoulder. "I don't know who it is you spent the night with, but it wasn't Jerry. He's been dead two days now. The cops just found his body, but they said two days. Something about bugs inside a person's body tells you how long they've been dead. Some kind of thing that crawls. I don't want to remember."

My legs went numb, and my head felt light. I could have used a bowl of cornflakes myself. I still didn't believe her.

Capri said, "Two days gone. We're holding his *pomana* soon. I came for clothes, coins, to get whatever is important for his spirit."

"Who told you he was dead?"

"My mother. The cops called her real early and had her identify the body."

My mind went blank. I fell onto the couch, taking a Chinese lamp with me. I wasn't concerned about my robe, or my dignity, anymore. Capri sat next to me. I put my knees to my chest and held on tight.

I had no idea who I'd made love with the night before—hell, maybe it was just the realest dream I ever had. It didn't matter. Sleeping with a stranger was nothing compared to losing Jerry. The part that had belonged to him was a giant hole, and that hole was swallowing everything. I don't cry often. When I do it takes me by surprise.

Capri stroked my hair. Her voice lapped the shores of my consciousness. "The police said a mugging, then a heart attack from it. We don't believe them. We know Pinky, they don't."

She whispered to me. "Maybe you just imagined you spent the night with a man. That wouldn't be bad luck at all."

"The man was Jerry. He was alive last night." I didn't sound so convincing to me.

I put my head on her shoulder. She hummed and wrapped me in her arms. It was warm there. I understood why Jerry had loved her, and now it was too late to tell him.

Reality hit, and it shot me off the couch. "I've got to get out of here." Capri stayed put and pulled cushion threads.

I zombied my way into Jerry's bedroom. The covers were a mess. Sheets and blankets tossed around, small dark feathers, pillows on the floor. Some wild dream.

I sat on the bed. I rocked back and forth. The room sort of disappeared—I was in the center of my own storm. I talked to Jerry and told him what a jerk he was, that this time he'd really gone too far. That if he was really dead he didn't have to mess around with my head by coming back from the other side for one last fling. I talked to my mother and apologized for having been a pain sometimes. I talked to the walls and told my daughters I loved them. Life felt short, dizzy, unreal.

Out the bedroom window was the Golden Gate Bridge. I wanted to go home. There was a wicker chair sitting under the window that led north to my world. I scanned the room, hoping its corners and hard edges would help me feel solid. The world slowly came into focus, askew, but no spinning. Paintings on the walls, albums on the table, my purse on the wicker chair, a small square bottle of red oil, ribbon tied around it, sitting alone on the dresser.

It hadn't been there the night before. I picked it up, opened the lid—a musky smell that raised my heart rate. I replaced the lid, turned it over. The label read HUMMINGBIRD OIL. It was bottled by Madame Mina's Mystic Café. Next to it was a note that would have been a love letter had it been written by someone I actually knew. It was signed, The Hummingbird Wizard.

As dawn had filled the window that morning, a wedge of first light kissed a man's smile in what I'd thought had been a dream. No more. I'd seen him cross the bedroom on soft feet. In that dim light he'd left something more tangible than a voice spoken in the dark or a forgotten sock. He'd left the image of a half-smile hidden between the pages of my sleep.

"Capri, come in here." I shouted louder than I'd meant to. I even startled myself.

"Okay, I'm coming! You sound like you saw a ghost. This is what comes of having sex in a dead man's room."

"Would you cut that out, and what are you wearing?"

"This thing? Work clothes."

She'd changed into a black body stocking with silver sequins sewn on the calves. She still had a perfect figure.

"I was afraid it might be mourning attire."

"I'm going to work."

"After Jerry's death and all the tequila it took to wash down your cornflakes?"

"If I don't work today, I'll lose my mind."

"You can't do trapeze stuff with a stomach full of cornflakes and tequila."

"I'm not drunk. There's nothing sobers you up like death. Besides, hanging upside down will get rid of any alcohol left up here."

She pointed to her head. "Upside down brings fresh oxygen to the brain." She pointed upstairs again. "But, like I said, I'm not drunk."

I'd have to take her word for it, but so far I'd seen no signs of sobriety.

"Call work and cancel," I said. "We're going to your mother's."

"You want to see my mother?"

"I didn't say I want to see her. I need to see her."

"Two different things. I feel the same way about her."

The way I figured it, nobody would be sneaking around Jerry's bedroom at dawn unless they were pretty sure he wouldn't be home. And nobody'd leave an anonymous gift for me unless they wanted to creep me out to the point of running. A character named Pinky might have been involved with Jerry's death, or he might have been in Vegas or Tahiti at the time. I did know one thing: a stranger had left me a letter and some perfumed oil, and I wasn't running. A friend I'd loved one way or another most of my life was gone. The oil was bottled by Madame Mina—she was a place to start.

I handed Capri the bottle of oil and showed her the pseudo love letter. "Do you know anything about this Hummingbird Wizard?"

Capri's eyes got big. She handed me my purse, tossed me my clothes, and told me to get dressed. She grabbed a coat from Jerry's closet that was long enough to cover her black-sequined sizzle. I noticed she had a pretty sizable wardrobe hanging in there.

She was already on the move. She glanced over her shoulder and said, "We gotta go right now. I won't even call work."

Capri stopped, held up the bottle of oil. "This is not great news. Things get worse over worse. Poor Jerry." Her face crumpled up.

"Don't start crying again." I grabbed her arm and pulled her down the hall. As we passed the kitchen, she reached out to drain the last corner of tequila.

"Stop pulling on that bottle. We'll get you a new one."

I know from firsthand experience, nothing motivates a drunk like the prospect of a new bottle.

I held the door open for her, and she locked it behind us. "I don't really like to drink. It's just that I need to relax," she said. "It's been a tough twenty years."

Seven

San Francisco is lousy with hills and grinning tourists who wear T-shirts despite skin-blasting wind and fog. They are relentless in their desire to climb halfway to the stars, and they line up at every corner to ride the cable car to the wharf and back.

Regular people take cable cars to get around the city and do ordinary things. Today I couldn't count myself among the ordinary. I was with a trapeze artist, on my way to see my fortune-telling mother-in-law, seeking information about my friend's death, and hoping her hummingbird oil would provide a clue about who'd been tiptoeing around my sleeping body and sneaking into my dreams.

Capri and I picked up the Powell Street line at the pier and rode it downtown. Madame Mina's home and private consulting office was one block inside the gates of Chinatown. I was glad to be moving, glad to be in any kind of motion. I held tight to the vertical bar and bounced on the polished wooden seat.

I wanted to ask Mina where they'd found Jerry. If they'd found Jerry. Part of me was in denial, I knew that, but it was hard to count Capri as a reliable source. We'd already made one stop for a pack of Benson & Hedges cigarettes and a pint of Jim Beam.

She didn't want more tequila. Evidently breakfast was over.

The hills rose before us, fell behind us. I trusted that the conductor was a vet, that he wouldn't panic and pull Big Red, the emergency brake that shuts down the whole line. I closed my eyes. Behind them I could only see Jerry alone in death. It made my stomach hurt. I opened my eyes. Garbage spilled onto the sidewalks. Another workers' strike. I closed my eyes. Jerry was waiting inside my head again.

When he left Los Angeles Jerry went straight to Cal Berkeley. I didn't have the patience for school, but he was good at it. He blazed through his undergraduate degree, burned through the law books.

Sometime during the night of my wedding, Jerry proposed marriage to Capri; she accepted. Maybe she proposed marriage, he accepted. I don't know. All I know is the next morning Capri worked the phone in my kitchen. She cut a deal with an all-inclusive resort trading trapeze lessons for a free beach bungalow. They had a Vegas wedding and a Mexican honeymoon. Those two had one hell of a ride.

Their baby was born after Jerry passed the bar, and Capri kept teaching circus arts. They seemed happy. The whole Szabo clan seemed happy.

Then Stevan died, and Mina went crazy with grief. She blamed me for his death. *You should never have let him drive that car with only two wheels and no roof!* She bombarded me with spells and curses. I didn't have the energy to go crazy. I dived into an emptiness so black it ached and moaned and held my head under the water. I drank myself into the void.

Mina wanted to take my kids. It was Jerry who kept her at arm's length. He stayed with me until I swam up through the black. Jerry got me sober. It was hard, not just the getting there, but the reality waiting for me at the end of the tunnel. Capri defied her mother and supported him one hundred percent. I looked at Capri sitting next to me on the cable car. I'd forgotten how she'd helped Jerry, helped me. She and I—we'd lost each other, too.

When I came around, I had three kids to support—I barely remembered giving birth to the baby—enough money to buy groceries for a month, and ten acres in Northern California with a mortgage and a run-down cottage. I worked hard and held onto our piece of the planet. Jerry cheered me on. Capri smiled from the sidelines.

Jerry opened a hole-in-the-wall law office on Haight Street. He took cases on a sliding scale, and he fought corporate giants for the little guys. One day he flipped the money coin and began working for corporations instead of against them. Capri left. Jerry tore off his training wheels, hardened up, and reverted to the supreme capitalist he'd been as a kid playing board games.

He made money, lots of it. He made so much money I think he almost scared himself. He merged businesses; he bought and sold them. He stitched them together with legal thread and un-wound them with delicate precision. He spent his life with people who were perched on the edge of ruin or excessive success. He walked a tightrope higher than Capri ever dreamed of.

The first time I saw Jerry after his transformation was in a corner suite of the Continental Hotel in Los Angeles. Like now, it was autumn. Santa Ana winds whipped the scrawny sidewalk trees below. We opened the windows to feel their power, and the winds' hot breath blew childhood memories back in my my face. Popsicles and Jujubes. Tree houses. Some bratty neighbor kid who teased Jerry about not having a mother. I slugged the kid, and he ran home.

Jerry'd cried. I put my forehead against his. We sat there, brain to brain, until the sky turned purple and the streetlights came on. The Santa Anas tossed the last taste of summer around my ponytail and his crew cut. We didn't talk about Jerry's vanished mother. She was off-limits.

When our grown-up papers blew off the hotel desk, we closed the windows. The past we shared receded. I'd just published my first major article and was experiencing my first major money. I was relieved. My family would survive. Jerry had taken a shot at playing with the big boys, and he was winning. He liked the feeling.

Romance had been a stranger since Stevan died. Jerry was safe. Jerry was dazed by Capri's sudden departure. I was safe. And so we agreed, in the nicest possible way, to use each other.

I chatted, sort of nervous, Jerry didn't say anything. He started to close the drapes, then changed his mind. He watched the traffic below. He wore the peaceful expression of a man gazing over the Colorado River running through the Grand Canyon instead of Sunset Boulevard running between skyscrapers.

"Can you smell the money as it rolls by?"

I stopped fluttering around. I had to admit I could.

"The Money River's complete with its own ecosystem," he said, "and it flows between immense glass buildings. I'd rather be swimming in the middle, I'd rather be white-water rafting, than sitting on the shore reading T. S. Eliot watching it all rush by."

I kissed his cheek. "Remember to wear a helmet when you take on a level-four rapid."

"I'm serious," he said.

"So am I."

Jerry stood behind me, put his arms around my waist, and rested his chin on my shoulder. We gazed below to the headlights blurring Sunset Boulevard, a smeared Milky Way.

"What are we going to do with each other?" He ran his fingers along the curves of my face. He knew every inch.

"Enjoy each other," I said.

"That's it?"

"That's a lot."

We enjoyed each other on the plush burgundy carpet until we had rug burns, then we moved to the bed under the stars that weren't stars, but were the glimmering man-made lights above us in other hotels and office buildings. We fell asleep listening to the Money River lap the concrete curbs. That was a very long time ago. Over the years, when times were good, or when life got rough and lonesome, we ran to each other, each understanding there was no romance.

No romance, but there was love.

The cable-car conductor rang his bell on Powell Street near Grant. This was our stop.

Eight

Capri and I walked between the two dragons guarding the entrance of Chinatown. Once inside the gates we had crossed the border that separates Chinatown from the rest of the United States.

On the left was a store selling silk kimonos, embroidered slippers, and cherry bombs. On the right side of Grant Street was a store selling cameras, CD players, luggage, and porcelain goddesses. Next to the techno-goddess store was a narrow flight of stairs, stairs I would have missed if Capri hadn't pulled me up short. On the wall was a sign with an arrow pointing up. The sign read MADAME MINA IS IN.

The only door was street level, wrought iron, and had three locks. It was open. Purple carpeting covered the stairs, two flights of them, and continued into the apartment. Two couches sat on the purple carpet and faced each other. They were covered in dime-store zebra. The black, white, and purple effect was startling, violent.

Against a far wall between the couches was an alcove shaped like a miniature Taj Mahal. Inside this shrine were two large embroidered pillows, a short-legged table, and a plaster Virgin Mary. Incense burned. In the living room the television was tuned to the country music network. Mina had all her cultural bases covered. Capri and I sat on one of the couches and waited for her.

Mina was busy with a client inside the Taj Mahal.

"So what's the deal, Mrs. Liu? One day you want to kill him, the next day you're looking for a charm to win back his love," Mina said. "I can't make the universe row in two directions at once."

"Oh, today I just don't care one way or the other."

"It's your money, but I have to ask—if you don't care, what are you doing here?"

"I'm here because this morning I wanted him dead. Fooling around with Old Lady Wong! So humiliating. I've lost face. I came here to have you get rid of him forever. But, on the way over, I remembered how handsome he was when he was young, how much he loved me. That's why I'm confused."

Mina put some herbs in a bag. She said, "This is the trouble with love. It *can* go two directions at once. Take this bag and sew it inside your nightgown. Sleep with it next to your heart, understand? Night after the full moon, come back. You'll know by then which direction your heart wants to go. That will be $75 for the reading, $100 for the herbs. I'm now taking MasterCard for your convenience."

"I'll pay cash. I don't want my husband to see the bill."

"Good choice. Ten percent discount for cash up front."

Mina rolled up the wad of cash and stuffed it down her blouse. This was the grandmother of my three kids. They shared the same DNA. I didn't want to wrap my head around that one.

She said to Mrs. Liu, "Full moon, come back and bring the herbs. If you're still not sure, we'll burn five candles, one in each corner of a pentagram, $30 each. You sprinkle the herbs on the largest flame, and I'll read the smoke. It never fails."

"Thank you so very much."

A grateful Mrs. Liu walked out of the shrine and didn't pay

attention to Capri or me. She dabbed her eyes and put the herbs in her purse.

Madame Mina plunked down on the other couch, but didn't take us in. "So many troubles in the world, so much work." She rubbed her hands together.

Laundry was piled in one corner of the room. An open box of Oreos and a case of Diet Coke, apparently part of her steady diet, were on the kitchen counter.

When Mina turned her face to me, her eyes rushed to an angry torrent. I'd seen that face years ago, less wrinkles then, but the same face.

"He's dead," she said to me. "You're too late."

"Too late? What could I have done?"

"There was trouble when Jerry was still alive—you ignored it. Trouble that was too much for me alone. Trouble that you helped cause. You go home, we have arrangements to make."

"I'm not a scared kid anymore, I'm not getting lost, and I'm not taking any blame for his death."

"It don't matter if you take it or not. The blame is there weighing you down. Soon your body will shrink because the jelly in your backbone will disappear. You will be four feet tall from the weight of blame. This is one death too many."

Capri, sounding quite rational said, "Mamo, Annie doesn't need this. Be nice with her."

Mina scrunched up her face, but she didn't explode. She inhaled, exhaled.

"Is this nice enough for you?"

"It will work. And I don't need this fighting either," Capri said. "You and I are the ones to blame for Jerry's life getting so messed up."

Mina was shocked. "What! We are *not* the ones to blame."

"We are. Especially you. Why did you ever let Pinky Marks near Jerry? You should have dusted him out of our lives like cobwebs in a corner."

"You think I didn't try? That man is impossible."

"You even met with Pinky in Jerry's office! That's trying to keep them apart? Pinky owns a scrap-metal business down near China Basin, what's he need a lawyer for?"

"How would I know? Him and Jerry said I got to go. To keep peace I even rode a glass elevator that makes your stomach and your head feel like they don't know each other."

I asked, "What did Jerry talk with you and Pinky about when he had you trapped in the same room?"

"I already told you. All kinds of stuff I didn't understand. Pinky either, but he pretended to. He hates to look dumb. When we met in that office it turned out terrible. Pinky asked Bill Wells to come in, like Jerry would only be on my side or something, and Pinky wanted things all even. Before you know it, everybody gets into a big fight, and Berva has to call the security cops from downstairs. Only Pinky could go to a high-class place and cause so much trouble."

"Maybe," Capri said, "Jerry thought you could learn to act nice with each other."

"There's only so nice I'm going to be, ever, especially to Pinky the Worm. If Jerry expected different, it's because he doesn't know all the details of our past."

"You and Pinky got too much past to hide. Maybe you got to missing Pinky. And maybe you thought of some excuse to get Jerry involved so you could see Pinky and keep your pride. You have to face what your plans brought Jerry—don't pass blame any farther than where you sit."

Mina went horrified. "What kind of daughter is this?"

Capri set her jaw, and crossed her arms. Mina got up, sat next to Capri, and put her arm around her. "Listen, my mad shouldn't have flown in Annie's direction, but as for Pinky? I wouldn't hook Pinky Marks up with my worst enemy. With Jerry, never."

Pinky was part of their lives, that was clear. Since I didn't know what part, I couldn't understand why they thought he had anything to do with Jerry's death. But reason had nothing to do with Mina's boundless ability to hold a grudge and blame every calamity on the object of her malice. No one knew that better than me. Capri was about to reply, but I interrupted her. Jerry's death was getting lost in the middle of a family skirmish. I wanted the facts.

"Mina," I said, "tell me what happened with the police."

"They call me up. They got a mugging, a heart attack, a body. Will I identify it."

"Why you? I mean, how did they get your phone number?"

"I'm in his address book under MOM."

I thought about Jerry and his no-mom status. He had picked one heck of a woman to fill the bill.

She said, "So, I go down there, and it's Jerry all right. They say *this body* was found in an alley, an anonymous tip led them to him. *This body* like he was not a person who walked the earth loving and eating." She looked at the ceiling, looked at the floor. More hand rubbing.

I touched her knee. "When do they think he died?" Mina looked at me like she'd forgotten who I was and where we were.

Her voice was soft, flat. "They said he'd been dead two days, since Friday night. It's a business area down there, not many people around during the weekend. With the garbage strike and piles of junk everywhere, nobody noticed the body. Come dawn today people start arriving for work. By then they notice the smell."

Capri lost her breakfast all over the wall-to-wall purple carpeting. Mina ran into the kitchen for soap and water. "Jesus Christ. All over my new rug. I hope this don't stain or take out the color."

I grabbed some paper towels and started wiping up cornflakes, tequila, everything else. I tossed the mess in the bathroom and got a cool cloth for Capri's head.

If she wasn't careful, Capri would be joining Jerry. None of us were kids, and at some point a body gets tired of the abuse. I never thought I'd worry about Capri, but there it was—I was worried. Capri put the cloth on her head. I rubbed her shoulders. She curled up on the floor and either fell asleep or passed out.

Nine

Mina and I each took one end of Capri. We tried to lift her onto the couch. Mina had difficulty with Capri's arms, and my half, the bottom half, was at an odd angle because Capri tried to turn over as we lifted her.

Mina said, "This isn't going to work."

We laid her on the floor. Mina lifted Capri's head while I put a pillow under it. Capri turned over, the move she'd been trying to make in thin air, and Mina covered her with a blanket, even tucked it around her toes.

"How long has Capri been like this?"

"The first thing that comes to my head is her whole grown-up life, but that's not true. It snuck up on her little by little. She'd get better, then she'd get worse. Better when she had a solid thing going with a man, best when she had Jerry. Worse these last few months. Right now, worse than I've ever seen her."

"Sometimes beautiful women get used to having their emotional needs met by a man. When he's not around, life falls apart."

Mina was amazed. "Look at me! I been beautiful from the second I was born, and I never let my life go up and down a ladder because a man was around. Or wasn't."

"Either have I."

"That wouldn't be in the cards for you."

Mina was a pro at double-edged remarks.

"I'll just assume that was a compliment and say thanks."

"Sure, why not. Anyway, Capri's problems with Jerry didn't have to do with her looks. Jerry wanted her to need him, so he treated her like a wounded bird. The more he treated her like one, the more she became one. The way we make each other change is a strange kind of magic."

"Not a good one."

"Not a good one, and now we gotta keep our mouths closed. You never talk about people newly dead; they might misunderstand what you're saying and get mad. You can't believe how cranky some dead people get!"

"Mina, wherever Jerry is, he's not hovering over our shoulders listening to us."

"That's true, his spirit could still be where the cops found him."

"You said they found Jerry in a downtown business area. Where *exactly?*"

"Jerry was behind the Dumpster in the parking lot of his own building. They think he was taking his garbage out late Friday night before he left the office and got mugged. He had a smash on his head. They think the shock could have given him a heart attack and he fell over dead with his garbage. This is what comes of working too much, that's what they're thinking."

"I guess getting mugged could give you a heart attack."

She considered my face. "You're not saying what's on your mind."

"It sounds stupid."

"When did that ever keep you quiet?"

I decided to be quiet.

"Sometimes I think you invented stubborn. You got something on your mind, say it."

"I don't understand Jerry taking out his own garbage. They have maintenance people who do that."

"Sure, it's a classy place." She ran her thumb along the end of each fingernail. "I hate to admit this, but it's not a stupid thing to wonder. Here's what I think—the only reason you'd take out your own trash is to get rid of something you don't want anyone to see."

"Why not use a paper shredder?"

"Life is more than paper, even for a lawyer, and nothing bigger than paper's gonna go through one of those things. Anything else, forget it."

I wanted to move out of our speculative world and back to the merely surreal territory of law enforcement. I wanted details of the possible mugging, the heart attack. Anything that would turn this nightmare into a stack of facts. I heard a soft snoring. Capri. Except for the noise, she resembled part of the furniture.

I said, "Tell me what the police are planning to do about Jerry."

"They used all kinds of words that mean Jerry's just one more death, no big deal. Poison tests cost too much, no need to do that, blah, blah, blah. They'll check out the Dumpster and see if anything matches the dent in his head. The coroner's got to look at his heart. They wouldn't bother doing that except he hadn't seen a doctor for so long. Jerry didn't even have one."

"No doctor? He sure knew plenty."

"It's like I told the cops, why did he need a doctor? He had me. Besides, you could have ten doctors. They're not gonna do you any good if someone hits you over the head in an alley."

That was for sure.

"Any lines on a mugger?"

"They're digging around his office, going through stuff around the Dumpster. Talking to a few bums who live in the parking lot."

"And?"

"And that's it. I wished them luck."

My turn to study Mina's face. "Okay, give. What else did you say to the cops?"

She let out a big sigh. "When they tell me he was mugged and had a heart attack I ask, 'How do you know which came first? The bash on the head or the heart attack? It's a very important question.'"

"What did they say?"

"They got a body, it's dead, the end. They don't care about any ideas a crazy old woman has."

I could practically hear the wheels whir inside her brain.

"I care."

"Okay. If the heart attack was *first*, not the mugging, where did the heart attack come from? Cops don't know anything about that." She shrugged. "What can I say? It's the method I would have used to get rid of him. Easy. There are 214 combinations of herbs that cause a heart attack. Pinky only needed to use one."

Mina kept talking. I didn't hear her words, just watched her mouth move. This woman had considered me an enemy for a long time, had a volatile nature, a self-proclaimed lousy disposition, and apparently she knew 214 herbs that could make anyone, including me, drop dead. I wanted to leave.

Mina was still talking, but I'd missed the middle chunk of conversation. ". . . then you get chummy, give him a drink, and wait for him to keel over from a heart attack. You haul him to the Dumpster so it looks natural, and nobody's gonna notice for a while. Then Pinky smashes him over the head just like it was a mugging, to confuse the cops, who are plenty easy to confuse."

With or without a mugging, Jerry's lifestyle made him a heart attack waiting to happen. Mina believed Jerry'd suffered a drug-induced heart attack and was then hit over the head to make it look like he'd been mugged in the alley. She saw murder, and the villain was Pinky Marks.

Capri stirred and sat up. She watched the country music channel with no focus. I hoped it wouldn't give her an urge for Southern Comfort.

I said, "Why would Pinky want to kill Jerry? Who is this guy, anyway?"

"I can't talk in front of Capri. She's artistic, very delicate."

Capri rolled her eyes and groaned. She put her right hand over her eyes. Her desire to be numb made perfect sense.

Mina lowered her voice. "I will say this. When Jerry knew a person the way he knew Pinky, the way he knew me, your life was like a piece of glass. He'd have known every crooked corner of Pinky's business like it was his own, just the way he knew mine."

"And what you wouldn't tell Jerry, he'd figure out."

"No kidding! Of course, how much Jerry had to figure out and how much he was told, I don't know. Like you probably guessed, Pinky used to be a friend to this family." Mina cast an eye in Capri's direction and shook her head. "A lot more than a friend to me, I'm ashamed to admit."

I'd almost come to imagine that Mina popped kids out on her own. Early on I'd asked about the father of her children, the identity of my daughters' grandfather. I'd been given a vague answer. I'd asked a few more times and was stonewalled into silence.

"When were you and Pinky . . . ?"

Mina looked annoyed. "He's no relation to your kids, just to a few of mine including that one who likes booze and Grand Ole Opry. That's all you need to know."

I guessed I was glad my kids weren't related to someone named Pinky.

She put her hands together like she was praying. Opened them, closed them.

"The things you do when you're young, do them even more than once! I left Pinky when something better come along. Pinky was one of the only legal things I've ever done. I should have known it would turn out bad."

"And Stevan's father?"

"I don't want to talk about him."

Same dead end for my girls' heritage. The wall around Mina was ten feet thick on this one, and I wasn't going to press. No point. Besides, Mina was enough heritage for anyone.

As for Pinky—he was a semi-permanent fixture in their lives. He'd been Mina's lover, husband, and fathered some of her kids, including Capri. Then he became the brunt of abject disgust, hate, and paranoia. Not an unusual path for a relationship to take.

"How's Pinky been? As a father?"

"When Capri was little she was his fairy princess. He took her to work with him . . . I don't know—somehow they went in different directions. I guess when she was too big to be his princess."

Mina's eyes were moist. She stood up and shook off the past. "We got to call Zoltan. I should have called him as soon as I lost track of Jerry."

"Zoltan?"

"Zoltan Perger, a Gypsy PI. He'll find out what the cops won't—he's the best in the business."

The best in the business? How many Gypsy PI's could there be?

Footsteps up the stairs. Mina turned her head toward the doorway to face the latest request. More clients wanting their spouses to go away or come home, lovers to be faithful, money. She looked exhausted.

It was Bill Wells. He blew into Mina's apartment like it was Home Sweet Home. This was an interesting development. He gave Mina a big bear hug. She went stiff, but tolerated it.

"When I got to work, the police were there," he said. "I knew I had to get over here. How's Capri handling it?"

She motioned to Capri, whose snoring had taken on a deeper tone.

When he turned away from Capri and let go of Mina, he noticed me. Waves of greetings and condolences tossed across his forehead and were discarded. His mouth opened and closed. Nothing came out.

Since his mouth wasn't working, I was also treated to a bear hug. And a chuck under the chin.

He glanced again at Capri, soft and vulnerable, someplace far beyond sleep. I didn't like the look I saw.

Mina picked up on the same thing. "Put your eyes back in your head, Bill Wells," Mina said. "This woman is off-limits."

"What are you talking about?"

"Don't kid with me. Annie and I went through some hard times because I thought she hurt one of my kids. If anyone hurt Capri . . . Jeez! I don't think I could work up the energy for all that revenge again."

Mina had a lot less confidence in herself than I did.

This morning, with Capri, I hadn't felt clear enough to drive. Now I was good to go, and I wanted my own wheels.

"I'm going to the police department, see what they've turned up. Then I'm heading back to Jerry's to pick up my car."

"You think the police is such a good idea?" Mina said. "Justice won't be found inside the system."

"The coroner's report may be finished. I'd like to know the results."

She looked at me as if I had no idea what a hairball the world was. "They probably went over it while they ate sandwiches and talked about how the 49ers look this year."

"You don't want to see it?"

"Yeah, I do. I'm just feeling low. Soon we'll hold the *pomana* and all evidence will leave the earth with Jerry. And the cops won't have done one thing to set things straight."

"An ordinary heart attack with a blow to the head on something lying next to the Dumpster when he fell," I said. "It's a simple explanation for Jerry's death, and probably what the coroner discovered."

Bill decided to act like what he was, a lawyer on familiar turf. His height grew by a few inches.

"I agree with Annie. He was young, but a heart attack is not unheard of in a man Jerry's age."

I wished he hadn't agreed with me right in Mina's face, but the words were comforting, even coming from someone as ridiculous as Bill. Labels make death and disease easier to handle. They apply makeup to tragedy's face.

"Although," he said, "if there was a mugging, and it caused his death, we are talking possible murder." Bill's words sat heavy in the room like an uninvited guest.

"Mina, who'd you see at the police station this morning?" I said. "I don't want to start all over with someone new."

"Detective Lawless. It's a name even I couldn't make up, so it happens to be the truth. A man I never heard of before."

In the old days Mina had a cop in each pocket. Putting spells on one cop's wife to keep her knocking out babies like clockwork, charms on another to keep her faithful. One by one her cops retired or went to jail. These days there were mostly honest cops in San Francisco, ones you couldn't develop a relationship with. I didn't expect much luck with those guys either, but I'd probably get further than Mina.

She perked up for a minute. "You tell them you're Jerry's sister," she said to me, "and have them release his body to St. Theresa's. That's where we're holding the *pomana*, it's tomorrow afternoon. I already told St. Theresa's we're cremating him. No point in filling up the planet with a bunch of dead people—I got it all arranged with a priest I know there. The cops just got to let go of Jerry's body."

I wasn't sure if I could get away with the sister routine, I didn't even know if it was necessary. Still, it didn't seem like a bad idea to be family.

I headed to the door and Mina said, "Hey!"

I turned around. She threw me her car keys. "You don't look so hot. Take my car."

"I need to catch a bus so I can pick up my car."

"Later. No more public transportation. This city has gone all to hell. You never know what kind of nut you'll run into on the bus. What's so interesting that those people got to talk to themselves about, that's what I want to know."

The keys belonged to a Buick Regal.

"No Lincoln limo, no Caddy?"

She shrugged. "Cars are easy to come by, like candy wrappers littering the sidewalk if you know where to look."

I took the Buick. Maybe I was driving a stolen car across town, but I wasn't in the mood to care. The seats were plush, the steering wheel was one foot in front of me, and the Buick drove as smooth as a boat slicing water. It made me feel large, invulnerable, and a little embarrassed.

A small foreign number cut me off—it turned left right in front of me. The embarrassment was gone. I laid on the horn. It blasted the first line of You Are My Sunshine . . . Not hostile, but loud, and it worked. It was the first time I'd laughed in days.

Ten

The police department was housed in a building that looked like it was made of huge stone-gray Legos. The wood inside was dark brown and heavily varnished. The varnish was chipping off the banisters, the walls were thick layers of pale mint paint. The oil paintings on the wall ran the gamut from Drake's pirate ship, to the fire of '02, to the World's Fair. There were also several portraits, the two most notable being Tony Bennett's likeness hovering above the Golden Gate Bridge among glittering stars, and Harvey Milk lying prone on a marble floor with a Twinkie flying out of a gun like a bullet headed straight to his heart. Modern funding for the arts.

There were rows of Formica desks. Behind them sat uniformed women talking on phones. There were shoulder-high clear cubicles where handcuffed men sulked, spoke, and gestured at suited-up guys with briefcases. In one corner stood a woman in a silk suit, impatiently tapping the tip of her high heel and checking her watch.

I was starting to think this was a bad idea. I had residual cop paranoia from my youth, and this place was feeding into it like crazy. I breathed deep and tried to get my pulse rate back into the normal range. Not much luck.

The noise was incessant, the movement confusing. To the left was a long corridor of doors, each door bearing a name plate. A secretary was stationed at the hub of several corridors. She juggled a constant barrage of calls and protected the time of the people behind those doors.

I asked her to page Detective Lawless. She did. I was told to cool it a few minutes, that he'd make time for me. I paced. More mint paint on the walls, but down the length of this hall was a mural, a WPA project if ever I'd seen one, depicting the era of Chinese junks sailing the Bay, actually filling the Bay. Chinese men and women hauling fish into their nets at sunset. It was by far the best piece of art in the place. There was less confusion down at this end of the building, but still the constant hum of voices and phones. I was feeling a little more calm, but by no means close to normal.

I was given a nod by the secretary. The nod said, "Walk that way."

Midway down the hall was his door, half-open, a brass plate that read DET. AUGUST LAWLESS. I knocked and entered at the same time. He'd dragged another chair in front of him, an old red leather one, and had both feet, large, resting on the cushion. He pushed it toward me with his right foot.

I sat down. "Detective Lawless?"

"That's me." He pointed to his badge just in case I didn't believe him.

He said, "I don't usually have time to talk to civilians, but since you're the deceased's sister, I made time."

"I told the lady at the front desk I was his sister so you'd see me."

"Lover?"

"Old friend."

"Oh." He rubbed the side of his face, cocked his head and looked at me. He stood and opened a window. Lawless lit a cigarette and blew his smoke outside to mingle with the fog.

He said, "This is a nonsmoking building, you know that?"

"It doesn't surprise me."

"Most days I've got all hell breaking lose in five directions, and I'm not even allowed to smoke."

I wanted to be on his side. "Doesn't seem fair."

"Damn right it doesn't. This city has turned into Fascist Heaven for people who make up laws governing every inch of our lives. And we're supposed to uphold those laws. Like we don't have enough to do, new guys on the force have to ticket kids on the street for smoking cigarettes. Regular middle-class kids smoking regular cigarettes. A stupid waste of manpower."

He shook his head in disbelief. "You're an average citizen. You think that's stupid?"

I did.

"We've got people breaking real laws. Murder, robbery, domestic violence, sex offenses, and we're supposed to make certain every barkeep in town keeps ashtrays off the tables."

He tried to look threatening or fatherly. I couldn't tell the difference. He said, "You believe in breaking laws?"

"Not me."

"You lied to get in here."

"Is that against the law?"

"If you lie to me again, you'll find out."

I got it. He was the boss. His badge said so, and now I would be a good girl and tell the truth, nothing but. I gave him my most sincere smile knowing I would lie in a heartbeat if I needed to.

He looked me squarely in the eye. "All right, then."

There was a computer log, hundreds of bound green pages that sat in front of him. He riffled through the pages. He picked it up and waved it at me.

"Know what this is?"

I assumed it wasn't the latest best-seller, but was keeping my comments to a minimum just in case being a smart-ass had become illegal in the city and county of San Francisco. Then I said, "The latest best-seller?"

He actually smiled. Thin, bitter, and minuscule, but I caught him smiling. I'd gotten away with smart-ass once, but I wasn't going to push it.

Lawless thumbed through the pages. "Yeah. The plot's a little thin, but it's got a cast of thousands. Too bad. All these people are dead, deceased. Some are presumed dead, you know, just disappeared."

I got it. Sort of a telephone book of the dead, and everyone in it had the same phone number.

"Lots of these people are found in little apartments over in the Castro or in the Tenderloin. Some in alleys off Haight or Hayes Valley, some in Union Square right across from the fancy hotels. Others fall asleep in doorways of expensive department stores and never wake up. And others are found in cardboard shacks in Golden Gate Park."

"I'm not . . ."

"Some Jane, some John, all got the same last name of Doe."

"Is Jerry's . . ."

"But, when I find a nice businessman who turns up in a parking lot, I get to actually feel like the plot," he slapped the computer ledger against his other hand "has a front, a middle, and a possible end."

"Jerry was not John Doe. He was a real person."

"All these people"—he caressed the cover of the bound papers—"believe me, were real. What distinguishes your brother or friend or whatever, is this—he is one of the few alley characters who had a real ID on him."

"Where do you go from here?"

"I've sent one of my men to his house to look for anything suspicious, sent a rookie with him, too. They'll also cover Baumann's office, and ask questions. Two guys is a lot in this city. Like I said, the times I get an alley death and get to close it up are a thousand to one. Maybe more. His death raises my red flags."

"Lots of people have heart attacks. Did something unusual turn up in the coroner's report?"

I knew he wanted to tell me and didn't want to tell me at the same time. I also knew if I said anything, my chances of him speaking were zero. I've learned He Who Talks First Loses. I sat quietly.

Lawless bit. "Nothing too unusual. We got some funny stuff that turned up in the Dumpster with Baumann's fingerprints on it. Someone else's prints on the stuff, too. Also some indications that Mr. Baumann was participating in activities that used to be illegal. But these days? Kinky borders on the ordinary. I'm one month from retirement. I'll be glad not to deal with this anymore."

Evidently I'd been living a pretty boring life because I only had the vaguest idea what he was talking about. Jerry hadn't shared the underside of his life with me.

"What *indications* were there, what kind of *funny stuff* was in the garbage?"

"Hey, I've worked this city too long to pass judgment. And there's very little I see that surprises me."

"You're not going to tell me what you found, are you?"

"I'll tell you we tested for semen samples, and they came back negative. None in the digestive system or anus. There were signs of restraint, some bruises—no big deal. Lots of physical details you wouldn't understand. The contents of the Dumpster—sorry, not in the middle of an investigation."

I must have been looking at him the same way I looked at cops in the old days.

He leaned across the desk, made a tent of his hands and said, "Don't look for a fight where there isn't any. We're on the same side."

"Which side is that?"

"The truth. Fooling around with strange people and strange

objects leads to stranger fantasies and weird hangouts. Any of the above can lead to several kinds of death, heart attack and mugging included. Someone, probably a person the deceased never mentioned to you, may have been involved in his death. That's why I've got two guys investigating.

"His death and the blow to the head were closely related in time. Truth is, we'll do our best."

"Seems like you'd want toxicology reports instead of telling"— here I averted my eyes to the ceiling—"telling his mother they were expensive and unnecessary."

"Actually, I told her getting the information we'd need from the body, including the tox report, was a fast procedure that we'd handle in our lab before the body's released by the coroner. Lab results will be in soon, and release of the body will occur thereafter."

He pulled out his lighter, lit another cigarette, and sat on the windowsill.

"By the way, we didn't call Baumann's mother, hadn't had time to when she showed up. She said she had a vision that sent her here. If you've got any pull with that woman, keep her away. This place is loony enough without grieving ethnic types banging around. Before she left, she actually leaned over and blew on top of the deceased's head."

He gazed at the ocean, sighed, and exhaled smoke. "Jesus Christ," he said. He looked for all the world like a lone lighthouse.

"She wants the body released to St. Theresa's. If you can handle that pretty quickly, I don't think you'll hear from her again."

"Done."

"One more thing."

He looked over his shoulder at me, but didn't really see me.

"I'd like to be kept informed of the progress of your investigation," I said.

"Don't get yourself in too deep. Death is hard to deal with."

"Death I can deal with, unanswered questions I can't."

He wiped some fallen ashes off his pant leg. "A word of advice. I never stop investigating. And I'm good."

He looked me up and down the way you'd inspect vegetables at a produce stand, completely without emotion. "It's why you've gotten so much of my time."

"You're suspicious of me?"

"You lied to see me. That's cause enough for suspicion. Then you come in here wanting to know exactly what I've found pertaining to the death. I'm wondering if you're worried about being linked to what Mr. Baumann tossed in that Dumpster, something in his office . . ."

"I was up the coast at the time of his death."

"Don't get all shook up. I can verify your whereabouts. When did you talk with him last?"

"Friday night. On the phone. Long-distance."

"He mention any clients, meetings?"

I thought about Mina and the invitation Jerry'd given her to come to his office that night. "We didn't talk about work," I said.

"How would you describe his state of mind?"

"He was Jerry. Overworked, stressed out, sweet, considerate."

"If I need to talk to you again, I'll know where to find you."

He had a printout of my address and phone number from the lady out front who'd run my driver's license before I was allowed in. I had walked right into the lion's den with the stupidity and arrogance reserved only for the innocent or psychotic.

My belongings were still at Jerry's. The cops would rummage around and find the new toys he had by his bed, and the God-knows-what-all he might have stashed other places. Also a home video we'd made a decade ago when our bodies still laughed in the face of gravity. Great.

Lawless turned and looked back out the window, watching his latest cigarette butt as it plunged to earth.

I broke into a cold sweat. I backed up mentally on our conversation, tried to remember if I'd tripped into anything I shouldn't have. I wanted to collect my things from Jerry's house.

I stood up to leave. "I have some makeup, other odds and ends, at Mr. Baumann's house. I'm headed over there to pick them up. Maybe I'll run into your guys."

"Give me a list and we'll pick them up for you. It's distressing to go into a dead person's house."

I declined. A policeman had never worried about my stress before. "Is there some reason I can't go to Jerry's myself?"

"No reason. You're free to do whatever you want, including incriminate yourself or put yourself in danger."

We each knew our place. At that moment we were as far from being on the same side as any two people could be.

Feeling responsible for events we've had nothing to do with is one of the most common of human failings. The Great Unearned Guilt Syndrome. I'd bet Detective Lawless had been pushing people's guilt buttons for years in order to gather information.

He'd turned me into a nervous wreck and made me want to spill my guts when my only crime consisted of having an old friend die when, according to the police department's estimated time of death, I was sixty miles away sweating out my bills in my rented room by the sea. Lawless was good at his job, I had to give him that.

This is why you don't talk to cops without a lawyer around. It's a cop's job to make you blab, and it's a lawyer's job to make you shut up. They're each playing their best game, and you're just the tennis ball bouncing over a legal net hoping to stay in the court. Or in the case of real life, out of court.

Eleven

A maroon car was parked in the middle of Jerry's driveway, the right rear tire having careened in at an angle, leaving a short trail of wet soil and flattened foliage on the cement. I drove Mina's Buick around the block a few times deciding if I wanted to find out who belonged to the car, or whether to come back later when it was gone. Within five minutes I got sick of cruising Bay Street, and pulled in next to the car. I took out the other side of the flower bed.

I heard Jerry's front door slam, looked up, and saw Berva. She blew full steam down Jerry's stairs, her head down, carrying a couple of file boxes, destination maroon vehicle. She was large, black, in her midfifties, and had been Jerry's secretary since he started his practice in the Haight. As was not usual, Berva looked scared.

When first she saw me, she froze. Then she recognized me and advanced. Berva opened her trunk and set the boxes inside. We met in the middle of Jerry's drive with a hug. This was not Berva's basic hug, it was a big-time comfort hug. She held me, she patted the top of my head, patted my face, and squeezed my hands. She wore beads of sweat on her forehead.

I started to talk. Berva hushed me and took one hand. We ran across Bay Street, toward Fisherman's Wharf, and didn't stop until we reached an outdoor cafe and plunked our butts into aluminum chairs that sank soft into the spongy grass. The cafe had a blitz of round tables covered with Italian umbrellas that flapped like tethered birds against the wind. Berva grabbed a napkin from a neighboring table, leaned back, and wiped her forehead.

"Listen," she said, "and don't interrupt me until I get through."

She began telling me of Jerry's death. It was an agony. I stopped her.

"I know about Jerry. Capri told me first thing this morning."

"Capri told you?"

"Yes."

Her face formed a question, *How did that come about?* And my face answered back, *Let's not get into it.* We didn't.

A waiter brought us iced tea. No sound but the barking of bull seals protecting their territory from other males. I thought of football.

Berva sipped her tea, stared across the endless gray-blue water cut with frothy waves. "The cops were at our office asking questions first thing this morning. Bill sent me here to get a client file in case the cops toss the house. A thick file he said, *Ozro v. Ozro*, probably a code, no one I've ever heard of. I grabbed what I could and split. I don't like sneaking around Jerry's house." She looked into the sky, bit her bottom lip. "I do not like Jerry being dead."

Berva's eyes, large, deep brown, whites faintly yellow, filling with water, looking back to the ocean. Berva holding herself together. Not wanting to talk because she might cry. Same reason, I was glad for the silence. We sat together, cushioned in it, knowing any words might carry us farther than we could go in that public restaurant full of laughing people.

She cleared her throat. Her voice was soft. "Jerry's house was a mess. Some woman's stuff was all over the bathroom. His bed wasn't even made."

No need to come clean on that one. I changed the subject. "You never heard of the file Bill wanted? You know everything that goes on in that office."

"Not lately. There's been lots of things, too many things, I either didn't know about or wished I didn't. That place has gotten to be as much circus as law office. Capri dropping by any old time wearing those outfits, you know, like it was 3 A.M. on Columbus Street. Half the time drunk as a skunk. Bill kind of leering at her and almost going nuts when she was around, especially when she and Jerry were alone in Jerry's office. I honestly thought Bill was on drugs, then I saw some television show and decided he needed to *be* on drugs."

"What was happening over there?"

"With the firm, I haven't got a clue. Lots of business with those Gypsies. Even I can't tell or remember who's related to who, and I'm not supposed to talk about confidential business anyway. Although what it matters now, I don't know.

"And with me, my blood pressure was through the roof. I would have asked for a big raise to cover the expense of my new medicine except that I already have health insurance. I'm even covered for going to a shrink if the medicine doesn't kick in."

"Jerry had health insurance, too?"

"Everybody in the office did."

"He ever see a doctor?"

"One time when he had some depression, I asked him to go. I heard about depression and new drugs on newstalk radio. Jerry said the medicine made him sick. That was two or three years ago."

She looked back out to sea, to the barking seals. "I'll work there long enough to close up a few pending cases."

She lit up a small brown cigar. This was new. "Bill is snake oil," she said, "Jerry was heart. I stayed at Baumann and Wells as long as I did because of Jerry, and still I gave notice three different times in the last few months. Jerry said he was making plans to go off on his own, that I should hang in there with him."

Berva crawled inside herself and spoke in a voice I could barely hear. "He went off on his own all right, as on your own as anyone gets."

I flashed back to a dinner last summer, Jerry at my house, full of too much wine, going on a rip about Bill. He and Berva'd discovered that more than once Bill had taken an estate nightmare and turned it into a dream, Bill's words, a real moneymaker for the law firm—Bill in particular. Not only did Bill screw the heirs and place the firm in deep legal liability, the heirs left Bill's office feeling like they'd just won the lottery.

Jerry ranted about unwinding his association with Bill, that it couldn't happen overnight, but damn, it would happen. Nothing ever happened, so I'd assumed that Jerry's resolve faded when he sobered up.

I wanted to ask Berva more questions, like if she thought the Ozro file might be one of the estate nightmares gone gold, but I couldn't barge in on her pain. She was undone to the bottom of her soul. I leaned across the table and touched her arm, kind of uncomfortable, wanting to fix her, and not having a clue how. I needed fixing myself.

As if reading my mind, she said, "Honey, some things don't take fixing. What they take is time." Her volume was up, she sounded a little like Berva again.

She'd known the Szabo family almost as long as Jerry had, so I took a shot in another direction.

"You ever hear of someone called the Hummingbird Wizard?"

Berva's lips cut a tight line across her face.

"You do know him."

"I know him, but I don't believe in saying bad things about people."

I drank my tea and waited for Berva to stop feeling virtuous and talk. It didn't take long.

When she let go, it was fast and furious. "He and Tyrell got into trouble some time ago. You know my Tyrell's a good kid and wouldn't do anything wrong unless it was someone else's idea. Hummingbird, his normal name is Jozef, is real smart, full of ideas, just the kind that my boy needs to avoid."

Tyrell must have been closing in on forty. From what I'd heard, he'd been in trouble since he was old enough to escape his playpen.

"How long ago did this trouble happen?"

"Tyrell was about seventeen fortunately, or he would have been tried as an adult. I told him then, 'Stay away from that Gypsy boy, he's all the bad parts of those people put together.' Jerry and I fought over who was to blame until we got sick of it. You know how Jerry is, loyal to that family like a big dumb dog. Sometimes it made him think badly about Tyrell when there was no cause to."

We were talking about Jerry in the present tense and hadn't noticed.

"Do . . . did, Hummingbird and Jerry still see each other?"

"Once in a while that birdman shows up."

"They get along all right?"

"I guess so. They're all a little spooked by Hummingbird. He's the only, and I mean the only, person in this world Mina listens to better than Jerry. Hummingbird tells her to do something, she does it. It's bothered Jerry some, and believe me there's been more than one fight between them. Men and their power struggles . . . you know. Anyway, Jerry's gotten used to it. To him."

I couldn't believe so much of Jerry's life was news to me. I took another shot and scored.

"What about Pinky Marks? You know him?"

Berva hooted. "Sure, the guy with a big head!" Here she gestured with her arms over her head like she was describing a Sunday hat.

"Last time I saw him was at work," she said. "Jerry asked me to call a cab and bring him to our building. Mina was already inside Jerry's office. Pinky finds out Mina's there and smiles like he's got a date for the prom, and he's scared stiff about it. He goes inside the office after spitting in his hand, laying his hair down flat, and making no effort to control his big goofy grin.

"Pretty soon Jerry sticks his head out the door and says Pinky wants Bill. I get him, they close the door. After a while I hear voices yelling right through Jerry's solid-core walnut door and paneling. Next thing I know the door bursts open. Pinky and Mina roll out fighting like a couple of wild animals, all arms and legs and lips and one big head.

"I'm trying not to laugh, which is pretty hard, and Jerry tells me to call security, but I wait a little because this is the most fun that's happened around there for ages, and I can see nobody's going to really get hurt. What I see is two people who love and hate each other with equal amounts of energy. That's a mighty rare thing. Jerry yelled at me to call security again. He was mad, and he meant it. It was the only time he ever raised his voice to me, but it was worth it."

"What brought the fight on?"

"Only one thing I could figure—Jerry was in the business of turning thin air into money. Maybe he'd figured a way to fix the family financially, and for some reason he needed both those characters to cooperate in order to pull it off."

"And maybe one party couldn't be pushed into cooperating."

"More likely neither could be pushed into anything."

"If security hadn't come, who would you have bet on to win that fight?"

She got serious. "I'd never in my life bet on Mina to lose. I don't care if a man is ten times her size. She's got a power makes you know she's gonna win, so a little bit of you just gives up and lets her."

"Except with Jozef, with the Hummingbird Wizard."

"Except with him."

"Berva, tell me something about him."

"What for? Where'd you even hear his name? You think he had anything to do with Jerry?"

"Just humor me."

She folded her napkin in her lap, the part she hadn't shredded. "It's like I told Tyrell long ago, and my opinion hasn't changed. Jozef is trouble, someone you don't want to be associated with, someone you don't want to meet in a dark alley. I also said if anything happened, and they were together, Tyrell being black, he'd take the heat, not the white guy, even though the white guy was a Gypsy, which is just about as tough a break as being black when it comes to the law."

"Trouble is your main take on the guy?"

"Trouble that comes in a mighty fine-looking package—tall, dark, curly hair, eyes that make you want to give it up."

Trouble in a fine-looking package. The fatal dynamic duo.

"Last night I was at Jerry's," I said. "Some guy named Joe phoned, said he had the wrong number, and hung up."

"Sure, he'd use that name if he wanted to sound like some all-American guy instead of what he is."

"Why?"

"Baby, I haven't got the faintest idea."

"Berva, I thought I slept with Jerry last night, but I couldn't have because he was dead. So I thought it was a dream, then I wasn't sure, and I thought maybe I slept with some guy who looks the way you've described Jozef. But I really didn't, at least I don't think I did. He walked through Jerry's bedroom and smiled at me while I was wrapped up in the covers. I *am* sure of that."

"You can't tell when sex is real or if you just dreamed it?"

"It sounds stupid, but honestly, the line's a little blurry on this one."

She leaned over and laid her hand gently on my wrist. "Honey, I wish I had your dream life. I dream about people chasing me or about going to the grocery store. Once in a while I dream about Jesus. That's it."

Berva looked past me down the street, and I followed her gaze. She was focused on Jerry's house and the cop car that was now parked in front. We each ordered food, even though we weren't hungry. We sat, listened to the seals, and threw the gulls our meals bite by bite. We didn't leave until the birds finished eating, and the cop car drove away.

Twelve

Berva's car disappeared south of the Marina. I walked up Jerry's stairs, backsided in Mexican tile. My bootheels made hollow sounds on the stucco steps. I lifted the potted geranium. The old Schlage that everyone seemed to use was there, but I didn't need it. The door was unlocked.

I stood in the doorway and wondered for about five seconds if I should go inside. I decided it wasn't a good idea, but that I was going to do it anyway. Probably the cops had just forgotten to lock up when they left.

I opened the door and stuck my head in. I called into empty space. No answer. No sound of footsteps on the hardwood floors. I checked behind the curtains, under the bed, in the closets, and on the balcony. No one there.

The house smelled vacant, the silence was dense. How does a house know when someone's dead? I'm not sure, but it does. After the death of a person they are never empty. They are full. Full of death. It was the first time it hit me, the first time I truly believed he was gone.

I had tears, plenty, but they were all stopped up. I spoke to the ceiling as if Jerry were on an ascent to somewhere, an airplane taking off for flight, a bird about to leave the telephone pole of existence and soar toward the unknown.

"You should have come to my house and learned to want things less. I would have kept you there until you did. This is a family house, you should have sold it. It framed your loneliness—it's too much like the house you grew up in. I stopped paying attention to you in the ways that counted, the ways I used to—I lost you, but not before you lost yourself. We buried that connection.

"When my last baby was four months old you said, *You've been drunk six months. Your mother's moved a pink trailer into the orchard, and she's named the baby Abra. Pull it together, Buddy.* You sat next to me in bed while I shook and cried and shook and sweated and didn't drink and I hit you and I bit my lip and looked at the baby I didn't know, but you did. And you put the baby in my arms when you thought it was safe, and you didn't leave until I could stand the sight of my mother, which wasn't easy. Until I could stand the sight of anyone."

I stopped talking to that place beyond the ceiling where I thought Jerry might be. He saved my baby, and he saved me, and I didn't do anything for him when I could have. Mina was right. If he asked me for help, I didn't hear him, and now it was too late. No wonder I couldn't cry. There weren't enough tears to wash away the guilt I felt.

On the coffee table were old photos of him and Capri at the beach. She must have been looking at them while she drank her cornflakes.

In the middle of the table was a vase filled with fresh flowers. They hadn't been there earlier. Roses you could miss, even carnations. Not a vase filled with one dozen bird-of-paradise flowers. Stems two feet long rising to meet an obscenely bright orange petal with deep red and yellow exploding from the center. My favorite flowers had indeed arrived. Jerry'd probably arranged for their delivery last week. The dead bringing flowers to the living.

He would have enjoyed that strange irony. Thank you, Jerry.

I gathered my makeup and creams off the bathroom counter. I definitely needed to get out. I called E. B., overdue, to tell her about Jerry, asked her to tell her sisters. I thought about Mina lying in wait for me the afternoon I got to Jerry's. I asked E. B. when Mina had called and why she'd told her where I'd be.

"Are you kidding?" she said. "I didn't talk to Grandma. And if I had, I sure wouldn't have told her where you'd be, particularly considering exactly where you were and what you'd be doing."

She sure was wordy. "How did Mina know I'd be here?"

"Mom, some of the stuff Grandma feels is real. Would you please come home? You can't bring Jerry back no matter how long you hang around San Francisco."

I promised her I'd be home soon, and that I'd stay in touch. I considered telling her about Jozef, the Hummingbird Wizard, and I wondered if she knew the guy. But I didn't want to drag her into that particular scenario. Not now.

Jerry's living room didn't look right, almost like it had been vandalized and put back together. The police or Berva or who-ever'd brought the flowers hadn't been very tidy.

The cabinet under the television was open. Videos were scattered on the carpeting. I didn't care if the video Jerry and I filmed in various stages of undress was gone. I'm too old to blackmail, and I have no reputation to uphold. Several family members and friends might be amused, but not surprised.

On the refrigerator were the tickets for *Phantom of the Opera*. Actually, on the refrigerator there was now one ticket for *Phantom of the Opera*. The other was missing. Maybe it disappeared during the police invasion. And maybe it was an invitation. I was going to the theater. Maybe I'd have a date waiting for me. A *very* long shot, but I've learned to follow up on everything, including temptation. I tucked the ticket in my pocket, gathered my belongings, and called my favorite hotel, the Chancellor, to book a room. None was available.

"Every room's taken?"

"Every room in town is booked. Tonight's the Red and Black Ball, which kicks off Drag Queen Pride Week."

I put my cosmetics back on Jerry's bathroom counter and mentally prepared myself to spend another night there. I lay down in his crumpled covers to nap.

I tossed and turned.

I couldn't do this alone anymore. I rolled on my side, picked up the phone, and dialed the best hotel in town, room 2022. I was put right through.

"Can I speak to Cynthia Sloane, please?"

"She's in the bath and can't be disturbed."

"Lana, I've known Cynthia since her first push-up bra. When are we going to stop doing this? The Marquis has phones in the bathroom. She won't even have to move one manicured toe. Just tell her it's Annie."

High heels thonking across a marble floor, then muffled by plush carpet.

Cynthia's voice sounding lethargic and blue. "Hello."

"Cynthia, how long have you been in that damn tub?"

"One or two hours."

"You're going to turn into a prune."

"When I quit taking tranquilizers, I started taking baths. Long ones."

"Tranquilizer replacement therapy—I guess they've been dunking nutty people in hot water for centuries."

"Thanks."

"If you were still popping pills, what would be the reason?"

"I'm lonely. I'm depressed."

"Cyn, snap out of it. I could use some company and some cheering up."

I told her about Jerry, about Detective Lawless, about Madame Mina, about my mystery midnight encounter, about the missing theater ticket invitation, about everything else I could think of.

She made an internal judgment that my life was more of a mess than hers, and she cheered up. Her voice grew strong, she offered me comfort, fed me clichés, nursed her own shock, and I appreciated her support.

"Cynthia, I need something from you."

"Anything."

"Does your suite have an extra bed? Other than the one occupied by Lana?"

"Sure, this place is huge."

"Mind if I crash there? All the hotels are full. I thought I could handle staying at Jerry's, but it's too much."

"Mind? God, no. We can order up room service, eat chocolate, and watch trashy movies on Pay-Per-View."

"Boy, you movie types lead glamorous lives."

Taking care of me became her mission, and she decided part of her mission was going to the theater with me the next night.

". . . in case you run into the mystery man and need moral support."

I didn't want Cynthia tagging along with me to the theater because Cynthia never tagged along with anyone. Most of the time it was fine, even fun, but I didn't want her center stage in this slice of my life.

"I've changed my mind about the theater," I said. "I don't want to think about him, Jerry's death is enough, and that other ticket probably just fell off the refrigerator."

"Annie, we need to go. On the possibility the man shows up we have to find out who he is. Maybe he had something to do with Jerry's death! You need to face him."

She had now inserted the *we* word into my life. I was sorry I'd mentioned it to her.

I said, "I only have one theater ticket, and I'm sure the show's sold out."

"And the problem is . . . ?"

"What was I thinking? You can probably sweet-talk or buy

your way into the seat next to mine, or at least one pretty close by."

"Absolutely."

I didn't have the energy to argue. Cynthia would be my date for *Phantom*.

"Okay," I said. "Time for you to get out of the tub. My life has made yours look good."

I looked at the bird-of-paradise flowers on the coffee table. I had one more call to make before I left Jerry's. That was to Detective August Lawless.

Thirteen

There'd been something about his lonely stance in front of the cracked double-hung office window that yanked at my heart and helped ease my cop paranoia. Several rings, and his voice was connected to mine by the secretary.

"Is this Baumann's sister?"

"This is the sister, if we're sticking to that story."

"Why not? You hit me in a good mood."

"I have a name you might want to run."

"Connected to Baumann's death?"

"A chance."

"Shoot. Wait, this pen is out of ink. Try to save money on these damn pens, and the ink runs out in one week. Okay, got one the works."

"Run Jozef Szabo, Jozef Marks, Jozef Ozro." I spelled the names for him.

"What am I looking for?"

"A criminal record."

"If you have information, don't withhold it. I need to know why I'm running these names."

"I'm not withholding anything. I'm giving you a possible lead based on a hunch. And let's forget the sister routine. Consider this an anonymous call."

"You're lucky I'm in a good mood."

"Catch a crew of underage cigarette smokers?"

"Nope. Just closed escrow on a little cottage on the Russian River."

The Russian River. We would practically be neighbors.

"I'm counting down the days," he said, "until my life is a slow river, a close ocean, and lunch with my wife."

"I've heard once a cop, always a cop."

"It's a tough life to live. For some guys it's tougher to give up. Not me. I've been cop enough for three lifetimes. Now I want to fish, and the wife wants me home. Although I can't imagine why."

"Maybe she wants to get to know you."

"Stranger things have happened."

I pressed my luck. "You'll call and let me know if anything turns up on those names?"

He already had them, but I gave him my pager number and my home phone number on the off chance I'd ever get out of San Francisco.

Something was nagging at me. "Detective Lawless, why are you agreeing to do this, no questions asked?"

"Number one, I have good instinct. Number two, I'm feeling mellow and lucky to be alive after twenty years in homicide. Number three, I ran you. You're clean as a whistle. Not so much as a traffic ticket in twenty years. Anyone that clean is either close to someone on the inside who's a lot higher up in this machinery than I am, or is squeaky clean due to fear. This means you're unlikely to hand me a real whopper of a lie. And if you try to hide something from me, I'll know it. Using you will be easy and may even lead to a resolution in this case before I turn in my keys and badge."

Because he trusted me so thoroughly, it also meant it'd be easy for me to use him, but I didn't mention the flip side of that coin.

I put the receiver down, started to pick up my bags, and stopped. I don't know why, but I kissed Jerry's kitchen table. I stood in his doorway smelling him, saying good-bye, being alone with him one last time.

Fourteen

I drove Mina's Buick across town. The motorcycle-sized streets in Chinatown almost squeezed me out, but I found a parking spot. Someday I'd get my car back from Jerry's place.

I put Mina's keys on her counter and told her about my meeting with Lawless, played up my disdain for the cops, and said he'd made me want to confess every unsolved crime in the Bay Area since the time of my birth. I didn't tell her about phoning and asking him to run down various Jozefs, aka the family's Hummingbird Wizard.

"Phaa. You got to ignore those cops. I shouldn't have told you to lie about being Jerry's sister. You're not used to the pressure. It's hard to carry off even the simplest lie when you're not used to being sized up like you're less than human."

"Anyway, they said Jerry had a heart attack, and . . ."

"This we already knew. Anything new?"

"They're doing toxicology tests, tests for poison, after all."

"Good. Any trouble getting them to let go of his body? St. Theresa's is ready for it."

"None."

"It's settled, then. We'll move ahead with the *pomana* tomorrow. Capri can spread the word."

I didn't know how to broach the subject about whatever it was they found in the Dumpster that might have excited Jerry to the point of death, or that led him to be around some questionable people. Sometimes Mina was outrageous. Sometimes she was a moralistic prude. I knew it was cultural, but I'd never been able to figure out the pattern.

I jumped in feet first. "You were right about Jerry throwing out his own trash."

She looked confused. "What?"

"Remember we wondered why Jerry had taken out his own trash? Turns out there were things he didn't want anyone to see, things definitely too big for a shredder. And it could have given him a heart attack. Too much excitement, fear, something."

She was very impatient. "I still do not have any idea what you're talking about."

"I'd give you more details, but I'm not sure what they found, and I don't know enough to fill in the blanks. I know it had something to do with unusual sex, and they thought it belonged to Jerry. It had his fingerprints on it, someone else's; too. Whatever it was."

"Oh *that* kind of stuff. Listen, I hear people's private lives all the time. In this city that's saying a lot. Believe me, I wish I didn't have this information in my head, but it's part of my duty in the universe to keep living so people can unload. Wild living carries a burden. Sometimes it's me they confess it to."

"So you know what the cops might have found?"

"All kinds of anything. God almighty! Don't you ever talk to your kid? E. B. could tell you things that would curl your hair. Sometimes I got to pretend she's no relation to me, or I'd worry myself to death."

I got a knot in my stomach thinking about E. B. Some of her rich, artsy clients were pretty strange; maybe she'd become part of a dangerous underground sex scene.

"Mina, is E. B. okay?"

"E. B.? Sure, she's fine. It's those kids she hangs around with who are nuts. I wish she didn't know them, but what are you gonna do? She brings them to me, and I got to hear stories that would make Detective Lawless blush right through his uniform."

I didn't know if that was good news or bad.

Mina said, "What about the smash to Jerry's head?"

"Too soon to tell. Contractors had been overhauling the ducting and plumbing system in the building, so there was plenty of material waiting for Jerry to fall on or get hit with."

"They leaning more one way or the other?"

"I believe Lawless thinks Jerry was mixed up with the wrong person. Someone we don't know. They've got two guys checking out his life. If someone was with him when he had his heart attack and didn't call for help, that's a crime. And they're not ruling out a mugging. In that case the crime may go unsolved."

"If someone pushed Jerry toward his death, they'll pay for it. The world works this way."

I tried to imagine what brought Jerry to the place death found him, and I couldn't.

"Mina, Lawless suspects, from whatever they found, that Jerry'd gotten involved in some pretty kinky stuff. What do you think was going on with him?"

"I think he wanted to be numb like Capri. She chose booze to get numb, he chose sex."

Fifteen

Mina and I had no words to give each other, none that were kind, none that were cutting. Unusual for the two of us. I sat on her couch and rubbed my hand against the grain of the zebra-skin fur. She sat across from me on the other zebra-skin couch.

Her voice broke the silence as if we were in midconversation. "Here's another picture. Pinky could have gone to Jerry's office, followed him to the trash hollering all the way, there's a big fight, and Jerry keels over from the strain of being around Pinky. And I'm not ruling out a heart attack caused by poison until I hear how those tests come out."

"Why do you keep dragging Pinky Marks into this?"

"He'd think he could get away with anything, including murder. He has more nerve than ten men put together. That's why we got together to start with."

"You thought he had a killer instinct and it excited you?"

"Jeez, no. He hadn't grown into that, yet. We met because he was such a nervy little rooster. It was at a Gypsy camp outside Barstow. Some of us were trying to fit into being American, but lots of us, that was the last thing we wanted.

"Pinky, he wanted to fit in. He had a job selling insurance.

Croak insurance he called it, and he sold it to Mexican migrant workers and to Gypsy families. Can you imagine the nerve of that? Two peoples who don't even know where they're going to live, never mind where they're going to be planted.

"He came to my tent, your Stevan was a tiny baby. Stevan's father had just died, and I'd borrowed money to pay for his *pomana*. Pinky said, 'Look! We can fake the date on his death certificate, and we'll date the insurance policy back to before he died. You just bought croak insurance on your dead husband and you can pay off all your loans so the relatives don't hound you! A beautiful woman like you shouldn't have to worry about money.'

"So, I paid everybody off, Pinky asked me to marry him, and we went into the courthouse in Barstow. He wanted to be an American, like I told you, so we had to do this marriage all legal.

"And that's how I met Pinky—he sold me croak insurance and got me benefits on my husband who was already dead, but hardly cold."

Her voice was reverential. "You can certainly understand this— I was very impressed with his mind."

Berva was right. Mina was still fond of Pinky. No matter how much she pretended to hate him, regardless of what she thought he'd done or was capable of doing. I understand wanting the worst for someone when things don't work out between you. It doesn't make them a killer.

She shrugged her shoulders and offered her final piece of evidence. "Jerry's found dead in a pile of scrap metal, it's kind of like the mark of Zorro. Pinky's the biggest scrap-metal man in this part of the state."

"It's far-fetched, Mina."

She'd lost Jerry, and she'd loved him. Mina was grasping for sense in a situation that could never make sense, because the only person who knew the answers was dead. I understood how she felt, and I knew it was hard.

When Stevan died, I wanted to ask him, *When you drove that motorcycle too fast, did you forget you had a wife and kids who counted on you? Did someone tailgate you into oblivion, or were you as surprised as we were when you flew into the ocean?* I couldn't stand thinking Stevan had been careless with us. I'd been angry with him, and felt guilt beyond imagining for my anger.

It's hard knowing you'll never have the answers. Mina had to struggle with her questions and hope for answers that would give her peace. I had to do the same, and I had to do it without her.

Time to leave, and I said so. "I'm staying with a friend in a hotel downtown. I'll leave you the number in case you need me."

Mina gave me one her looks.

I said, "The friend is a woman."

"Did I say anything?"

"You didn't need to."

"Good. When I need to say something, I'll let you know." She slammed her mouth closed. I knew the quiet treatment wouldn't last long.

"Okay, now I'm letting you know. It's dumb to pay for a hotel room when I got all this space. Why don't you stay here?"

I wasn't sure what space she was talking about. Capri alone took up half the floor. "I appreciate the invitation, but the hotel room is free, and I need to get away from Jerry's death for the night."

"Sometimes I think you're unnatural to the human species. Your connection to family is hardly there at all."

She flung racing forms and clothes off the couch she was occupying. She slapped it with her right hand. "See here? Nobody hardly uses this couch. No lumps or sags. We got to take care of each other."

"Mina, maybe I am unnatural to the human species, but tonight I need an old friend and a nice, anonymous hotel room."

"So you prefer friends to family. I don't understand, but I believe you feel this way."

She shook her head and looked mildly disgusted. Mild disgust and misunderstanding summed up too much of our relationship.

Mina hadn't quite finished chewing me out, I could feel it. I was saved from this by her ringing telephone.

She picked up, said hello in a very cranky way. She listened and didn't sound cranky anymore. Her face flew between fear and dread. Her end of the conversation only consisted of *fine, sure*, and *I'll be there*.

"That was the cops," she said, "well, not the cops. It was that guy Lawless. He wants me down there for questioning. What do they think, that I killed Jerry? I don't want to go, but if I don't, they'll work themselves into a fit."

"Mina, I'll go with you to the police department."

"Thanks," she said, "but I got an appointment pretty quick. Mrs. Liu again. She can take me down to the cops when we're done."

I stood and kissed her good-bye. "I'll call you tonight and see how things went at the police station." She patted me on the cheek, but her mind was elsewhere. It was with Lawless and being grilled.

I walked down her stairs. A man with his head down passed me on his way up. All I saw was the top of his hair, dark and curly. That described all the Szabo males. I kept walking, then turned to face his back. But I didn't get a view of his back. He'd stopped climbing the stairs and was waiting for me to turn around and see him. He smiled at me. I scooted down the next flight of stairs. If Mina was lying to me and she was really waiting for the Hummingbird Wizard, she wouldn't have to wait long—I was pretty sure he was heading up her stairs.

Sixteen

I took the bus back to the Marina and retrieved my little car. There were three tickets under the windshield wipers. So much for my squeaky-clean record.

I hadn't told Cynthia Sloane what time I'd arrive, I hoped she was there, and hoped it wouldn't be a hassle getting in. I wasn't counting on Lana's hospitality, that's for sure.

I parked in a public lot three blocks from the Marquis Hotel to avoid the price of valet parking. I walked fast, skirting men wrapped in sleeping bags or old blankets, men hovered against doorways, men invisible to themselves, invisible to others. Most of them had learned to sleep without letting go of their paper cups.

Some held signs declaring themselves veterans, although a few looked young enough to be the children of Viet Nam veterans. These were the victims of a more personal war. One man had a border collie with a healthy coat while the man was shabby and too thin. I went into Nate's, bought the man a sandwich for his dog and two for him.

Cynthia had left a key for me at the hotel's front desk. I entered her room quietly and heard an old movie playing in Lana's room. Lana got up when she heard the door open, looked at me, said, "YOU," and went back to her room.

Cynthia was sitting at a table in the kitchen reading a pink and purple book. On the cover a woman was being tortured by a too-tight blouse. She was in the process of ripping it open to give herself breathing room.

I sat down across from Cynthia. She closed the cover. "Men!"

I knew exactly what she meant, but I wasn't in the mood to go there with her.

She pulled back from her book, stepped into my life. "I'm sorry about Jerry."

"I'm sorry, too."

"Any final word about what happened?"

"The final word is Jerry's dead. Whether it was a natural death or not, I don't know. We might never know."

"That's rough."

"Cyn, could we skip the girls' night? I'm beat and feel like I've been through four kinds of hell. I need to disappear."

"Bedroom's to your left, it has its own bath." She gave me a kiss. "If you can't sleep and want to talk, wake me up."

I said good night, and she went back to her book. As I was filling the tub, I saw the romance novel fly. It hit the kitchen wall hard. Another *Men!* section.

I lay down on the fourteen-inch mattress while the tub filled. I closed my eyes and drifted to a place with no people. Silent as snow, a large white room. A voice. Cynthia's.

"What are we going to do if we find him?"

Life came collapsing in on me like four sides of an old box. I worked to remember where I was. Cynthia's hotel room. What she was talking about?

"If we find who?"

"At the theater. If we find the guy you saw creeping around Jerry's when you were asleep. The one you thought you had sex with but didn't. Probably."

Her pillows, soft, wonderful goose down. Too many words in the world.

"Annie?"

"If we find the guy . . . I don't know. I wanted to do some rational thing like ask if we had sex or if I dreamed him. When I say it out loud it sounds moronic."

"It's not."

"And ask if he knew who he was leaving the perfumed oil for."

"That's not stupid either."

"Okay. That's what we're going to do if we find him."

My voice was a drone, my eyes were closed. "Fantasy or real—I had an indescribably beautiful, erotic, surreal in-and-out-of-body experience in Jerry's bed while he was lying anonymous, uncared for, dead behind a Dumpster. I don't know how to deal with that."

"You'll reach inside and find a way, then you'll put it down. You can't move in the world carrying a pack of guilt on your back. We both know that."

I opened my eyes. "I'm using a movie star as my reality check. This is a new low."

"Talk about low? I use you the same way, and you're a rag reporter. Thank God we know our professions don't define us."

"Of course they do."

Cynthia looked amazed. "Oh, shit."

"Tell me about it."

She turned off the water for the bath I was too tired to take, picked up the book she'd flung against the wall across the hall, and walked to her own room. I climbed under the covers into the cool crisp sheets of expensive hotel bliss. Sleep found me quickly and it was merciful. No dreams.

I awoke to the sound of two women complaining at each other. Lana and Cynthia. I rolled over and looked at the clock, it was the middle of the night. Lana stomped into my bedroom, shook me on the shoulder, and said, "The telephone is for you. You may pick up on your bedside table."

My voice was most of the way asleep. "Hello?"

"They want to arrest me."

"Mina?"

"Who else? They want to arrest me."

"What for?"

"Jerry's death."

"God, Mina you really must have pissed them off."

"I just acted like myself. I told the truth as I see it."

I turned onto my side. "That's what I was afraid of."

"This is not the time to act cute."

"They really want to arrest you for Jerry's death? They have to have evidence that links you to the crime.

"Mina?"

"Well, not for the crime exactly, but I did see Jerry before he died. Just before. Remember I told you he wanted me to sign some papers Friday night and that I'd said, 'Forget it?' I lied to you. I did go down there and see him, but I didn't sign those papers. I told Jerry when he could write them in plain English, I would sign them. Or not."

"Who told the cops you were at his office?"

"That big dumb security guard. He remembered I'd been there. I asked the cops, how could that man have identified me? I'm no different than any other good-looking woman on the street."

"What did they say?"

"They laughed. Listen, you are my one phone call. They say if they can't get me for murder, then there's all kinds of scams they can hold me for. I'm in trouble over here."

"You need a lawyer. The only one I know is Bill Wells."

"Jesus God, don't call him. I'll be in the electric chair by next week. Call Zoltan Perger, that PI I told you about. He's almost the same as a lawyer. He's smart, nothing shakes him up, and he can lie with the best of them."

She gave me Zoltan's number, and I promised to get him on the stick. I called E. B. and told her to check out a bailbondsman in San Francisco. She wasn't surprised when I told her why.

Seventeen

The one thing Gypsies forgive above all else is poor judgment in love.
—Jozef Farkas, *The Gypsies*, 1843

Unfortunately, poor judgment leads you smack into birth, death, and other big trouble.
—Madame Mina Szabo, 2003

I woke up at 6:00 A.M., and I wasn't worried about Mina. She's made out of space-age metal—indestructible. If I were of the law-and-order persuasion, my sympathy would have gone out to the law enforcement officers who had to deal with her last night.

Cynthia's not a morning person, it would be hours before she woke up. In spite of life's sudden left turn, I still had bill collectors who expected my life to go on as usual. I left Cynthia an embarrassing note. In my entire career I'd never made the request I was now making of Cynthia. It was necessary, but I was mortified and made a hasty exit.

Will be back late this afternoon to get ready for Phantom. *Avoid long baths, eat lots of chocolate. I've never done this before, but could you interview yourself? Questions are on the counter. Make up answers, make up new questions. Whatever works. Love, A.*
PS: Thanks for the space and the peace.

Time to see if Mina was back in business or headed to San Quentin. I'd stop by her house, make sure Zoltan had cleaned up the legal mess. The route between all points in San Francisco and Chinatown was becoming automatic. I passed the Sutter and

Stockton garage, a concrete homage to the ability of man to take a vast space and transform it into something ugly and dreary before it's had a chance to acquire those characteristics through time.

I squeezed between two rental-looking cars on Stockton Street. The early, narrow streets were double-parked with rattling delivery trucks. Their cargo, crates of live fish, table linens, fresh vegetables, shark fins, and elk antlers, was tossed out the back and to the sides. I avoided all delivery projectiles.

I arrived at Mina's just as morning hit Capri. She groaned and leaned her head back on the couch. She was in pretty much the same spot she'd been when I left the day before. Pretty much the same condition, too.

Mina stroked Capri's hair. "How are you, baby?"

"I'll live. I don't know if that's good or bad." Capri's skin looked like it was trying to make up its mind, too.

Mina waved a wordless hello to me. She wasn't really present for my hello or for petting Capri. She was looking down a distant road, some past indiscretion or success. Wherever she was, it wasn't someplace here and now. She gently laid Capri's head down, and motioned me into the kitchen. Capri rolled off the couch and curled up on the floor.

"Zoltan have any trouble getting you out?"

"Nah. Zoltan said unless they wanted to charge me with something, they had to let me go."

"And . . ."

"And they let me go. Let me tell you, cops act like they're so tough, but they are some of the most suspicious people you'll ever meet. I sang a few songs in my own language, made up a bunch of silly curses, told one of them his foot troubles would only get worse if they didn't leave me alone. The man was hobbling around all over the place—it didn't take a genius to figure he had troubles there. Then they got the big boss, Lawless. Him I didn't mind. He actually had some brains between his ears, also common sense. Anyway, we talked about Jerry with Zoltan sitting right beside me the whole time. When Lawless was done he called the young cops a bunch of clowns, and he escorted me outside like a real gentleman. Then he told me not to leave town. So here I am."

Lawless was experienced, Lawless was smooth. Mina does not know the meaning of restraint, and I was sure he'd gotten more out of her then she knew. I only hoped it wasn't anything that would come back to haunt her.

"E. B. called while I was down there and talked to Zoltan," she said. "She had bail money set up when and if I needed it. What a kid!"

I agreed.

Mina made tea, and she used her good china. I made a tray of food, and we took it into the living room.

When Capri saw me her eyes popped open. "Jesus, Annie, you're here. I wondered where you went last night. We almost forgot to show my mother the bottle of red oil you found. Show her that love letter, too."

Capri gave me the opening I'd decided I didn't want.

"Capri, it's nothing."

She tugged at my shirt. "Go on, show Mamo the oil and the note."

She pulled the small bottle of red oil with the drawing of a hummingbird on the label from my purse.

Mina studied it. "Oh this. Sure, you get this oil over in the Latino part of town, Central Americans like it. Hummingbird oil, *chaluparosa* oil, they call it. It attracts love. I buy it and put my label on. Business is complicated enough without making my own products."

She turned the bottle over in her hands. "Where did you get this stuff?"

"Mamo, this was left on Jerry's dresser for Annie Sunday night, you know, the night she spent at Jerry's when she thought she was with him but wasn't."

Mina's eyebrows shot up to her hairline.

"What is Capri talking about? Capri don't make sense some-times."

Here we go. I looked at Mina and gave her the whole dumb story. "Sunday night I was waiting for Jerry. I'd been jittery, and drank some steeped valerian root washed down with white wine. It gave me a picturesque wham. I had very intense dreams, intense to the point of reality. Come first light I saw a man walk softly across Jerry's room. I'm pretty sure it was the same man I saw walking up your stairs yesterday. Anyway, Monday morning I found this hummingbird oil wrapped up in a bow, sitting on Jerry's dresser. It hadn't been there when I went to bed."

Mina put her hand to her mouth and gasped.

"Annie," Capri said, "you got to show her the note. That one he left you. You put it in the zipper pocket of your purse."

I didn't know why all of a sudden Capri's memory was clicking along like a well-oiled machine.

I got out the note and handed it to Mina.

She held the note at arm's length. "Let me get my glasses."

She studied the handwriting. Mina muttered the words under her breath. She read it again. This note probably meant more to her than it had to me because, unlike me, she was familiar with the person who wrote it. Her skin was now approaching the color of Capri's.

Gypsies like the color red. It's good luck. Madame Mina wears red underwear. I know this because when she walked into the kitchen to put the note under a stronger light, she forgot her daughter was sprawled out on the floor in front of the couch, and fell over her. Mina's skirt, all seven layers, went with her, end over end, showing flashes of red. She didn't move.

Capri climbed out from under her mother and got the Jim Beam she'd been nursing on the cable car. She puckered Mina's cheeks and poured it down her throat. Mina's eyelids fluttered. Mina rearranged her clothes and recovered her dignity. As much dignity as you can recover after you've exposed your red underwear. She got to her knees and used the kitchen counter to help her stand.

I said, "You know who wrote this."

"Of course. We all know this person."

"I need to find him."

"Sssshhh. You think of him, *poof*, he will appear."

"Good."

"Listen to me. This is my boy. No one knows him better than me. His father and I were a terrible combination for making babies. My other kids' fathers—one was older than God, and the other was a horse's ass. At least they didn't help me pass along power too big to handle. This one is too much responsibility."

Mina stared at me. It was not comfortable. She said, "Annie, you've already met this son of mine."

"I can't say that we were actually introduced."

"I mean before Sunday night."

I went through my mental list of romantic attachments and friends. I came up blank.

"Get that blank look off your face. He's the kid who threw up on you at your wedding."

I tried to remember the wedding boy's face, but it was just an annoying blot. I tried to place him at parties, but he was always the kid on the fringes watching people, listening to them. What I remembered was that he moved like vapor through family gatherings.

"The kid who drove you home that night?"

"Yes, Jozef."

"Joe for short?"

"When he wants to feel all-American, yeah, Joe. I hate that name."

"He called Jerry's Sunday night."

"I didn't think he got into town until yesterday morning."

"If we're talking about the same man, he was in town by Sunday night. How much earlier than that, I don't know."

"We got to stop messing around," Mina said. "Jerry is having a terrible time as a dead person. So many questions around him, so many people hungry for what he had. So far his death is just like his life. We got to make things peaceful for him."

"How do we do that?"

"Simple, we find the person who killed him and even things out. And we go see Zoltan to help us get started."

"You think he can figure out why Jerry died?"

"Zoltan's very strong. He's the one who sniffed around and found Jerry, the one who made the anonymous call to the police. He can smell Gypsy blood from a thousand miles off."

"Jerry wasn't a Gypsy. Jerry was a Jew."

"Jerry hung around us long enough for the scent to rub off on him. And, like the cops said, Jerry was two days gone. Zoltan wasn't the only one smelling him, just the first."

She took the bottle of Jim Beam away from Capri. I didn't know if she needed a shot, or decided Capri didn't need one more.

Eighteen

*M*ina said, "Capri, stay here. I mean don't go nowhere. Anyone comes in, look at their palms and read their fortune. You can handle that much of the family business."

I picked up my purse and put the note and hummingbird oil back inside.

Mina said, "What do you want with that stuff? Leave it here."

"It smells good."

"Unless you want to attract love or trouble, make sure the lid's on tight."

We opened the door to leave, and there stood Bill Wells on the landing.

Mina smacked her head with her hand. "God almighty, Bill, not now."

She looked at me. "See what I mean? That oil attracts trouble like there's no tomorrow."

Mina closed the snap on her purse. "Listen, Bill, I got other things to do than pretend to tell your future while you weasel family secrets out of me."

"What are you doing here?" I asked him.

Bill put a crushed look on his face as easily as a woman slips into a silk dress. "I just wanted to know if there's anything I can do for the family."

Mina looked at Capri, her hand on the doorknob. "Capri, don't talk to Bill about nothing. In this state your tongue is looser than Mira Zabronski's daughter. You need to start spreading the word about Jerry's funeral."

Capri's mind had stopped working. "His funeral."

"Tomorrow."

"Right, tomorrow."

"Bill, maybe you can make yourself useful and help Capri with this."

Mina slammed the door in Bill's solemn face. We stood on the landing outside her apartment. She was flushed, she was breathing heavily. Mina shook her finger in my face. "That Bill! He has a crush on my daughter, and says he loves me like a mother. All nonsense! What he says and does are very different than what's inside him."

"He has a crush on Capri?"

"I don't even know how she can breathe under it."

"How did Jerry feel about that?"

"Same as me, not great."

That was probably an understatement. Divorced or not, living together or not, Jerry was still attached to Capri heart and soul. At least he had been.

"Capri?"

"She hardly notices him, which only makes Bill worse. Let's leave it like this, I don't like Bill. I don't guess you do either. I never trusted him with Jerry in business. I sure don't trust him with my daughter's heart. Or her body."

"You feel okay about leaving Bill alone with Capri?"

"No, Bill's a stray dog who picks at bones until he worries them to splinters. Capri could say the wrong thing, you know, toss him the wrong bone, but we got no choice. Forget Bill and move your legs. We got to talk to Zoltan about you and the

Hummingbird Wizard before he leaves his office, and we got to find out what he knows about Jerry."

E. B. was right. I shouldn't be here. I wanted the police to find Jerry's killer, not a Gypsy PI. "I want to go home," I said.

"Move your legs."

For a big woman she was hard to keep up with. Her layered skirts flew behind her like flags from seven countries.

"Where's Zoltan's office?" I shouted at her back.

No answer. I followed her past a Clean Well-Lighted Place for Books, down Van Ness and straight into the Haight. There were odd shops with tiles falling off, gay couples making out on street corners as they waited for the light to change, photos in store windows of guys doing things that, I don't care if they do it, but I don't want to see it any more than I'd want someone looking at me in a shop window.

We walked eight blocks up Haight Street and stopped in front of one of the storefronts. There it was, Madame Mina's Mystic Café. I'd heard of it for years, but I'd never been there, never even quite believed it existed.

A man paced outside the cafe. He wore a black fur jacket, full-length, and a tall fur hat. The fur had fallen off in tufts. Zoltan Perger looked like someone from another continent of time.

On a blanket spread before him, in front of The Mystic Café, was a ratty quilt. Some of the fabrics were the same as those in Mina's skirt. One was yellow with bright red thunderbolts passing through at lightning-quick angles.

Lying on his quilt were two cats. They weren't tied to anything, and they weren't caged. They slept. Leaning up against the window was a poster board sign that read Psychic Cats—$1.00 For Reading. Zoltan had a parrot perched on a stick about five feet high fastened to a thin wooden base.

Patting his chest, Mina said to Zoltan, "You're wearing my favorite coat. It carries the scent of life."

He sniffed his sleeve. "You don't know where this coat has

been. This is not the scent of life. This is the stench of existence."

He turned to me. He was warm and layered and kind and strong and masculine. "You'd like your fortune?"

Mina rolled her eyes.

He caught the look. "You stay out of this, Mina. Sometimes you act like you're such a big shot."

"Have I even said one word?"

"You don't need to say nothing. You just roll those eyes, and people fall off the chairs they aren't even sitting on."

Zoltan faced her fully. His cheeks were deep red, he had lost the ability to speak. He opened his jacket like he was ready to fling it on the ground. I thought we were in for an all-out fight of the sort I'd heard about between Pinky and Mina.

Nope.

Zoltan took Mina inside his jacket, wrapped her against his chest, and kissed her. Passionately. Mina kissed him back with the same enthusiasm. Apparently Pinky wasn't the only man in Mina's life. I tried to look elsewhere, anywhere. To the store selling five-hundred-dollar silver platform shoes, across to the old woman huddled in a doorway with a hamster on a leash, up the street to two hunky men, their arms around each other, kissing as passionately as Zoltan and Mina.

Zoltan's voice. "So, which cat do you want to read your fortune?"

I turned around. They'd come up for air.

He said, "Go on. Pick a cat, he'll tell your fortune. Don't tell anyone what it says, or its magic will run right out."

Mina straightened the front of her blouse, and I picked the fat orange cat. Zoltan put tuna on a lever. The orange cat pressed his paw on the lever and then licked the tuna off his paw. When he lifted his paw, it released the lever, and a fortune rolled out of a wooden box. The fortune was straightforward. It read, *The trouble with resisting temptation is that it may never come again.*

Zoltan's parrot squawked on his perch. Zoltan said to the bird, "Felix, bless the lady."

Felix fluffed the bright turquoise feathers around his neck. He looked down at me and sang, *God Bless You!*

Mina said, "Enough. Now we three go inside and get serious."

"Getting serious sounds like too much time," I said. "I want my car, my friend's hotel room, a decent meal, then home."

They both looked at me as if I were a spoiled child. Mina shook her head. Zoltan told me to bring the cats. He took Felix the parrot, and Mina folded his quilt.

He bowed and opened the door to The Mystic Café. "Come into my office."

Nineteen

*T*arot cards were laminated onto the tabletops and chair seats. No matter where you put your ass, you sat on a Priestess, Knight, Fool, Death, or Transformation.

Computers sat on the tables closest to the walls, and they were plugged into phone jacks. Each table was occupied, and each occupant was having his tarot read via a virtual psychic on the Internet. In the back of the cafe stood a dark wooden counter layered with shellac. On shelves behind the counter were rows of teas and oils stacked six high to invite strength, brain power, love, and luck. That was just the first row.

I noticed that most people working out their futures on the Net had chosen the tea deemed to make their virtual hope become reality. Many were eating odd muffins or stuffed pita bread. Depending upon how complicated your life was, in other words how much computer time you needed to sort out the details, an afternoon in that place could add up to a healthy chunk of change. Good thing. The neighborhood was funky, but it was high-rent.

Zoltan pulled out a chair for me. Mina nodded in approval. It was plastered with The Fool card.

She said, "The Fool is a good card. In *King Lear*, The Fool is the only one who gets to tell the king the truth and live to say, 'I told you so.'"

Mina never ceased to amaze me. "You know about *King Lear*?"

I shrunk under her stare. "My family was very theatrical. We traveled Europe. When we moved here during the war, we performed around the States. Who doesn't know *Lear*?"

"I don't know him," Zoltan said.

"You wouldn't," she said.

Mina smiled in the smallest way, and her eyes actually sparkled when she looked at him. His joy squished him flat against the wall under a photo of a naked man wearing a fruit bowl for a hat. The naked man had a wide-open grin and held a Chihuahua in his lap. The title was in large letters—ADVENTURE IN PARADISE.

Zoltan wriggled in his seat and started playing footsie with Mina under the table. I know because he got me once by mistake. I moved my feet as far away from him as I could. His foot kept going up and down Mina's calf.

She moved her chair back. "Zoltan, stop screwing around and act normal. We got important business. Annie's an outsider, but right now she's on the inside."

I looked around The Mystic Café. "I don't want to be on the inside of this."

"The choice is not yours. It was decided before you were even born."

Arguing with Mina was pointless.

"Zoltan, Annie is a very old friend to Jerry." She stopped here and took a deep breath. "She is my dead Stevan's wife, who I've talked to you about."

He stroked his beard and twisted the ring on his middle finger. "E. B.'s mother? Holy God."

He sized me up and said quietly, "The two men in your life? What happened to them both is a true tragedy."

Mina said, "Stevan lived his life in a careless way, and he paid the biggest price because of it." She turned to me and said, "I'm sorry to say this in front of you, his widow, but since I'm his mother, it gives me the right to say his faults."

Turning back to Zoltan, she said, "Jerry's different. Somehow Pinky pushed him into death, you and I both know that. We know something else. Pinky has brains and nerve, but he don't have the concentration to plan much on his own."

Mina was still obsessing over Pinky's role in Jerry's death. It struck me that I hadn't taken her seriously, and I didn't know why. She'd known the man for years. I'd never heard of him until the last few days. He might have been an abusive husband and father, a man capable of murder, a man with reason to want Jerry gone. One of my habitual thinking patterns was shattered—just because Mina believed something didn't mean it wasn't true.

As long as I was consorting with the law, and the law was feeling mellow, maybe I'd ask Lawless to see if anyone around the department had ever heard of Pinky Marks.

I looked at Zoltan and Mina with their heads together. Whatever they were cooking up, the SF Police Department was no match for them. If Pinky was responsible for Jerry's death, I was certain those two would dispense a justice more swift than any set of bureaucratic wheels could. I wouldn't want to be in Pinky's shoes for all the world.

"I'll find out who helped Pinky with the thinking part." Zoltan put one hand on Mina's and one hand on mine. "The truth will find us. It always does."

Mina looked comforted.

While we were on Pinky, I had a flash. "Mina," I said, "didn't you say you and Pinky got married in Barstow, that it was the only legal thing you've done?"

Zoltan went ramrod stiff like I'd just stuck a piece of rebar down the back of his shirt all the way down to the seat of his pants.

"Don't remind me," she said.

"This means you never had a legal divorce?"

"Legal according to the United States of America? No."

"And you live in a community property state."

"If you say so."

"Mina, do you have a will?"

"God no, bad luck."

"Do you realize that if anything happened to you, Pinky would automatically inherit anything you own?"

"I think Jerry mentioned that."

Zoltan furrowed his brow at her.

"Okay," she said, "I'm sure Jerry mentioned that to me. But I don't own anything worth getting into a sweat about."

Zoltan's furrowed brow rearranged itself into surprise, but he didn't say anything.

Maybe this had something to do with Jerry's late date with Mina Friday night. If so, Mina could be in trouble. The woman drove me nuts, but I didn't want her to suffer any actual damage.

"Zoltan," I said, "would you keep an eye on Mina?"

"I have for years."

"Not that kind of eye. I mean tail her, protect her. And follow up on anyone if you think it's necessary. Taking care of Mina may give us some clues concerning Jerry's death. I'll pay your standard rates."

Whoa. That just slipped out. I wasn't sure where the money'd come from, and I had no idea how much PIs charged, but we'd figure that out later.

"I couldn't charge you. You're family."

"You're a professional. I won't take your services unless I pay you."

"Zoltan, like I told you, she invented stubborn," said Mina. "She says she won't budge, believe her."

And so it came to be that Zoltan Perger came into my employ.

*   *   *

"You want me to start in with Mina like she's a stranger?"

"Yes. Dump any ideas you already have. They might cloud your reason."

He took a deep breath and closed his eyes, like he was trying to empty the trash bin in his head.

"Okay. Let's go."

He took out a pad of paper.

Mina said, "Zoltan, this is stupid. You know as much about me as I do."

Zoltan was all business. "Mina, I've been hired to protect you. Don't give me any grief, okay?"

Mina folded her hands in her lap like a prim schoolgirl.

"Fine," she said. "Here's a place to start, Mr. Perger. Hummingbird is in town. Sunday night he paid a visit to Annie. I don't know how long he was in town before he went to her. But he hits town around the same time Jerry leaves forever? This can't be a coincidence."

Zoltan squeezed her hand. "Nothing's a coincidence. That's how this whole thing"—he spread his arms to encircle the world—"has worked for so long. We can't live right if we forget that."

Zoltan had dropped his Romeo role, and was all concentration.

"You have no idea when Hummingbird got here, Mina?"

"No. He usually calls first, not this time. He showed up long enough to make himself known to this one"—she pointed to me with her thumb—"and he came by and took me to the police yesterday, just like I'd called him or something. He dropped me off and disappeared."

Zoltan kept his eyes locked on Mina's. "Maybe he was trying to warn Jerry off Pinky, and he got here too late."

He turned to me. "When exactly did Hummingbird visit you?"

"This is really speculation. I'm assuming it was Jozef, your Hummingbird, because of the note he left, but I've never met the guy, well not for a long time, so I couldn't really say I knew who walked through Jerry's bedroom around dawn on Monday. Also, I'd been having a big dream, and I thought at the time I was in bed with Jerry. And then, in the morning, I wasn't sure. This is not much help."

"So, you can't identify Jozef as the man in the bedroom?"

"Pretty hard to positively identify someone you haven't seen since he was a teenager."

"Couldn't you smell if a Gypsy was in the room? It might have been a regular prowler."

Mina said, "Zoltan, she don't know from smells. She's Irish."

"Oh." He looked sorry for me.

I said, "I was tired, lonely, had an herbal blast, fell asleep, and started dreaming. Pretty soon I'm flying with a handsome man, I'm close to bliss, and I'm losing track of gravity. And some guy walks across the room and out the door."

They both looked at me. "He took you flying?"

I was truly in the Fool's seat. Foolish to be there when I could be home having my regular old life instead of sitting at a fortune-telling cafe with bad art on the walls, apocalyptic chairs, and two Gypsies discussing my life in relation to my oldest friend's death. One more hour and I'd be soaking in Cynthia's tub, the soak I didn't get last night.

"He didn't take me flying. It was a dream about flying and sex, and the person you call Hummingbird sneaked into it."

"This is bigger than I thought," Mina said. "You didn't say nothing before about flying, not even on airplanes, which I hope to God not to do in a long time, like maybe after I'm dead."

I was at the end of my rope. "Listen, you two. I'm not one hundred percent sure about the sex part—part of me still believes Jerry died later than the cops think he did. But the flying part was a dream. That's it."

Zoltan slammed his fist on the table. "How often do you dream of flying with a man and wake up with feathers in your sheets?"

"There were just a few, probably from the pillows, and how did you know about the feathers?"

"Hummingbirds must have feathers to fly. That must be obvious even to someone who can't smell right."

I was confused, pissed-off, and tired. "I can't think right. I need to leave."

Zoltan gently took my wrist and lowered me back to my seat. "Let's calm down. Did you lock the door before you went to bed?"

"Sure, but that house key under the planter made Jerry's place home-away-from-home to any number of people. And dogs. Hummingbird either knew about the key, pretty likely, or he broke in."

"Lot's of people put their keys under a planter. An easy way for a prowler to get in."

"That's true. But what about the body oil? Prowlers usually take things, not leave them."

"Annie, if it *was* Hummingbird, he gave you the protection of his wing. But he's moody." Zoltan ran his fingers through his beard and turned to Mina. "I agree with Annie," he said. "She should go home. We'll take care of this by ourselves. It's our way."

Mina insisted I stay. I liked the way they argued about me as if I weren't there.

"Zoltan," I said, "try this on for size. A kid, my dead husband's brother, throws up on me at my wedding. Years later he hits town when Jerry dies and doesn't let his family know he's here. He skulks around Jerry's house in the middle of the night and leaves me a love letter and some red oil that fortunately hasn't stained my purse. This guy has got to be damaged."

My stomach tightened up, and a rush of fear charged me.

Mina held my face in her hands. "What's with you? You're even whiter than usual."

"What if Hummingbird was responsible for Jerry's death?"

"That's crazy talk—and Hummingbird is anything *but* damaged."

Even nearly normal families mess each other up, no way you could grow up in the Szabo clan and be left unscathed. Stevan was wild and fast and loved danger. That's attractive, it's also a disaster waiting to happen. Jozef was intense and quiet—they're the truly scary people.

"Mina, families damage each other. You know that."

"Maybe that's true of your family, not ours."

Mina was a mother. She'd lost Stevan. She'd believe anything or ignore anything to protect the son she had left. Zoltan was busy taking notes, probably wanted me to think I was getting my money's worth.

I'd done my bit: The cops were on the case, Zoltan was on the case. I was going home.

Twenty

$\mathcal{T}$he door to The Mystic Café opened. A man walked in, ordinary clothes, no feathered dream cape. The light from the plate-glass window behind him tossed his soft dark curls. I wanted to bury my face there. I wanted to breathe him. I wanted to sneak out the back door. His skin was pale brown, completely clear. He carried a bouquet of roses. I hate roses.

He bent down, kissed Mina on the cheek, and gave his mother the flowers. He shook hands with Zoltan.

The young woman across from us was having her tarot read by one of the two human fortune-tellers in the cafe. Hummingbird used his smile, the early-dawn smile I remembered, and said to her, "Excuse me. You're sitting in my seat."

She fluttered around and relinquished her chair with a weak grin. A revolting display of submissive behavior. He pulled up the chair he'd claimed and joined us. It was laminated with the first card in the deck, the Wizard.

He ordered three sandwiches, a large salad, and a slice of double chocolate cake. How he'd stuff all that food into a pair of size 32 waist jeans I didn't know. Either a fast metabolism or a long time since the last meal.

I placed the note from him and the small bottle of perfumed

oil on the table. I pushed them toward Hummingbird. Mina and Zoltan moved their chairs back. I looked in the man's eyes, looked behind his eyes, looked right through his skin.

I couldn't feel evil, joy, melancholy. I could not get inside him. He was an expert at concealing himself.

He locked on to my eyes just as hard.

He unfolded the note, didn't read it, refolded it. The veins along the back of his hands were fine cords. His fingers were long, not thin, hands that worked, hands that could sculpt. They were like Stevan's hands, they made me ache, I stopped looking at them.

He tossed the note across the table. "Just now, when I walked through that door you knew me, and you hated me. I don't understand."

"How did I know you in broad daylight wearing jeans and a toss-away smile like some average guy? Because you're not an average guy, and because I felt my body's reaction to you. It was almost cellular. I don't know why I want to hate you."

"A piece of truth. Thank you."

"The truth. Were you in Jerry's room around dawn on Monday?"

He looked at his fingernails, then met my eyes. "I was."

"Were you next to me in bed?"

"My mother's here. This is not the place. I left you a gift. For now, leave it at that."

"You crept into bed with me while I was zoned out, didn't you?"

"I don't need to sneak into a woman's bed."

I was sure that was true. He was gorgeous, but something more.

"Jozef, we have a big problem here. If we actually had sex, it was rape. Most of me was not there."

"What?"

"You heard me."

"If you believe that, why didn't you talk to the police about it?"

"The police? I'd drunk too much valerian, and I washed it down with wine. I was asleep, but not quite, and didn't know if what was going on was real. At least real with someone other than Jerry. It's embarrassing to spend the night with a stranger and not know they're a stranger—you felt familiar. What, exactly, could the police do about that? Nothing. That's not true—they could laugh me out of the building."

"Embarrassed? I don't think so. You're no innocent heroine swept away by lust. You're a grown woman who knows what you want. You saw me, you opened your arms, you invited me in."

"This cannot be true."

"I'm sorry to be an embarrassment to you. It wasn't my intention."

My head was going like a carousel, each rotation turning into one more round of neurotic speculation. Throughout my mental ride Jozef and I sat in a silent face-off that weighed ten tons. He tried to read the thoughts running quick across my face and gave up. He couldn't follow them. Who could?

Maybe Lawless would turn up something on him. If not, I had a few other sources I could try. I might even sink so low as to pump Bill for information.

His thoughts were easy to read. Jozef was out of patience. I wanted to ask him his version of what happened with us, maybe it wasn't the same as mine, and talk to him about Jerry. What was he doing in Jerry's house? When had he hit town? We couldn't talk at The Mystic Café, or in front of Mina. I was about to suggest a place, a time, when he jerked out his chair and stood up, the chair legs scraping across the concrete floor like raw fingernails on a chalkboard.

He turned to Mina. "Mamo, I'll see you later."

Jozef stroked Mina's cheek and kissed her. He loved her in a tender way, that was obvious. Big deal. Lots of wackos love their mothers.

He bent down and put his face in front of mine. Astounding intensity. "When I want you again, I'll find you."

"Don't count on it."

"In a world full of beige people, you're easy to find."

He stormed toward the double glass door. He looked over his shoulder at me, walked back to the table, and put his face into mine, his hand on my cheek.

"I envied my brother for you, I thought how I'd love a woman with such flash and passion. You don't know that part of yourself anymore, you're even embarrassed when that part of you wakes up. What a waste." His jaw clenched. His anger went interior.

He gave me his back again and pushed through the door into the world on the other side. Mina broke loose from Zoltan and followed her son.

Twenty-One

"**Z**oltan, I'm paying you to keep an eye on Mina. Shouldn't you follow them?"

"I know where they're going."

"Want to clue me in?"

"No."

Quiet sat at the table like a third person between us.

Zoltan said, "You weren't the only one who was embarrassed. He was."

"I didn't see it."

"What do you think that anger was about? He gave you love, you denied it. You even pretended it wasn't real."

"I should talk to the cops about him."

I was mumbling, looking down at my lap, acting like I thought the cops could fix my love life or nail a man for murder with no evidence. And maybe I wanted Hummingbird to be a villain because he'd made me feel things that I thought were dead, or at least comatose.

Zoltan lifted my head up, held my chin in his hand. His skin was hard, I felt the knuckles time had turned into knots. "Annie, you don't understand who he is. Hummingbird's the wizard of our *kumpania*. He wouldn't want any harm to come to Jerry. Just the opposite."

"What if he got tired of a non-Gypsy being in the center of his family's life? Jealous of Jerry's relationship with his mother, unhappy with the way Jerry treated Capri, ticked off that Jerry'd dragged Pinky back into their lives."

"Dealing with Pinky was strictly business."

Yeah, right.

A waitress flowed by wearing tie-dye and scarves. She offered us a menu, recognized Zoltan, and kissed his cheek. She flowed back into the otherworldly place she inhabited behind the cash register.

I said, "Jerry putting together a business deal with Pinky and Mina may have seemed like a final humiliation for the family."

"I don't know anything about Mina's business."

I doubted that. Zoltan had an eye for Mina, which meant he noticed her life, all of it.

Zoltan said, "You're angry and humiliated, not that I blame you, for sleeping with a man you thought was someone else. This doesn't mean the man had anything to do with the other's death."

I'd already covered that internally. It also didn't mean Hummingbird was in the clear.

"What was he doing at Jerry's house?" I said.

"Probably to talk about the family, he saw you in bed, and couldn't resist you."

"I'm past the age of irresistibility."

I waited for Zoltan to argue with me. He didn't.

I wasn't quite ready to dump Zoltan yet. I figured if nothing else I could get a story line for *The Eye* out of him. "What exactly is the wizard of a *kumpania*'s job?"

"It's very important. He feels people down to the middle of their bones. Feels them the same way Gypsy men feel fish and catch them. You know this technique?"

"I missed that issue of *Field & Stream*."

He threw his hands up in the air. "You don't want to know who you're dealing with, okay by me."

"Sorry."

He settled into his seat and cleared his throat. All the symptoms of a tall tale. I could hear Cynthia's posh hotel room calling my name.

"It's like this—Gypsy men lie on the bank of a river, stick one arm in the water, and wait patiently for a fish to swim by. They tickle the fish belly, soft, until they feel the rhythm of the fish, until they become the fish. They pull the fish up as easily as they would pull themselves out of the water.

"Jozef has this ability, but big. He touches a person and finds their pulse, feels their heart. He can feel the rhythm of a body, jump into it, fix it if you're sick, and heal you. He can also slow it down, stop it. If you stop the beating of a person's drum, they're dead. He is rebirth, he is absolute destruction."

"As far as dangerous characters go, that would make Pinky Marks small-fry compared to Jozef."

Zoltan looked as if I'd slapped him across the face. He was probably sorry he'd mentioned that part about screwing around with heart rhythms. I didn't know if he was playing me for a fool, or if he believed what he was saying.

He looked me squarely in the eye. "Jozef protected you Sunday night, be certain of that. Maybe you wanted to look for Jerry, and he kept you from the horror of finding him. I wouldn't know. I do know this—to be inside you, to pulse with you in that dance between men and women, is the strongest force in the universe. It makes babies cry to be born. He took you to the center of power and protected you there."

I looked around The Mystic Café. People reading fortunes to helpless people looking for a boost into a hopeful future, others working with computers for a helping hand out of their present life. This was not a world I wanted, nor had it ever been.

I took myself on a trip back to what I consider the real world, and I stood firm on it. I discarded the smoke and mirrors and said what I needed to believe.

"Jerry's too young to be dead. That part's very hard. I'm not crazy about what happened between Hummingbird and me, but I doubt it's the first time two strangers became intimate in the middle of the night. Especially when one was partially asleep."

No more Mystic Café, no more universal truths. I stood up.

Zoltan said, "You're leaving? Where would you go that's safer than us?"

"I'm getting my car, going to my friend's hotel. Tomorrow I'll head home. All those things are safer than you, at least for my sanity." Home. E. B. My pierced and tattooed daughter seemed as solid as Mount Rushmore.

Zoltan said, "You shouldn't be alone. I'll drive you."

But I needed to be alone. After Stevan's death Mina invaded my life until I couldn't breathe. Now, with Jerry, I'd hardly had one real moment to feel the depth of my loss without the Szabos butting in. Once again they'd taken a terrible situation and made it worse for me.

I put my purse over my shoulder. Zoltan helped me on with my coat.

"What about the cops and Hummingbird? Are you going to mention him to them?"

Here I had to scoot around the truth. I'd already given Lawless a first name with a choice of possible last names. No details, no aka Hummingbird Wizard, nothing about our encounter at the time Jerry's body was discovered. I measured my words so I wouldn't fall into an out-and-out lie.

"Zoltan, I'd like to think of cops as the guys in white hats. Kind of like my dad riding his horse over a ridge to save the day. Truth is they've never done one useful thing for me other than suggesting I install locks on my front door when I thought I'd had a burglar. I never got around to putting in the locks, and it's been ten years.

"Also, I'm liable to get myself into some kind of trouble that I didn't even know existed if I talk to them." That was certainly true. "I've got faith that the universe will take care of those who need to be taken care of." That was true, too.

He patted my hand. "You know how to think right. You're a good girl."

I'd loved my mother, but things with her were always complicated. My dad was different. Easy. He'd been gone so long he was beginning to feel like a faded black-and-white photo, a smile on some other kid's lunch box. But when Zoltan patted my hand, letting me know I was doing my best, I remembered my dad and I missed him. It made me feel kind of bad about slightly lying to him. I told him where I'd be staying, and to keep in touch.

Three blocks and two bus transfers later, I spotted my car. It was the one with pink and yellow parking tickets flapping under the wiper blades, the one parked in a forty-five minute zone.

My car, my freedom.

It started right up. My rearview mirror showed a scene of government confetti following in my wake. Within two blocks the last parking ticket had flown out from under my wiper blades.

Twenty-Two

I pulled in front of the Marquis Hotel on Powell and Geary Streets. A uniformed man flurried over. He wore a gold name tag with his name embossed in Old English script. Poe. Poe looked at my car as if it were a four-wheeled disease. He offered to park it for me, and I let him. Unlike the night before, I was bringing up my bags, and I didn't want to hoof it from a parking lot up the street.

Before Poe drove off in my car, he got out a handkerchief so he didn't have to go skin-to-skin with my steering wheel. I'm sure he makes more per year in tips than I make writing for *The Eye*, plus my work on the side. Not too many old cars spend the night at the Marquis unless they're classic. Mine's anything but. Once I tried buffing it, but the cosmic blue paint started rubbing off, so I left it alone.

Extraordinary women turned and led with their long legs, each emerging from one in a line of Mercedes Benzes and BMWs. Their cars were whisked away by Poe clones. The Marquis is across the street from Union Square, and inside Union Square there is one wrought-iron bench visible from the hotel. The rest of the square is surrounded by bushes and trees. I walked across the street.

The man lying on the bench wore a tattered coat that was expensive thirty years ago. Newspapers were spread on the bench beneath him, and one yellowed sheet was open across his chest. His skin tone was gray. I thought about Detective Lawless, his log of the dead, and wondered if this man would soon be among them. I got down on my knees and watched his face to make sure he was breathing. His eyes flew open.

"Hey!" he yelled. "Were you checking to see if I was alive?"

"Yeah."

"Thanks," he said.

He rolled over, taking a sheet of newspaper with him.

I crossed the street again. Men in cashmere sweaters arrived at the hotel holding the elbows of their beautiful women, and, as far as I could tell, not one set of their beautiful eyes strayed to the man on the bench. I walked into grown-up Disneyland.

A bellman took my bags, and we climbed into a glass elevator that rode high above the man on the bench. It takes a particular key to make the elevator stop on the penthouse floor. No one is allowed merely to wander outside the rooms of the rich.

Average room rates start at $225 per night. This is for the old part of the hotel, where rooms are the size of extra-large closets with a view of the ducting and tar-paper roofs of other buildings. Cynthia's quarters were larger than most people's apartments. I put my electronic key in her door and three green lights lit up while the bellman hustled in with my bags. He refused my tip.

The human guard dog, Lana, looked at me like a sort of vermin on the skin of life. I don't know why it's so hard for some people to act decent.

"Lana, I'm only going to be here one more night. This shouldn't be a big deal for you."

"I don't like Cynthia to be disturbed. When she's disturbed, the cameras pick it up."

"I didn't know she was shooting a film right now."

"She's not."

"Then she's allowed to be as disturbed as life allows."

She ran this through her head.

"We'll have a truce then."

"Thank you."

"Besides, Ms. Sloane has given me the rest of the day off."

She held the strap of her expensive leather bag in the crook of her elbow. She was half-in, half-out of the door, when she turned around. "I'll be back tonight, though."

Hooray.

Cynthia was stretched out on the living-room couch wearing reading glasses, no makeup, sweats, and socks with holes in the bottoms. On the floor lay the torn and crumpled pages of a mutilated magazine.

I pointed to the mess. "What's with this?"

"I tore out the fat pictures of me. Plural. Tomorrow I am going to call that editor and ream his sorry butt from here to Mars."

She was eating a Reese's Peanut Butter Cup and reading a Ross McDonald mystery. She'd either given up on the pink and purple book or finished it.

This is the kind of photo *The National Eye* pays a bundle for, and it's why people like Cynthia have people like Lana. Without the Lanas you get guys pretending to deliver flowers busting in and snapping pictures. The pictures go to the highest bidder. The more unflattering the photo, the bigger the payday. Catch a roll of flab or a ripple of cellulite caressing a thigh, and you've got enough dough to live on for a month.

Most women, those with eccentric hobbies, heroic pets, or obnoxious ex-husbands, like having their pictures in print. But, just like movie stars, they want to be warned in advance. Nobody wants their picture taken when they're lying on a couch surrounded by empty candy wrappers. That's one of the reasons I do very few movie star stories. They're not quite fair.

I sat on the arm of the couch and scanned the cover of Cynthia's book. I'd read it. It was about an actress whose death was made to look like an accident so her new husband, who fooled around behind her back, could get her money without having to get yelled at or be dumped and wind up broke for fooling around behind her back.

I said, "If I had your job, I probably wouldn't read that."

"Why?"

"Never mind."

"You have a very Pollyanna attitude toward life," she said, peering at me over her lenses. She looked like a cynical high school teacher who's fed up and dreaming of wide beaches.

"Right now I need to muster all the Pollyanna attitude I can."

Cynthia said nothing in reply. She flipped a page.

I said, "I'm going to take the bath I didn't get last night. I need to relax, and you're in one of your moods."

The tub was white and copper-veined marble. It was big enough for four small people, three good-sized people. It had two faucets, Jacuzzi jets, and would not run out of hot water. You don't run out of hot water in fancy hotels, only at home.

Cynthia's hair-care products were natural and herb-infused. Her bathing toys included floating pillows, iced eye shades, and a rubber duck. There was a small refrigerator in the bathroom that held two bottles of champagne, a six-pack of Coke, and a small roll of French cheese. Ritz Crackers and Cheez Whiz were on the counter next to a little television set. Inside this bathroom Cynthia had built a womb-like getaway, complete with good champagne, in a very short period of time. I tossed my purse on the counter.

I took off my clothes and caught their limp shape. It had been too long since I'd bathed. There I was, naked, in the full-length mirror. I don't own a full-length mirror, never have, in order to avoid this specter. The fact that I didn't work out was apparent. My knees weren't as tight as they should be. There was a hint of loose skin under my arms. My boobs were okay. My hair was still red, although now I had slim gray racing stripes on either side. I had all my own teeth, uncapped, white and straight, and a large smile. Some crow's-feet. If I concentrated on my face, the rest of my body was easier to take, or at least ignore.

I poured a small bottle of apricot bubble bath into the tub. The foam was as fierce as if I'd poured Dawn detergent under running water. I looked at the label. Use one cap only.

I sank into two feet of hot water and six inches of bubbles. My body felt as slick as a seal's. I put my head back, closed my eyes, and laid a folded washrag over them. I craved heavy retreat. Little specks of colored light buzzed under my eyelids. I felt warm, my muscles, what little I had of them, loosened up. I could almost taste the void, deep and beautiful.

There was a vibration that rattled and echoed the walls, a vibration that sounded like an electrical short somewhere. I jumped from the tub, laying several inches of water on the tile floor and awaited electrocution. The sound stopped and started again. I traced its source. My purse. My pager was on *vibrate* and was dancing my purse across the countertop, a mamba of electronic communication.

The number on the small screen was unfamiliar, a San Francisco one.

I picked up the pink phone next to the john and dialed.

"Lawless here."

"Annie Szabo here."

"You got my page. Good. I didn't know if you'd respond."

"I didn't recognize the number; otherwise, I might not have." I was beginning to like our relationship.

"Ha-ha. Got some information on the names you gave me. It means nothing to me. If it means something to you, particularly in relation to Baumann, you'll tell me."

"Of course."

"No Jozef Tsabo, Marks, or Ozro has a record that I can find. Jozef is spelled unusually. Eastern European or something."

"Something."

"I ran a few names connecting any person in this case to a Jozef."

"Including me I assume."

"Naturally. One name did come up in relation to a Jozef, although this Jozef's surname was spelled S-Z-A-B-O."

"That's the way I told you to spell it."

"You want to know the connection or give me an F in ethnic spelling?"

"I want it."

"Person he's connected to is Baumann."

"Baumann?"

"Baumann. You know, your dead brother."

"I know who we're talking about."

"Some time ago Jozef Szabo was charged for swiping a fancy motorcycle, owner had left it parked on the street, keys in the ignition. Szabo had no priors as an adult. Before trial Baumann paid for the motorcycle, twice its value, and the owner agreed to drop charges. Baumann, an attorney and related to this guy, agreed to be his custodian during a period of time agreed to by all.

"Unusual, but Jozef was from a Gypsy family. Those people get handled by the system a little differently. More lenient in some areas, tougher in others. I don't know the drill. I do know that vice has its own unit working with the Gypsy population. They know what's going to heat things up and what may help these people move into mainstream society. When a Gypsy has someone accountable for them in the outside world, we tend to keep our eyes on the situation, let things slide, and hope they'll join the great American melting pot."

My heart was pounding. A motorcycle. I stood naked, soaking wet, frozen in place, for once not noticing how I looked in the mirror.

"Anything else?"

"One minor thing. He threatened Mr. Baumann, felt hemmed in, they had a slight altercation. Mr. Baumann ended up with a black eye and didn't press charges. Mr. Baumann was aware this wasn't unusual behavior. Jozef was no kid, but he was young, and lots of times the person a kid'll blame is their savior. Christ, look at all the kids who hate their parents when all they've done is love them from the second they were born. I got a daughter. Never mind. Lucky for me I got another."

"Sure." My voice sounded like Lauren Bacall's, but like it was blowing through a foggy mist two blocks away instead of sexy.

"Why'd you ask me to run this guy?"

Now I could talk to Lawless about Jozef. I wouldn't protect someone who'd strong-armed Jerry, regardless of how long ago. There was one threatening incident on record. Maybe there'd been others. *Loyal to that family like a big dumb dog*, Berva'd said about Jerry. I'd give Lawless Jozef's recent whereabouts, my suspicions, swallow my pride, and cop to my night with him, plus the timing. Anything. Everything. If Jozef had a record, they could compare the prints on the Dumpster porn items against those in Jozef's file and see if there was a match.

I said, "I believe he might have had something to do with Jerry's death."

"Not possible."

"I thought you were suspicious of everyone."

"Not this one. Your Jozef Szabo died in a motorcycle accident. He drove that fancy bike he stole into the ocean some years ago."

That wasn't Jozef, that was Stevan. I spiraled into a chamber deep and too close.

"You still there?"

"Still here." Barely.

"You got any other hot leads, like other dead suspects, make sure you let me know. I love rummaging through microfiche down in the basement. Three hundred and sixty-five days of mildew per year. I risked my health for that dead end. Thanks."

"You're welcome."

"Hey, you okay?"

I leaned against the toilet tank, held the phone receiver in my hand, looked at it as if it were an animal incongruous there in my hand, a hamster. *You okay?* His words spun on their heads and did a somersault on the wet tile. *Not Okay. Help.* Couldn't push words out. I hung up the phone in the middle of his concern and curiosity, in the middle of my inert call for help.

I picked the pink phone back up and dialed Zoltan's number. No answer. I left a message. I told him what I'd found out, and where I'd be that night. If Jozef did grab that other theater ticket off the refrigerator, I wanted someone large to know where I was.

Twenty-Three

"**C**ynthia, give me fifteen quiet minutes in the tub. I need to find a place where I can handle death and sex and deception and I don't-know-what-else at the same time."

"Okay."

I didn't hear her leave. I cracked my eyes open. She sat perched on the side of the tub.

"Time to myself while you're counting down the fifteen minutes doesn't work."

"I'm not leaving. You look sort of weird."

"This is how non–movie stars look naked. Sort of weird."

"No song and dance with me. What happened between the living room and now?"

I asked her to pop one of those bottles of champagne, and told her I didn't need a glass. I took a long drink straight out of the bottle. I could feel the buzz to the end of my toes. Fortification. My heart flew around the news Lawless had given me, diving, coming up again to ride the currents. I'd hold it close I until I came to my own conclusion.

"I can't talk about it."

"Sure?"

"Positive. Not yet."

Cynthia took the bottle off the edge of the tub and chugged. Her skin was pinker than usual, she was intense, she had the air of a hunting dog.

"What are you staring at?" she said.

"I was thinking you look kind of weird, too. The mad kind of weird."

"Tad was supposed to spend the evening here, but he's canceled, again, some business deal. He gets a call, he works late. Same old, same old."

"The calls aren't from other women pretending to be secretaries?"

"No. That I'd understand. I'd cut him off in a minute, but it's part of my human-behavior repertoire."

Cynthia met Tad Jones, this year's contestant for love of her life, at a party some neighbors of mine had thrown to celebrate their anniversary. Cynthia was visiting me, licking her wounds over another love gone rotten. I'd dragged her along to help her recover. I didn't like Tad and his French cuff links then. I liked him less now. I'd never help anyone recover from love again.

"Do you love Tad?" I said.

"He proposed to me the first night we met. He kept proposing until last month when I said yes. He's fifteen years younger than me, and I was flattered. He seemed like the best of both worlds— a solid businessman who was handsome and exciting."

"That should have been a tip-off. Con artists are exciting. Solid businessmen aren't."

"Maybe. All I know is that now that I've said yes, he seems pretty uninterested. I feel stupid and used."

"So Tad is yesterday's news."

Cynthia said, "I'd like to give him one more chance to redeem himself by doing something spectacular. And believe me, it would have to be truly spectacular."

"Why bother with one more chance?"

"Unfortunately, the sex is great."

"That's a drag."

"You're telling me."

She was playing my bathwater with her fingertips, making the bubbles reach the marbled shore, then shushing them into the center of the tub again.

I studied her face. I didn't like what I saw. "You gave Tad money, didn't you?" Cynthia took money seriously. Very seriously.

"Yes."

"And?"

"I don't have the slightest idea which toilet it went down. His business has an enormous cash appetite."

Cynthia was far inside her head creating columns of liabilities and assets and negative net worth. When she finished her emotional balance sheet, that relationship would be dead in the water with or without a spectacular redemption. Cynthia could find great sex elsewhere.

She opened another bottle of champagne.

"I avoided getting involved with a film person because I wanted someone normal. So, instead, I hooked up with a man who's taken my bank account for a ride."

"It looks that way."

She opened another bottle of champagne, probably heavy into plotting revenge.

I ran a little more hot water and refolded the washrag over my eyes.

My brain burst bubbles of thought into the air and shaped them into various puzzle pieces. I tottered on the verge of comprehension—it felt like throbbing on the edge of orgasm—but I couldn't reach that final climax of understanding.

Too many puzzle pieces. Jerry discovers Bill's been scamming, he wants to leave his practice, and turns up dead by a Dumpster loaded with X-rated goods. Pinky and Mina realign in his law office, but Mina's final word, according to Berva, will come from

Jozef; Jozef who took me and shook me, woke me, and gave me back myself. Why, I don't know. Jerry's worried about Capri, with good reason, and Bill's harboring a tremendous crush on her.

I heard Zoltan's voice in my head. *No coincidences, no random events.* My gut was screaming that he was right, with the volume turned up full blast, and I'd come right back to Jozef. Jozef was related to all these people, related to me. And the law considered him a dead man.

"Cyn, I don't want to see Jozef tonight."

"I know. That's why we're going."

"Maybe that theater ticket fell off the fridge and is lying with the rest of the crud that lives under refrigerators."

"That's a good possibility. We're going anyway."

"It's a bad idea. I was married to his brother and I loved him like crazy. They look too much alike. Their hands . . ."

"They're brothers, there's bound to be similarities."

I wasn't ready to talk to her about the motorcycle death. I took a drink. I took a deep breath. This I could share with Cynthia. "It's no wonder I thought that whatever happened Sunday night was a dream. Making love with him was like making love with Stevan."

"Annie, you need a new love interest. I mean it."

"I know that, but let me finish will you? There've been plenty of men, and don't worry, I'm sure there'll be more. But there hasn't been a single one since Stevan who knew every one of my buttons. Not until Sunday night."

"Is this a good thing we're talking about or a bad thing?"

I took another pull. "I haven't got a clue. It's outside the realm of good and bad. It just sits there and is. And what if this man's a killer? I couldn't tolerate what that would say about me."

"Now you're really getting carried away."

I passed the bottle back to Cynthia. "He wrote me something," I said, "left it on Jerry's dresser. It was either a deranged thing to do, or a passionate and brave thing to do. It's the kind of thing

Stevan used to leave around the house for me to find. But Stevan was my husband."

I motioned to my purse, and she found the note. She read it once, read it again:

I am greedy for you in all ways. I want to eat your moans, lick your sighs. I'm greedy for you in ways that can't be explained in words, these pale shadows of opaque lettered light. Pale shadows don't cover the ways I'm greedy for you. I'm greedy like wind kicking up a storm, like an ocean of salt water, large and hungry— full at once to breaking. Howling. I want you in a place where there's nothing but the ways I am hungry for you.

Cynthia opened a drawer under the sink and pulled out a pack of Lucky Strikes. "Do you want to start smoking again?"

"No."

"Me either."

She pulled the red cellophane strip from around the pack, lit a cigarette, took a drag, and put it in my mouth. I blew smoke to the ceiling, took another drag and blew smoke into the bubbles.

My voice resonated in the hollow of water and ceramic tile. "I know why I'm so mad at the Hummingbird Wizard. I did invite him in, invited him in some way I don't want to remember, can't quite remember. I'm not mad at him for what happened. I'm mad at me for wanting him. I'm mad at Stevan for not hanging around long enough for me to get tired of him."

Cynthia flicked an ash into the tub. *Thanks, Cyn.*

She said, "We're too old to keep doing this stupid dance."

"We're never too old. Who'd want to be? I want to feel that some ecstatic or disastrous romantic encounter is waiting around the next corner any minute. I want to feel like that until the day I drop dead." I couldn't believe what I'd just said, could not believe it was true—it was—and I was thinking about the man with soft dark curls when I said it.

"Not me. I want a stable life," Cyn said.

"Get over it. There's no such thing."

We emptied the second bottle of champagne and dressed for the theater. Cynthia loaned me a dark red dress and a velvet wrap. I looked good, and the looking good made me feel strong and ready for whatever was waiting around my corner. Death or sex, violence or forgiveness. It was all part of life, and it was all good.

The phone rang, Cynthia answered it, wore a puzzled expression, and passed me the phone.

"Perger here."

"Zoltan?"

"Are you on your way to the theater?"

"We're just headed out," I said. "Are you keeping an eye on Mina? We're not worried about me. We're worried about her."

"I've got it covered."

"Where are you?"

"I just bought this cell phone, here's the new number. It's real good even from inside this mall, isn't it?"

"Where is Mina?"

"She disappeared into a Frederick's of Hollywood ten minutes ago. That place keeps her busy for at least half an hour."

Twenty-Four

The St. James Theater is old, very old. It is ornate, it is round. There are enough angels drifting on the pale blue ceiling to fill several small parts of heaven. The draperies are spun gold threads, real gold. There are bizarre box seats that, because of their angle, appear to be the worst seats in the house. They aren't.

I was front row balcony. Jerry paid big dollars for these seats, and the Phantom would be flying past my head at some point in the production. The last time I saw *Phantom* I fell asleep. This time I'd stay awake, despite the bath and the champagne.

It was nighttime, but Cynthia wore dark glasses. She also wore a blond wig and a designer dress tight enough to talk anyone out of their seat. I felt like I was on a date with a high-priced hooker.

"I don't know why you bother wearing dark glasses when you've got on a dress that attracts a ten-mile radius of attention."

"Tricks of the trade. The dress attracts attention to my body, not my face."

"It's almost embarrassing to be with you."

"We need an extra seat, right? I'm not going to sit in your lap. One of your colleagues might make me, and I'd be front page in the supermarket as the star who dates women on the side. Although you do look pretty hot in my dress."

"Cynthia, knock it off. I don't care what you look like."

She pinched my cheek and kissed air in my direction.

The place was packed, this week was the end of *Phantom*'s run. We elbowed our way to the lobby bar and each got a cup of black coffee. The champagne was edging me toward sleep before the show had even begun.

I spotted Bill and Capri on the far side of the lobby. They were dressed to kill. Capri was using a column for support on one side, and Bill's arm on the other. What the hell were they doing here? Had Jerry planned a group date when he bought our tickets? Who was trying to piss off whom when these tickets were purchased?

Cynthia lifted her sunglasses a moment and narrowed her eyes in their direction.

I winked at Bill across the lobby. He didn't see me, or he ignored me, I don't know which. I winked again.

Cynthia pulled me back against the flocked wallpaper. "Stop winking. You look like you're having a seizure."

"I'm trying to get Bill's attention."

"Why?"

"I don't know. Maybe just to throw him a curve."

"This is juvenile, and it's stopping right now."

I escaped Cynthia and took another look. Bill was wrapped up in Capri, and wouldn't have seen any farther than her chest. She made what looked like one feeble attempt to fend him off, then caved in. Capri was out of it. I imagined the theater manager could have had his head in her chest for all she knew. Or cared.

Cynthia lifted her glasses again. "They do look cozy together."

"Bill looks cozy with every woman."

The lights dimmed, we found my seat. The seat to my right was empty, waiting for the ticket holder, maybe waiting for Hummingbird. That or waiting for a future maid to find the ticket for seat 4A under Jerry's refrigerator and toss it.

A married couple had the two seats to my left. They were from out of town. They were not interested in changing seats, they were not interested in leaving the theater. They were staying right where they were. The woman was adamant. The man was mostly struck dumb by Cynthia's curves. Cynthia was smart. She ignored the husband, pulled out several large bills, and handed them to the wife. The couple was gone as soon as the cash hit the woman's palm. Cynthia took the seat next to my left. She removed her sunglasses.

"I haven't seen a show in years. This is so exciting."

"You're an actress, for God's sake."

"It doesn't mean I go to plays. Film and stage are very different mediums."

Fortunately the music came up before she could launch into a full-scale lecture concerning the merits of film over live theater or vice versa.

Ten minutes into Act I, I remembered why I'd fallen asleep the first time I'd seen *Phantom*. Fifteen minutes into it I felt warm and drowsy. My next memory was of light and voices filling the theater. Intermission. I cracked my eyes open a slit. Cynthia patted my hand and told me she was going to the ladies' room.

The seat on my right was still empty. This had been a stupid idea. I'd gotten dressed up just to nap in a hard seat with dried gum on the armrest. The theater lights blinked off and on. People returned to their seats. I sat up straighter in an effort to stay awake for the second half of the performance. This was Jerry's last gift to me. I'd make an effort to enjoy it.

The lights went down, actors on stage, dialogue, a burst of song, a body next to mine. I felt Jozef like a crimson shot. I kept my eyes glued to the stage.

My velvet wrap rose off my right arm as if caught in a sudden breath. I turned to him. He was handsome, nearly beautiful. I felt naked, shy, excited, scared, voluptuous, all those things. He held one corner of my stole in his hand. He ran the velvet across my lips, down the side of my face. He put his hand on my knee, the silk fabric of my dress ran smoothly along my skin shaped by his hand. He leaned over and blew his voice in my ear.

"Go home. You're too much in the middle."

"I was put there when Jerry died."

"That can't be undone. Go."

"I really didn't want you that night. I barely remember it." I couldn't look at him when I said that.

He put his lips around the fine edge of my ear. My skin shuddered down the back of my legs like a first sip of hard booze.

"You're not lying to me, you're lying to yourself. That's okay. This afternoon at Mina's Café I was angry. How could something so surprising happen and you be mad about it? Then I understood. It was the surprise that made you mad. You like to know what's going to happen. Me, I wasn't surprised to be swallowed by you. I expected it."

"*A surprise?* That's kind of putting it mildly. We really do need to talk."

"What happened between us, it's big. It may happen again, maybe not. But it goes into the background now. Annie, it's time to get serious—I can't keep protecting you." He leaned away and held my face in his hands. "You're too full of life to deal with death. And that's what's going on here."

"I'm full of life because I've fought with death for years. It doesn't scare me."

"You haven't dealt with your own death. Leave."

He stood, ran the back of his hand along the curve of my neck. I closed my eyes and heard a soft moan. Mine.

I pulled him to me. "The night we were together when I was mostly asleep . . ."

"When you were partly asleep . . ."

"Whatever. Did we actually have sex?"

"We made love."

"Did we practice safe sex?"

I thought he might laugh at me, but he didn't. "In the way you mean, yes. In another way, no. Nothing can be safe between us. Huge and vivid, I look in your eyes, I want you, I've always had you, and I've missed you all at once." He smiled. "Compared to that, who wants safe?"

I believed him on the first count, and the rest I understood. My response to him was old and comfortable, pulsing and new-born.

I held his face between my hands. I went inside to the place where people recognize each other, and he welcomed me in. He wasn't someone else, not an imitation model of his brother. He was Jozef. Feelings, old and new interwoven, bashed heads inside my bones, jockeying for position. In the midst of that confusion I felt both his power and his danger. I was drawn to him, but I pushed myself back from his edge. In this internal landscape could trust have a home? I didn't know where to put this.

He rose and faded up the steps. I arranged my wrap higher on my shoulder and rubbed the back of my neck. I smelled his fingers on my cheeks. I tried to focus on the show, and where was Cynthia?

It was past time for my own nest. Jozef was right, there were too many things I was in the middle of that I didn't understand—the police might not be the only place where I could stumble into trouble. But I was tired and wired, too much so to drive home that night. I'd sleep one more night at Cynthia's hotel and drive home in the morning. I'd call Mina before I left and give her my good-byes. I'd tell Zoltan to check in with me several times a day. I wished I'd told Jozef that I had Zoltan on the job watching out for Mina. There were many things to leave behind.

And one other thing to do before I left town. I intended to hit the parking lot behind Jerry's office. The cops interview for a living, but so do I. I figured I had a lot better chance of getting a few bums to open up than the cops did. It was a slim shot, but maybe I could find a person who'd been in the area when Jerry died. I didn't mind being in the middle of a few bums. Except for my borrowed clothes from Cynthia, I was beginning to look pretty shabby myself.

We were into the finale, still no Cynthia next to me. If she didn't show, she'd have to get a cab. The lights went up and filled the theater. If I closed my eyes, I could still feel his breath like July desert blowing across my ear, like the color of evening down my neck.

I got tired of waiting for Cynthia. I grabbed my wrap and left the auditorium. I saw her next to a pillar just inside the theater. Acres of people swarmed past her out the door. She still wore the blond wig, but she'd changed into a turquoise polyester pantsuit and white patent leather shoes with chunky heels.

"Is this your idea," I asked, "of being discreet?"

"During intermission, when I was in the ladies' room, I traded my old outfit for this one."

"You traded your Valentino dress and Pappagallo pumps for that?"

"Absolutely. I'd have to pay a fortune for this outfit in LA. It's very retro, very cool."

"Cool does not begin to describe you. Let's get out of here."

"Go? Please. I want to poke around in the dressing room, look at the costumes, talk with some of my fellow artists."

"Why?"

"Because I'm an actress, and I have to keep learning my craft."

"Cyn, Jozef showed up and . . ."

"I saw him. He's hard to miss. If you don't want him, I'll take him."

"Men aren't articles of clothing that you pass around to your girlfriends if you don't want them anymore."

"What planet are you from, anyway? Of course they are."

"You can't have him."

"You want him?"

"I might."

"Even though you think he may have been involved with Jerry's death?"

"I'm revising my opinion."

"If you change your mind about him, let me know. Come backstage with me?"

"I'll wait in the lobby for you."

"Fine. Tonight when we're back at the hotel, maybe you can help me figure out some way to get even with Tad. Put your imagination to work. Anyone who can write alien love stories can certainly help me figure out a way to humiliate Tad. I wish you could take an unflattering shot of him with me. Of course I'd look good, but not him. Something."

"Cyn, bad idea."

"He needs to suffer, at least a little."

"Would you stop?"

She gave me her shoulder, and then the *oh drop-dead* look of a rebellious teenager. I guessed I'd want Tad to suffer, too.

She walked down the steps past the area with a sign that read AUTHORIZED PERSONAL ONLY. Nobody stopped her. The way she walks, nobody would. Cynthia found a short flight of concrete steps and disappeared within the innards and muscles of the theater.

I returned to the lobby and ordered a glass of wine, then switched to a cup of coffee. Up seemed better than down. I paced the lobby, and it emptied out. An old woman cleaned the ladies' room. A young carpet sweeper worked on the last debris left by respectable adults who'd created a mess resembling the aftermath of a slumber party.

Twenty-Five

I got antsy, tossed away my coffee, and descended the same steps that had gobbled up Cynthia. It was dingy downstairs, far from the fairy tale that had been enacted on the stage above. The floor was old cement splattered with years of paint. Cynthia probably thought the floor was retro.

There were narrow alleys of dressing rooms on either side of the hall, men and women in various stages of undress, clothes cluttering the floor and furniture, and not one square inch of quiet. A woman yakked about motivation. I tuned her out and scoped out as many naked men as I could.

Farther down the hall were several open doors. Light poured out these rooms into the dark hall. I assumed they were the offices of those who did the marketing, produced the show—all the goings-on that make the show go on.

I heard Cynthia's high laugh, the one I knew as phony and charming. I followed the sound to one of the rooms that spilled light into the hall.

Bill had his back to me, Cynthia sat with him, perched sideways on a threadbare velvet couch. She was curled around him like a cat around a mouse.

Cynthia caught sight of me, put her finger over her mouth

telling me to hush, and motioned for me to back off. She ran her hand down his face in one continuous movement, concealing the hand sign she'd given me. I backed into the darkened hallway.

She gazed into his eyes with a look approaching adoration. She brushed a few of his stray hairs into place.

Cynthia said to him, "It's so great to have this time alone. I can't believe we ran into each other down here!"

"I can't believe you remember me."

"Are you kidding? I'm very attracted to powerful men. For one thing, they understand money. I've got it, but I just don't have a clue about it."

HAH! Cynthia knew how much change she had floating around the bottom of her purse.

Bill was slightly drunk. Where he'd stuffed Capri, I had no idea.

He put his finger on the end of Cynthia's cute little nose. "Money? No mystery there—just a big game. You win, you lose, but you never let it get you down. Always think of the next project."

"It sounds very similar to the movie business. One bad review? Forget it, you think about your next part."

"Exactly so!" He looked in either direction as if they were in a crowded room. "Can you keep a secret?"

"Are you kidding? If I couldn't keep a secret, I'd never have gotten *anywhere*."

"I've got a project going now that will net me enough to retire on, and I mean comfortably, if I play my cards right."

"But money can't be the only motivation, Bill. Your heart and head must both be fully engaged."

"Oh sure, I mean, this project is fun!"

"Great!"

"First project—I'm acquiring Madame Mina's Mystic Café. It may be the first of many."

"A string of Gypsy cafes? I love that place!"

"Who doesn't? But this one is purely a real-estate transaction."

"Wow, you must be loaded. Like I said, I don't know anything about money, but this is one pricey town."

"I have a method of picking up property at bargain-basement prices."

"Lucky you!" She laughed and tickled his chin. "Just who are you stealing this land from?"

"The cafe owner, Mina Szabo. She owns most of that block. The recent property appraisal is close to eleven million, lots more if the area attracts urban development funds. I've had preliminary discussions with Mina, and I'm trying to ease her into cooperating with us. She has no idea what the property is worth."

"Well, there's certainly no reason for you to enlighten her."

"None at all. Most of the time she forgets she owns it, doesn't even want it—she'll let it go for peanuts. Now that Jerry's not a problem, that sounds terrible, but you know what I mean. Her parcel will be easy to pick up."

"You're off to a great start!"

"It's a win-win situation. She can retire, she won't even have to hassle with realtors and inspections. None of that. We're also tying up other loose ends for her."

"Listen, I have a friend, Tad Jones, who has money up the wazoo. You two should get together."

She gave Bill Tad's home and work number. Good idea. Those two deserved each other.

Bill was so enraptured by his own life at that precise moment in time it spread across his countenance like rain after a long drought.

If someone had snapped a picture of my face, what they would have seen was the pure shock of *Holy Cow! Mina, a property owner in San Francisco! How'd that ever happen?* Something Jerry must have set up for her, the only possible explanation. I'd bet anything that when Bill found out about the land there had been one hell of a fight between the partners at Baumann and Wells.

Cynthia stretched her long legs on the couch. She planted a big, juicy kiss right on his cheek, and ruffled his head like he must be tired from all that heavy thinking and convoluted planning. Bill looked like he'd just won the lottery.

"Great talking to you, Bill. Any more business and my head will start positively pounding." He had been dismissed.

She autographed his wrist and kissed his hand. Her eyes twinkled with delight. GAG. She was one hell of an actress all right.

Twenty-Six

I waited until Bill the Boil disappeared down the hall and turned the corner. I sat on the edge of the couch with Cynthia.

"So you threw Bill and Tad, the two piranhas, together."

"Maybe they'll kill each other."

Cynthia fussed with her makeup and clothes. Teasing Bill had been a messy business.

"I'm ready," she said. "Where to?"

"You are staying here while I look around for Capri."

"I thought Jozef said she was fine."

"I need to satisfy myself that she's okay. Find some of your fellow actors and commune or emote or something. I'm on my own."

"Even the Lone Ranger had Tonto."

"This is why you're staying here. You have trouble maintaining a clear line between fantasy and reality. Right now reality is the need to keep my ass hidden and in one piece. Which means you stay out of the way."

"I don't like it."

"Look, you may have temporarily fooled Bill into thinking he was a captain of industry. When he recovers from your reflected glow, he may remember you and I are pals, and that he just spilled a bunch of very toxic beans. In which case your ass is in lots of potential trouble."

"Christ! My ass is part of my livelihood. It's even insured."

"Pardon me?"

"I'll wait here, but hurry up. Being left out of things is one of my issues. That's why I have to be center stage."

"Center stage doesn't work while I'm sneaking around. Staying relatively safe is one of my issues. Tonight we're honoring my issues as opposed to yours."

She tried on a pout, and I interrupted before she had time to push out her bottom lip. "And I do not have time for your wounded inner child."

She accepted her defeat, not gracefully, but at least quietly. I left her inspecting pots of greasepaint, an ancient-looking black feathered cape that had been flung on the floor, embroidered velvet shawls, red ostrich boas, sequined slacks, and stacked heels. God knows what she'd look like when I returned.

I took off my heels and crept down the dark hall past dressing rooms and offices, some empty and open, some locked. In stockinged feet I did not make one sound. I heard faint voices, then stronger voices. Soon the voices ebbed and flowed between loud rage and heavy silence. They came from an office at the end of the hall and to the right.

Deep amber lamplight oozed out the door, a door that was slightly ajar. I flattened myself against a wall and peeked inside. Bill and Capri stood on opposite sides of a desk. A funny-looking round guy stood against a far wall trying to look like furniture, but looking more like one of my daughter's sculptures padded with foam rubber. This appeared to be a party he wanted no part of. I pulled back into the shadowed hall.

Bill eased around the desk next to Capri. She was angry, he was trying to smooth her out. Bill knew where the power lay in getting that property from Mina.

Capri'd had enough of whatever Bill was pushing. Her anger and the length of the play had sobered her right up. Her voice began low and harsh, it raised the hairs on the back of my neck. Certainly a curse perhaps a litany of them. Her lithe body lunged toward Bill, a leopard about to chow down its prey. Every inch of her spoke fire. Bill staggered back a few steps, went into emotional shock, and closed his mouth. He never knew Capri when she was young and was startled to find she had that kind of fire. I was relieved to see it again.

Bill slit his eyes, a lizard in a silk suit. "Capri, let's talk about this in the morning when you've calmed down." Bill turned to the round man. "Pinky, I think you should leave, too."

There really was a Pinky.

Pinky grinned like he'd just been granted a pardon from the governor and edged to the door.

Capri looked at Pinky. "You stay put. You are right in the middle of this and have been from the start." He stayed put.

She turned to Bill. "You! This is my family. How dare *you* get in the middle of this, the middle of our business. You are trouble, terrible trouble. Interfering and juggling people's lives, I hate to tell you, is a sure ticket straight to hell."

Her eyes flew back and forth between the two men.

"Pinky, I don't want to, but I love you. Bill, your words are useless, empty, pathetic. Just like the inside of you. I don't want you near me again."

Bill had thought she was easy, a piece of pretty flesh to be sculpted and used. He was wrong. Bill turned on his heel.

She called his name. "Bill, I expect you at my back, but I don't expect you there for long. I think I have an amazing will to live. Who would have figured?"

He stormed out like the king of darkness. Pinky stood next to Capri, looking at her, looking at Bill's retreating back, looking completely clueless—a pathetic jester hoping to keep his head. I slid to the safety of a shadowed corner, but there was no chance

Bill would spot me. He carried enough anger to darken an out-door ballpark on a Saturday afternoon.

My heart was beating a million miles an hour. I imagined shadows and shapes around me, converging upon me. One giant bear, another shape, this the largest and most surreal, resembled a Russian version of Abraham Lincoln cloaked in dark shadows, long cape, tall hat. Above me a woman as wide as she was tall hushed the St. James Theater ghosts of productions past into silence.

My feet screamed, *Run!* Between spying on Cynthia, although that was by invitation, and spying on the Szabo crew, I was beginning to feel like a warped Nancy Drew. I pulled away from the door, but found it hard to move. My feet were frozen to the floor. Tried it again. I walked fast, then ran down the hall in my stocking feet, headed to the dressing room where I'd left Cyn. An arm shot out from behind a curtain and grabbed me. It pulled me inside folds of heavy velveteen.

Twenty-Seven

I was smothered by ancient damask lining and dust. If I was claustrophobic, I would have been on full tilt. As it was, I was woozy with fear, and my heart beat rings around my chest.

"What are you doing here?" Hummingbird said. "I asked you to leave."

"I *was* leaving until you grabbed me." I batted my way out of the velvet cocoon, and Hummingbird stood next to me against the wall.

"I meant leave this whole mess, but there you were where anyone could see you."

What was wrong with this guy? I would have missed the most important parts of my life if I'd avoided every mess that came along.

"You were there?"

"Of course I was there," he said.

"I didn't see you."

"Neither did anyone else, but you were in plain view."

Once freed from the fabric I started to breathe again.

"Listen," I said, "nobody tells me when to come or go or ignore trouble."

He put his hands on my waist, stood back, and studied my

face. I studied him in return. He was preparing his lecture, I could feel it. He had one hell of a nerve, and I was about to tell him so when he put one arm around my waist and pulled me toward him. He held me close until I was inside him again. Smell of desert rose, of ocean tumbling down moist mountains with water in the air to breathe—couldn't I just stay against this chest? I hated this meltdown, and I loved it. Both.

He spoke into me, his cheek against my head. "No one bosses you around, it's strong and it's sexy. But people get killed for a Rolex watch, even a pair of expensive shoes. What do you think happens to someone who stumbles into the middle of a shady eleven-million-dollar deal?"

"I don't want your mother to get shafted, or worse. Jerry's death has worked out nicely for Bill. He'd like to marry Capri, deep-six your mother, and inherit the dough. When did you find out about the deal?"

"It doesn't matter. I'm going to put an end to it, and when it's over I want you in one piece."

I said, "We can't leave Capri with Bill. Nowhere near him."

"I've taken care of Capri; Pinky, too."

I found my bones, not easy, but I did, and we went to get Cynthia. She was wearing her retro outfit and discussing Ingmar Bergman with a guy in drag who hadn't even been born when Ingmar was big. He thought black and white was a total experience. I had an old Zenith television in my barn that was his for the taking any time.

Hummingbird said, "I'm walking both of you out. I want you gone, and now. I have to check on Mina."

"Zoltan's watching her."

"Zoltan?"

"I hired him."

He looked surprised. "Okay, that's good. I'll check on both of them. Now let's get you out of here."

Cynthia looked at Jozef with goo-goo eyes. She said, "I'm with him."

"No chance." I answered.

Cynthia rolled her eyes like a teenager making fun of her girl-friend with the stupid crush.

In the rolling of her eyes one bone-rattling metallic shot rang out, then in the distance, perhaps another shot, that or an echo of the first. Cynthia's eyes grew large, then they were still. She held on to the front of my dress, and I held her arm. Jozef's arms wrapped us both. The sound rolled endlessly down the corridor, pinging off concrete floors and stone walls.

He turned and ran toward the sound instead of away from it. I watched his figure disappear down the hall, toward disaster, and I followed in a fugue state somewhere in the wake of his shadow. Cynthia did not move, could not move.

When I got to the end of the hall, I didn't see Jozef, I saw footprints. The footprints of someone who'd walked through splattered blood that mixed its darkening red with the old purple and orange paint flecks on the floor, blood-smeared steps leading to an outer door that was bolted. A jumble of pain.

Bill Wells stood staring at the blood, too. He had a smirk on his face like someone had just told him a dirty joke. I didn't know who the joke was on, but it wasn't funny.

"What happened here, Bill?"

"How the hell should I know?"

"Because you're standing in blood and you have a sick smile on your face."

"Everyone handles shock differently."

I scanned the hall, wondering whose body this blood had escaped from.

"Have you seen Jozef?"

"Only the old man."

He must have meant Pinky.

"I'm calling the cops," I said.

"No cops."

"Sorry, but there's blood all over the place. I'm calling the cops."

He took a step closer to me.

"There's nothing for them to do. This was a mistake. I was handling a prop, or at least I thought it was, and it fired."

"That's your blood? You shot yourself?"

"By mistake."

Bill showed me the ripped flesh of his calf, the back of one pant leg torn to tatters.

"You need to get to a hospital," I said, "and how did you possibly manage to shoot yourself in the back of your leg? I knew you were an idiot, but this really takes the cake."

Bill advanced on me, wincing slightly, but for someone with a bum leg the guy was quick. He grabbed my left arm and pinned it behind my back.

"Get out of my frigging face." My teeth were clenched. I hated this man beyond all rational limits. Hate gave me a big advantage. I was not the least bit scared of him. But I wanted him to think I was. I needed to get out of there.

I put my face close to his and pressed my body into him, trying to give my numbing arm a little breathing space.

Not surprisingly, Bill got the wrong message from my body closing in on his.

"You like it a little rough sometimes?" he said.

I laughed. "Bill, you weren't enough for me when you were in one piece and relatively sane."

"I'm enough for any woman."

"Keep telling yourself that, Bill."

Now my arm really hurt because he'd moved away from me, but hadn't loosened his grip. I made another move that took me into his chest.

"If you tell anyone about this," he said, "or about anything you may have seen or heard, someone you love will pay."

"Someone already has," I said. "Jerry."

He put his mouth next to my ear and whispered. "I mean someone you really love ... like your daughter. She's very beautiful."

My daughter. My head felt light, but I couldn't afford to blow up or get scared. If I didn't keep my heat turned down, I'd lose.

"Bill, I believe my daughter, half your size and half your age, could put you away."

He let go of my arm, I fell back a few steps. He flushed red and smacked me across the face, full force, with the flat of his hand. Colored lights sparkled and whirled under my eyelids. I squeezed my eyes hard, ready to meet my maker, prepare for the next lifetime, or free-fall into the eternal black void. But I was still standing.

Bill wore his sick smile, this time laced with disgust. He pulled back his hand, ready to slam me again. For some reason he changed his mind, grabbed my arm, and pulled me close again. For a lying wimp who sat behind his desk all day, Bill was strong. A second blow probably would have taken me out or done some kind of permanent brain damage. I didn't know why he changed his mind. I did know there was someone who truly wished me dead—the man who now held me. I was not happy about that.

I looked at him without blinking an eye. Tomorrow my eye would be swollen. I'd deal with it then.

Chest to chest, we locked wills. I could have kicked his wounded leg, but it seemed petty. I gave him a hard knee to the groin instead. Much more appropriate. The tatters of his pants, now sticking to the ooze that was his leg, were clearly visible as he fell to the floor and went fetal. Between groans, he cut loose with a string of swear words.

"By the way," I said, "I don't like it rough. Ever."

The guy was pond slime.

Bill could rest assured of one thing: His leg was nothing, that little jolt to his groin was less. I wanted to make him understand pain, and I wanted to do it in a big way.

I looked around, saw no one, and heard nothing but Bill. I wondered where Pinky was. When you can see trouble coming, you've got a chance of avoiding it or knocking it unconscious. Trouble that sneaks up from behind is blackest.

I'd had enough of the fairy-tale world of the St. James Theater. I'd go back to the dressing room, call Lawless and tell him he'd almost had another customer. Then I'd grab Cynthia by her blond wig, and get us back to her hotel. Grown-up Disneyland felt lots more real, and certainly more safe, than this place.

I took one last look in Bill's direction. The lights had been doused. Dark shadows nibbled at his edges, and I heard a far door close. Bill, still prone, called out to me.

"Remember," he yelled, "keep your mouth closed. And no cops."

"Whatever you say, Bill."

Twenty-Eight

*D*etective Lawless showed up tired, his face looking like pre-shrunk corduroy. Two of his men tore the dressing rooms apart, although they were already such a mess you couldn't tell the cops had even been there. Lawless questioned Cynthia and me separately, and not for long. I told him about the conversations I'd overheard, both of them, and about my encounter with Bill, plus his threat against my daughter. I told him the first shot I'd heard was real, and that there'd possibly been a second. Because of echoes and distance, it was hard to tell.

I wasn't certain I included all the characters, and knew for a fact I didn't mention Jozef's presence. I didn't know if Cynthia had. Lawless was too pooped to grill us well-done, but would probably make up for it later.

The cops didn't find a weapon, real or otherwise, nor did they find Bill. They scraped a smattering of blood off the floor, bagged it, and tagged it. Lawless said good-bye to me from the doorway. He looked straight ahead, not at me, and waved with a slightly Queen Elizabeth wrist-turning gesture. When a cop takes on Queen Elizabeth's mannerisms, you hope someone else is driving him home.

I had a bad feeling about Pinky's disappearance. I suspected that either Pinky shot Bill in the leg and ran, or that someone else, maybe Bill, had shot Pinky, then exited his bleeding body from the building. That would have required some help, which left another nagging question. Who at this point was on Bill's side, so much so they'd help him cover up a shooting?

I collapsed on one of the old dressing-room couches. The Bergman fan offered Cynthia his chair. He tossed his silk scarf around his neck, checked his makeup one last time, and left to join the drag-queen party filling the city streets. Cyn ignored the chair and plunked down on the floor across from me. She took off her patent leather shoes and rubbed the soles of her feet. Despite the rank odor of the smoking gun, probably gone but still imprinted on my brain, despite the police, I still smelled him, Jozef, a lush jungle in my hair. I needed a shower.

I stared at the floors painted purple and streaked with red. Gray cement peeked through the colors. No blood on these floors. I didn't want to look at floors and think of splattered blood.

Cyn wore a puzzled look, like she'd woken from a weird dream and couldn't remember where she was.

My voice was a monotone. "We heard a gun being fired."

"Who and why? My brain's too fried to fill in the blanks."

"I don't know the who. I've got a pretty good idea why."

Mina had property, lots of it, and was supposed to be easy pickings. Someone didn't like the way things were working out— too involved, dangerous, who knows what else. That shot was probably meant to simplify things. I didn't know if it had.

I thought about Jozef running down the hall, flying toward that shot. My last sight of him was his back, his thick hair streaming out behind him like the dark tail of a comet.

"I hope Jozef's all right," I said.

"How do you know Jozef isn't up to his eyeballs in this?"

I didn't know, and I didn't want to think about it. My body tensed.

Cyn said, "Look, forget what I just said. I told you my brain is fried. I feel like I'm going to be sick." She wrapped her arms around my knees and rested her head there.

"I saw blood," she said, "real blood."

"Yes, on the bottom of my shoe. I saw it leaking out of someone who was skating in it."

"I wish people could check in and out of scenes as easily as they check out of hotels." She sounded uncharacteristically philosophical.

She looked up at me, eyes all wide and vulnerable. "Why don't you keep my hotel room for the night, and I'll drive to your place. I'd like to relax, breathe some real air, maybe recover a little before I head back to L.A."

"Not this time. You're high-maintenance, and tomorrow I'll be back home. I need absolute solitude."

"I'll be low-maintenance."

"I don't know how to say this in a nice way, but you don't know how to be low-maintenance."

"I'll stay in your trailer. You won't even know I'm there."

"E. B. lives in the trailer."

Cynthia sighed. "I wish I'd had kids when you did, when I was too young and dumb to worry about raising them right. I'm very alone in the world."

"Alone? Most of the Western world loves you." That was a stupid knee-jerk consolation, I knew, and entirely meaningless.

"I have good press, a few years left in film, then I settle into friends, family, and financial security. The trouble is, I have few friends that like me because of who I am, whoever that is, and no family."

I patted her head. "Take some of my family. I've got them coming out my ears."

"No thanks."

She stood up, straightened her shoulders, and did some stretches. "Okay, let's go to the hotel. I'll pack and catch a plane to LA. I can shake off the dust of this disaster at home."

"Now I feel guilty about not offering you hospitality."

"Don't. I understand."

"Come up in a week or two when everything's settled down."

"Sure." It was the kind of sure that meant *Forget it. The chance was now and we lost it.*

She asked me to stay put while she went to the bathroom, possibly got sick, and freshened up. I rummaged through the exotica on the dressing table. Greasy stage makeup. Liners and lip gloss and shadows and feathers and nylons and glitter and cold cream. I moved things around, then tried to put them back in their exact spots as if the man whose table this was had a map and knew the position of everything on it. More pots of makeup, a cropped red wig, small brushes, and what the hell was Cynthia doing? God, she could be exasperating.

I walked to the ladies' room and listened. Nothing. I waited. I knocked on the door. No running water, no answer. I called her name. Nothing. I opened the narrow door a crack and peeked in. The door opened straight onto Golden Gate Boulevard. Cynthia had shaken me. If she'd sped off with my car, she was a goner.

As the word *goner* streaked through my head, my chest tightened. I pictured a very sick and smirking Bill standing in the hall of blood. Cynthia could be in trouble right up to her insured ass.

I ran two blocks to the parking lot and spotted my old Austin Cooper. There was a note under a wiper blade.

Am taking care of my ass, took a cab straight to the airport. If Tad calls the hotel, tell him you don't know where I am. I want him to wonder what my money can do to hurt him. Love, C.

She and I corresponded by e-mail and phone. I hadn't seen Cynthia's handwriting since we were in high school, written in large round loops, and dotted i's with hearts. I had no way of knowing if someone had forced her to write this note, or if she'd written it at all. Injured or not, Bill was a loose cannon. No telling what he might do if their paths crossed. I thought about calling Lawless, but didn't. I wasn't used to running to the police like they were benevolent daddies.

I repeated this mantra: Cynthia was being Cynthia—doing what the hell she felt like when she felt like it. I reached inside my purse. I still had the key to her hotel room. Tonight it would just be me, Lana, lots of worry, and very little sleep. The female Rottweiler would be thrilled.

Little traffic, easy access to the room. On my hotel bed was a list of the interview questions and answers. I'd forgotten all about them. Cynthia left a note saying she'd already faxed them to the magazine. Now I really felt guilty. I read the questions and answers and my guilt subsided. She'd done a pretty good job of making herself sound like a cross between Auntie Mame and the Dalai Lama. I didn't know about the magazine, but her agent would love it.

At 3 A.M. the phone rang. Lana shuffled in with her hair in rollers and green cream on her face. She handed me the phone without saying a word, turned, and closed the door.

It was Cynthia.

"I'm home safe and sound."

"Thanks for letting me know you're okay. Good night."

She gave me a wan good night in return. I heard water running.

"If you're having a tub-a-thon, dry off and go to bed."

"My life is a disaster."

"Remember we talked about you being high-maintenance? Stop driving me crazy and go to bed."

"I'm sorry."

"And stop sounding pathetic. I'm not buying it."

"I miss Tad."

"What?!"

"Not Tad exactly. I miss the idea of a Tad, the idea of a partner. I witnessed violence. I'd like to be comforted."

"I understand. Could you have a relationship crisis at a reasonable hour?"

Her wan sniffling stopped. "Tad's a fool. He could have had this, and he blew it."

"This?"

"I am currently pointing to the length of my naked body in the tub. He could have had this plus my wallet, and the man blew it."

"Lucky for you. Find a nice guy, and give him everything you've got. I am currently pointing to the length of your body and the width of your wallet. Get out of the tub and go to bed."

"Thanks. I knew talking to you would help. By the way . . ."

"What."

"When I got home there was a message waiting from your editor."

"At your house? Which editor?"

"The editor of the magazine I interviewed myself for. He'd been trying to reach you, but wasn't having any luck."

I could feel my income decrease by half. If only it were that easy to lose weight.

"And?"

"And he said it was one of the best interviews you've ever done, and that he'd like to discuss doing a monthly with you."

"Are you serious?"

"Isn't that great?"

"I guess so. I feel kind of weird about it."

"That's silly. Who would know better than me how to interview me delicately and get to the most important issues of my life without exploiting me?"

It sounded right, and it sounded confusing. Especially in the middle of the night. I thanked Cynthia for the possible new gig. I might take it—I'm good at being sensitive and all those other things women's magazines thrive on. I said good night to Cynthia; I heard bathwater spiraling down the drain.

I hung up and called my daughter. She sounded wide-awake.

"What are you doing?"

"Painting."

"E. B.? I heard a shot, saw blood, and I don't know what it was about. All I know is that the shot's still ringing in my ears."

"Are you okay?"

"I truly feel okay. I'm deeply calm."

"I don't think you should be."

"Me either. I think I've shut down."

"That could be a problem."

Twenty-Nine

> You want to give God a good laugh? Tell him you got plans.
> —Madame Mina Szabo to Annie Szabo

I woke up later than I'd planned. Before saying my good-byes I was going to hit the Embarcadero, drive over around Townsend and find Tony Tiger. I'd done a story on Tony last year. He was the cream of the crop of street people. If it was happening, Tony knew about it. And Tony was not a bum. He not only had a self-created job, he had a mission. His mission was to make the world feel better. Over in that business district, they needed Tony.

I pulled into Jerry's parking lot. I didn't have a sticker, but I wasn't going to be there long enough to get towed. I hoped. I walked up one block, and there was Tony at his usual corner.

Tony's one of the blackest men I've ever seen. He is tall and he is broad and he'd be imposing except for his clothing. He wore a tuxedo that was made out of tiger-striped fur, complete with tux tails. He wore a black shirt and an orange cumberbund. He also wore a tall stovepipe hat covered in the same tiger-striped furry fabric.

He stood at least one head above every man and woman who passed by. To each passerby he extended his hand and shook it. People stuck out their hands to him. It was nice to see a smile first thing in the morning, nice anytime. That smile sailed all the way across his face.

" 'How you doin' baby? Have a good day.' 'How's it going, man?' " This was his patter all day.

"Hey, man, what's up?" Tony shook the hand of a worried-looking businessman. His face was pinched, slightly gray. "Not so great today, Tony," he said.

Tony gave him a hearty pat on the back put his arm around him. "You got to take the bitter with the sweet, babe, got to take the bitter with the sweet." And Tony beamed that smile of his.

The small gray man looked like a load had been lifted from his shoulders. I thought the city ought to put Tony on their payroll. He was the *Ain't It the Shits, But I'm Okay, You're Okay!* of street people. God knows how much money had been saved, how many deals pulled out of the toilet, because Tony was right there cheering everyone on in the arena of life. And the arena for these folks was business. Tony told me he chose this area for his mission because these people had lower spirits than just about anyplace else in town.

Tony gave me one of his greetings. I felt my immune system grow stronger. What a guy.

I asked Tony about Jerry's parking lot, about whose usual hangout it was.

"Man, the cops ask the same thing. What'd Skiz get himself into now?"

"Nothing, Tony, it's about what he might have seen."

"*That* thing. Well, he didn't tell the cops much. When they came around Skiz got me before he talked to them."

"You were there when they questioned him?"

"Yeah, like I said, Skiz didn't say much, but he still said more than I thought he should. Talking to cops is nervous time, though."

"I know exactly what you mean."

"Yes you do, I know you do." Tony patted me on the back and gave me one more smile. 8:00 A.M., people going to work, the streets were filled. Lots of them probably would have traded places with Tony. He seemed one hell of a lot happier than they did.

"Skiz is the man's name who lives there?"

"Yeah, but you missed him, baby. He leave before all this business riffraff show up, and he don't come back until most of the cars is gone. Did you park in the place where you got that boot put on your tire before?"

"Yeah."

"We better keep this short. I haven't got time to undo one of those things right now. Skiz told the cops that Friday night he'd seen a woman and a man. Description of the man sounded like Jerry. The two were arguing all the way from the outside office door clear across the parking lot. Jerry, he had a garbage bag. He set it down, and the two stopped yelling at each other. Skiz said he thinks Jerry and the woman say good-bye, and she leaves, but he's not exactly sure of details because the yelling scares him. He knows he was scared, not much else."

"That's it?"

"That's all Skiz told the cops. Whether that's it, and whether that's true? I don't know. I got a job to do here, and as soon as the cops left, Skiz headed over to Union Square, and I went back to work."

Sounded like Jerry was alive when the woman left. When *some* woman or another left.

"I gave Skiz the eye while he was talking," Tony said. "Like, *You said enough man, shut up.* Could be Skiz making this whole thing up. Cops came back once more, Skiz pretended to be asleep. They don't even notice him. They tagged a bunch of garbage. Man I hate to see that. It's so personal, going through people's trash, you know?"

"I'd like to talk with Skiz. Could you put in a word for me?"

" 'Course I can, but you got to come earlier than this, or else get here real late. He leaves when the circus starts, kinda wanders.

I worry about that man, but I got my hands full here. There's only so much worrying 'bout people I can do.

"I try to make life better for people, they mess it up, then I got to start all over again."

Tony saw the second wave of people arriving for work.

"Back to work for me, baby. It never ends. I'll talk to Skiz for you."

Thirty

I walked to the deli across the street, bought myself a cup of coffee and a muffin that cost as much as a sandwich. I used the ladies' room, and then I used their pay phone. I wasn't looking forward to this call, but I'd promised myself that before I left San Francisco I'd call her. My need for time and distance didn't negate what now felt like family duty. I'd be making another drive into the city early tomorrow to talk to Skiz, but today I really needed my home.

I had no intention of telling Mina about meeting Hummingbird at the theater, and none to disclose the plans to cheat her out of her property. She certainly didn't need to hear that it would be 'easier to pull off' with Jerry gone, didn't need to hear it any more than I had. I might have to lay this on Mina sometime, but it could wait.

Mina answered on the first ring. "What?"

"I'm going home."

"All this death and lying and cheating I smell and what do you do? Run off like a scared rabbit."

"Mina, if I could fix things I would. Right now I want to sleep for a solid week."

"Today is Jerry's *pomana*. You're in the circle with us, and you'd leave without attending his funeral? It's not possible. You were his family."

"I'm not his only family. He has a father, a son, you, Zoltan, Capri. Others."

"This is true. We found Jerry's father, but he's working on some movie script in the middle of no place and probably can't get here. Jerry Jr.? I have no idea where he is. You're the only family Jerry had on the outside."

"I don't know how you tracked down Oscar Baumann, but I'm leaving."

"At least come to my place in Chinatown and help me get Capri ready for the funeral. Do this for Jerry, okay?"

"As soon as she's dressed, I'm going home."

"That's a good plan. After the funeral take Capri with you. She could use some country air." Mina hung up.

I'd give Capri a few hours before I escaped, but she could get a dose of country air elsewhere or at my place later.

I drove to Chinatown and parked on Sacramento Street. A Chinese man ran into the street, darting between cars and screaming what I assumed to be obscenities at no one in particular. He climbed up on a vegetable bin and, in very plain English, proclaimed himself President of These United States. He must have fallen through the family cracks, or done something so terrible everyone washed their hands of him. I dodged behind a delivery truck to avoid him and got myself to Mina's.

The door was unlocked, Mina was gone. Capri was asleep on the couch wearing Mina's bathrobe. Five Capris could have fit into her mother's robe. Drunk again. Seemed like Capri had two speeds—off and on. When she was on she was incredible—bright, strong, so strong, and clear. When she was off she was completely gone. I started to think that she used booze because she couldn't handle the full force of her personality, and couldn't cope with what her words brought in the way of response. How had this happened?

I nudged her a couple of times. I encouraged her to get up and get dressed. No response, I gave up. I pulled out a book from Mina's shelf, Milos Zlatos, *The Gypsy Guide to Dreams*, and made myself comfortable. Soon I was dozing with Capri.

I woke to the sound of honking horns. Out the window was a caravan of three gold Cadillacs, late model, two Lincoln Town Cars, one white Lincoln limo with the license plate MADAMEM, and a black hearse. Cars and pick-up trucks in various states of repair and disrepair were parked on the street below, a few with their engines running. I didn't spot one foreign car.

Mina climbed out of the white limo with Zoltan right behind her. I didn't see the psychic cats, but Felix the parrot was perched on his shoulder. Zoltan had traded his weary black coat for a tapestry jacket and black silk pants. He wore red cowboy boots. Zoltan was a striking man, nearly magnificent.

Mina looked up to the apartment window, raised both arms, and waved them back and forth. The loose skin under her arms followed a moment behind her bones.

She put her hand up to her mouth. "Come down, come down here." Her voice took up half the block. I rested my forehead in my hands and unsuccessfully willed this spectacle to disappear.

Gold coin bracelets hugged her wrists. Pushed up over her elbows were heavy silver bracelets. Around her neck she wore the gold sheriff's badge welded to a chain I'd last seen at my wedding. Apparently it was reserved for special occasions. She had on a pleated purple velvet skirt and matching satin sling-back shoes. A shawl with thin silver threads woven into the red fabric was tossed over her shoulder in an off-hand manner. No black for this funeral. People on the street did a double take when they saw her. In San Francisco that's saying a lot. Mina was quite an exotic animal.

I told Capri to take a shower. She sat up, took off Mina's robe, curled up, and went back to sleep. We started over. Getting her off the couch was one thing, standing up was another negotiation.

On the street below Mina yelled my name. I ignored her. She yelled again. Capri was propped against the wall, and I held her upright. I refused to start from ground zero.

I stuck my head out the window and hollered back to Mina. "Keep your pants on. I'm trying to get Capri to the point where it doesn't look like we're having a double funeral."

"How much longer?"

"I don't know. If you can't wait, go ahead. We'll catch up and meet you there." A second thought. "Where are we going?"

"First to St. Theresa's Church of the Incarnation. They agreed to hold the ceremony even though Jerry was not a church member."

That was an understatement.

Zoltan whispered something in her ear. She looked up at me again. "We can't leave without you. We go as one, or we don't go at all. Time is one thing. Unity is another. We wait for Capri until she's ready."

"Why don't you come up and help me?"

"What? You raised three girls, and you can't get one girl ready for a funeral?"

"I raised three girls and got them ready for school. I never dressed a drunk woman for her ex-husband's funeral."

"I've got my hands full keeping order down here. You can take care of one small woman."

Mina observed the chaos of cars and people. Her people. One man was parked in the middle of the street. He leaned against his Lincoln and picked his teeth with a slim pick. It reflected the light off his two front teeth, both gold. The woman with him had spread her blanket on the sidewalk and began shuffling her tarot cards. Her blanket was pink and red, with butterflies embroidered along the edges.

The butterfly woman had just spread her tarot cards for a passing tourist when a Chinese man working the Techno-goddess store ran out to the sidewalk flailing his arms, yelling in Chinese.

His shirt was white with black buttons, heavily starched, and he wore slim black pants that his rear-end didn't quite fill out.

Mina'd already told the couple to ditch the cards quick, I'd heard her aggravation two stories high. When the Chinese man went into a tirade, Mina changed horses. First she fired back at him in English, then, when she ran out of American swear words, she went off at him in several other languages. I slammed the apartment window shut and decided Capri did not need a shower. I hustled her toward a closet and rummaged through her clothes.

She said, "I don't want to wear black."

"As far as I can tell you own no black."

"That's because I have good taste."

"Your sense of style doesn't mean diddly to me. What I see is a naked woman standing between me and getting the hell out of this asylum."

I heard someone coming up the stairs. Maybe the fashion cavalry had arrived. It was Mrs. Liu.

She said, "I tried these herbs around my neck, and I can't stand the smell. I want my money back."

Great. A dissatisfied customer. I wasn't going to stand around arguing with her. I jumped into the Szabo mode with frightening ease.

I said, "You don't want the magic to work, fine, but no money back. You paid for a potion, not a bouquet of roses. You don't like the smell, buy a clothespin for your nose."

She slammed her fist in her palm, shook her head, and took a few steps forward. When she did, she got a full view of stark naked Capri. Mrs. Liu's eyes got big.

"What? You've never seen two women in love?" I asked indignantly. "I put a charm on this woman to win her love. She sees me and tears off her clothes. Never even been with a woman before! And you're telling me you don't think the magic will work? You don't want to wear the herbs, fine. But, like I said, no money back."

Mrs. Liu backed out the door. "I'm sorry I interrupted you."

I mumbled under my breath. "Fortune-tellers, we're just like doctors. People think we have no private lives at all."

Mrs. Liu turned and ran down the stairs. I peeked out the window and saw her tear up Grant at full speed. The circus continued below. Felix flapped his wings and relieved himself down the front of Zoltan's clean shirt.

I turned away from the window. "Capri, no more crap. I don't know where your underwear is, but here is a tight blue dress. It's turquoise, Jerry's favorite color. I'm giving you five seconds flat to get this zipped up, or you're going to the funeral naked."

She must have believed me. She got into the dress and didn't argue about the underwear.

I said, "Keep your legs crossed."

"Gypsy women can take or leave underwear. Our men like to watch us walk when we don't wear it. I learned that from my mother."

Not only was Mina rich, she was a regular love goddess. That aspect of her personality had escaped me until the last few days.

Now that Capri had her dress on, she was struggling with a pair of three-inch heels.

"You can't wear those."

"What's wrong with them?"

"What's wrong is that they'll kill you or seriously injure you by the third stair, and I do not, repeat, do not, have the patience for a trip to the emergency room. Take them off."

I perused her closet. "Don't you have any flats?"

"Flats? No style at all."

I threw clothing out of her closet like a burglar fighting the clock. I tossed her a pair of soft-soled shoes that looked like ballet slippers.

"Wear these."

"Those are my tightrope-walking shoes."

"Great. Jerry fell in love with a circus artist. Wear them today as a tribute to him. He would have wanted it that way."

She looked at me skeptically, but she slipped them on. Those shoes were my only hope of getting her down the stairs.

"I wish we could have found the ones covered with sapphire rhinestones." She sighed. "Those he used to love me to wear in bed."

"Capri, this is called oversharing. Let's go."

On the street Zoltan was keeping his cool, and he wiped the bird poop off his shirt. Mina picked up the tarot cards that belonged to the young woman. She told the woman this was her personal territory, and not to think she could weasel her way into Chinatown just because a funeral happened to let her through the gates.

A policeman walked out of McDonald's golden arches with a cup of coffee in his hands. He checked to see what the commotion was about. Hooray! Order. Sanity. I was actually glad to see a cop. This was becoming an alarming thought pattern.

He said, "Mina, my wife still hasn't come back. Do you think . . ."

"Eddie, I'm headed to a funeral. Join us if you want, but today I'm not working."

Eddie bounced into his squad car and revved his engine. He joined the procession down Grant to St. Theresa's. I'd gotten into the limo with Mina and Zoltan after we crammed Capri into the back. The engine started up, and I was going where I hadn't planned to go—Jerry's funeral.

A guy I didn't recognize was our driver. He smoked a brown cigarette, hummed, and beat time on the steering wheel to his inner music. Capri was slumped against the rear door. The color of the carpeting was that of a nursing baby's poop. It ran up the sides and the doors. I suppose it's hard to manufacture carpeting that's a true gold color. Ed the cop was right behind us.

Capri was passed out cold, snoring lightly, and a thin line of drool ran out her mouth down her chin. Even now, stuffed into a dress that was ten years old, drool and all, Capri was a knockout. She sat up suddenly and said, "They aren't in season this time of year." She put her head back down and passed out.

Mina and Zoltan glanced at her, at each other, and for a split second they almost looked concerned. I didn't know if Capri was talking about melons or white shoes or Christmas turkeys, but when she'd opened her eyes and spoken, something behind those eyes raised the hair on the back of my neck.

Felix flew to Capri's lap, cocked his head from side to side, and sang, 'God Bless You!' to her. I was in agreement with Felix. Capri could use all the blessings available. Mina laid a scarf on Zoltan's shoulder to protect his shirt. She held out her finger for the bird, who climbed back onto Zoltan. Mina and Zoltan put their heads together and talked.

No one took Capri seriously, I realized that, but why no one showed concern about her health—I couldn't figure that out. I was beginning to understand the major reason Capri needed Jerry. When Jerry was in the room, Capri was never invisible. For Jerry she was the room. Last night at the theater, even without Jerry, arguing with Bill, feeling her full power, she'd been the room.

We continued down Grant to St. Theresa's. I wondered how we would all find parking places. We passed the church.

I said, "We just passed the church."

Zoltan nuzzled Mina's neck.

Mina said, "At the last minute Father McCabe decided not to hold the service. His parishioners would be jealous. Such a big turnout for people who've donated so little money to the church. We're not rich, you know."

Right. Most of those cars were worth more than a wealthy person donates to a church in one year. The money for them came from somewhere, and none of these folks had the kind of credit that permits easy financing. The cars represented one heck of a lot of cash, ingenuity, or change of vehicle ID numbers.

Mina scoped out the alley behind the church. "We just got to go in and swipe Jerry's body, then we'll head out and do the service somewhere else."

Thirty-One

"Tell me you're kidding," I said.

"I'm kidding."

"No, you're not."

"I thought for once I'd try and make you happy by being agreeable. Look, it's no big deal—we just collect Jerry, and then put him to rest."

"People collect baseball cards and stamps, not bodies. It must be against the law."

"Since when are you so big on law?"

I was wondering the same thing. "I'm big on not going to jail," I answered.

"Oh, that."

"That."

"Listen, I been through this routine more times than I want to count. So much death all the time! I promise you're not going to get in trouble. You can even ride with the body if it makes you feel better."

"No thanks."

"I'm just trying to be considerate."

"Forget it. How do we collect Jerry?"

"See the big car in front of us?"

"The hearse?"

"The really big Cadillac that's good for hauling every member of your family anywhere you'd want to go?"

"The hearse."

"Sure, okay. The rest of the cars, they go straight. We follow the big family wagon into the alley behind St. Theresa's. I talk to the priest, tell him I got so many troubles he wouldn't believe it. While I'm doing that, four of our men take the box that's holding Jerry out the side door and push it inside the wagon."

"You've done this before and gotten away with it?"

"I know the priest on a first-name basis. He don't want any trouble from me, like the evil eye pointed in his direction. I don't want his God pointed in my direction. We're in kind of a standoff. Because of this we help each other out."

"Jesus H. Christ."

Mina surveyed the stained-glass windows and lowered her voice to a whisper. "Yeah, he's everywhere around here, isn't he? You don't want to make evil eyes in this place. They'd come flying right back at you."

We rolled into the back of St. Theresa's. Mina emerged from the limo and straightened to her full height. She wasn't someone to argue with. The priest marched out of the chapel wearing an enormous crucifix. If the man had to deal with Gypsies on a daily basis, he'd have chronic back pain. I watched them talk. Behind the priest's back the chapel's side door opened and four large men wearing black boots shouldered a wooden coffin. The coffin slid into the back of the family wagon, otherwise known as a hearse, and the door was slammed.

Mina kissed the priest's ring, he made the sign of the cross above her head. They were balanced in the world of blessings, and we took off down the alley. The rest of the party had pulled into a commercial parking lot and waited for us to pass. As we did they fell in behind us.

Mina sized me up, head to toe. "Stop looking so nervous, would you? It's bad luck."

"Stealing a body isn't?"

"How can you steal a body when it don't belong to the person you're taking it from? You think Jerry'd rather be with strangers or with us?"

I settled into the backseat. I looked at Capri. Not a flutter from her direction. Even Zoltan's parrot was quiet.

It occurred to me that, once again, I was with the Szabos and without my car, in other words, without any means of giving them the slip. I groaned out loud.

"What was that groan about?"

"Where's the service being held? I'm wondering if there's any chance I'll get my car in the near future."

"The service will be at the ocean."

We were circling the Bay, we were completely surrounded by water. "Could you narrow that down?"

"It really don't matter what part of the coastline we pick. We want to be close to the water so we can take Jerry's body, plus his precious possessions, and put them in his *vardo*. We'll set it on fire and roll it into the Bay. The ocean avoids attention, lots of isolated places. Besides, we don't want to catch anything important like buildings on fire."

"Set his *vardo* on fire?"

"Sure, you wouldn't want his enemies to get hold of his bones or his possessions."

"Jerry's gone. His bones and belongings don't matter anymore."

She spit on her hand and put a dot on my forehead. "Say you didn't mean that."

"I didn't mean that. Can I wipe your spit off?"

Mina heaved a sigh of relief. "Sure, it's done its job."

She may not have been worried about the attention a fire would bring, but I was. "Mina, is this burn necessary?"

"Jerry may be cursed with bad luck if we don't purify everything with fire. This includes him."

"What kind of bad luck can a dead man have? Someone kills him all over again?"

"Who can say? I've never been on the other side. Not that I remember, anyway."

I let it go and moved on, or sideways, or under. Elsewhere.

"Jerry, as far as I know, doesn't have a *vardo*," I said. "What is a *vardo*?"

"A *vardo* is your wagon, your transportation, your way of moving through the world."

I got the picture. Sometime after dark we would drive Jerry's cream-colored classic Mercedes Benz to an anonymous shoreline and roll it toward Japan. The car would be stuffed full of Jerry, his videotapes, CDs, toiletries, and Jockey briefs. We'd torch his Mercedes *vardo* and send the cinders of his life flying into the Pacific Ocean to swim forever with great white sharks, sea lions, and barnacles. It was insane. I wouldn't have admitted it to Mina, but Jerry would have loved it. At least the old Jerry would have.

Headed north, almost out of the city, we took a sudden turn east and detoured south through China Basin. I was a passenger on a trip that had a mind of its own. Warehouses, some busy, some abandoned, hugged the shoreline. We came to a halt in front of a corrugated building that looked pre–World War II. The sign above the roll-up door read: MARKS AND BROTHERS ANYTHING YOU WANT METALWORK. A phone number was hand-painted in pink paint below the larger sign. We were the only funeral procession in China Basin.

We pulled in first, then cars and trucks behind us followed and stopped in front of Pinky Marks' warehouse. Madame Mina got out of the limo and laid different herbs on the four directions of the cracked asphalt. We stood huddled in a group. She lit the herbs.

Mina talked to the sky, she talked to the metal building. She raised her fist in the air like a nineteenth-century revolutionary.

"This is to protect all us good people from what I'm about to bring on you. Pinky Marks, if you can turn invisible or become a bird and fly away, this would be the time to do it." She put both hands around her mouth. "YOU HEAR ME, PINKY?"

She considered the mourners squeezed into the area we'd been herded and made eye contact with each of us.

She lifted both hands to the sky, her fingers spread wide. "Jerry Baumann, I invoke your spirit. Come and see the man who caused your death; but when you do, leave everybody inside this circle alone, okay?"

She placed candles—east, north, west, and south. To the east she lit a yellow candle. "Jerry, you're gonna wake up with the sun. When you wake up, spit on the sleeping face of Pinky Marks.

"To the north, make Pinky feel the ice and snow, freezing him off from all family and friends. Say to him, *You are now a man alone.*

"To the west, may the last thing you think of be those who love you. Imagine yourself putting Pinky to bed. Cover him with a quilt of old vegetables so all rotten insects will find him.

"Last, to the south, may your soul find sweet blue beaches. Relax there, hear the waves. Call your enemy to join you and drown him in the tide if you feel like it. We won't mind one bit.

"PINKY, COME OUT HERE NOW! We are releasing Jerry Baumann's ghost to haunt you where you work and live."

A man peeked his head out the door. Pinky Marks. It looked like he'd survived his evening at the theater with Bill. Of course, I didn't know if Bill had survived his evening with Pinky.

"Mina?"

"Come out, you coward!"

He opened up and stood in the doorway. Pinky was short, round, and reddish-colored. Except for massive forearms from years of metalwork, he appeared to be a pretty benign villain.

"For godssakes, Mina. What are you up to?"

"We are seeking justice!"

He sniffed the air. "What is that!? You set fire to my tires or something?"

"What you smell is burning herbs. They'll send you where you belong and protect the rest of us."

"Mina, someone should have burned you as a witch when you were a young girl. Like three centuries ago!"

"Don't act as dumb as you are. You killed this lawyer who's sleeping forever in a wooden box."

"What lawyer's dead?"

"Jerry."

"Jerry's dead?"

"Thanks to you and your lawyer."

"I ain't got a lawyer. Unless you count that blood-sucking mosquito, Bill Wells. How come nobody mentioned this to me last night?"

"What was last night?"

"Me and Bill and Capri were trying to figure things out, but I didn't understand what. All I understood was that there was trouble, and somehow you'd blame me for it."

"Pinky Marks! Don't try to change the subject."

"What subject!"

"The fact that you killed Jerry."

"I wouldn't harm one hair on his head. Not for anything, not even big money." He leered at Mina like a hungry beast. "Baby, I take that back. You, I'd do anything for."

Mina raised her face to the sky, then turned in his direction. "You are impossible, Pinky Marks. Someone comes along and puts screwy ideas in your head about what helps me, what doesn't, and next thing you know Jerry's dead."

"Hey, Bill's the one has it in for Jerry. Just because Bill says he's my lawyer doesn't mean I'm gonna do what he says."

"You forget what the truth is."

"Baloney. It's Wells who stirs up trouble left and right." He stepped closer and tried to peer down Mina's cleavage, but he was too short. "I never did one thing to Jerry. As a matter of fact, hearing that he's gone makes me feel like someone tossed a knife straight into my heart."

Mina's silence was directed at Pinky. It was as loud as the Pacific waves crashing against the giant black rocks behind the warehouse. Mina turned her back on him and circled the four herbs. She blew Pinky's name on each pile.

His face raced back and forth between mystified and mad.

"Saturday night you're honey all over me," he said. "Wednesday you curse me to four directions of hell in my own parking lot. And all I did was get four days older. Witch! Get out before I burn you at the stake myself!"

"Saturday night? You don't make sense," she said to Pinky. "What else is new."

She turned in Zoltan's direction for a brief instant. His chin was raised, he gazed at some far-off point. This was Zoltan's only reaction to the news that Pinky'd been with Mina Saturday. Maybe he refused to be baited, maybe it was a familiar game.

On her way back to the limo she shook her fist at the nuts, bolts, screws, and bent fenders covering Pinky's yard, and decided to leave him with one parting gesture. She flung open the back door of the hearse.

She climbed onto the huge chrome bumper, bounced up and down on it, and beat on the hearse's roof. She said, "Jerry, you don't have to be scared of Pinky no more. You're dead. Come out and set things right."

Pinky emerged from his side door, locked it, and started an old pick-up truck with his company name advertised on the tailgate. He pulled into our caravan as if he were one more welcome mourner.

The Gypsies honked their horns, and I disappeared into the fuzzy upholstery, longing for a mind-numbing drug or the sudden ability to teleport. I didn't feel so hot.

Mina looked at me. "With you it's kind of hard to tell, but your color don't look right."

She put her hand on my knee. "You've been around more magic than you're used to. Don't worry about Jerry. We're still taking him to the ocean, but we wanted his spirit to wander around this place so he could take care of unfinished business. Sometimes when you're a spirit, it's hard to find your way around. You need a little help."

She handed me a hard root to chew on. "This will make you feel better."

Mina looked at Capri slumped against the carpeting inside the limo and said, "Honey, you have one of these, too." It fell out of Capri's open mouth into her lap.

I don't know what she gave me, but it didn't seem to have any effect. I was still in the processional headed somewhere in San Francisco for the service. We skirted the piers, the numbers got larger.

When we passed the carousel at Pier 39, Mina stuck her head out the window. "Hey, Pier 39 merry-go-round! Jerry Baumann is inside a box now, but he always liked you. I'm sure he'd want to pay you his last respects." We pulled over for several minutes.

The tourists barely noticed Mina. They did notice the line of cars, trucks, and aged limos tooling up the Marina and blocking traffic in the intersections.

"Why don't you turn on your lights?" I said. "They'll know we're in a funeral procession, and they won't get so pissed off at us."

"Listen to that language, you're too old to talk trashy. There's no need to put on headlights when you got a perfectly good horn."

I slumped farther down in the seat and noticed we were heading straight for the Golden Gate Bridge. Straight out of the city. North. "I thought the service was in San Francisco. There are isolated beaches just south of the Bridge."

"Things are a little hot for us in San Francisco. We'll burn the *vardo* at Drake's Bay and then head to your place."

"Things are hot, so you're heading to my place?"

"Hot's not a big deal. Just a matter of jurisdiction and time."

"I'm so relieved."

"It's got nothing to do with you, and no cops involved. I'm talking Gypsy jurisdiction. I got word on the street while we were waiting a million years for this daughter," she pointed her thumb at Capri, "to get her clothes on—don't she look like a movie queen or something?—and I hear some of the Badras think we're hogging the space between Chinatown and Haight. It's a good idea to give them time to cool off."

She picked at her fingernails. "The girl I yelled at who had the tarot cards on the sidewalk? Badra's favorite daughter."

"Mina, Gypsy jurisdiction scares me a hell of a lot more than the police do."

She patted my hand. "We're lighting the *vardo* tonight when it's almost dark, then we'll just keep going north and stay at your place. Nothing to worry about."

"What makes you think you're welcome in Sonoma County? We have Gypsies there, too."

"Rosa, Lola, and Tommy Geza. Good people. They're having a little trouble with the *gaje* police, so they'll probably be over at your place, too. I told them to make themselves at home."

"Mina, you know I have a small cottage. Very small."

"But you got lots of property around it. You and Stevan did good when you got that place."

"I've also worked my butt off to keep it."

"Boy, when I worked that wedding at your place . . . what a tragedy. I knew Stevan's lifeline was running out, and there wasn't one thing I could do about it. I saw Jerry and Capri would stick to each other. This I also knew would be a disaster, but I saw my grandchild in Jerry's eyes, so I shut up. He was gonna be a nice boy. The only person there with any sense was your mother.

Good strong lifeline, one who takes care of everybody, and she loved her family. She's a lot like me."

"My mother died last year."

"I know this. Who holds you together, now?"

"E. B. and I make it work together. She's out in mom's trailer."

"Always lots of work for the mothers and daughters. Sometimes it seems like that's what everything's about."

"Mina, you changed the subject."

"Which subject?"

"Too many Gypsies with too many problems staying at my place."

"I could have fixed your wedding so it wouldn't have come off. No heartbreak from a dead husband, but you wouldn't have those three girls, either.

"I also could have fixed it so Jerry and Capri never saw each other again. See how much responsibility I carry? I do this every day of my life, always trying to make things better for people. Think about that."

"WHAT HAS THIS GOT TO DO WITH STAYING AT MY PLACE?"

"You owe me for those three daughters. Second, you got plenty of room. I'm thinking of that nice apple orchard giving free fruit to everyone and lots of room for camping. We won't bother you, we won't even use your bathroom."

"No, you won't."

"Don't feel bad. We're used to making outside. We only need our tents and our music."

I opened Capri's purse and found the bottle of Jim Beam. It was empty. I swore off hard booze years ago, but now and then I'm tempted to fall off that wagon. If ever there seemed like a good time to jump off and wave good-bye to the dust as the wagon wheels scooted over the hills, this was it. I guessed I was glad the bottle was empty.

I pulled out my cell phone. A warning was in order. "E. B., we've got company coming."

"Good. I'm making a tofu loaf, there's plenty of food."

"Not even close."

"I'll add more vegetables."

"Trust me, it won't be enough."

"How many people are you expecting?"

I counted the cars and figured how many people there were per car.

"About one hundred, give or take ten."

Thirty-Two

The troops assembled at the water's edge, Drake's Bay, a spoon of a bay protected on three sides by grassy cliffs. The hearse and Jerry's Mercedes were driven to the shore. Four men emerged from the hearse, opened the back door, and pulled out Jerry's coffin. One of them stepped into a pile of seaweed. A giant bladder kelp, thick and strong as ancient vines, wound around his ankle. Over he fell, flat on his face, with the casket landing almost on top of him had it not been for the quick moves of the two men in front.

The man freed himself of the seaweed, pulled his pants up higher, and knocked his fist on the lid to make sure it was secure. They carried the coffin to the Mercedes. They opened its doors. The casket wouldn't fit inside. They laid the casket on the hood of the car, and it slanted at a precarious angle. I half expected Jerry to roll out onto the sand.

A man from the crowd ran to shore wearing a tool belt around his waist. In no time Jerry's front passenger seat was gone. They crammed the casket as far as it would go toward the back. A few feet of the mahogany coffin stuck out the door, but they seemed satisfied, a job well done. They shoved Jerry's shirts and an old guitar back in the car. If he'd bought the convertible he really wanted, the procedure would have gone a lot smoother.

The men boarded the hearse, now empty of its cargo, intending to join the rest of our group. The driver turned too tight, and they got stuck in the sand. A tow truck engine fired up, and it rumbled down to meet the hearse, a giant hook dangling from the truck's grille. They attached the hook to the rear bumper of the hearse and freed it.

Jerry's Mercedes stood alone to meet the tide. It looked out across the vast slate ocean. A priest waded into the water, although not the priest in San Francisco, not like any priest I'd seen before. He waved some incense around, crossed himself, and threw some plants into the Pacific. He wore the standard black robe and collar, but under the robe the torn hem of blue jeans and the tops of old PF Flyers were visible. Both sneakers were left feet.

People lined up to throw things in the car, on the car, under the car, in the trunk, on the hood. They whispered small prayers, and asked Jerry to help them out while he was on the other side. I joined the Gypsies and tossed in a photo of us taken at a county fair. Mina stood beside me with a shopping bag full of papers. She mumbled a few words and placed the Macy's bag in the trunk. We drifted back to the beach and to the cliffs.

This ceremony seemed fitting for Jerry. A Jew who didn't practice Judaism, an avowed atheist who believed in fate and karma and, if really pushed into a corner, did believe in God, at least God's wrath. He loved his friends and family, and lots of us were with him. It was relevant and unintentionally irreverent.

We stood in a perfect crescent of sand, water, and first moonlight. The cliffs protected us from view by those on Sir Francis Drake Boulevard, although by the time that boulevard winds its way west through the Marin hills to Drake's Bay, where it meets Highway 1, it is a deserted farm road. No one would have seen us but a cow coming late to the barn. In a middle gray light the moon sat on one side of us, the last sun on the other, and made shadow puppets of us all.

On the hill above I felt something warm. I turned and saw Jozef concentrating on the Mercedes. When I looked at him he turned his head from the car to me. More a sense than a sight, but in the dusk I felt him smile. I turned my face back toward the ocean. I hadn't seen him since the shots at the theater.

The tow-truck driver reappeared and made sure Jerry's tires were free of sand. He pushed the car from the shoreline toward the ocean until it rested on hard-packed sand. Small waves tickled Jerry's tires. The driver pulled a can of gasoline from the bed of his truck. He poured it on the Mercedes' hood. Jerry would have had a fit about that.

A figure appeared by the car. It threw sand wildly on the hood. The truck driver grabbed the person by the shoulder and pulled them away. The person left, took a turn, and searched the trunk. The person wrestled something out. The driver and thief were mere outlines, unrecognizable, and the ocean carried their words away before they reached me. I looked up the hill to measure Jozef's reaction. He wasn't there.

I saw him just before he reached the shoreline. The moonlight tore his curls apart. Now, counting the tow-truck driver, there were three people. Hummingbird grabbed what looked like Mina's shopping bag from the person standing near the open trunk, and gave him a shove. Judging from the size of the shadows, the intruder was outmuscled. The truck driver slammed Jerry's trunk closed.

The man who'd fought over the shopping bag huffed away from the shore toward me. He favored his right leg. He came within fifteen feet of me and didn't notice I was there. Bill. He was the one frisking Jerry's car, and apparently he had survived Pinky and the theater. Too bad.

Bill continued his rampage in my direction. By the time he reached me, he was walking, hopping, and cussing. His leg made rampaging difficult. I sat hunched with my back to the wind like a granite boulder fallen down the hill. Bill almost bumped into me.

The tow-truck man went back to work, pouring enough gasoline on Jerry's car to obliterate everything inside and out within several minutes.

Bill spoke to me as if we were good pals, like it was him and me against the world.

"These crazy people want to burn everything. Wrecking Jerry's car, a piece of fine machinery worth close to $80,000 is nuts, but I guess that's their business. Seems like they could have sold it instead of destroying it, though. Those papers are different. They belong to my law partnership."

After the Gypsy emptied his gas can, he tossed a torch in the middle and ran like hell. The blast blew flames into the sky, along with parts of Jerry's steering wheel and windshield. It was a little late to worry about destruction now.

"Bill, you don't have a partnership anymore. Your partner's dead. And I doubt there's one paper that Jerry didn't have on disk or in his file cabinets." I pulled my sweater around me. "That leg's going to get infected if you don't stay off it. You could even lose it."

"The police questioned me, thanks to you. I thought we'd agreed—no police."

"They must have believed whatever story you made up. You're not behind bars."

"That's because there's nothing I'm guilty of."

Bill hoisted himself up and left. I'd become a boulder on the beach again. I watched him climb the hill to his car. I watched to make sure he was alone, that he hadn't hoodwinked Capri into joining him. He *was* alone, and climbing the hill was a slow process of step, drag, hop. He fumbled through his pockets. Looked like he couldn't find his keys. He knocked on the door, he pounded on the roof. The sound whomped across the hills like a

Jamaican drum. Suddenly the door flew open, and Bill started the engine. He roared north up the highway.

Hummingbird had his arm around the tow-truck driver's shoulder. The wind came up and blew a few papers out of the shopping bag he held. Apparently Hummingbird had spared Mina's offering to the trunk from the burning. I looked into the blaze, and saw him turn his face toward the sky and laugh. Charcoal haze blanketed all, then a stiff ocean wind pushed it to the hills. Hummingbird was gone.

I walked to the ex-Mercedes and the ex-Jerry. Billowing black smoke and bright orange flames tossed the last debris to heaven. Mina and Zoltan stood in the ocean, just far enough for small waves to wet their feet. I joined them. Ed the cop stood with them. No ticket for littering, or whatever laws they were breaking. At least Mina had one cop she could count on.

Zoltan stroked his beard, and his face wore surprise. "That car went off like three kinds of Christmas plus the Fourth of July all thrown in together."

What had they expected? A nice little campfire?

I said, "One huge explosion is what you're going to get when you dump gas on a car and toss a torch in the middle."

Zoltan became aware of the ever-widening cloud that filled the sky. Also the acrid smell of metal mutating from a solid to a liquid. He said, "We're going to have cops and firemen up the rear-end pretty quick. I've got to tell everyone to move it."

Zoltan didn't have to bother. Headlights from Gypsy cars and trucks, and there actually was one horse and wagon clanking along, snaked their way out of the Pacific inlet back to the highway. Every one of them had their left blinkers on, all turned north, all in the direction of my home, none turning back to San Francisco.

The mushroom cloud that rose from the rubble of Jerry's car was orange at the bottom, smoky gray and black toward the top. The smoke hid the moon and turned the ocean a murky mud color. The sun had set. Mina leaned against Zoltan.

"Zoltan," I asked, "where did the Hummingbird Wizard go?"

"He flew off somewhere. When you'll see him again is anyone's guess."

"What were those papers he and Bill were wrestling over? They were the ones you tossed in the trunk, Mina."

Zoltan didn't let her speak up. "Bill is an idiot. There's no piece of paper worth arguing about, especially with a man twice your strength."

"Bill thinks the entire legal system is on his side," I said. "Although that may change. His law partner's dead, and last night he was wandering around in fresh blood."

"Fresh blood? What's this about? Why didn't you tell us about this right away?"

"Mina, I called the cops, and they're on it."

I didn't want to go into the details, like Capri's whereabouts and the company she was keeping last night, and then march back over the details in case they'd missed any. Zoltan didn't look surprised, didn't look anything. He dismissed violence as easily as you would an uninvited guest. He paused to look at the last of Jerry and his Mercedes becoming one with the cosmos.

"Phoo," Zoltan said to me. "Legal system. Police. All playground stuff humans invented to amuse themselves. It's got nothing to do with real power. How did someone get to be as old as you and know so little about important matters like power?"

Thirty-Three

*T*hey pulled up my drive between the trees, around the barn, anywhere there was enough bare ground to fit a vehicle. My daughter was waving, happy as can be, like a pack of Gypsies shows up at our place every week or so.

I met her in the doorway.

"You okay?" she asked. "What's with the eye?"

"Later. I'm tired, but okay. I wish all these people weren't here."

"Aren't they cool, though?" This was supposed to cheer me up.

"Yes, way cool. What have you got going on the stove?"

"I'm cooking for everyone."

Every parent has moments when they're absolutely certain their kid is on some new drug that will send them to the outer edges of space and will never bring them back. This was one of those moments.

"E. B.," I said patiently. "There are over one hundred people coming. See the cars pouring through our gates like ants on a counter covered with cookie crumbs? They don't expect to be fed."

"Mom, they are our guests."

Her hair was colored an outrageous deep burgundy. She wore chunky-soled shoes, had a tattoo on her right shoulder, and regarded me with her hands on her hips. How she got off looking like that and sounding like my mother was beyond me.

After I'd called E. B., she had driven to Food for You. She'd purchased ten two-gallon cans of SpaghettiOs, five cases of Hostess Ding Dongs, paper plates, Hawaiian Punch, and plastic forks. The first batch of SpaghettiOs was simmering inside a large canning pot. E. B. blopped a spoonful of noodles, a sprig of parsley, and a Ding Dong on a paper plate.

"Start handing these out while I heat up the next batch," she said.

"We'll put the food on the picnic table and they can serve themselves."

"God, you're a miserable hostess. It's a wonder you have any social life at all."

My oldest daughter is one of the most stubborn humans who ever walked the earth. Considering the waves in her gene pool, it's not surprising. I knew I'd give in, but I acted like I might not. These were the unspoken rules we operated by.

She said, "Could you just pass these plates out? Is that asking too much?"

I supposed it was not.

"Also, wheel the two giant garbage bins into the orchard so they can toss their trash when they're finished."

Not only stubborn. Bossy.

I handed one young woman her food and asked about her clothes. She wore a wide skirt, and the fabric was black. It was heavily embroidered.

I said, "That skirt is fantastic. Is it from Hungary?"

She shrugged. "My boyfriend got it for me when he was in LA, Olvera Street, he said." Her dog lifted his leg and peed on a man sitting next to a campfire playing guitar. She chased the man off.

I went back to the kitchen for more food. The Gypsies did appreciate the food, and they started trading each other guitar picks and metal charms for their Ding Dongs. A few of them looked at my palm, one touched the bumps on my head. Musical instruments were everywhere. I was getting into it. Someone tossed a joke at my back, and I laughed out loud. I went for more food.

At my kitchen table sat The Newly Lame Bill Wells, Madame Mina, E. B., and Zoltan. Capri was on the floor sitting against two chair legs. Someone had changed her into one of my sweat suits. The table was littered with papers, and a Macy's shopping bag sat on the floor next to Mina full of more papers.

I said, "This looks like a regular powwow."

Nobody said anything. The laugh went right out of me.

There was a familiar-looking guy scraping the last bit of SpaghettiOs out of the pot. He turned around and made a sweeping gesture with his arm. "This is a nice thing you done here. For everyone."

"Thanks," I said.

Mina spoke up. "Don't look into his eyes when he talks to you. You might go right down your own drain."

The man made a movement with his hands like he was brushing away an annoying fly. "My name is Pinky Marks. I came to pay my respects to the deceased."

Mina's villain supreme.

Pinky motioned to Bill. "Ever since this guy tells me he's my lawyer, I never even knew I needed one, my life hasn't had one moment's peace. Nobody's has. I'm sorry for your loss." One round noodle hung from the corner of his moustache.

One death, one bloodletting, and a funeral. The last thing I needed was some controversial character who might have contributed to the catastrophe. "Pinky, I don't want you in my house."

"Okay by me. Thanks for dinner."

At least he was agreeable. Pinky left, walked out my back door into a night filled with barking dogs, Hostess Ding Dongs, fireworks, and guitar music.

Capri said to the back door, "My mother's ex-husband. One of them. My dad."

Mina stuffed a Ding Dong in Capri's mouth. "Why do kids got to remind us of the stuff we did? They think we're too old to remember on our own?"

I left them all behind, every one, and ambled though my orchard. Sometimes the fringe of a party is the best place to be alone.

I breathed in the kind of air sliced in half by October, hard on the outside, juicy in the center—crisp and fine. I pulled an old chaise lounge out of the playhouse, shook off the cushion, and laid it back flat. For an hour or so I studied the stars, and they winked back at me. My chest rose and fell. I breathed and I listened. I could feel me again.

I'd done my part. I'd played hostess, I'd risked being at the wrong end of the law to send Jerry heavenward, I'd brought Capri home with me. I'd heard threats and plots and seen blood the night before. I now wished only bad things for Bill, a man I'd slept with once in a desert of desperation. And I'd made love with a stranger thinking he was someone else. I hadn't had a chance to understand any of it, never mind let go.

Time to reclaim my domain. My space had been taken over by people who, for the most part, drove me crazy. I launched off the chaise lounge and headed for my house. I opened the door, and they were all there.

"No more talks at my table. Everyone out."

E. B. stood to leave. "Not you, sweetheart." E. B. sat down.

Bill studied his fingernails and tried to look like he belonged. The sight of him in my home infuriated me.

"Bill, go. Now. I believe you've finally created some form of legal hell for yourself that you won't be able to squirm out of. If you haven't created it, I will."

I poked his sore leg, just slightly, but I did. "Also, your health seems to be failing."

I started in on the next two. "Zoltan, keep watching Mina, but take her and that parrot back to the city. I can't tolerate an animal who talks more than I do.

"Mina. I want you to write me a Christmas card each year so I know you're still around. The year I don't get a card . . ."

E. B. interrupted me. "Mom, stop. She's my grandmother."

She was right. I had no right to go off like that, but I also wanted my house back. I wanted my old life back, but that wasn't going to happen. Not soon. I wanted Jerry to enjoy the circus in the orchard. That wasn't going to happen. Ever.

"I'm sorry. Not that she's your grandmother. Sorry about the way I talked to you, Mina. I'm so tired they haven't invented a word that describes it." I could barely hear my own voice. "Even though I'm sorry, I still want you all to leave."

Everyone either had something under their fingernails, a speck on their pants, or a need to study the ceiling. No one looked at me, no one moved.

"Why isn't anyone leaving?"

No response, no eye contact. You know the expression, you could have heard a pin drop? You could have heard something lighter than a pin drop—a flea drop, dust drop, a sound wave drop.

Mina spoke, but she didn't look at me. "I don't send out Christmas cards, but I get plenty. Birthday cards, those I like. While you were out in the orchard, Lawless called and asked for you. I pretended to be you; otherwise, he wouldn't have talked to me. Believe me, sounding like you isn't easy."

"What did he want?"

"He said those tests on Jerry come back. First he threw up by that stupid Dumpster. He'd been drinking curanero and dupatra, then he had a little heart attack. There wasn't much tissue damage to his heart, just enough so he probably thought he had gas—that's why he drank those herbs. Did he make the tea himself? I don't know. The cops think he would have been fine, except afterward someone hit him on the head. Very hard. That's what finished him off."

"No heart attack then an accidental fall?"

"He was killed. Absolutely. Also they got a fix on the time of death. Sometime in the middle of Friday night."

She must have been making this up. "Curanero and dupatra?" I said. "It sounds like a dance team that went crazy on his chest."

"You always joke. Life is not a joke. It's got a real attitude, but it's not a joke."

The silence got heavier. It weighed a solid city block.

Jerry murdered. This made no sense. I leaned against the door-jamb. I think the only people who believe murder is real are those who could do it, and those who've experienced it up close. It's choosing death over life for another human being, it's pushing them into the blackest place possible. The ones left behind feel they should have noticed something big and terrible was on the horizon, spotted the trouble, bought the person a nice lunch, vanquished the enemy. All impossible.

I pictured the round red man with battered fingers and large forearms scraping the last SpaghettiOs out of my pot. I could imagine him poisoning someone, maybe bashing someone over the head, those large arms looked strong. His harmless quality must have been a front, and I'd bought it. They'd all been certain he had something to do with Jerry's death until Lawless called.

"Mina, you thought Pinky had something to do with Jerry's death. Would Pinky know about these herbs?"

"Sure."

"A bodywork man?"

"I learned most of what I know from Pinky's mother. She was my mother-in-law for a while, right? She and me, we liked each other pretty well until Pinky and I broke up. Soon after she dropped dead, and that was really the end of our relationship forever. But Jerry's death probably had nothing to do with those herbs, get that out of your head."

Bill didn't make one move. His strategy was to remain invisible and hope that his invisibility would provide him immunity.

"Mina, was he mugged?"

"Jerry still had his wallet on him, and there was cash inside. Plenty. Definitely not a mugging."

I said, "Pinky's a big guy. Jerry was not. He could have killed him easily."

Mina was steady and firm. She was handling this better than I was. "Believe me, we cannot hang this one on Pinky."

Mina sincerely believed Jerry was murdered, but the killer was a mystery to her. I knew this because she wasn't directing anger at anyone. Her face was ruined. Her body a devastation. I felt again for the reassuring, solid wood of the doorjamb and leaned against it.

Mina joined me there, pulled me to her. She lifted my face and held it between her hands. "Here's what we know. The police say Jerry was murdered. They're sure of that. The little heart attack had nothing to do with anything. We've got to deal with this— Jerry must have been someone's last straw."

"Maybe Pinky's," Zoltan said.

Mina inhaled deeply. I felt her breath rise in and out. She let go of me, turned to Zoltan, and looked at him as if he'd just won first prize in the idiot contest.

"It is not possible."

"Of course it is."

"No more pretending. When I went to Jerry's office Friday night," Mina said to me, "Pinky met me there. Jerry wanted both of us together. We were about to finish off what got started long ago, but instead we got into another fight. Pretty soon we made up, and one thing led to another. Pinky went home with me, he stayed with me Saturday night, too. I did not want anyone to know about it. Now I don't care."

Zoltan looked like he'd been run over by a truck. Maybe two. He started to sputter his indignation.

"Zoltan," she said, "this is not about you. I'm not worried about your feelings right now. I'm worried about that daughter of mine who's wearing Annie's clothes. Jerry murdered? I don't know how she's going to live with this."

"Capri's stronger than you think." I said. "It'll take a while, but she'll be fine, and she can stay here as long as she needs to."

"You tell Lawless that. He's on his way over. That fink-cop Eddie, it turns out he went to the funeral just to keep an eye on us, he's hanging around here somewheres, making sure nobody takes off. Capri in particular."

"Capri?"

"Lawless says he has enough evidence to bring her in for Jerry's death."

"That's crazy!"

"You talk to him about it when he gets here. It was hard to keep sounding like you when that man told me he thought my daughter had killed the love of her life. You think you're worn-out? You don't know the meaning of *worn-out*."

Mina put her head down on the table and did what I'd never seen her do, not even when Stevan died. She cried into her own arms.

Thirty-Four

My little house nestled in a hollow of Moon Mountain Road had held so much—births and deaths, holidays and love, pain and surprise, growth and horror. I didn't know how the simple bricks and mortar, redwood and stucco, had remained intact.

I sat on the edge of my bed, looked at the telephone, and rehearsed what I was going to say. I dialed Lawless' direct number.

He picked up on the second ring.

"Lawless here."

"You can't be serious about Capri."

"Hello, Mrs. Szabo."

That took me back. I thought he'd mistaken me for Mina.

"Isn't that your name?"

"Just call me Annie."

He knew the first time around he'd been talking with Mina, not me, and he wanted to make sure I knew. This man had a mind like a maze. Following the paths wasn't easy, but it wasn't impossible.

"I heard you were on your way to my house. Aren't I out of your jurisdiction?"

"Not in a murder that occurred in my city. I have every right to pick up Capri Baumann, wherever she is."

"What makes you think Capri is here?"

"Because Eddie Florentino's been with you since the funeral, he's in your orchard, and he's keeping an eye on our suspect."

"He's not allowed here without a search warrant."

"He was asked by the elder Mrs. Szabo to join the funeral procession. He's an invited guest."

"That is low. This is my home, and I didn't invite him."

"Let's not split hairs."

"This is bigger than a hair."

"When I get there I'll have a search warrant in hand."

"When do I expect to see you?"

"I told you," Lawless said, "we have a special unit that deals with the Gypsy population. I had to wake up the guy so I could take him with me. This isn't just some politically correct issue. We can't go on private property and stir up a hornet's nest with those people."

"As far as I'm concerned you already have."

"Listen, I have evidence, and I have a witness who fingered Capri, or someone who matches her description, as being with Mr. Baumann at the place and time of his death."

"I don't believe it."

"Also, ask Capri Baumann if she owns a pair of blue rhinestone slippers. They were in the Dumpster. They had her prints on them; Jerry's too, and it wasn't hard to trace them to her. They were custom-made."

"Those were the only prints?"

"The only ones that count, and they connect her to the scene."

"What kind of witness could you possibly have?"

"A man named Skiz who lives in the parking lot."

"The street guy, possible junkie. He told you he saw Jerry with a Capri-clone woman who hit him over the head?"

"I've already said too much. This is serious—you're harboring a possible murderer. As soon as we put her in a line-up and Skiz positively IDs her, we start building a case."

"She loved Jerry. Where's your motive?"

"Motive? You've got to be kidding. Mr. Baumann was seen in several clubs around town. The expensive, out-there kind including a very exclusive dominatrix club patronized by high-ranking politicos—male and female. All the while he led Capri Baumann to believe he wanted to work out a reconciliation. If she'd discovered the details of his life and confronted him with them . . . Also there's reason to believe that she was good and tired of his legal maneuvers concerning her mother."

"Have you ever seen Capri Baumann? She's small. She couldn't kill a man using brute strength if she wanted to."

"Capri Baumann has taught circus arts her entire adult life. A trapeze bar weighs twenty-seven pounds. When you've spent years catching and releasing one of those, you have incredible upper body strength."

He knew where Capri ordered her shoes, he knew Jerry's hangouts. He'd discovered an impending reconciliation. He knew about Jerry's and Mina's legal meanderings. Lawless even knew the weight of a trapeze bar. The man told me he was good at his job—he wasn't kidding.

"Are you checking out his partner?"

"Bill Wells?"

"I believe he's the only partner Jerry had," I said.

"Of course I'm checking him out."

"He had motive, opportunity . . . the whole nine yards."

"He was up in Mendocino at the time of death."

"How about a murder for hire?"

"We're getting a little melodramatic, aren't we?"

"We're talking about money, and a man, now dead, who stood in Bill's way of getting it."

"I told you I'm good. This means I am checking out everything. Including Bill, even though he has an alibi. But crimes of passion are a lot more common in this world."

"More common than murder caused by greed? Boy, I'd like to see the statistics on that."

"You have access to stats. Get them yourself."

Lawless and I were back on opposite sides of the fence. It was easier when I liked him.

"When you come here," I said, "you'd better have that warrant. And, as of now, Eddie is an uninvited guest."

"Play it however you want. I'll be there an hour after that clown from the Gypsy unit shows up here."

"I can hardly wait."

"And, from what I hear, there are over one hundred people on your property. Finding Eddie in order to evict him may be difficult for you."

I'd already come up with one idea to save Capri's butt while he and I were talking. I'd just thought of another possibility.

"Hello?" he said.

"It's nothing. See you later."

The later the better. I'd calculated the amount of time I had to find Eddie and lose him or turn him around. Also the time to hide Capri someplace where she couldn't be found regardless of the number of search warrants. If none of that panned out, I'd make an anonymous call to the local sheriff's department as my own irate neighbor complaining about noise. I'd let the local sheriff's department clear out my orchard, redwoods, and Gypsy guests—including Eddie.

I hung up the receiver in my room. I wanted to curl up on my bed and go to sleep for a long, long time. Like until all this was over. I hadn't killed Jerry. I knew that much. My daughter was in the clear. I knew that much. It seemed like I had a right to sleep through the final curtain call.

I walked back into the kitchen and sat at the table. I glanced at the full moon propped above my windowsill. Mina's eyes were red, but she'd pulled herself together.

"I just talked to Lawless," I said. "We've got some plans to make."

Mina turned to Bill. "This isn't my house, but I'm asking you to leave. I've got things to say about Pinky, and you're his lawyer. I probably got things to say about you, too. We know Capri is not a killer. We need to talk before Lawless gets here."

Bill looked hesitant.

"I really mean it. Go."

He stood to say good-bye, but no words came out. He made eye contact with everyone at the table, and with that contact he implored us to let him stay. When he reached E. B., he lingered too long. Mina caught the look.

She said, "Bill, how much trouble do you need anyways? I will pull tricks from the dusty corners of my head that I haven't used in years to get you out of here."

He looked horrified, then he composed himself. His ice-blue eyes matched his cashmere sweater. He should have looked handsome, but he didn't. His eyes were cold and incongruous with the arm wrapped protectively around Capri. "Pinky's a client, but I'm practically family. I should be here."

"Pinky, sometime-worm from the hole in the center of the earth, is one of us. You are not. And Pinky is not sitting at this table. You are."

Mina motioned for Bill to be gone.

He made his way around the table and even had the gall to play up his limp. He bent down and kissed Mina on the cheek. He touched Capri lightly on her head, stroked her hair, and patted her tenderly on the shoulder. In the midst of this gross insincerity he made every effort to examine the papers in front of Mina. He bent down to plant one final kiss on Mina's cheek. Surprisingly she opened her arms to wrap him in a hug and rubbed him on his back.

"We'll figure out how to fit you in when this mess is over. Now is not the time."

Bill hobbled out the door.

Capri had hoisted herself to a kitchen chair, and she lit a cigarette. The smell of stale tobacco would be floating in my cereal bowl the next morning.

Capri said, "Mamo, you hugged Bill."

"I'm sad and shook up. Maybe I shouldn't have been so mean." She shrugged. "He was the lawyer of Pinky Marks. Other than that he could have stayed all night, what do I care for?"

Bill's car pulled out of the driveway and crunched across my gravel onto the main road.

Mina pinched Capri's cigarette and took a drag. She stubbed it out right in the middle of a Ding Dong sitting on one of my good dishes, and blew the rest of the smoke out her nostrils.

"Also I got to wonder," Mina said, "why is Bill so interested in these papers that he'd slobber all over me and act more like a horse's ass than usual just so he can get a peek at them? What's he looking for? If I'm nice, I got more chance of finding out. The more I find out, the less the cops will be in your life. That I'm sure of."

Capri smiled. "Thank God, I thought you were losing it."

"Capri, I lost it a long time ago. That's why I got all these kids, all this heartache, all these men in love with me, and family mixed up with the police plus everything else left and right."

Mina opened the shopping bag she'd had by her side. "Jerry'd been sending me papers for months, and I ignored them. I tried to burn them in his *vardo*, like asking him take them back, but these papers don't want to let go of me."

She handed the oversize Macy's bag stuffed with wadded-up and folded papers to E. B. She volunteered to begin the process of sorting and searching and figuring out why this flurry of paperwork was generated on a weekly, sometimes daily, basis. Some papers fell out of the bag and remained on the table. They were covered with letterheads and too much language. E. B. retreated to the living room where she could spread out.

"Hummingbird swiped those papers from Jerry's *vardo*. Nobody touches anything in a funeral *vardo*. When he saw Bill wanted them, he decided they were worth saving."

"Did Hummingbird give them to you at the beach?"

"No, he gave them to me after we got here. Out in your garden. You didn't see him?"

"No."

"I guess he's lost his interest in you." Mina arranged a few loose papers like a large deck of cards.

"Anyway," she said, "Hummingbird didn't want to give them to me, but the papers got my name on them, they're mine. Since I'm his mother, he could hardly say no."

"My kids say no to me all the time."

"You raised them wrong. Not enough guilt. Guilt makes for very responsible-acting children."

She looked at Capri. "Unless you got someone who don't pay attention to one word their mother says no matter how good a mother they are."

Capri didn't reply. She'd been hearing this kind of stuff from Mina for as long as I'd known the two of them. But tonight there wasn't time for banter. We had to stash Capri someplace safe and do it fast. Alibi or not, I was certain Bill was the person who had shown Jerry the door to eternity. I had to talk to Skiz, and I had to figure out where those rhinestone shoes had been. Anyone could have planted them in that Dumpster.

"If I believed in such things," I said, "I'd swear Bill had made a pact with the devil to dump Jerry, get off scot-free, and end up with a load of money." I didn't tell Mina the money Jerry was fighting with Bill about was hers.

Mina turned her hands into wings and fluttered them over her left shoulder. She spit on my floor and rubbed it into the linoleum with her shoe.

"What was that about?"

"You want to sleep with the devil?"

"I don't think so."

"Good. I just told him to get out of this house for keeps. You shouldn't have mentioned his name."

I heard a car driving over the gravel toward my house. Too soon for Lawless. Probably Bill pretending he'd forgotten something.

We waited to hear his story. It would be a doozie. A car door closed gently. Maybe he was trying to sneak up hoping he'd catch a snatch of conversation. The sound of each bootheel tapped hollow on my old wooden steps. The screen door opened slightly, gnats buzzed around the porch light.

It had been five years since I'd seen Oscar Baumann, but I'd known the curve of his shoulders, the tilt of his head since I was a kid. He stood in my doorway with two duffel bags at his feet. He wore three layers of dust and a face so old and worn it shocked me. Oscar walked straight to Mina. Tears filled his eyes. They held each other without a word. They were tender, loving.

Mina poured him coffee, Capri roused herself and tried to comfort him. He pulled her into his lap and held her like a child. Relief poured over her. It felt intrusive to watch them, but I couldn't pull away.

Sadness speared me. Jerry'd had this family who loved him. No matter how their world was spinning, he held the quiet place in the center for them. In return they gave him passion and color. Jerry had what everyone wants. He was needed. He'd let it all go long before he died. Why had he let it go?

Mina smoothed his hair. "How are you doing, Oscar?"

"My only son is dead and it's my fault. How would you be doing?"

Thirty-Five

"**O**scar, you're bone tired," I said. "We would have picked you up at the airport . . ."

"I got into San Francisco late this afternoon, rented a car, got stuck in commuter traffic. I ran the horns and traffic of our lives through my head. I needed to be alone."

Mina said, "I will never understand all this needing to be alone."

"Obviously that alone feeling passed pretty quick. Here I am."

Oscar and I held hands across the table. He brought my hands to his face and kissed them, he held them against his cheek. I loved him. Behind his eyes I saw Jerry's eyes, a sad but funny humor, like you were waiting to see what part of your butt life was going to kick next. For Oscar there was no wondering.

"Capri, where's J. J., my only grandchild? Isn't he here for his father's funeral?"

Capri looked lost, like she thought he was in the next room, or she'd forgotten who J. J. was, or she'd gone on a bender and hadn't picked him up at school. Oscar waited for an answer.

I said, "We sent word to the Mandarin Palace in Vegas, the last place we heard he was working."

Oscar sank deeper into himself.

"Oscar," I said, "you know Jerry and J. J. haven't spoken for years. We're doing the best we can to find him."

Oscar squeezed my hand and kissed it again. "If I can't keep track of my own grandkid, I can't expect anyone else to."

He poured himself another cup of coffee, filled it to the top with milk and sugar.

"I caught the first plane out, but I missed everything—the plans, the funeral, being with family—everything. This unraveling is my fault, and I haven't been here to help pick up the pieces."

"Stop blaming yourself."

"I don't know how to stop. I got him into the mess that became his life, so much stress that it gave him a heart attack. He wanted to be like me, work in the movies, write screenplays. I said, 'No way, kid! Get yourself into something stable. Be a lawyer, you're that kind of smart! Too smart to live your life like me.'"

Oscar put his head in his hands. His hair was combed to the side to hide the bald spot covering most of his scalp. The thin wisps of hair dyed dark reddish-brown didn't cover the age spots on his skin. I hoped he and Jerry had parted on good terms. They'd had their ups and downs.

"When was the last time you and Jerry saw each other?"

"Three months ago. When I flew to Asia, I went out of San Francisco so we could visit. At first it was strained, then I mixed a batch of margaritas. We got drunk, told stupid jokes, watched *Bonanza* on TV and thought it was the funniest damn thing we'd ever seen. We spent the next three days eating in seedy restaurants. We even went to a strip joint! I got too chummy with one of the gals, and a bouncer kicked us out. Jerry looked proud of his old man, like I'd won some kind of award or something."

Oscar had tears in his eyes. He pulled out a handkerchief, wiped them all aside, and blew his nose.

"Jesus, Oscar," I said. "That's probably the best time Jerry's had since he was a kid. It's a lot more important than missing his funeral."

"Yeah, it is, of course it is." Eventually he'd convince himself this was true.

I thought about Jerry's Mercedes going up in flames, exploding, and sending its heavy German metal parts into the stratosphere. Jerry would have loved it, but not Oscar, not even the funny Oscar. Oscar would have considered it a sideshow, and no one wants to think of their kid's final bow as a carnival act.

How could I tell Oscar what we'd just learned from the cops, that his son had been murdered? That he hadn't died of a heart attack?

Mina said, "Oscar, the cops called this evening. Actually just one cop, name of Lawless. He told us something you don't want to hear, but you got to know it. Jerry was killed."

Her words were a blunt instrument that knocked the air right out of me. Oscar cringed. His shoulders sank low on his body. The man who sang and danced his way through life with corny jokes and politically incorrect pinches was not the guy sitting at my table.

He ran one hand down his face shaping the skin into a strange fleshy mask. He shook his head. "Just like his mother."

I didn't understand. "What?"

"Just like his mother." He studied the mottled skin on the back of his hands. "She was never in Europe or traveling or visiting galleries or relatives or mad at me. She died when Jerry was four years old. Killed by some nut she'd met on a movie set, one more man she had to sleep with who wasn't me."

"Did Jerry know?" I asked.

"I don't believe in family secrets. They hurt you, they take hold of your life by the tail, swing you around, then you can't figure out why you're dizzy."

"Jerry knew about his mom and never told me?"

"All those years you kids had your heads together—his grief was a package he couldn't bear to hand you."

"He probably never heard it from you. Not really."

"Could be. I know I got tired of talking to him about it. Finally, I let him believe whatever he wanted about his mother. It seemed easier that way."

Mina shook her finger at him. "Sometimes the easy way comes up and bites you on the rear, Oscar."

He put the palm of his hand against her cheek. "Mina, I love you."

"God in heaven. Spare me one more man who's in love with me."

Oscar mopped the last stray tear from his eyes, even laughed a little. Mina'd taken five years off his face. He finished his coffee and surveyed the human wreckage at my kitchen table. "I'm surprised Wells isn't here."

"He was," Mina said. "We kicked him out."

Oscar said, "Going into partnership with Bill was the worst thing Jerry ever did."

"Bill's dirt under your shoe, even compared to Pinky."

"Pinky still sniffing around you?"

"What else?" she said. "Oscar, Pinky and Bill had some kind of plan that caused Jerry's death. This is the one thing I'm sure of. There's money hiding somewhere, and Pinky smelled it. Bill fell in love with it, then they both needed Jerry to get it. Jerry didn't want to help them out. I told Jerry high ideals were heavy baggage to carry, but I could never get him to dump them. In the end those ideals made Jerry say good-bye to everything beautiful, ugly, loud, and bright."

"I'm not crazy about Pinky or Bill, but killers?"

"I didn't know all of Jerry's life, but a mugger or Pinky or Bill, that's what I thought right off. I mostly blamed Pinky as the usual root of all trouble. Then I find out Jerry was killed when Pinky and I were together. But even without knowing that, I was starting to think maybe Pinky was in the clear. I can smell this trouble like smoking wires, which is not Pinky's usual choice of cologne," she said. "And of course it's not Capri. Oscar, I want to know who did it so I can get even."

"What had Jerry gotten into?"

"We've got a stack of legal papers that people have been fighting over," I said. "That's a start. And Jerry had a procession of strange characters marching in and out of his life toward the end. That's another place to start. I want to get even, too."

"That's not like you."

"Oscar, Jerry and I had a date. I'd like to find the person who robbed me of one more night with Jerry."

Oscar's eyes sparkled, and he put his hand on my knee.

"You get them, kiddo."

Mina was not amused. I had pushed her disapproval buttons, but she kept her mouth closed. She was letting me slide on Oscar's account. Also on Capri's—she was smiling at me, too.

We nursed our mugs of coffee.

Capri leaned her head against Oscar's shoulder. "The cops think maybe I did it, and they're coming to pick me up."

He put both arms around her. "That's ridiculous. We'll get it straightened out."

"But maybe I did kill him. I know I wanted to plenty of times. And I know I got a hole in my head that leaks out the things I do or think when I drink too much."

"You couldn't kill anyone. Especially not Jerry."

"I hope you're right."

Thirty-Six

E. B. and I walked into the orchard. We were on a double mission. Get rid of Ed and find a spot to hide Capri until we flushed out the real killer. E. B. would keep Ed busy, I'd find the hidey-hole.

We told Oscar to keep Capri away from windows, out of Ed's sight, until we could hatch a plan. Mina was sick of Zoltan. I was paying him to tail her while she was doing her best to give him the shake. *Adios* money.

Mina was appalled that E. B. was going to use her wiles, Mina's words, to keep Ed busy.

"This is a job for a pro, honey," she said.

"Grandma, I know you've got a wild past, but tell me you were never a pro in that department."

"Of course not! I've got real talent."

"Same with me. We're even."

"Not quite," Mina said. "Ed's had a crush on me for years. The man is married, was married, so I kept him at arm's length, but it wouldn't take much to light a match under that one."

Pinky was on the loose, but I couldn't worry about him. Operation Hide Capri was in full swing.

E. B. and I each put on black jeans and black sweaters. After

I'd found the perfect place to hide Capri, I'd sneak back into the house for her, maybe through the apple cellar—I hoped that door still worked. I'd dress her in black outfit number three and get her tucked away. The Ninja gals. I was pretty sure when I got over being scared I would think this was funny.

E. B. and I crept around the back of the porch and saw nothing. We both looked pretty great in black, I've got to say that. About fifteen feet from the porch I saw a light spring up from the flip of a Bic lighter. The person with the cigarette was not interested in hiding from anyone. It was Mina. She had Ed cornered. Literally. He was backed into a space where the shed meets the barn and makes a ninety-degree turn.

E. B. started to laugh. Ed Florentino was about thirty-five, not tall, but definitely an Italian stud with a small, well-shaped behind. I put my hand over her mouth, but the sight of Mina luring this stud into her web was pretty entertaining. Ed was a helpless fly trying to escape. The harder he pulled away, the stickier Mina's web became.

Mina held his right hand in hers. She held her cigarette in her left hand and blew smoke out to the stars. Mina looked sophisticated in the way only Frenchwomen or movie stars do when smoking. I couldn't hear what she was saying, but Ed's eyes were big. He was trapped between the future written in his palm and his present, which was in the control of Madame Mina. I'd have been scared, too.

It was obvious Ed was going to duck under her arm or find some other way to escape pretty quick. His desperation was jiggling his legs. If he escaped back into the midst of the Gypsies, we'd have a hard time finding him again.

E. B. took the lead. We pretended we were just out for a stroll. She bumped into Mina, slightly nudging her against the hip. She apologized, put out her hand, and introduced herself to Ed. Ed couldn't have looked more relieved than if he were a shipwrecked man seeing an ocean liner come into view.

Mina smiled, but it was phony. She put her smoke on the ground and stubbed it out with her left shoe.

"Good night, darling," she cooed to E. B. Turning to face Ed, Mina said, "Ed, you come into my office as soon as possible. If you can't afford it, we'll work something out. Your fate line is screaming down the middle of your palm like a tornado. We got to do something about that pretty fast."

"Sure, Mina. I'll be in my first day off."

"I don't work evenings, but for you I'll make an exception. Don't put this off." Now Ed looked plenty scared. She headed to the house.

I turned to Ed. E. B. had his full attention. This is a family of women who are not ignored by men. As long as that was our truth, we might as well use it.

"Ed, I spoke with Lawless," I said. "He doesn't know when he'll be able to show up."

"What's the problem?"

"He's waiting for a man from the Gypsy unit. Orders from above, standard operating procedure. I don't know."

Ed groaned. "The Gyspy unit consists of Victor Bosch. That guy doesn't even own a watch. And it's getting cold out here."

"E. B.," I said, "why don't you take Ed around and introduce him to people. I'm sure it'll be a lot easier for him to do his job if people think of him as an insider."

"Would you really do that?"

"Of course," E. B. said.

"But I'm supposed to keep an eye on Capri."

"Ed," I said, "what did she look like when you last saw her?"

"Drunk out of her mind."

"Then you'll believe me when I tell you that she is currently passed out in my dog's bed."

"No one could make up a story like that."

"Also, Capri and I haven't got a great track record. If she's guilty of Jerry's murder, I want her to pay for it. I'd make a pretty good watchdog. Should she come around, which seems unlikely, I won't let her out of my sight."

"Well, I guess it wouldn't hurt to take a little walk." He looked at my daughter. "Let's go."

I pointed to my cheek like I had when E. B. was a little kid. She didn't miss a beat, just leaned over and kissed me. I whispered in her ear. "Keep him away from the well near the old water tower."

"Love you too, Mom," she said.

I climbed back up on the porch and sat on the front steps like I had all the time in the world and not one worry. As soon as they were out of sight, I bolted into the house.

"Capri! Capri!"

Turned out I had not been lying to Eddie. Capri was curled up in the dog bed sawing logs like nobody's business.

I splashed her with water, held out a cup of coffee. "We've got to get you going, fast. And you're going to have to be agile. What works best to get you sober? Coffee or a cold shower?"

"Hot coffee, lots, and my head in the sink. Also a bottle of tequila. I'm not drunk, just tired."

I poured a pot of hot coffee in a thermos, and pulled a bottle of Sauza from the top shelf in my kitchen.

"Hey, this is the really good stuff."

"Only the best for you, Ms. Fugitive."

I gave Capri some clothes. I told Oscar to break into a show tune if Ed or Lawless showed up. I opened a window next to the couch so I could hear him. Mina was sitting on the other end of the couch. She'd lit another cigarette and was talking to Oscar about old times, old movies, you name it. She didn't harbor any resentment against me or E. B. for taking her away from Ed.

"How's E. B. doing?" she said.

"Remarkably well."

"We're a good team, us three. I lure the men in, she takes over after they're heated up, and you do the brain work."

I thought this sounded like a combination that could get us on *America's Most Wanted* or a pilot for our own television show. Capri came into the living room, dressed and ready for work. Her feet were bare.

"Capri, you're going to freeze or get stickers in your feet."

"You said agile. You want agile, I got to have barefeet or the right kind of soft-soled shoe. I looked around your closet. Nothing, so I'm wearing bare feet. I know my body. No arguing."

The excitement of the chase was on Capri. She was wide-awake, even comprehensible and together.

She kissed Mina and hugged Oscar. All of a sudden I wondered if she was planning to run. I couldn't worry about that. If she ran, it would be Ed's problem with Lawless, not mine.

We skirted the edge of my property. There was an old well that hadn't been used since Stevan was alive. A man had come out once to check our well. When he emerged he looked at us with awe, and asked if we'd been drinking the water. *Sure,* we'd told him. *That,* he said, *is not water. It is salamander juice.* We got the paperwork to hook up to county water the next day. I remembered the man had lifted a cement slab to get inside the well and check it out. It was a perfect hiding spot, at least temporarily. But it was more dungeon than well.

It took longer than I'd counted on to stay in the shadows and work our way around the property line.

We got to the well, and tried to lift the cement slab. It was hidden under years of blackberry bushes. The stickers pierced our skin. Capri had stepped right on a bramble in her bare feet. She didn't holler, though it must have hurt. She was operating on nerves and that old part of herself, the Capri who didn't take a backseat to anyone.

"This," she said, "is not going to work. I could lift that cement slab, but I cannot stand in the middle of berry bushes while I do it."

"I don't think we could hoist it up even without the bushes.

That man must have had a long pipe he used for leverage to raise the lid. It feels like it weighs a ton."

"Don't be silly, I could lift it. But not at this angle." Lawless was right. She was strong. I hoped I wasn't making a mistake.

She studied the area. "Well, there's no one over here, and no reason to be here—that's a good thing."

She spotted the water tower about twenty yards away.

"What's that?"

"An old water tower. Stevan converted it into a studio. Sometimes he'd spend days up there painting—he'd work and sleep. He'd call over to the house now and then to make sure we were all still alive. I don't even think he ate while he was out here. I split off the property and sold that part to my neighbors. Too many memories, and they wanted it for a writing studio. That was several neighbors ago."

We walked to the fence line. One neighbor ago, I'd had some kook who put up a wire fence with curled barbed wire around the top. The neighbor didn't last long, just long enough to leave a tetanus buffet for anyone who tried to climb his fence.

"Going over won't work," she said. She tried to lift the wire. "Not under either."

We backed up. I watched her line of vision as it climbed an aging pole. "That pole, it's the one for the phone. Yes, I see the wires to your old water-tower studio. They lead straight to your house. These are still your telephone wires?"

"No, when we became part of the county they gave us new wires and buried them."

"Good." She rocked the old pole covered with tar. It shook a little, and it was split, but after decades of rain that wasn't a surprise.

She shinnied up ten feet before I had a chance to get a word out.

"What are you doing!"

She called down to me in a loud whisper. "I'm climbing to the top of this pole. When I reach the wire, I lift myself up and walk on this wire straight to that old tower. It's not even on your land. Perfect."

"Capri, you could break your neck."

"I been doing this since I was ten."

God, I should have handed her to Lawless. There was no way she would have killed Jerry; she'd get off, and at least she'd be in one piece. Right now she was destined to be splattered on the west end of nowhere.

"Please. Forget this and get down."

"Hush. You want to make me nervous?"

"No."

"Good. You can't anyway. Up here in the air, this is my true home, the place I am me."

"You get inside the top room of that tower and do not move until we come and get you."

"No problem. Hey, save that Sauza for me."

"Done."

I was shaking from head to foot, then I felt his arm around me. "Do you worry about a bird when it flies?" he said.

"I worry about a woman walking on an old wire. One who's upset and not thinking straight."

"She's an artist. This is the place she goes to leave the upset part behind. She's fine."

We stood together and watched her silhouetted against the moon. She was beautiful, truly part of another world. It was a place of grace that I would never know.

She climbed into the tower. Capri waved from the window— she was safe. I turned around and punched Jozef in the arm.

"Where have you been?"

"There are one hundred people here. How easy do you think it was to find Eddie for Mina, and how easy do you think it's been to keep an eye on Zoltan and on Bill? Where I've been is three places at once."

"Bill? He left long ago."

"He is here."

"Let's go someplace quiet and talk. I have a few questions to ask you."

He looked up to the water tower and smiled.

"No thanks," I said. "I was thinking of someplace planted on the earth. Like my bedroom."

Thirty-Seven

$\mathcal{E}$veryone who mourned and celebrated Jerry's departure was either passed out, partying, or talking. My bedroom was an oasis of peace and quiet. It was a miracle, and probably a short-lived one. It was a good time to ask Jozef about the bombshell Lawless had laid on me.

Jozef sat on the edge of my bed. He stood up, then sat down on the chair at my desk. He traded standing for sitting once again. The moon, now a small slice of yellow, sat perfectly above my bed. Jozef could not be still.

I put my hand on the back of his neck.

"Jozef, just settle yourself somewhere. We haven't got much time."

He tried the edge of my bed again, and I sat down next to him.

"You make me feel like a teenage boy."

"Do not throw up down the front of my shirt again."

He cleared his throat. "I'll try to control myself."

"Lawless gave me some confusing information," I said. "Jozef and Stevan must be mixed up in the state's files. A man named Jozef Szabo flew off a cliff into the Pacific and ended my run of kids. Also, the records list Jozef as six years older than me. What happened to Stevan? I am certain of very few things, but my marriage is one of them."

"This is one of the favors Jerry did for this family. He erased Jozef, me, my family's Hummingbird Wizard, off the face of the planet."

"What?"

"All Stevan's information was given to Jozef—social security number, birthday, everything. Then Jerry called all that information by a new name. He called whatever was attached to the dead man 'Jozef.' Jerry did a switch on the death certificates, and on any other records."

"Why?"

"Because Jerry always did good for this family. We had a tragedy that couldn't be changed. My brother, your husband, died, and it was terrible. But Jerry saw an opportunity to name Stevan's death 'Jozef' and give the still-living Jozef a free ride in the United States of America. No tracking me, no finding me. Here I sit, right next to you, but according to the authorities I died years ago. Can you imagine the freedom he gifted me?"

There've been several times I'd wished my girls didn't have social security numbers. I wished they were free of the government, and free of computer junkies intruding on their lives simply because they could.

"Jerry knew the value of living between the holes and cracks," he said. "He built a home for me there, a place I can fly from and never be found."

I was dumbfounded by Jerry's understanding of this family's needs, and his willingness to go out on a limb and create an identity-limbo that Stevan and Jozef shared.

"Lawless also told me you'd had a fight with Jerry," I said, "that you'd assaulted him."

"I was too young to understand the name changes. Or care. Too young to understand the hoops Jerry must have jumped through, the women at county offices he must have charmed . . .

As for fighting with Jerry? I was headstrong and stupid, I hated my life. I loved Jerry, but I wanted so many things. He represented a world that would never be open to me. We fought more like father and son than like two brothers." He looked right into my eyes—he'd learned the freedom to do that, too. "I don't know what will happen to us without him. He's barely gone, and I miss him."

He lay back on my bed, his hands behind his head. I didn't say anything. I felt the same way, also a little conflicted because this family had given Jerry his life, and they'd also taken it away.

"This gift Jerry gave me, this being invisible—it carries a lot of responsibility," he said. "If I were on the wrong side of the law or my people, no one could find me. The trust he placed in me was wonderful, also a kind of burden," he said. "On the other hand, Gypsies are often invisible. He just made it official."

"I would hardly call your mother invisible."

"That's because you're part of her life. Did you know there are one million of us? We're right under your noses, invisible to you, but not to each other. You can imagine, there's good and bad in that, too."

I could see a lot more good than bad. I'd chosen my own way to be invisible. At last count I had nine fictitious business names registered in just as many states. This has gotten out of hand, but somewhere along the line I'd decided that in this brave new world it's nearly impossible to hide, but I could at least make it difficult to find me. That's as close to invisibility as a card-carrying member of this society gets.

Gypsies are better at going around the system than reporters, private eyes, and most government bureaucracies. Because of this they've always had my utmost respect. At least in a general way.

"Jozef, I want to enter your mother's name in my computer and do a fast search. I know there's land involved in this mess, I learned that at the theater. I don't know the details, but maybe I can find them."

"You don't need my permission."

"I feel like I do."

"Do it."

Mina Szabo had a credit file. A big one. No surprise. Mina's Mystic Café was a bustling enterprise, too big to work on a cash-only basis. She had suppliers, rent, and taxes to pay. Mina's credit was impeccable. I was sure this was due to Jerry, always anal about paying bills. (He went into near cardiac arrest each time he saw the backseat of my car. It had been used to transport my bills and notices from collection agencies most of my adult life. Also, he wasn't crazy about the petrified sandwiches that were part of the wildlife inhabiting my car. When he put on his self-righteous horror, I tuned him out. He knew what was lurking back there. If part of him didn't enjoy it, he wouldn't have looked.)

I found Pinky and Mina's marriage, but couldn't find the when or where of their divorce. Mina was right—there'd been none. And Mina's Mystic Café, was not, as I'd thought, something Jerry had arranged for her. She and Pinky owned the property in joint tenancy since the late sixties when the Grateful Dead was trying to clean up junkies on Haight and Ashbury, when kids from the Midwest had landed in droves, then departed after several bad acid trips. Who had Mina bamboozled out of that parcel? It must have been one hell of a scheme.

I looked up her place in Chinatown, one of the few areas where Chinese had been allowed to own land in the state of California, in the entire United States of America. It was owned by a Mr. Chen Wong. It was his father's before him. Mina was their tenant before she came into possession of the Haight Street property. How an outsider got into Chinatown I didn't know.

Land in San Francisco is at a premium, always has been. The city is surrounded by water on all sides except one, and there's never been a way for San Francisco to muscle its way south. There's nowhere to build but up, and earthquakes make that dicey and expensive. Bill Wells had poked around the law office and found the potential gold mine on Haight—he'd expected to pick up Mina's Haight property after taking her for a quick trip to the cleaners. Jerry had ruined his plans.

How much of a gold mine was the Mystic Café? It would depend upon which way the wind was blowing at the planning department. Their business is public, entry is easy. I took a dive into their web.

After perusing babble about various ethnic groups' demands to name parks and grade schools, I stumbled onto the plans for a multiuse complex in the heart of the Haight. One that was in the early planning stages, one that was under wraps until it had been pulled together, one that would enlist a spectacular architect, the new Frank Lloyd Wright, the man who'd designed museums and city buildings around the world.

Early plans called for the structure to span both sides of Haight. A covered sidewalk one story high would bridge the street. It would teem with shops. The third floor would be comprised of condos, a gym, and an atrium. The street would be an open mall closed to traffic. The project would be, the architect declared, a celebration of the sixties of this entire historic area.

Several well-knowns and many unknowns had overdosed there, acid rock had hammered nearby Golden Gate Park every Sunday, a few kids on R & R from 'Nam had blown their brains out in the Haight, a few others had tripped out and never come back. It was a landmark piece of property, and The Mystic Café had seen it all. If you considered it something to celebrate, you probably weren't there, but time views pain, confusion, and anger through a romantic lens.

And Mina's property was smack in the middle of all this celebration. It was the only parcel left to be obtained.

I now had a clear picture of what was going down at The Mystic Café. Bill had discovered the property, Jerry was scrambling to salvage it all for Mina, trying to come up with a date of separation for Mina and Pinky. And I'd bet anything that Bill was under the table trying to slip Pinky cash to buy her half outright from Mina—Pinky had no more idea of its value than Mina did. Bill could then turn around and sell the entire chunk to the city for a handsome profit.

No wonder Mina was confused by all the legal work that flew in her direction. This was a complicated issue.

Mina had to be told that she was the victim of a major con job. Also that she was a red-blooded American with a credit history providing many personal details of her life. That would send her into temporary shock. It was a good thing Jerry was dead. She would have killed him for putting her on the map in such a big way. Pinky's plight was worse. He'd started this whole trail when he dragged her to the Barstow courthouse and made her get a legal marriage. Unfortunately for Pinky, he was still alive.

I looked at Jozef. "Do you want to lay this on your mother?"

"We'd better do it together. There's safety in numbers."

Thirty-Eight

Jozef and I had every intention of having a heart-to-heart with Mina until we saw her, then we both chickened out.

"We'll know when the time is right," I said.

"Maybe we'll be lucky, and get hit by a bus first."

My kitchen had just been used to prepare food for one hundred Gypsies and it was the picture of order compared to the explosion in my living room. I was surprised to see Eddie Florentino sitting cross-legged with E. B. on the floor.

Mina read my surprise. "Do you know Eddie has Gypsy blood?"

"Really?"

"So few of us around, we have to take care of each other. They wanted to put him on the Gypsy unit, but they thought he didn't know enough about his heritage to do any good. Turns out I knew his grandmother down in Barstow."

"You're kidding."

Eddie grinned just like he'd been given a new lease on life.

"I knew I was drawn to Mina for some reason," he said. "I kept seeing Mina about my wife, she tells me 'don't trust her.' One day I came home and she was on the couch with some guy from the force."

"It's been a hard time, Eddie, but at least you got a bunch of new family to make it better."

"What happened to Lawless?" I asked Eddie.

"Victor was just booked for accepting bribes. Lawless wants me to remain on surveillance. As long as no one's leaving, and he hasn't found Skiz, there's not much he can do."

"They have Capri's shoes."

"They *had* Capri's shoes. They're not in the evidence room anymore. I wouldn't want this to get out, but it's not unusual for things to 'disappear.' Maybe someone thought his wife would like them."

I believed that drugs and money might disappear. Shoes, forget it. But then again, Eddie worked there, I didn't.

"Eddie, I never understood what the big deal was about them, anyway. Capri could have left them at Jerry's two years ago. Maybe he was getting rid of everything that reminded him of her. Who knows?"

"I told my boss the same thing. But Lawless has terrific instinct, and a twenty-year track record of breaking cases. All I know is that without placing Capri at the scene, one pair of shoes is the start of an investigation—it's not the end."

Mina continued flipping tarot cards in front of Eddie.

"He asked me to do some initial questioning," Eddie said. "Lawless gave me a list, he said you'd cooperate. Maybe he's losing his enthusiasm now that he's about to retire."

No way. Even though Victor Bosch was behind bars, Lawless would be rattling his brain for information. Also tracking down Skiz or anyone else that could identify someone at the scene during the time of death. That's what I'd be doing.

"Eddie, this isn't personal," I said. "but I'm not big on cooperating with the law. And since you don't have a warrant or probable cause, I have the right not to answer questions. I also have the right to ask you to leave."

Eddie looked crestfallen.

"Ask him to leave! He's practically family!" Mina said.

"Mina, he's a nice-looking man who's sitting in our living room waiting to see if one of us slips up and hands him something. No offense, Eddie."

"None taken."

"What if he were here in an unofficial capacity. Like as a date?" E. B. said.

What was wrong with my daughter and Mina?

I cleared my throat and said to E. B., "How's Capri doing?"

"Still curled up in the old dog bed."

"Let's go check on her."

E. B. had moved the bed into a corner of the kitchen, near the woodstove, and had folded up a bunch of blankets with some clothes and sneakers sticking out. It looked human to me.

I'd wanted a word alone with my daughter, but Eddie wasn't far behind.

"Capri must have really tied one on," he said.

"She was very much in love with Jerry. This has been a terrible shock."

"I can see that."

I gently led Eddie back into the living room. Mina raised her eyebrows at me and flipped two more cards. She gave Eddie a stellar reading.

"See here? You are to take Victor's place on the Gypsy unit. This card says no direct experience, but blood is thicker than water. You'd do good for all of us, both sides of the fence."

E. B. sat cross-legged on the living-room floor wearing tight jeans, a tank top, and bare feet. I was used to her, and I still never got over how beautiful she was.

Eddie seemed safe enough to leave with my daughter, but it was not safe to leave a bunch of blankets wadded up and pretend they were Capri. If Eddie knew we were playing him for a fool, all that camaraderie would fly right out the window. I suggested to Eddie and E. B. that they go outside and enjoy the party.

"I agree. So much dancing. Where are you going to hear music like this?" Mina said. "You want experience for the force? What better time? And we'll be here when you feel like questioning us. Or at least me."

Eddie was happy as a little clam, and E. B. didn't look so unhappy herself. She went into my room, applied new red lipstick, fire-engine red, and grabbed a wide skirt. She twirled around for Eddie and said, "Let's go, Copper."

After they left, Mina flopped back in her chair. "Whew. I thought we'd never get rid of those two."

"You didn't seem any too anxious."

"When did looking anxious ever help around the police? We just got to be glad that things worked out, and Victor's in the can; otherwise, we'd have Lawless up here. Him I can't handle." Another one of her thin smiles.

"What?"

"What *what*?"

"What are you smiling about?"

"Look, the thing with that Gypsy unit is they put guys in there who are more part of us than part of them," Mina said. "I was blowing Victor's nose when he was three years old. I saved his mother's life when she was being beaten by his father. I hit that old creep on the head with everything I could find until he passed out. Now—I ask Victor to sneak around the police department and get something, he's going to do it. What does he care about Capri's shoes? He cares that I saved his mother's life."

"You threw Victor to the sharks, and he went willingly?"

"Sure. He'll be out in a day or two. It's not much to pay for your mother's life."

There was one file on my floor called Ozro. The name of the file Berva was sent to recover from Jerry's house. "Ozro Marks," I said to Mina.

"Yeah, I told you this, Pinky's real name."

"Pinky's filed a new paper against you almost every week for the past year. Actually, Bill's filed them in Pinky's name. Some of these allegations are outrageous."

"I had Jerry to take care of this. He's dead. What do I do about it now?"

"I also see lots of blank spaces with your name typed underneath. There's only so much a lawyer can do if you don't sign their papers."

"Jerry said that, too. I told him number one, I never sign anything, especially if it has to do with *gaje* courts, and number two, I don't remember number two. Yes, I do. Number two, the Gypsy courts said our marriage is done, that's enough for me.

"Me and Pinky haven't been together for a million years," she said. "I asked Jerry, 'Why all of a sudden this push for a legal divorce?'"

"You have no idea why Jerry wanted you to get a divorce, and do it fast?"

"No. I only knew it was a real sore point for him. I tried to listen when he'd explain it, but I'd get bored, then I'd tune him out."

An unfiled divorce would have driven Jerry nuts, especially when the joint assets were huge.

Mina tossed the few papers she held on the floor with the rest. "All this legal mess can't have anything to do with me. Only a big shot deserves this."

"Mina," I said, "you are a big shot. It's possible someone wanted Jerry dead because of your money."

"What are you talking about? Sometimes I got to borrow money from the cash register at The Mystic Café just to buy groceries."

This was not the perfect time to break her millionaire status to her, so I edged around it. She was having a hard enough time grappling with things she couldn't understand.

"Mina, the money has to do with why Jerry wanted you and Pinky to make a clean break."

"It all comes back to Pinky, doesn't it?"

"And Pinky's lawyer."

"Can you imagine them wanting so much evil for me? With Pinky it's a matter of the heart. This causes people to act nuts, and you can forgive them. Almost. With Bill, it's just another job. It's cold, it makes anything possible."

Oscar, as subtle as Mina, asked, "Why do you hate Pinky so much? Did he dump you?"

"Dump me? No one has dumped me in my entire life since I began with my first marriage when I was fifteen years old."

Mina cleared her throat. "Actually I was the one kind of left Pinky."

I knew that understated tone. "Kind of left Pinky?"

"Not kind of. I did."

"So you left Pinky," Oscar said, "and you've been mad at him ever since."

"Pretty much."

Oscar understood Mina completely. "It doesn't make sense, but love's like that."

Mina nodded her head in agreement. "No kidding. Decide to head for the door, and a man can ruin your life. A woman, too, I guess.

"I was *marime* for a long time because of the fuss Pinky made when I left. He dragged me through the Gypsy courts left and right until my hair practically fell out. Of course, I was pregnant during this time, so that had something to do with it."

Oscar said, "What did Pinky do that made you leave him?"

"He caught me fooling around. As my husband he had the right to look the other way and end the marriage, to look the other way and keep the marriage, or to get the whole community involved. They'd follow his lead."

I said, "If he caught you fooling around, it seems like he had a right to be mad."

"He did some fooling around himself. We never talked about it, I wasn't interested enough to care. No, it wasn't so much me fooling around, but that it happened in front of everyone. It hurt his pride."

"In front of everyone?" Even Oscar, who thought he'd heard everything, had amazement plastered across his face.

"Jeez. You want the whole story or something?"

I knew enough about Mina's love life already. "Not really."

Oscar piped in. "I do."

"Okay. I'll tell you. There was this *pomana*. Funerals make you feel like, you know, maybe tomorrow I'll get struck by lightning or something. Better enjoy myself while I can.

"This was an old-fashioned European funeral where they put the body in its box on a table in one room and the guests are in the next room having a party. Anyway, Zoltan and me are standing together next to the box, we hardly know each other. We're looking at the peaceful expression on the dead man's face thinking how he wouldn't be happy or sad or anything anymore, and we're not thinking about each other at all, just that dead guy, and Zoltan turns to say something to me, and I kiss him right on the mouth. I'm very passionate."

Oscar looked at my coffee table and traced a grain of pine with his fingernail. Zoltan. He'd also been a fixture in Mina's life a long time.

"Zoltan kisses me back, we're kissing like the world was gonna end or begin, and then we fall on the floor, and we're rolling around under roses that are in big baskets around the dead man. We roll under the dead man's coffin, and by now there's no shame or reason involved. The world explodes. Zoltan gets up a little to pull up his pants but the casket falls over, thank God not right on top of us, and the dead man rolls out.

"What a noise. Everyone in the other room who's been drinking wine and playing guitar and talking about the dead man's life, comes running into the viewing room and finds the corpse in the middle of all these flowers lying on its side, half-in, half-out of the box, Zoltan with his pants still down, and me with one leg pinned underneath the wooden box. I mean not even the best liar in the world could talk themselves out of that situation. There was no point in even trying.

"So Pinky, he did have the right to walk out of that room and pretend he saw nothing, but he couldn't do it. He dragged me into the dirt; himself, too. Because then I had to talk about all the women he'd fooled around with when he did bodywork on their cars. And lots of those women were my friends."

Zoltan walked across the room and stood behind Mina. Except for Jozef mentioning he'd been keeping an eye on Bill and Zoltan, I'd forgotten about him. I wondered if he was on the clock. If Zoltan was doing his PI job, I shouldn't have forgotten about him. There should have been reports. Pictures. Something.

He looked at Mina with regret. "I'm the one who ruined your life. I should have kept my pants zipped up."

"Like I would have let you! Zoltan, our fates are like the braids on a young girl's head. You can't undo them, and you don't want to. Everything would come tumbling down around me without our lives woven together."

Right then Mina looked soft and vulnerable, and I believed she did love Zoltan.

"Mamo," came Hummingbird's voice, "if Jerry got himself into a mess because of Pinky, or any of the rest of us, I want to know. Taking care of you will be a big job now that he's gone."

Jozef's soft voice commanded more attention than one twice its volume. Mina let go of Zoltan's hand and touched her son's head, touched it gently like a butterfly on a beautiful flower. He sat on the floor near her chair, his breathing was quiet, as soft as a bird's wings against the sky. The only other sound was the clock ticking off time, the wood snapping in the fire.

I thought I heard a knock on the door. I tried to ignore it. We all tried to ignore it. Who knew what new disaster might be out there? Another knock. Oscar got up and faced it. It was the round, red man with Popeye arms.

He put out his hand and Oscar shook it. "Mr. Baumann, I'm Pinky Marks. The man they thought killed your son but didn't."

Thirty-Nine

"Pinky!" Mina said. "Annie already kicked you out once. This is like when you sold that croak insurance. You got more nerve than a rooster."

"I been sitting on the bench under the open window listening to my name get bashed around left and right. I'm not gonna sit out there and get raked over the coals."

He crossed the room and patted Jozef on the back. "Hello, old friend," he said.

"Mina, maybe we can straighten out this mess together," Pinky said.

Zoltan looked horrified, Mina looked relieved. "Okay," she said.

"Besides," Pinky said, "there's a car parked on that hill, a white Oldsmobile with US government plates. I'd just as soon keep a low profile. Like none."

I peeked out my window. An anonymous car that yelled *government agent!* If I'd ever seen one, up the short slope and on the public road. Now I had Gypsies, a big-city cop, and the feds encamped in and around my property.

I said, "Pinky, before we start cleaning up Mina's mess, can I ask why that agent is following you?"

"Brother, you know how the government is. I'm a small businessman. It's a wonder us little guys stay in business with the feds riding our tails day in, day out."

"Are you involved with the mob?"

"No way. They're worse than the government as far as sticking their noses in your business."

"Do you have a gun on you?"

"I don't carry a gun, never have."

"Those guys are after you for something, and it's not for being an entrepreneur."

"I'm no criminal. They think I'm guilty of white-collar crime? Pretty funny—I never been involved in a white-collar business, and I don't own one white shirt."

I could see the fed had a pair of binoculars and was scoping out my property inch by inch, foot by foot.

"How long has he been here?" I asked.

"Don't worry. He didn't spot me. I knocked on your door as soon as he pulled up. He's sitting there thinking since everyone in the world is here, I might show up, and he was right."

My head started pounding. I'd had a mild throb earlier, now I had the mother of all headaches.

I'd ignore the federal agent as long as he stayed off the legal limits of my property, and I'd sneak Pinky out when we finished sorting through the paperwork that wound its way through his and Mina's unconventional relationship. If we needed to, we could stash Pinky in the water tower with his daughter. But maybe, with him and Mina in the same room, we could sew this up.

"Pinky, Mina," I said, "did you know anyone was interested in buying the cafe?"

"Is that what this is all about? I would have sold it, no big deal," Mina said. "I most of the time work out of Chinatown."

"They couldn't buy it from you alone."

"Why not?"

"Because what they wanted was the land."

"The land belongs to me. They could of bought that, too."

"It's also got Pinky's name on it."

Mina was mad. "Pinky, you got to make such a stink out of everything, even in that run-down neighborhood. That cafe could have burned to the ground for all I cared!"

"Hey, I'm not to blame on this one," Pinky said. "Fine with me if we sold it. I didn't even remember my name was on that joint."

"Not until Bill told you?" I asked.

"Right. Bill says to me, 'Listen, I've been going through office files, and I see Jerry's trying to file a divorce for you and Mina. He's filled out papers that lists the cafe and property as Mina's asset. If we don't get busy and contest the divorce, you're going to lose a lot of money.' "

" 'Go ahead and lose it!' " I says to him. " 'Let Jerry file the papers. Mina's a witch.' "

Mina was incensed. "A nice thing to say about the mother of some of your children!"

Things were heating up. I'd gotten a feel for Mina's rhythm. When Mina starts fighting with a man, they end up in a hot clinch. I didn't need that in my house, especially in Zoltan's presence.

"You two cut it out and behave."

I gave them a moment to settle back in their seats and calm down.

"Mina," I said, "do you know how much you own?"

"I own whatever that old lady left me in 1968. I don't want property, I never did. I told Jerry that. Every once in a while Jerry'd ask me for the tax bill, I'd say, 'What tax bill?' 'Stop pretending you don't own land,' he'd say. 'You want the government to get it?'

"That's the last thing I wanted. Mrs. Smyth's spirit would jump up and kill me if I let the government take her property. Owning land was very important to her. She didn't like the government of California. She thought Ronald Reagan was a communist, and that Pat Brown before him was two communists put together.

"Anyway, Jerry had the tax bill sent to his office so he could pay the property taxes behind my back. He hired people to run the cafe, he and Zoltan did, and I went there once in a while to meet Zoltan and drink a free cup of tea. I pretended it was free just because they liked me. And, like I said, sometimes I'd take a little money out of the cash register.

"Mrs. Smyth was one of my first clients. I respected her. I didn't have any use for communists either. She thought her family was a bunch of lost pinkos. She didn't like them, they didn't like her, and she left her property to me. Her family fought me, but Jerry took care of them. The land ended up mine, and I became my own landlady. Pretty funny."

I said, "Mina, do you know how much that property and the attached rental units are worth?"

She groaned. "I forgot about those rentals. Like I said, that neighborhood is old and run-down. The cafe is shabby. It can't be worth enough to fuss over."

I said, "It's worth approximately eleven million dollars. Minimum."

Mina fell back into the chair cushions. "Jesus H. Christ. That's enough to get sick about. Who'd want that kind of dough?"

"Lots of people. Bill for starters. Maybe Pinky."

I'd hit Pinky's hot button. "Not me! I'm proud. I don't take nothing that don't belong to me, especially not from a woman who used to be my wife. Or still is."

"But, Pinky, that land does belong to you," I said. "Half of it, anyway."

"It's a stupid legal detail because we were married one sunny day in Barstow. That old lady left it to Mina, not me. She didn't even know me."

"Then why didn't you sign the divorce papers giving that property to Mina as her asset?"

"Number one, I never sign anything, number two, the Gypsy courts said our marriage was over. That was enough for me."

Boy, those two were right in sync. Mina looked at Pinky the same way she looked at Zoltan. Things were not going well here. Pinky either still loved Mina, and maybe the feeling was mutual, or he was sweet-talking her into getting that property by pretending he didn't want it.

Mina said, "Why this one piece of land? There's plenty of broken-down places around San Francisco in bad neighborhoods."

I told her about the city wanting to build a multi-use complex. Her eyes glazed over, and she went elsewhere, probably just the way she had when tuning out Jerry.

I said, "Mina, come back."

"Uh? Okay, I'm back."

"And, Bill wanted your land because he believed he could cheat you, easy because you had no idea what it was worth. He'd buy it from you for a song and sell it to the city for an entire Broadway musical."

She said, "With Jerry gone there'd be no one to stop me from selling it cheap, right? His death came in handy."

"Yes, it did."

Mina leaned back in the chair and heaved an enormous sigh. She hadn't wanted money, but it rushed to her headlong with all the misery that sometimes accompanies it.

"I wish Jerry wouldn't have worried so much about me," Mina said. "The last century has been good for people in my line of work. I never had trouble making money, did I, Pinky?"

"No, Honey, you didn't. Money likes you."

Oh good. Now they were acting nice and calling each other Honey in front of Zoltan and everyone else. Zoltan fidgeted on the couch. Hummingbird sat next to him and monitored him, ready to restrain him or comfort him. Mina was oblivious to the men in her life.

"Think about the problems people needed help with! Two world wars, not only a depression but a Great Depression, you got a stock market that falls through the floor, you got one that goes through the ceiling, then another that hits the basement.

"You got kids who act loony and take drugs left and right. They pretend they hate their parents who gave them everything in the world. These kids grow up, and their kids stick earrings in private places and get tattoos all over their bodies and don't know whether to act like boys or girls. They think they love everybody. The truth is they love nobody, including themselves.

"THEN you got a whole generation of people who should have died twenty years ago, but they just keep living, and they can't figure out why they're hanging around. They hardly know anybody in their family, and they regret all kinds of things. Like I said, this has been a good time for people in my profession."

The twentieth century, as distilled by Mina Szabo. Busy, but grim in the human-relationship department.

"Whew!" she said. "I got to take a breather. Zoltan, want to come outside and look at the stars with me?"

He was on his feet before she finished delivering the invitation. Mina was right. Men fell in love with her left and right.

Mina said to Hummingbird, "Want to come outside with us and visit old friends? Maybe find a nice woman?"

"I'm staying here with Annie."

Mina tousled her son's head. "There's lots of pretty young girls out there . . ."

"Not interested. It's not until a woman gets loose and comfortable inside her own skin that she's comfortable wrapping it around a man."

Mina smacked him playfully upside the head. "Tell me about it!"

I didn't know if that interchange was complimentary or not. I did know Jozef wasn't leaving me alone with Pinky, and I was glad about that. I can take care of myself, but sometimes it's nice to play the board game of life and land on a free space. That's what Jozef felt like.

Hummingbird sat in one place. His quiet awareness of his surroundings was huge. Nothing could go wrong when nothing went unnoticed. Feeling that safety gave me the room to voice what was on my mind after Mina and Zoltan walked into the night.

"Pinky," I said, "do you and Mina still have something going on?"

Pinky looked surprised. "We never stopped with something going on."

"Is that the real reason you didn't sign the divorce papers?"

"Nahh. I didn't think those papers were worth a hill of beans. I also knew one thing—if there was any way that schmo Bill could take advantage of us, he was gonna do it. He puts a paper in front of my face, I'm not gonna trust it, I'm not gonna sign it."

"Jerry wouldn't have let anyone take advantage of Mina."

"Sometimes things fall through the cracks, even when you think the world of someone. If the papers were wrong, how would we know? I figured, don't sign, we're safe."

"You didn't care if Mina got everything?"

Pinky rubbed his chin. "Sure, I did. I didn't want her to get my auto body shop and the other businesses I got, and she didn't want them. But that land? That was hers, but she'd have been lucky to get a dime on a dollar if she signed any papers that Bill filled out with my name on them. Which is why I never signed them."

"Then why did you hire Bill?"

He cringed, looked pained. "It had nothing to do with Mina. I hired Bill because I started having trouble with every kind of law you can imagine. That guy sitting up on the hill is one tiny example. The first time one of those guys showed up, Bill called a couple of hours later and says, like he's just checking in, 'How you doing? You need anything?' I ask him to make those guys disappear. He does. For a little while. Pretty soon it's, 'By the way, you and Mina own one heck of a lot of property together. Want me to take care of that, too?' "

Bill had played Pinky raw. He'd created problems for Pinky, a phone call here, a fax and photo there. Bill had provided government harassment so Pinky would need him. After he needed him, Bill slipped in the joint property as a side issue.

Pinky said, "I told Bill, 'Forget the property. That old lady left the land to Mina, not me, because of how Mina helped her.' That lady was a pain in the neck. Mina deserves whatever she got from her."

I said, "Would you sign the papers now giving everything to Mina that's hers?"

"Sure I would. If those guys get me," he pointed to the Oldsmobile. "I'm not gonna be able to hold on to anything I got anyways."

I handed him the papers and he signed them. Oscar witnessed them. I'd talk an old friend who worked at the bank, a notary, into stamping them.

"That's it?" Pinky said. "All this heartache and stress over something Mina and I didn't give two hoots about? How come lawyers aren't against the law, that's what I'd like to know."

"Jozef thinks there's more. Mina and I are going to look around Jerry's office tomorrow."

"Listen to that kid." He pointed with his thumb at Hummingbird. "If he says there's something going on, it's more than intuition. It's because Jerry told him so. Get into that office and find it."

Pinky talked about Hummingbird as if he wasn't there, and Hummingbird seemed more interested in Pinky's body language than his words.

"Without Jerry around, what's Capri gonna do?" Pinky said. "She is sick in her heart, and it's made her body sick."

"We'll help her get well."

"She's needed help a long time. A couple years ago she showed up drunk at my place with Bill Wells, of all people. I figured he was using her for something, maybe just to lord it over Jerry. With Bill it had to be something."

He rubbed his palm across his forehead. His hand was large and red and rough. The creases were filled with dirt, the kind that never comes out. He said, "I wanted to get rid of Bill, get him away from Capri, a thing that's practically impossible."

I thought about Bill's arms around me, horrifying, and how hard it'd been to dump him after a lousy one-night stand.

"So then I made a stupid mistake," Pinky said. "I called Jerry. I wanted him to come over and rescue Capri from Bill. I didn't think what a disaster it would be."

"What happened?"

"What do you think? When I told him Capri was with Bill, and she was drunk besides, Jerry went nuts. The kind of nuts that makes you smash someone's head in. Jerry must have broken every speed limit getting to my place. I played it down, tried to smooth it over when I saw how crazy he was. I told him they were just pals, other dumb stuff. He didn't believe me."

"No fooling him about Capri."

"He loved Capri like a man possessed, divorce or no divorce, running around or not."

Here he looked up at the ceiling, drank a glass of water, and wiped his mouth with the back of his hand.

"I got to tell you, I heard there was a dead lawyer in this family, I was surprised it was Jerry, not Bill."

"Jerry didn't have that kind of temper," I said. "His anger was turned on himself, not others."

"Every man has a temper when it comes to his woman. I been through this with Mina over and again. I felt like killing someone a couple of times, believe me. But Mina would have turned her back on me forever. As it is, I still get her love now and then.

I'm not a hungry guy, I need business more than I need love. I settled.

"Also," he said, "I'm mature enough to know these things happen. Jerry didn't have that kind of maturity. Smart like nobody's business, but emotions are different than brains. I always thought it was just a matter of time until Jerry gave Bill what he deserved. I'm sorry he didn't hang around long enough to do it."

He coughed and folded his hands across his knees. "You got everything you need to make things right?"

"Everything that leaves each of you with the property you have in your possession and the final dissolution of your marriage. Berva can file these papers."

Hummingbird said, "Pinky, for now, don't tell anyone what you've signed. Not even Mina."

"No problem. Boy, I could wring Bill's neck a couple of times."

"You and everyone else around here," I answered.

"When are we going to take him out for what he did to Jerry? We waiting for something in particular?"

"You're pretty sure he killed Jerry?"

He raised his arms. "Who else?"

"Lawless said Bill was one hundred miles away at the time of Jerry's death."

"That's a stupid reason to think someone's innocent."

I thought about Bill and that skewed smile inside the theater, blood on his legs. He hadn't seen Hummingbird, he'd said, *just the old man*. If Bill could be guilty from a hundred miles away, Pinky could be guilty from across town with a sleeping Mina as his alibi.

"Pinky, anyone ever call you 'the old man'?"

"I don't get that kind of respect. Mr. Oscar Baumann could be called that, Zoltan for sure. Jesus, that guy's got to be older than God by now."

He leaned forward, put both elbows on his knees, and talked to Hummingbird.

"Kid, keep taking care of your mother. Stubborn people need lots of watching. You been doing a good job. I hate to admit it, but Zoltan has, too. Much better than I ever did."

"Pinky," I said, "Mina's blamed you for everything in the universe with the exception of typhoons, earthquakes, and assassinations. And I'm not so sure about the earthquakes. You're being very decent about everything."

"Mina hasn't had an easy life. She needs someone to hang her struggles on. If that's me, who cares? I've blamed plenty of trouble on her. Of course, in most cases she really *was* the one to blame. But, you get older, you stop caring about the little things. I just want to retire quietly."

Pinky bent down and kissed me on the forehead. "Mind if I sleep in your orchard, somewhere the government-issue Oldsmobile can't see me? Maybe there's an old friend, a nice woman, who'd like Pinky tonight. I could use some arms and legs around me."

I thought about asking him to check on Capri while he was out there, but decided she was a secret I needed to keep.

Forty

I don't know if the Ding Dongs gave the Gypsies a sugar rush or what, but the music was getting wilder and louder. Mina said Zoltan was pooped and that he'd gone off to sleep in her limo, leaving her temporarily manless. E. B. had disappeared into her trailer some time ago, presumably with Ed. That left me, Hummingbird, Mina, and Oscar in the kitchen drinking coffee.

More coffee. I would be awake for the next three years. Oscar teetered on his own ragged edge, but Mina was fresh as a daisy. She would outlive us all.

She said, "Oscar, you want to come with me and Annie to snoop around Jerry's place tomorrow?"

"I'm going to the ocean and talk with Jerry. I'm not up for anything more."

"Okay." She stretched her arms, arched her back, and yawned. "I gotta get a good night's sleep." She patted Oscar on his cheek and used the bathroom down my hall.

Oscar wondered if there was a motel nearby. I did not want him to be alone.

I pointed him to E. B.'s trailer. "Stay here with us, Oscar."

"E. B. might have company."

"She has a bedroom door. She can shut it if she wants."

He scratched his head. "Is that stuffed horse of your dad's still out there?"

"Yep."

"Still got all its hair?"

"Yep."

"I'll be damned. He's doing better than me."

Oscar carried his duffel bags into the orchard toward the trailer's soft lights, picking his way between the hot pink flamingos, plaster elves, and penguins my mother had decorated her patch of grass with.

I was just beginning to relax when Zoltan appeared at my door. "I don't mean to bother you, but I can't find the limo. I been wandering around in the dark getting more and more tired."

"Zoltan, the car's probably surrounded by twenty others. It's out there somewhere." I started to close the door.

He put his hand on the door. "You remember where I parked it?"

"Sure. It's between the two largest redwoods . . . Never mind, I'll walk you there."

"Thanks, little one." He looked around the room. "Where's Mina?"

"I don't know. In the bathroom. Asleep. Somewhere. I haven't kept track of her."

"Zoltan," Hummingbird said, "I'll help you. Annie was going to bed."

Zoltan refused him, but Hummingbird insisted. They each took a flashlight. Ten minutes passed, fifteen, still no Jozef. I'm not good at waiting. I grabbed my jacket, but had no need for a flashlight. I know every inch of my property, with or without a moon.

I walked about two hundred yards and saw Jozef. He was pressed inside the hollow of a redwood burned out by fire fifty years ago. On hot summer days I love standing inside that deep red heart of fragrant wood. I joined Jozef there.

"What's going on?" I whispered.

He pointed to Zoltan standing perfectly still, perfectly alone, some distance in front of us. His back was to us.

Jozef said to me, "Zoltan didn't need help finding the car, what he wanted was you. He has radar for that limo the way some women always know where their husbands are. Zoltan stopped acting lost and ditched me. I followed him to this grove."

"And?"

"And nothing more than you see. He just stands there."

"Let's go inside the house. I'm cold, I'm tired, I'm spooked, and I don't want to share the inside of this tree with any nocturnal beasts or spiders."

Jozef put one arm around me, then the other. We stepped out from the wounded tree. The night held a cold that threatened to turn first frost by dawn. The obstacle course of trees, fenced garden areas, and E. B.'s crazed metal-man sculptures created shapes that danced in the windy night. One dark shadow moved around a tree and bumped into Zoltan. It was Bill. This guy was a walking scourge. We slid back within the safety of the tree.

"I've been waiting for you," Zoltan said.

Bill pulled at his pant leg. "Why? So you can shoot me again? What was that all about?"

"I just wanted to put a scare into you. I didn't mean to hurt you."

"You're nuts. We're supposed to be on the same side."

Zoltan turned his head in our direction. He explored the air, he sniffed it like a black bear, then he turned his attention back to Bill.

Bill was pained. "Zoltan, whatever you want to talk about can wait. I'm trying to hook up with an empty bed."

Zoltan shook his head, he put his arm out and held Bill's arm firmly in his grip. "You've failed this family, you failed me. I told you I wanted Pinky out of our lives, and I've paid you plenty to make that happen."

"You're kidding. I've made every criminal agency in the United States aware of Pinky and his business dealings. The heat is turned up on him so high he's going to be out of here any minute, out for good."

"Without signing one thing."

"Zoltan, when he's gone, I can forge his signature, I can forge a marriage certificate for you and Mina, I can file any form or paper necessary."

"And what about selling that property? I was supposed to get part of it before Mina discovered how much it was worth. Now she knows."

"We can still get her to sell it cheap. You and I will split the difference between what's really paid for it and what Mina thinks is paid for it," Bill said. "You have a brain. Use it."

"Don't talk to me like I'm stupid. I'm not." Zoltan scratched his head and cleaned his bootheels against the gnarled roots of a tree stump.

"Bill," he said, "what should I do with you? I wanted Pinky gone, he's not. He's here, and I don't know where Mina is. Saturday night I caught them having the kind of lust most men pay for. I went into the bushes and threw up. That's on the personal end.

"On the business side you got a big bunch of cash from me already, and you'll screw Mina as soon as you can. I could be left without a dime or a woman," Zoltan's eyes narrowed, he looked like a beast who hadn't eaten for too long. "I should have been a man and taken care of this situation myself."

Bill was wary, almost scared. "What are you going to do?"

"Get another lawyer."

Bill started laughing. He kept laughing and couldn't stop. "Your family is crazy. You're lucky to have one lawyer who'd take this on." His laughter stopped, and his face froze. Bill's voice was hard as chunks of concrete, and just as gray. "Back off. I can have Mina arrested for so many things it would make your head spin. I can also have you brought in for Jerry's death."

"What?"

"Please. I can find a law that will override any other law. That's what a good lawyer does, and I'm good. I can build a case that will make it look like you killed Jerry. And I'm starting to think it's a possibility."

"You could never prove that."

"More than a possibility. A likelihood," Bill said.

"But I didn't."

"Explain that to a jury after I finish presenting my case."

"You are a bastard."

"Unlike many people in your family, I came into this world in quite the conventional way. Not a bastard."

Bill turned his back and walked toward the orchard, toward the party, toward the laughter. Zoltan stood alone in the dark, his figure a black hole darker than the dark around him. He clicked on the flashlight and wandered in the opposite direction, away from the laughter.

Hummingbird and I held each other within the fuzzy bark of the redwood. I didn't want to hear that conversation. I'd spent years building a nest that was a safe sanctuary from hidden motives and dark greed. I felt like a stranger in my own world. The damp of the redwoods, usually a cool and gentle rustle of peace, felt sinister and suffocating. I wanted my bed and the warm cover of quilts, flannel sheets, and easy dreams. I held Jozef's warm hand to my face, and we left the dark behind.

Forty-One

My house was filled with the smell of two woodstoves and an underlying note of cigarette smoke. It was a haven from the clash of voices and emotions gone wrong among the trees and vineyards. I was tired to the inside of my bones.

I wanted to cry, but I was all cried out. I wanted to sleep—too much coffee. I wanted to stay up and talk—not a thing to say. Jozef stared into his tea looking for an answer or a way out. I missed my mother; I missed my kids being little. I wished it was Christmas, or some other happy time, and we were all together baking cookies, having flour fights, watching reruns of *It's a Wonderful Life*.

I brushed my teeth and padded down the hall, far past ready to fold, only to find that Mina had made herself comfortable in my bed. I stood straight and still in my polar-bear flannel pajamas holding my toothbrush in one hand.

Mina said, "I'm too old to sleep on the hard ground, and I'm tired of men. There's plenty of room in this bed for you and me both."

I swallowed the Colgate foam in my mouth, an involuntary reaction to the idea of sleeping with Mina.

"That's okay. I'll sleep on the couch."

"You people are so funny. You go to bed with strangers and you don't want to sleep with people you've known for years. It's like you think sleep is more intimate than sex. This I don't understand."

"I don't understand it either, but I don't want to sleep with you, Mina."

"The bed is important, of course. You don't want other people loving in it, fighting in it, dreaming together, making babies in it. None of that. It's your private place. But an old lady and a single woman? Who cares?"

"I care."

Mina rolled over on her side and propped her head on her right hand, brushing a wisp of hair out of her face.

"Sometimes a bed is a place to spend your dreams. Stevan was so handsome, more than that, he had a beautiful soul. Men like that, sometimes they don't last long. I think old age, and the things that come with it, would be too hard on them. At least he gave you three kids before he left. A son would have been good, but you don't get everything."

She rolled over. In one minute flat she was snoring.

"For a sexy woman Mamo has a terrible snore."

The Hummingbird Wizard stood in my bedroom door.

Madame Mina stopped snoring. She lifted her arms out from under the covers and outstretched them. He walked to her and she wrapped him up.

"You came in late to your brother-in-law's funeral, and you missed the caravan. What kind of person is this?"

"I sat on a sandy hill above the ocean and asked Jerry's spirit to have peace. I asked him to forgive us for involving him in a life that wasn't his own—we sucked the life out of him until the very end."

"That's a terrible thing to say!"

"He loved us too hard, like we were a lost cause he had to fight for. It wasn't his place, and it wasn't right."

"You think we loved the life out of him? Love don't work like that."

"Love is wrapped in all kinds of disguises and costumes and names and vices and darkness and addictions and deep green pools of lust and longing. All these together killed him."

I watched him talk, watched the curve of his lips. That curve was a mystery that could have been a straight line to the truth or the coldest thing I'd seen on a person's face.

"You're my kid," Mina said to him. "I love you, but I don't want your words."

She closed her eyes and started snoring again.

We watched her bulk rise and fall, comforting in its rhythm. It was mesmerizing, like watching a baby sleep.

He said to me, "You're sure about going to Jerry's tomorrow?"

"Absolutely. And I have to pick my car up. It's stranded in the city."

"I'll get it for you."

"Forget it."

Jozef looked at me like a man discovering a new world, like a man deciding how to walk upon my landscape without losing his footing. That would not be easy. I wouldn't be easy for him to figure out, get rid of, or keep.

"First," he said, "Jerry dies, then we hear the tangled web of deceit Zoltan and Bill have woven around this family. How many dead bodies do you need? How many lies? This isn't settled. There are still hungry people and unanswered questions around us."

"Don't try to keep me from doing exactly what I intend to do. I might start thinking that maybe you're Pinky's son and you're not happy about the papers he signed tonight."

Mina spoke to the wall. "I don't know from papers, but he's not Pinky's son. He's the reason for the end of my marriage with Pinky."

Mina rolled over and started talking to us like we were in the middle of a conversation.

"Hey!" I said. "I thought you were asleep."

"Because you heard me snoring? Boy, are you a sucker."

These are the kinds of comments Mina uses to deflect conversations from going into the dusty corners she doesn't want you to see. I ignored her.

I pointed to Jozef. "Whose son is this?"

"You're lucky I'm too tired to be in a bad mood with you for being snoopy. He's Zoltan's, the child conceived at that funeral I told you about."

"A pretty strange beginning," I said.

"Yes and no. On one hand, hey, you're alive—that's a lucky thing. On the other, it's not the most romantic thing to have your spirit fly into the universe in the same place somebody's body is lying around waiting for their spirit to leave. It's probably kind of rude. Manners between spirits is beyond my understanding, but I know life comes nipping on the heels of death. It's God's way of evening things out."

"Mina, as long as you're lounging around on my bed, I want to tell you something, then I want to ask you something."

"You think I'm too tired to get mad?"

"Never. But I'm between you and the door."

"Trapped. Go ahead."

"This is between us only. You think Capri could have killed Jerry?"

She didn't seem surprised at the question. "I've thought about it, believe me. If he were my husband, I might have thought about it once or twice. But she's a lot nicer than me. I really do not think she could."

"Zoltan?"

"Zoltan is my best friend. I'm not saying he couldn't kill someone. I'm saying he could never kill someone I loved as much as I loved Jerry."

"You pretty sure?"

"I'm tired, and my head is full. No more talk."

Mina was agitated and just about to move into her insulting mode. Jozef preempted it.

"Mamo, it's late," he said. "Go back to sleep."

"Don't tell me when to sleep like I'm some kid who's keeping the grown-ups awake!"

"Fine, stay up all night," he said.

She waggled her finger at him. "And no arguing about Annie and me going to the city tomorrow."

"Jerry ended up dead because he walked where you're going. That doesn't matter to you?"

"It does matter. That's why we're going."

She rolled toward the wall again. "I'm sleeping right here with both ears open. If you two have monkey business to do, don't keep me awake about it. I'm an old woman who needs her sleep."

I went to the living room and curled into the crevice of the couch. I covered myself with a tattered tulip quilt my grandmother had sewn. The flowers were hand-embroidered on a calico background.

Jozef sat on the floor next to me. I closed my eyes and drifted toward sleep. With a drowsy voice I said, "I don't quite trust you, but I want you, and I'm going to trust that. I'm not making sense."

He stroked my eyelids. "Here's the sense—sometimes there is no sense."

"I love your voice." And I did.

"You were yourself with Stevan, there was fun, passion. You let it tear out and fly for him. I help you remember who you are, and you give me some ground to stand on. That's a good trade."

He touched my face. I could feel where this was headed, and I wasn't ready. Even though I'd already been there.

"I'm going to fall asleep, alone, and you're going to fly away and leave me my dreams. Your mother's in the next room with both ears open."

He put the back of his hand on the side of my neck and ran

his fingers down my skin, barely touching the soft place between shoulders and neck.

"I want to feel the inside of you again, even though you think you don't want me there."

I wanted him there, of course I wanted him there. Then the whole thing—desire, fire, you name it, came to a screeching halt.

I sat up. "If Mina were dead, Bill and Zoltan would figure a way to get everything she owns."

"That's right."

"She's in trouble, Jozef."

"Tonight she's safe. Tomorrow I'll make sure she stays that way."

"That's ominous sounding. It occurs to me that having no identity could make you one dangerous guy."

"It occurs to me, too. Because it came out of Stevan's death, I haven't exploited it. But I'm tempted."

I searched behind his eyes for him, watched him struggle with right and wrong, watched him try to give the two words definition. I understood the struggle, and I understood wanting to give it up.

"Jerry understood pain and loss," I said. "They're two animals that can make us forget the taste of joy and mystery. But they can also make us remember."

I put my hands around the back of his neck. "Your mother's right about funerals."

"What are you talking about?"

"Jozef. Come into my orchard with me."

Forty-Two

*T*he fusion was not union but reunion, this was not a man who danced inside my body for fast pleasure. This was Jozef.

We lay on the old quilt, dried leaves moist beneath us, churning the soil as the leaves turned to earth. His skin was sweet around mine, a ripe orchard, an autumn night filling the sky with the thick smell of fruit ready to fall.

Our touch was summers spent running through grassy fields, swimming in green turtle ponds. My ear to his chest, I could hear his steady beat. Night wind ran along my skin in places I'd long forgotten.

Beneath him my head fit into soft skin just between his shoulders. His hands slid behind my head and cradled it. Dark eyes opened into mine sharing secrets, dear and strange. His body was a tiger, mine an exotic snake.

The history of my heart shed its skin and lay beneath the trees, blowing and shredded for anyone to see. I didn't care, and I didn't want to bury it. That skin was old, used, and now belonged to the earth. My new skin was middle neon blue with a crimson underbelly.

Side by side, Jozef stroked my face. He whispered that my

cocoon was the safest place he knew. He snuggled there warm and close, listening to my heart, relaxed, serene. Me, I was bathing my new naked skin in the moon's light: white and water and mercury. I spoke his name once to a cloud blowing by and fell asleep.

Thin morning light filtered through gold-red leaves. I turned over, there he was. We turned to face each other, belly to belly, pressing fire to water. We'd be together again, we knew that. I licked last night's love from his fingers, we dressed and separated to be part of other people's lives, part of the world. I wrapped up in the quilt and walked to the house, the quilt was pressed against my face. I wore his scent like clothing. A house filled with people waited for me, and an orchard full of Gypsies was packing up and moving out. Jozef still moved inside the house that was me. He would all day.

Several rows of trees away from where we'd slept I saw Bill. Evidently he'd never been able to hook up with a bed. He leaned against a tree, asleep, a surprised smile on his face. I wouldn't want to know his dreams. I wondered why he hadn't left when he and Zoltan were finished with each other. I wondered if he'd spent the night listening to our love. It gave me the creeps.

Forty-Three

Hummingbirds break all laws of gravity, nature and survival.
Hummingbirds are symbols of magic and miracles, especially
the miracle of resurrection.

—*The Complete Book of Hummingbird Lore*
1989

I smelled strong coffee, a good autumn smell. E. B. and Madame Mina sat at the table holding their mugs. Mina was reading E. B.'s tarot cards, using the old deck Stevan had painted for me. I looked out the screen door. People were packing up their tents and instruments.

E. B. said to me, "Grandma and I decided that Capri's going to stay here and dry out."

Mina interrupted, "If it's okay with you of course."

"Mina, you've never asked permission from me for anything, or help either."

"I'm not myself at all. What I am is desperate to save my family, to save my daughter. It breaks my heart to see her in a million pieces like china that's fallen on a brick floor. Sometimes I wonder if there's enough glue to put her back together."

"As long as she's alive, there's enough glue."

Jerry had helped me, and it was Jerry who looked the other way when Capri was drowning and needed help. Life isn't as easy as *You do this for me. I'll do this for you.* The concentric circles of help and love are wider than that.

"E. B. says some of her friends go someplace where they rehab you. I'd put Capri there, but I don't like the idea of giving my family to anyone. Too many generations of losing people."

I could see the trail of people she'd lost, the generations that walked that trail, and I understood some of what she'd done to me in the past. A lot of her life had been driven by fear. Leaving Capri with us wouldn't be easy for her.

"Okay," she said, "it's settled then. You ready to hit Jerry's office?"

"As soon as I take a shower."

Mina spun me around, held my arms, and gave me the once-over. "You look bright pink and happy. Like you couldn't say something bad if you wanted to."

"I had a good night. That's all you're getting out of me."

"Hey, you're allowed to keep secrets."

When I turned around, she slapped me on the behind. Playful Mina was a new one on me.

"I think you'd better stay here and get more of what you got last night."

"Mina, we're going to San Francisco."

"I know, I know. I'm getting ready."

I noticed that my daughter wore the same bright pink look on her face.

"Eddie?"

"Still asleep."

"You wore him out?"

"God, you're nosy. It's barely light outside."

"And look at me! I feel all chipper because I spent the night alone!" Mina said. "Okay, enough about men."

Mina pulled a pair of bright red underwear out of my kitchen sink. Pink water dripped on the kitchen counter. "I didn't come prepared. I washed these in your sink last night, and I forgot to hang them up."

"You're not wearing underwear? I mean, I don't care, forget I said anything, it's none of my business, just rinse the sink when you're done."

"Sure, okay. I'm wearing underwear, though. It's a sexy kind, new to me. E. B. has a couple of red pair she loaned me."

Mina checked the room. "Only women in here, right?"

"Yep."

She lifted her skirt and I saw a pair of thong underwear stretched farther than Lycra was ever meant to go. It was practically invisible in its tug to manage its integrity. Her flesh fell around it in various lumps.

She smiled large. "These feel strange when you first try them, but I think the look is worth it."

E. B. gathered up the tarot cards, enjoying her grandmother thoroughly. "By the way, Grandma thought of a new name for me."

"What would that be?"

"Ever Bright."

How this was an improvement over her real name, or the other names she'd invented over the years, I didn't know, but it sort of suited her.

"Electric Blue matches your hair better, or at least it did last week," I said.

"I'll never understand why you and dad named me that."

"When your parents made love," Mina said, "they saw electric blue everywhere. Bursting electric blue flowers in vases, the bursting blue flowers of their imaginations. Your name is beautiful when you know that."

I stared hard at Mina.

"What?" she said. "You don't want your daughter to know where she came from?"

"I want to know how *you* know where she came from."

E. B. said, "Forget it. This conversation can end right now."

Felix flew off the kitchen curtain rod and landed on Mina's shoulder. He relieved himself down her front, she didn't seem to notice, then he blessed her. "Felix, baby," Mina said.

I petted the bright blue feathers around his neck. "Is Zoltan still around?"

"Sure. He spent the night here with everyone else."

I raised my eyes.

"Not in your bedroom with me. I wouldn't bring a man into your bed. It would be defiled. In fact, if Zoltan had spent the night in there, you'd have to take the mattress outside and burn it straight away even though it is a brand-new Sealy Posturepedic and a better mattress than I've ever had. We still make enough sparks to set your mattress on fire without even having to haul it outside."

"Zoltan stayed in the limo? When he knew you were in here and sparks were waiting?"

"Zoltan comes to bed with me when and how I say. And, of course, he understands the taboo about sex in another's bed."

"He just forgot the taboo against having sex under someone's coffin."

Hummingbird walked in and kissed me on the nape of my neck. "Thank God, or I wouldn't be here."

E. B. stared while trying not to. If I read her right, she was grossed out and squeamish.

Mina read her the same way. "Your mother has the right to a life, you know."

Mina pointed her thumb at E. B. "Kids. They think they invented sex. They don't know it's not until you have extra skin and wrinkles around your eyes that sex becomes the best part of living. Right next to eating, of course."

I nestled into Jozef's chest. The smell of him kissed me from the inside out.

"I thought you'd left," I said.

"I had someone to speak with, now I'm headed to the city. Then back tonight, if that's all right."

He walked out the door, and Mina looked after him. "He's polite, isn't he? I did good."

I whistled my way down the hall and changed my clothes. I was anxious to hit the road and get back home. I decided a shower could wait.

But life had other plans. A minor delay, an unexpected delay.

Forty-Four

I walked out of my bedroom fully dressed and ready to hit the road. There was Eddie. He sat on the floor in the kitchen on his knees. He was covering Capri, the real live Capri, with my quilt while E. B. and Mina looked on, Mina wringing her hands.

I said, "Is she okay?"

"I got up to have a cigarette just in time to see her sneaking into someone's trunk," Eddie said. "She would have left with them if I hadn't seen her climb in."

Mina might be right. Maybe there wasn't enough glue in the world to fix Capri.

"She was drunk? I mean, still drunk?"

"She was in that trunk clutching a bottle of Sauza like it was her last friend," he said.

Capri must have skittered down, found the bottle at the bottom of the pole, I could have kicked myself for leaving it there, and passed out for the night. Somewhere. She sure as heck didn't make it back up that wire tanked out of her mind.

Eddie was a kind man. He studied Capri like he wanted to make her better and didn't know where to start. We all felt the same way.

"Eddie," I said, "can you not mention finding Capri to Detective Lawless? She's been drunk for at least two days, couldn't have done anything dastardly, and I'd like to let her sleep it off and have family waiting for her when she wakes up."

Eddie talked to me, but he looked at E. B. "After last night, I'm reconsidering my career options. I don't have any problem keeping Lawless off your back."

His heart was in the right place, but I wasn't sure he could pull it off. I wasn't sure if he *should* pull it off.

"I don't want to get into it right now," I said, "but being able to move in both worlds would be a gift for everyone."

"And Eddie," Mina said, "when Capri wakes up, the family I want her to see is you. Can you do that for us?"

"I'd be honored."

She kissed him on the cheek. "Your grandmother would be so proud of you."

Mina and I got ourselves organized and tromped through a family of redwoods on our way to the limo. It was parked at the edge of the orchard. We saw Zoltan's profile inside the car, his head tilted back, his mouth slightly open. When we opened the car door, he jerked awake.

Mina put her mouth to his ear. "Hey, Baby! We're ready to go. Let's clear out of here and find some concrete."

"Could we wait until it's really morning?"

She handed him a travel mug of black coffee and rubbed the back of his neck.

"Someplace in the world it's morning. You want to eat before we leave?"

"If we get hungry, we'll stop at Burger King. I feel lost in the middle of these trees like I don't feel in skyscrapers."

Eddie and E. B. came out to say good-bye.

Eddie might have been evaluating his career options, but he was still a cop. He stuck his head in the back window.

"Where are you headed so bright and early?"

"To Jerry's office . . . here and there. Would you also keep an eye on my kid?"

"No problem."

"I mean it."

He took on a serious tone. "I do too."

"E. B., my gun is in my bedside table. Use it if you need to."

"Mother!"

"Can the theatrics. You know I've always had that gun out here, and I can still use a knife if I need to. So can you." I turned to Eddie. His face was a pure puzzle. "Maybe I'm just scared for my family, but there's more going on around here than you know. More than I know, too."

Zoltan said, "You done? I'm not kidding, these trees are giving me the willies."

Before I had a chance to answer him, the power window buzzed upward and shut off E. B.'s good-byes. She gave us a soundless wave.

"Good thing you knew Eddie's grandmother," I said to Mina. "What a coincidence."

"Boy did I ever know her. She was the most miserable person you ever saw. She was also one of the women Pinky snuck around with. I've got to say this much, she was in a real good mood during that time."

Zoltan floored it, and his tires spun wells in the loamy soil. He jammed it into second gear and the car bolted out of the trees, past the government agent, and into the river of road that poured us into Highway 101.

After thirty minutes of motor hum the coffee kicked in and Zoltan seemed almost subhuman as opposed to the cranky cretin who'd been driving us south. He'd been in league with Bill, he'd jerked Pinky around, and he'd planned to steal from Mina. Subhuman was the highest rank Zoltan could ever achieve. For the time being we were stuck in the car with him, and for Mina's sake I had to pretend Zoltan was a good man. It wasn't easy.

It was the first time Zoltan had been close to that kind of money, and he sold out for a chance at it. His values and priorities had been tested, and Zoltan flunked. Greed's an ugly animal.

He looked over his shoulder. "Where am I taking you ladies?"

I said, "To Jerry's office, to Chinatown to get my car . . ."

"Sure you don't want to pick up your car first?"

"Positive. I want you waiting outside ready to hustle us, and whatever we find in Jerry's office, away. Okay with you?"

"Sure, fine. I got nothing else to do."

There was a sarcastic edge to his voice. Too bad. I wanted to make sure he wasn't alone with Mina. Keeping him busy shuttling us around seemed like a good idea.

Mina massaged the back of Zoltan's shoulders. She thought she had him by the tail. It wasn't easy to be quiet, but the less she knew the safer she'd be. It was the only thing that kept me from telling her what she'd eventually have to learn about Zoltan. Besides, Mina's *Kill the Messenger* attitude was real. Hummingbird could tell her about Zoltan. Preferably when I was in a different state.

Zoltan exhaled one long exasperated breath, and we zipped through Marin County in the commuter lane. She had three one-dollar bills ready for him when we reached the toll at the other end of the Golden Gate Bridge.

The Golden Gate Bridge straddled gray water frothy with ragged waves. The Bridge is not really gold. It's the color of a California Poppy turned liquid and poured into a paint can. On a clear day few man-made things are more beautiful. Through the fog it stretches tall and spits its color to the sky in search of blue.

We sailed through the toll gates and kept to the left, taking the Marina route to Jerry's office.

Mina was up for this adventure. She wore a smile that was new to me, and she spoke with a voice full of mischief.

"Last night when everyone was sitting around talking about my own personal life, and other things I didn't understand, I was busy thinking about today and how to get into Jerry's office. I decided, no big deal, we just use the key and we can get in easy."

"You have a key to Jerry's office?"

"No. Don't you?"

"No. You have a plan?"

"Of course," she said. "You can't live without having a plan, and you sure don't get to be old without plans that work."

"What's the plan?"

"You wait in the car, and I talk Berva into letting me inside Jerry's office to get photos. He's got nice ones of the family with expensive frames on his desk, I don't even have to lie about wanting those. Berva'd never think I want to look at any of his papers, which normally I wouldn't."

"What if Berva doesn't let you in?"

"I'll just sneak in."

"Look at the way you dress. You can't sneak anywhere."

She blushed a little. "You don't have to compliment me all over the place."

"Why don't you tag along, but let me handle Berva. I've known her for years."

Mina raised her eyebrows. "We have to handle Berva together, especially if the cops have been there. I'm a wacky old lady, no trouble to anyone but myself, and you're just one more old girlfriend. Big deal."

She was right about the cops. Jerry was dead. Murdered. They'd conduct a search. Which means we needed to search more thoroughly than the cops would. I didn't know what we were looking for, but I figured we'd know it when we found it.

I said, "If the cops have been there and not conducted a search they may have sealed the place until they do. I'm sure there's some law we'd be breaking if we sneak stuff out. How are you with that?"

"How can I be guilty of stealing things that concern me? Besides, Berva is going to let us in, and the cops will never know.

You think you got a history with her? I've been hearing her troubles forever, usually for free. She'd be afraid I'd put a hex on her if she said *no* to me. Which may or may not be true."

We pulled in front of the Townsend Towers into a handicapped parking space. Zoltan took a handicapped parking plaque from his glove compartment, put it on the dash, and opened the doors for us.

Jerry's office is an eighteen-story brown building of tinted glass that looks like a skinny elevator to nowhere. It's impossible to imagine life-forms of any sort climb inside that spaceship and work productively every day. The offices are filled with lawyers, accounting firms, investment bankers, and a few shrinks who turn out money eighty hours per week. There's a street-level deli that serves fancy beer, smoked turkey on pitas, and lots of feta with Greek olives. The patrons and office workers spend several hours each morning before leaving home attempting to achieve a casual look.

We rode the glass elevator up. Madame Mina turned her back to the sidewalk as it receded below us.

"This is worse than flying in an airplane."

"I forgot you were scared of flying."

"Not really. I'm scared of crashing."

Made sense to me. Mina had her back turned toward the outer windows and white-knuckled the inner railing. The elevator stopped on the eighteenth floor, the last floor. The offices of Baumann and Wells took up the entire space. The metal doors parted, and Berva sat in wait. She smiled at Mina like a hungry guard dog with a ferocious appetite. I got the impression that Mina had an inflated opinion of her influence upon Berva June Mays.

Forty-Five

*B*erva's desk was a walnut crescent in the middle of the lobby directly in front of the elevator. Behind her desk, she was empress of the top floor. She wore an outrageous-colored print dress that emphasized her large breasts. No one could enter without seeing her and without being seen by her. Berva held clients at bay, handed them tissues, tossed them out, chewed them out, and asked them politely to wait. There were six women hidden in the back who kept paperwork flowing and deadlines met. They all answered to Berva.

The office had been recently remodeled. There was opaque glass etched with designs that were supposed to impart a feeling of serenity. The carpet was pale moss green, thick, and expensive. The walls were painted a warm, milky white. Good art hung on the walls, and large healthy plants sat below the paintings. In one corner was an oddity. I remembered Jerry telling me about a sculpture he had acquired, a trade for services he'd said, but his description of the piece did not do it justice.

Apparently one day Capri came waltzing in with Pinky. He was carrying a semi-obscene metal indoor fountain. Before you know it, he'd plugged it in behind Berva's desk. Water drizzled out of the demented sculpture's mouth, down his shoulders, and then it recirculated through its most obvious anatomical part. Bill had opened his office door and spotted the metal man—he was hard to miss. Bill went into a rampage and tore the plug out of the wall. He also yelled at Capri for coming in wearing trashy clothes. His words. Capri was crushed, Jerry stuck up for her and for Pinky, too. Jerry marched behind Berva's desk and plugged the fountain back in. When Berva gave him a look he'd simply said, *Deal with it.* Jerry walked Capri and Pinky outside and treated them to lunch.

The guy was still there, directly behind Berva, but his water had been turned off. I only had one problem with that sculpture— it looked alarmingly like one of E. B.'s

Berva intimidated most people, that's why she was good at her job, but her powers of intimidation stopped with Mina.

Mina marched up to Berva's desk, looked at what Berva was wearing, and nodded in approval.

"Nice dress, Berva. I noticed it at the funeral. You always got good taste."

I hadn't seen Berva at the funeral.

"Hello Annie, Mina. Can you two leave now?"

"What kind of thing is that? We just got here."

Berva was distracted. "Mina, you know as much about me as I do, and I know more than a little about you. Like I know you're going to try and get inside these law offices and nose around. It's not going to happen."

Jerry's office door had yellow tape across it.

"The cops have already been here?"

"Just long enough to put tape across those doors. They're coming back, and you're leaving."

"You think a door wrapped up like a Christmas present is going to stop me?"

"No, but the lock is, and I can't let you in. It's against the law."

Mina stood in front of Jerry's door and spit on the tape. "What has the law and plastic tape got to do with my family? Nothing."

I'd never seen Berva like this. She wore the wet smell of anxiety, and it was more than just Jerry. She strode across the lobby. Static sparks flew from her heels across the new carpeting. Her eyes met Mina's.

"My oldest boy, Rydell, has been in trouble with the law again. He's out on parole, hasn't checked in, and nobody knows where he is. Maybe."

We knew what that meant. Berva was hiding him somewhere and didn't want trouble with the cops.

"I told you what's wrong with that boy," Mina said. "He needs a permanent woman. Fluids have built up inside his brain and made him act crazy."

"Listen, right now my family cannot exist for the police."

Mina patted her on the back. "I know what you mean. Once cops see you it's like wearing a neon sign over your head that invites them to kick you in the butt and ask questions later. You and me, we wear the same skin in different colors."

While she was speaking, Mina'd eased her hand under the plastic tape and was rattling the doorknob.

"Mina, don't do that," Berva said.

"My family just wants a few pictures, things that are nothing to anybody." Mina lifted a corner of her skirt and wiped her eyes, although I hadn't noticed her crying. She tried the door again. "It won't open."

"Will you stop?"

"Sure, Berva, of course. Why won't it open?"

"It has an electronic lock, the kind you slide a piece of plastic through, you know, not a metal key."

Mina looked perplexed.

"Like in a hotel," I said to her.

"Hotels don't have regular keys anymore?"

I said, "Lots of them don't."

"Mina, the key is locked in my drawer, and it's going to stay there." Berva folded her arms across her chest.

Mina took Berva's right hand, held it palm up, and traced the lines that ran straight across the middle and down to her wrist.

"You need to stop smoking. I've told you this before. Your life-line splits right here"—she jabbed her finger in the middle of Berva's palm—"and this means an unhealthy old age. Do you think you can count on Rydell to take care of you when you're an old woman drooling in your bed and need to get up and go to the bathroom? I got herbs and one healing prayer can stop that smoking habit in two weeks. I'll trade you the herbs for that plastic key."

Berva looked doubtful.

"Berva, no one's going to take care of you but you. Being old is bad enough. You don't want to be sick about it, too."

Berva stood on one foot, then the other. She wavered, but not for long. Berva walked to her desk drawer. When caught between the law and Mina, Mina seemed the lesser evil. Maybe the greater. Anyway, she'd decided to let us in.

Berva removed the plastic key from a metal lockbox in the back of her top drawer. She ran the magnetic strip face down, fast, and turned the knob. No green lights. Nothing.

Mina said, "This is what you call a key? It's not opening anything."

"Sometimes it takes more than one swipe."

Berva slid it through the magnetic mouth a few more times. She tried it once more. No success.

"This kind of key don't work so hot," Mina said. "Every time they invent something new, it don't work as well as the thing that came before it."

"Someone changed the code on this door," Berva said.

"Why would they do that?"

"Because they thought I might cave in and let you inside."

"Berva, you're a strong person, no one could talk you into anything."

Berva rolled her eyes. "Honey, forget it. I can't open this door."

Mina opened a fold in her skirt and pulled out another plastic card. "Try this one."

I said, "Where did you get that? And don't try telling me you found it in the hall or in the ladies' room."

"Okay, okay. I got it from Bill last night at your place. You know, when he was acting like an idiot."

I must have looked blank.

"When he gave me that phony pat on the head and then bent over and hugged me. God help us, I think he even kissed me."

"He did."

"Bleck. Anyway, I felt this plastic thing in his jacket pocket and I lifted it. It was perfectly harmless. How could I know it was the key to this office? I just thought it was a credit card and we could charge a few things before he found out it was gone."

"You stole a credit card from Bill?" My face must have registered something between disbelief and glee. I looked at Berva. We were in the same place on this one.

"It's no big deal! I didn't know I was taking a private key. I just thought it was a credit card." She looked at us and added in a hushed voice. "And probably one with a very high limit."

Berva said, "Mina, you got every reason in the world to stay out of the cops' way. You make Rydell look like a Boy Scout."

Berva took the piece of plastic Mina'd hidden in her skirt and ran it down the middle. Three green lights lit up, I pushed the door open. Papers and pictures were strewn across Jerry's desk. Hummingbird Wizard sat in Jerry's chair.

Berva blew her stack.

"Mister, you and Rydell are cut from the same cloth. How you got in here, I don't know, but you're getting out. Now."

Two open windows with heavy draperies fluttered behind him. I said to Jozef, "How did you get in?"

Mina closed the windows and drew the drapes. "He's a bird, he flies in. What's the problem?"

Jozef ignored Berva, not easy, and held a paper up to his mother's face.

"Jerry had this divorce paper for you, you signed it, but there's a note on it saying you called him the next day and asked him not to file it."

Madame Mina feigned shock. "Someone called and pretended to be me."

"Don't pull that on me, Mamo. You still love Pinky."

Mina's face went pale, her hand flew to her cheek. "Pinky is a monster!"

"What woman ever stopped loving a man because he was a monster?"

"I did. He left me with an orphaned son, two little girls, and a baby on the way."

"And the baby, being me, was not Pinky's. You've also kept Zoltan on a string for years when he could have found a woman who'd love only him. It's turned him inside out and made him into a monster, too."

"Zoltan, a monster? You got to be kidding!"

"Mamo, you have to take responsibility. You didn't pay attention to your money, so Jerry had to. You've kept two men hanging, and didn't want the final piece of paper that would end Pinky."

"Jerry said Pinky would rob me, but since he was robbing me of stuff neither one of us remembered I had, I didn't see how it could matter."

"Well, it's over now. Pinky signed your final divorce papers last night, and you'll sign them today. Bill will be out of here, too."

He held up a fistful of papers clipped together.

"This is a list of client complaints filed against Bill. The last name on this list is yours—Jerry put it there for you. There must be close to fifty people who'd be more than happy for Bill to disappear. Professionally speaking."

I leaned on the desk, I pictured Jerry sitting just where Jozef sat. My body felt detached from my head, and my head felt dizzy. Jozef's voice warbled somewhere in the background. My mouth was dry.

"Annie, are you listening?" Hummingbird said.

"I'm listening, but I didn't hear you."

"You need to sit down?"

"I'm okay. What did you say?"

He held a package out to me. "Pictures taken by Zoltan, just a few, and they were taken with a telephoto lens. They're grainy and fuzzy. Zoltan's PI business name and phone number are stamped on the back of this manila envelope. I found it in Jerry's top drawer."

"Let me see those," Mina said.

"Mamo, for once you're listening to me. You're not to see these pictures, not ever. Understand?"

"It's very important?"

"Yes."

Mina weighed the meaning of her son's words and decided she'd let herself be protected without an argument.

He handed the envelope to me. "Annie, there are probably more like these. Find them and leave. I'm going back to your house."

"Not so fast," Berva said to him. "Baby, you made this mess and you're cleaning it up. You leave when I say so."

"Berva, you can yell at me later."

She put her hands on her hips, speechless with exasperation. She wanted to talk to him alone, and he didn't get the message.

He left the room and opened a side door leading to the eighteen flights of steps he'd race down to meet the sidewalk.

I held on to the photos Zoltan had snapped. My head felt like it was swimming again. I was jolted with jagged feelings, ones of pain and humiliation, crashing against each other like water against rocks.

Mina helped Berva clean the desktop, while Berva looked over her shoulder waiting for the law to arrive.

Berva's voice sailed across the office and hit me upside the head. Her voice was loud and clear. It sounded like it came from the front row of a Baptist choir.

"Take what you've got now and scoot. I want nothing more to do with this."

Berva gestured like she was erasing a blackboard that held all our actions on it, and she shook her head. Mina held a box of papers and photos that were leaving the office.

Berva spoke to the heavens. "God, I am paying for consorting with the dark side. I deserve anything I get."

"I've told Berva's fortune for years." Mina said to me with an air of confidentiality. "She thinks I'm on the dark side. I guess that's pretty bad."

Berva turned her attention from God to Mina. "It's the worse. I should have trusted in God, well I did, but you were added insurance, Mina. Besides my health issues, you got rid of a bad husband when he needed getting rid of, and you brought on a good one."

"Yes, I done all that. I like you, Berva."

"I owe you, but if there's trouble with the cops, I'm covering for myself no matter where that leaves you."

Mina patted her on the shoulder. "You do the best you can. You're a good woman."

Mina turned to me. "I think Berva needs some more of those hormone shots. I can't figure what sent her into this holy tizzy without it being something to do with female troubles."

"Would you do me a favor?" Berva said, "It would put my soul at ease."

"You name it."

"Come to church with me next Sunday. Reverend Wright would do you a world of good."

Mina cringed momentarily, but didn't lose a beat. She collected a few more odds and ends, including inserts from the Sunday *Chronicle* containing coupons for cheap toilet paper.

"Berva, I'd be proud to go to church with you. Maybe you'd let me borrow a dress. You got the best taste in this city."

This seemed to take a load off Berva's mind. She smiled warm and rich. The three of us did a perfect job replacing the yellow police tape.

Mina handed me the box. I lugged her plunder of photos and papers to the elevator. We waited for the doors to open, then Berva started all over again, but this time it was aimed at me. "Annie, I'm ashamed you're involved with thievery. I always had great respect for you."

The elevator pinged at each floor. Slowly.

Berva marched to her desk and grabbed a handful of invoices, memos, and binders imprinted with the firm's logo. She piled them on top of the papers I was holding. The elevator was on its slow ascent to rescue us.

Another trip back to her desk for more things we didn't want. When Berva unloaded her metal box of petty cash on top of the growing stack of debris, it teetered precariously.

One final trip for a handful of paper clips which she sprinkled on top, like cake decorations. "As long as you've become a thief, you may as well take everything!"

"Berva, that really wasn't necessary."

I was tipping at an odd angle to remain balanced and to keep the booty, mostly junk, from toppling onto the floor. One corner of the box was cutting into my hip bone. I wasn't even aware I still had hip bones.

Berva stuck her nose up in the air. What a mood! She'd either had a sudden attack of conscience, not likely, or needed some hormones like Mina'd said. This was the slowest elevator in the world.

"Mina, I'll pick you up at nine this Sunday morning. That gives us time to go to Sunday school before the church service."

"Thanks," Mina said. "Don't forget to bring a nice dress for me!"

After Berva'd busied herself with headphones and paperwork, Mina whispered to me, "Now I got to go someplace and get told I'm going to hell."

"They have good music at Baptist churches."

"That's something, I guess."

The elevator made dinging sounds. Soon we'd be saved from Berva's righteous virtue. I wanted us out of there as much as Berva did.

The doors opened, I shifted my weight under my burden and hoped nothing would fall. Inside, we turned slowly to face the doors, into the office, Mina still having no desire to watch our plunge toward the sidewalk. I pushed the CLOSE button with my foot. Nothing. The doors remained open.

Berva looked up and caught us trapped in the glass elevator box. We faced into the office, we faced her. She had a final thought and pulled the headphones off her ears. In a sweeping movement she gestured at the things we'd gotten out of Jerry's office.

"Annie, I'm allowing you to take those papers out of this office because you are the executrix of Jerry's will. Do you understand that?"

"Okay."

"You have a right to discovery of his assets; otherwise, I wouldn't have given you the time of day."

"Thank you."

The elevator arrived, the glass doors closed. Mina said, "Maybe if Berva sticks with that Baptist church, it will do her some good. So far I don't think it's working."

Zoltan was out front with the engine running. When he saw us he pulled the handicapped plate from his dashboard.

"Where to?"

"Just around the block."

"What's around the block?"

"The parking lot where Jerry was killed," I said. "I've got to find some guy named Skiz before the worker bees start arriving."

"Someone named Skiz? In a parking lot? I'm not hanging around some stupid parking lot."

"We have to talk to this guy."

"It may not have crossed your minds," he said, "but I have a business to run."

"And I am one of your paying clients."

"I quit."

He slammed out of the car and tossed Mina the keys. His irritation was brooding and massive.

Mina watched Zoltan in retreat. "God almighty. A few nights I don't feel like having him, and he throws a tantrum. Ridiculous." Zoltan tramped up the street, hailed a cab, and disappeared to the east.

"What sign is the moon in today? It's someplace that puts everyone in a bad mood," she said.

Mina didn't know Zoltan's real pout was about seeing millions of dollars fly out of his life.

There was a definite upside to Zoltan's departure. I couldn't keep my eye on him, but I could make sure he wasn't screwing around with Mina's head, pocketbook, or personal safety.

She looked at the limo and her mood lightened. She tapped the hood, and was happy as a little lark as she bounced around the car and into the driver's seat. She turned the key over. The limo's engine purred. I sat next to her. She bent forward and kissed the dashboard.

"Boy, do I love this car!"

"I guess it's that freedom of the road thing."

"It's also that bending the law thing. It makes me feel like a wild woman. I been too well behaved lately."

"Bending the law?"

"I never quite got around to having a driving license. I'm a good driver, and I own this car. What do I need a license for? It's more fun without one."

Forty-Six

*M*ina flung the bulk of her limo around the southeast corner of Townsend like she was driving a sports car. She didn't slow down when she drove into the parking lot, and the front of her bumper crashed into the rise of the driveway. That didn't slow her down, either.

She parked in the space reserved for office 1801. "Hey, this is Jerry's spot. You think he'd mind?"

"I don't think he'd mind at all. You stay in the car while I find Tony Tiger and Skiz, dig around, see what they know."

"I want to watch you work."

"Forget it. I want you to stay in the car."

"You've watched me tell fortunes plenty of times."

She emerged from the limo, and I checked her out. I didn't look intimidating, not like someone you'd hold back from. But Mina could pass for one of the street people, except her clothes were new. As a silent partner she could be an advantage. I told her to go along with whatever I said, and to remember who was running this show. Mina agreed.

"This is exciting. I never tried another kind of job before."

I hoped I would not regret this.

Tony Tiger was slipping into his pants, getting ready for the day. The rest of his clothes were neatly stacked, tiger-striped top hat and all. This parking lot was a good-sized piece of asphalt, one that ate up half the bock. The other half of the block was covered by the Townsend Towers. Tony wasn't worried about being half-dressed in a parking lot at the beginning of a brand new day.

After I'd written the article on Tony, and had gotten to know him, it was hard to stop worrying about him. Such a good man. I don't know if the world's tilted so the nice guys fall off first, it sure isn't in the movies, but real life is different. My real life, anyway. He had complete confidence in the goodness of human beings—if they'd fallen on hard times, they'd get back up or they'd die. Life would be better for them here on earth, or they'd be with Jesus. Either way, in Tony's world, it all worked out for the best.

Once upon a time Tony owned a Chevy dealership in the South Bay. That was the one area of his life he didn't share with me. What happened that led him from that place to this? I did know that Tony had a drug problem, that he was working on it, and some days were better than others. He dreamed about retiring to Oregon. After this big-city life he wanted to sit by a river and listen to the wind ruffle pine needles. I joked, said if I ever won the lottery, I'd get him a cabin. He didn't laugh back. He looked real dreamy, and said he'd turn that cabin into The Church for the Unknown Street Soldier.

I hoped he'd live that long. Street people have a short life expectancy. Five years ago the so-called legitimate press ran a series of articles on street people. They stated that at the end of the day worn-down men and women go home to their comfortable apartments to drink imported beer and watch satellite television on the dimes they'd bummed. Baloney.

Lots of these folks should be on meds. The drugs they had access to were illegal, dangerous, and robbed them of entire days. When you're on the street you stop feeling, not just to fight off the cold, but to forget where you're sleeping. I thought about their mothers, too. Some of these men had been the shine in their moms' eyes, had been the babies that kicked their moms' bellies from the inside out—each mom rubbed her belly, felt that baby, and smiled.

My article went national because not many women will sleep on the streets for a week. But Tony protected me, he protected everyone. I gave the money I earned from the article away. Making money off people's hard times? I couldn't do it. Bills were tough that month, but I had a house and a bed and a shower.

So, it wasn't the first time I'd seen Tony getting dressed or undressed, and he wasn't embarrassed to give me a hug in his orange briefs.

"I kept Skiz here late yesterday morning waiting for you. What happened?"

I looked at Mina. "Life took a sudden detour."

Tony smiled from ear to ear. "Don't it do that, though? This morning I told Skiz to wait again, none of the poor goons in that building shown up yet, and I said you'd buy him breakfast. He wants an Egg McMuffin."

Tony introduced me to Skiz. If Skiz were an animal, he would be a ferret—small, charming, nervous, shy, thin, in need of affection and afraid of it.

Skiz would not meet my eyes.

"You go on and take a walk with the lady," Tony said to him.

"Ladies," Mina said.

"Ma'am?"

"I'm with her."

Tony shook Mina's hand. "You have gonzo taste," he said. "I like people who wear colors that shout to the world. It makes this a happier place to be."

He'd won Mina over in one minute.

Skiz said to Tony, "You're not going to come with us? To get that Egg McMuffin?"

"I told you. Annie is the lady I lived with for a week. She's good people, nothing going to happen to you with her. She even brought her mother along. People who love their mamas are A-OK."

I looked at Mina, and she played it cool.

"Yeah, this daughter, she's real A-OK."

"Tony, afterward I'll head right to Union Square," Skiz said. "Watch my stuff for me?"

"I always do. Always do."

McDonald's was two blocks away. Even folks with money to burn are strung out on McDonald's. Except for a few vegetarians who're afraid to be near meat oil, or meat flavoring, or something. I could never be a vegetarian. It's too complicated.

We walked under the golden arches. I stood in line to order up our food while Skiz and Mina took a booth. I glanced at them. Skiz was thawing out, he appeared to be talking with animation. Mina shook her head like she understood every trouble in the world, particularly his. I wasn't surprised. Listening to problems was her job. And she was probably better at getting her clients to unload their inner lives than lots of well-educated shrinks who charged up the kazoo. I've got nothing against shrinks—I just think there's a place for anybody who's good at listening to people and really seeing them.

I carried the food to our table. Skiz' eyes went big. "TWO Egg McMuffins, a large coffee, and potatoes, too?"

Mina patted him. "You got to keep your strength up."

He slipped one of the Egg McMuffins inside his pocket.

"Skiz," I had to approach this gently, "did Tony tell you what I want to talk with you about?"

"A little. He told me don't be afraid to talk with you. Mostly that's what he said."

Skiz had a nervous twitch in his right eye that I hadn't noticed. Every now and then his eyebrow would bounce straight up like someone had pulled a string.

"I need to talk to you about last Friday night."

It's not like he had a Day Planner and could whip it out and pull up his past schedule. It's not like I had one either.

"Friday night?"

"That's the night you saw something in the parking lot that the police questioned you about."

"Oh. That Friday night."

"Right."

"I like Friday nights. A whole weekend with hardly anyone around. It's when I feel peaceful. I just float on the clouds rolling by. When you can *see* the clouds through the fog!"

Skiz was unwinding, feeling good. The food, the coffee, the company. It was like a step into a real life of comfort, of companions—a life he'd lost or never had. A life we all have a basic yearning for. A healthy yearning. Skiz was okay.

Mina reached over and put her hand over his. He didn't pull away. Another good sign.

"Tell us what happened that night," I said.

"It's like I told the cops."

"Do you remember what you told them? They won't talk to me. Not really talk."

He looked at me with understanding.

"I'm in the parking lot. I'm asleep," he said. "It's late. I don't own a watch, but I know the sky and the different colors it turns between midnight and dawn. It was kind of in the middle of those two places.

"I woke up because I heard voices and I got scared and I thought someone was going to hurt me, so I crawled deeper inside my blanket. I think my teeth started rattling, and it wasn't from the cold.

"I stopped pretending it wasn't real, and I listened. It's some woman's voice, and she's mad. She's hollering in a language I don't understand. She's not hollering at me, so I figure I'm safe. I sit up. She's thin. If she wasn't hollering, she would be pretty.

"Then I looked at the guy she's yelling at. I know him. He's the one who works here and parks in that place where you parked your big car."

"Jerry," Mina said to me.

"Jerry and Capri," I said to her.

"What happened next?"

"He yells back. They're still fighting. She reminds me of the way my mother used to sound. But I'm not going back under those covers. I'm a grown man. So I keep watching. I like the man who parks in that place. He's bought me coffee and given me food, and I don't like someone hollering at him. I call him the Nice Guy.

"Then the voices get lower. Then there aren't voices. I stand up to make sure everything's okay. Everything is okay. She's crying against his chest. He's holding her and patting her. They don't hate each other at all. They start kissing, very slow, like they really care about each other, like in the movies. Not nasty sexy, just like they love each other."

"And then she smashed him over the head?"

Skiz looked surprised and a little scared, like I was trying to trick him.

"What?"

"The police think she smashed him over the head."

"No, then she got into a car parked near his and left."

"You told the cops this?"

"Pretty much, not exactly . . . not all of it. Tony was giving me the dog-eye. Why?"

"Because they think she killed him, and they're looking for her."

"When that woman left, the man with the good parking spot was waving good-bye to her."

"Did you go back to sleep?"

"I started to, but then some other man shows up after that pretty lady leaves. He pats Nice Guy on the back and gives him a thermos. I wished I had something hot to drink. There's a full garbage bag, Nice Guy picks it up, and they walk to the Dumpster, laughing and talking.

"Nice Guy tosses the bag out. All of a sudden he falls over. But he's not dead. I hear him asking the other man for help, he's holding out his hand for help.

"I go and get Tony, but he's no use. Tony's just hit up, and he's higher than a kite. His eyes are a thick glaze.

"I don't know what to do. I'm creeping along by that fence where those guys can't see me, and I'm wishing there was a phone so I could call an ambulance or something, because the Nice Guy was really in trouble. I know that sound.

"I'm wondering why his friend with the thermos doesn't do anything. Maybe he's scared. I look at his friend. Maybe I'll be brave and talk to him. But then I *really* look at his friend. His face scares me, and he is big. He takes a chunk of something lying on the ground and he hits Nice Guy on the head with it. I hear a groan. He hits him again. The bad man stands there like he's waiting to hear if there's any more groans. There aren't any."

"Was the guy who hit the Nice Guy the man with the parking spot next to Jerry's?"

"No, no. That's Sneaky Guy. He's thinner, younger. This man was wrapped in some strange black coat, and it's not even all *that* cold outside."

Mina was white, but she didn't say anything. We both knew who Skiz was talking about.

"I waited until the big man was gone. I check Nice Guy out. I feel for a pulse, and there isn't any. I don't see any reason to call the police or an ambulance. When you're dead there's nothing they can do. I wandered over to Union Square. I spent the next night there, too. I didn't like being away from home, but that's what I did."

"Why didn't you tell the police the rest of the story?"

Mina didn't wait for Skiz to answer. She looked in his eyes and said, "Sometimes you don't know if what you're going to say is going to get you in trouble instead of the person who should be in trouble. That's why he didn't say anything."

"That's right."

"And you couldn't have done anything."

"Not anything. Tony usually takes care of this stuff, but Tony was too far gone. I was scared."

"It's okay now."

"Do you have to tell the cops what I saw?"

"No way," I said. "I'm going to lead them to the man who killed Nice Guy without getting you involved."

"Thank you."

I gave him a twenty-dollar gift certificate for McDonalds' that I'd purchased when I paid for our food. Mina pulled some money out of her blouse and folded it in his palm. "Sometimes you need regular cash, too," she said to him. We left McDonald's, we were headed in opposite directions. Him downtown, me and Mina back to her car.

We walked to the parking lot. We never turned back to look at him, but I could feel him standing still, looking at us, and I was sure Mina could, too.

Forty-Seven

M ina and I didn't talk about Zoltan. We didn't know how reliable Skiz was, we didn't want to believe what he'd said. Bill was a better villain, he'd want Jerry gone so he could grab whatever he could. But Zoltan and Jerry? Even if the Haight Street property was sold, even if Pinky was out of the picture, even if Mina and Zoltan married, Jerry would set up trusts that Zoltan would never be able to lay one finger on. Zoltan must have known that.

"Mina?"

"I'm deciding whether to believe a man named Skiz who tells time by the color of the sky."

"I want to talk with Jozef about this."

"Or whether to believe in a man I've loved most all my life."

"I think we need to talk with Jozef."

"There's one thing we know for sure now. My baby's in the clear, and at least she got to kiss Jerry good-bye. Let's put what we heard in the deep freeze—just for a little. I already don't remember half of it."

I patted the tape recorder in my pocket. "Me either, but I don't need to."

"I want to make tracks back to your place. I smell trouble

brewing in that orchard like there's no tomorrow."

Mina started up the car and directed me to climb through the inside limo window into the back and find a bag of old clothes in one of the cabinets. Now that she had her car, now that she'd met Skiz and Tony, she wanted to make a quick drop-off at Good Will.

She careened around corners barely missing several pedestrians, swore at deliverymen parked in the street, and ran several red lights.

I was on all fours searching behind the seats and through the cabinets in side panels. The streets of San Francisco bounced by me. I found candy-bar wrappers, an empty quart of Smirnoff's, and one quart that was half-full. I opened the drawer under the seat facing forward and found a few shopping bags and some clothes.

I held up one piece of clothing that was a fantasy of color and design. It was old and intricate, beads and coins were embroidered between the fine stitches. It was a black silk cape lined with jet-black feathers, and appeared to be floor-length. There was dried mud on the hem, still damp.

I ran my hand over the cape. "What are these? Raven feathers?"

She looked in the rearview mirror. "Yes, and believe me, ravens don't give up their feathers easily."

"Whose is it?"

"Zoltan got it from his father, who was the Hummingbird Wizard of his *kumpania*."

"It's incredible, beautiful."

"Beautiful with power. These capes are handed down from father to son, as is the tradition with the position."

"The position."

"Of course. Zoltan was the Hummingbird Wizard for our group until Jozef was old enough to take it on. I told you, Zoltan and I were a strong and terrible combination for making babies. Thank God there was only one."

"Does Jozef borrow this cape from his father?"

"No way. There's a big ceremony when it's handed down. When the cape is gone, it's gone from you forever. Jozef got tired of waiting—he has his own cape."

I ran my fingers along the muddied hem. "I guess Zoltan still likes to wear it once in a while."

"Not that I know of. He let go of the power, but he wasn't ready to pass down the cape."

I could imagine passing down the cape but keeping a corner of the power to yourself. The other way around didn't make sense. It's not like you could wear it to parties, not even Halloween parties. For one thing, it would never withstand a trip to the dry cleaners.

I thought about ancient times, the mantle of power. Passing it down had never been easy. It often happened with a struggle or death. Zoltan might have conned Mina into thinking he'd passed down the power. I didn't believe it.

We decided on one quick trip to Jerry's. I wanted those journals of his. Mina and I were a terrifyingly fast duo.

Mina rested her hands on the steering wheel. "Now where? Chinatown?"

"Yes, my car."

"You got it."

She breezed across town, glanced off one curb, nearly took out a fire hydrant, and came to a dead stop in front of my car. I got out, thankful to be alive. I didn't even have time to straighten my clothes, never mind my head, before she waved to me from the driver's window, an innocent toodle-ooo, and stopped traffic by flipping an impossible U-turn in the middle of Grant.

I shielded my eyes and watched her hopscotch her way down Grant, barely missing humans, animals, vehicles, and shop fronts. Several blocks down I heard a screech of brakes and blaring of horns. Mina would either total her car before she left the city limits or would be back in Sonoma County light-years before me.

My small blue car was buried beneath more parking tickets. I'd have to ask Cynthia to interview herself for another magazine article just to get myself out of hock with the city and county of San Francisco. Maybe she'd let me take an unflattering photo. That would definitely get me out of red ink.

Forty-Eight

Somewhere near the Sonoma County line I spotted the limo on the shoulder of the road. I pulled over, checked it out, no Mina inside. I walked into the bushes off the road and called her name. Nothing. The hazard lights blinked rhythmically. I reached inside and picked up the phone connected to the console on the driver's side.

The phone rang into empty air. I sat in the car, I paced Highway 101 up and down. I made circles in the shoulder gravel with my heels. I wrung my hands. I got into the limo. The keys were in the ignition. I turned the car over and checked the gauges. Radiator fine, oil fine, gas gone.

I climbed into my car. Two miles north I saw a patch of color flying to the right of the highway. A little closer and the patch of color became Mina's skirt. She walked the highway north and hitchhiked at the same time. I pulled over.

"Am I glad to see you! Nobody picks up hitchhikers anymore. This is what's become of the world. Everyone scared of everyone, even a harmless old lady."

"Mina, no one would ever look at you and think you were harmless."

"Yeah?"

"Yeah."

She settled into her seat looking greatly pleased with herself.

. Mina said, "What are we gonna do about my car?"

"The next gas station is ten miles up the road. We're taking our gas can and filling it. Then we're going to turn around and fill up your tank."

"You carry one of those cans?"

"I do."

"I'm used to men thinking about those things. I guess if you're not the glamorous type, you depend on yourself for everything." She patted my leg. "That's smart."

Her face was filled with adventure.

I said, "Can I ask you a question since we're getting along with each other?"

"I guess so. If I get mad, I'll let you know."

"When Stevan was alive, I didn't want the details of your convoluted family. Who needed it? After he died, I pretended those details never existed. Now I'd like them because they're part of my kids' lives."

"There's not a lot you don't know."

"Feels like I don't know anything."

"You really want this?"

"I do."

"First I got to say something. Mrs. Liu left a note saying she seen you and Capri together, Capri stark naked, and that you were lovers. Why would I care who loves each other? Love is love, it creates good feelings in the world.

"On the other hand, you start with one son, you move to my daughter as a brief fling, and now my other son's in love with you. For an ordinary woman, my whole family falls in love with you left and right."

"Mina, it was before the funeral. I was trying to get rid of Mrs. Liu. She wanted her money back, and I thought a minor shock would move her out the door."

"Her money back? She didn't mention that part."

"She said the herbs you sold her smelled bad."

"What am I? A florist? You did good getting rid of her. Also in keeping the money."

She noticed the passing traffic, everyone whizzes past me, my top freeway speed being fifty miles per hour up hills, and she smiled out the passenger window. I could see her reflection in the glass.

"Okay. Every good story starts at the beginning," Mina said. "My birth. I was too young to remember that, of course.

"Here's what I do remember. When I was a young girl, life was a simple thing. Now, this was the Depression in Europe, it was everywhere, you got to remember that. It meant nothing to us. Poor is poor. When the Depression hit, we didn't hardly notice. We didn't have a home to lose. Nothing to lose.

"We traveled to small towns filled with people almost as poor as us. Their houses weren't all that much bigger than our wagon, our *vardo*, and lots of them didn't have any more earthly possessions than we did.

"We'd go town to town, put up a sheet, and show movies. We charged not much, sometimes people watched for free. We didn't care. People appreciated what we gave them. If someone had a little extra money or a little extra trouble—we'd tell their fortunes after the movie. That was where we made our money. Life was poor, and it was good. Believe me, no stacks of paper.

"We had a dancing bear, did you know Gypsies really had those? I had a string of Russian blue beads. They'd been passed down in my family for five generations. It was like wearing a piece of clear August sky around my neck. Always, we had each other.

"Then life got bad. Gypsies were collected by the Germans out in the fields, they even took samples of our blood. Some crazy experiments. With family in the United States who collected money for us, we were lucky. We got out. Sometimes I think my family don't love this country enough. Over there? We would have died with the other million Gypsies who died during that war.

"Before the war, like I said, life was simple. There was beauty. There was food or an empty belly. There was music. There were fights over love, there were babies. I miss those days. Birth and death walked beside us on the roads. We knew them like family. Death didn't hide in alleys, it showed its face. This makes living a real life fuller. You understand?"

"I do understand."

"You want to know where our family comes from?"

I'd wanted this information for almost thirty years.

"Please."

"Your Stevan's father was a Polish Gypsy, he died before the baby was hardly born. Old age. The man was close to fifty years old. Then Pinky showed up and gave me Capri plus another girl who died. Pinky never knew what to do about them. Maybe he was disappointed to have daughters, although he treated them real good. Hummingbird came, literally, on the heels of death, at that funeral.

"I've been a single mother with three fathers: one a good human being, at least I used to think so, the other not so good, the other one old—none of them worth a damn as a father. In the end it's always the mother with the kids, the mother who has the responsibility."

She stopped and looked at me so hard it went right into my eye sockets, and nearly took us off the road.

"You should know this better than anybody," she said. "We got to love our kids, and we do. They're tied to us like kite strings. The father, he can fly off whenever and wherever he pleases. It's in a man to do that, and it don't matter if it's families with money or without."

I could feel her studying the side of my face while I pretended to study the wet, black curves of the road. I knew that road by heart.

She said, "You taught your kids how to tell the difference between a real life and a life someone else has invented. That's important.

"My father invented my life when he married me to Jack Szabo, a man old enough to be my grandfather, even though I had many suitors and one I was in love with. Next, Pinky invented my life. After him I decided no one was going to invent my life anymore. I do what I want and make my own life."

She stopped watching me and stared ahead at the open road.

She said, "You and me, we're kind of alike."

A Chevron station was two exits north. There was the sound of pavement rolling under the tires, and not one word passed between us. There've been times I've felt closer to another human being, but not many.

Forty-Nine

I pulled into the pole barn and saw the limo parked between two apple trees. Mina had beaten me home. She reclined across the trunk on her back. The light filtering through the branches danced across her body.

"I'm enjoying this nice patch of sun while I can," she said. "I got a real bad feeling that's turning my insides into a roller coaster."

We opened the trunk and loaded up until we had almost zero visibility ahead of us. I followed in her footsteps, and then walked right into her. She'd stopped and dropped the box she was carrying.

"Mina, are you okay?" I stumbled to her side but kept my balance.

There was Bill, legs akimbo, leaning against the same tree he'd been leaning against early that morning. He'd fallen deep into the sleep that never ends. He didn't look peaceful in death. His face had wonder and agony scrawled across it like graffiti. The blood leaked out his shirt and puddled beneath him like abstract art, something incongruous, something that shouldn't be where it was.

Bill Wells had enough enemies to fill a portfolio of suspects. Most of them were at my house or had been, and one of them decided to do everyone a favor. But violent death is a favor to no one. The haven that had been my home was now the scene of a murder, and a dead body lay beneath one of my apple trees becoming part of the nitrogen cycle.

Mina and I sat on the ground next to Bill's body, measuring our surprise and weighing our options. Part of me hoped if we stayed there long enough the problem would sort itself out, and we could continue as if nothing had happened.

She said, "Maybe we should shove him into the limo, drive him out to the pier, and throw him in the ocean."

"Mina, we can't pretend Bill didn't exist."

"He's a wild card. It would be like him to take off and disappear forever."

I looked at Bill. He didn't look much different dead than he had when he was alive.

"I just thought of something," Mina said.

"What?"

"Maybe Capri's the one who did this. If he followed me around like a dog with his tongue hanging out of his mouth, I'd want to kill him at least twice a day."

The branches rustled in a breeze carrying the perfume of fruit and damp ground. The earth was in the middle of slowly swallowing Bill into her eternal belly.

"Unless we're willing to ditch the body, we got to call the cops . . ." She spread her right arm out like a game show hostess presenting a refrigerator. "Ten whole acres you got here . . ."

"I'm not burying him in my backyard."

"You want to call the cops?"

"I guess so."

"Think about it, now. Ten whole acres with a guy planted who nobody's gonna miss for long."

"Get off that line of thought," I said, "or we'll both be in jail. Cops have dogs and who knows what else to find people who disappear."

Mina stood up and groaned. "My bones are getting tired of all this birth and death and rebirth. It's so predictable. One night a baby comes into the world, the next day a person leaves. Sometimes I feel like this planet is a giant train station."

"Mina, something's wrong with me. Here's a man, murdered, a terrible crime. Here is a man, murdered, who I have known for many years. Even known intimately when I was low and desperate. And I'm not sad he's dead."

"Maybe you'll feel sad when it sinks in."

"I hope so. That would make me feel normal."

"You want to feel normal or like yourself?"

"Like myself."

"Then don't worry about whether you're sad or not. You can't help the way you feel."

"Mina, how do you feel?"

"Scared."

"Honest to God?"

"Honest to God. I'm scared because people around me are dying quick, I'm scared the next one's going to be someone else I love like crazy."

The hole in Bill's chest made the cause of death apparent.

"Does Pinky have a gun?"

"How would I know?"

"Zoltan?"

"Hey, after the last few days it turns out I know a lot less about Zoltan than I thought. And none of the new stuff is good."

She took a last look at Bill.

"I don't know about you," she said, "but I'm going in the house. I don't like the company of dead men. And one of us better call the cops."

We didn't need to bother. Parked around the side of the house was a Sonoma County cruiser.

Fifty

Uniformed men sat around my kitchen drinking coffee just like I ran the neighborhood diner. These boys were from the county. One of them I'd known since he was in first grade.

"What are you guys doing here?"

They shoved more cookies in their mouths and passed a meaningful look to Eddie.

Eddie pulled me aside and put both hands on my shoulder.

"I have some rough news."

"Bill is dead."

"You already know?"

"Yeah, Mina and I parked around the side of the house and saw his sorry carcass waiting for an angel of mercy to take him away."

Eddie was worried about me. "You want an aspirin?"

I thought this was a pretty funny antidote to the sight of a dead body, and I laughed. And then I couldn't stop. Thank God. At least I wasn't feeling normal anymore.

"Sit down."

Eddie led me to one of my own chairs and eased me down. He poured me a cup of coffee.

"The police came here to arrest Bill for Jerry's death. They found him exactly where you did, but you can't arrest a dead guy. Capri looks like a suspect again."

I told him about Skiz and Tony Tiger. I told him Jerry had been alive when Capri left, and I described the man they'd seen committing the crime and leaving. Also about Jerry's pleas for help.

"If this pans out, it clears Capri in Jerry's death. But not Bill's," Eddie said. "Especially if she thought Bill killed Jerry."

"Have you mentioned Capri to the local boys?"

"Not yet. I'll wait until the local law leaves. They'll get nasty if I step on their toes. For now, neither of us says one word."

I checked my dog bed. Empty. "Where is Capri now?"

"I have no idea." That didn't sound good.

"Eddie, listen to this—you've got to talk to Tony and Skiz." I handed him my tape recorder. "Dress in torn jeans and an old T-shirt when you do."

"I will."

Even from the grave, or close to it, Bill had provided me with the means of meeting yet another arm of law enforcement—one of my nightmares come true. The weapon had not been found. Not yet. Because it was my house, I was treated like I'd committed a crime.

The cops searched my place, including my closet and drawers. I found one of them opening the top drawer of my dresser, and I hit the roof. Eddie was right behind me all the way. He was the first cop I was thankful for. If he was still a cop.

"I haven't seen a warrant to search," Eddie said to Officer Strunk.

"There's been a murder here."

"Actually there was a dead body on this property, not in this house. And Bill Wells could have been murdered somewhere else and brought here."

"I repeat. We are investigating a murder."

"I repeat. He could have been murdered somewhere else and brought here."

"The warrant's on its way."

Eddie said, "When it comes, you're in. Until then, stop your search."

He was my temporary hero, but now I wished we had dumped Bill off the pier as Mina had suggested.

The county officer in charge, Strunk, looked like he smelled something rotten. I think the rotten smell was me. Maybe Eddie, too. I wasn't cooperating by letting him and his men ravage my realm. And Eddie was taking my side.

I got out a pad of paper. "Officer, you failed to give me your name."

"Lieutenant Detective Strunk, Alfred Strunk."

"I want your badge number."

Eddie cringed. Evidently that was a no-no.

"I don't have a number. I am number one. Hear me? Number one in this county. The buck stops here." He thomped his chest with his index finger and poked his face into mine. He looked like a gorilla on the Wildlife Channel.

Strunk stepped back and smiled a weak grin. "You have my name and rank. Now may we please search your premises?"

"It doesn't matter if you act polite." Another cringe from Eddie's direction. "The answer's still no."

"Great," he said. "We'll wait for the warrant, and while we're doing that the killer gets away. Would you at least answer a few questions?"

"Maybe."

"When was the last time you saw Bill Wells alive?"

"Yesterday."

"SFPD says this is the second death in one law firm. They also said you were a close friend of one of the victims, Mr. Baumann."

"That's right."

"When you first heard about Baumann's death, did you believe Mr. Wells was involved?"

"No."

"Are you sure?"

"If you're going to ask any more questions," Eddie said, "she needs to call her attorney."

Strunk turned to me. "You have that right. Who's your attorney?"

"Jerry Baumann."

"Great. Look, you're not under suspicion. You're a good citizen who's had a bad time. We're not asking questions that implicate you, we're just looking for a place to start."

A deputy came in holding a handgun with a pencil through the trigger guard. Pinky looked over his glasses at the young man, at the gun, then disappeared back into my mohair chair and his newspaper.

"I think we've got a lead, sir."

"Where'd you find that, Johnson?"

"Found it on the other side of the orchard, under the trailer. Recently fired from the smell of it, an old .45 automatic handgun. Good guess that it matches the bullet lodged in the tree behind the deceased's body."

Strunk smiled at me. "The murder is now connected to this property."

The young man was so eager to please it was painful to witness. "Sir?"

"Yes?"

Johnson pulled out a piece of paper with a flourish. "Here's the warrant. We got it just before we found the gun."

"We had legal right to search before you found the gun?"

"Yes, sir."

"Good work!"

Johnson, still young enough to sport a healthy case of acne, was a satisfied young man who'd done his duty. This was quite a coup. Eddie stared the kid down, and wouldn't let up. We just might keep Eddie.

Strunk tried to intimidate me with a hard-edged glare. Probably practiced it in the mirror.

"You know whose gun this is?"

"No."

"Whose trailer is it?"

"It used to be my mother's."

"Used to be?"

"She's dead."

"You got a lot of dead people around here."

"She died last year."

"Anybody been out there recently?"

"I don't keep the trailer locked. Anybody could have been out there."

"This is an old gun."

"Probably belonged to my dad."

"And he's?"

"Dead."

"Your husband home?"

"Not for some time."

"Run off on you?"

"Died."

"Jesus, lady."

"It sucks, doesn't it?"

"Yeah. Life sucks."

"Life doesn't suck. Death does."

"You got any ideas about who wanted Bill dead?"

"You don't have that much time."

"Well, he won't be bothering anyone now. The body's bagged and on its way out."

"Good. I'm not crazy about having dead bodies around my place."

"You could have fooled me."

One of his men put the gun in a Baggie and labeled it. Strunk was told they'd dusted for prints, and there weren't any on the gun. Not anywhere.

"Damn," he said. "The killer wiped them clean or used gloves. A lousy break. We'll check for evidence near the crime scene."

He left to walk my property and take notes. He told his men it wasn't necessary to search through my personal effects, in other words, to leave my underwear drawer alone, at least for now. He was in his element, a happy man. Eddie stood between us, a good-looking champion.

My phone rang, it was for Strunk. He came in and took the cordless. I only heard his part of the conversation. It was quite simple, consisting only of *Shit, Dammit, Sure, Yeah*, and *Okay*. He hung up and handed me the phone.

"Without prints and a pile of suspects I'm four steps behind," Strunk said. "Make a list of the people who've been here during the last eighteen hours. We've got a grieving woman at the station who's driving everyone crazy. I'm going to talk with her, see what she knows."

"Grieving woman? What's her name?"

"She doesn't speak English, but she's crying and carrying on and lighting candles and doing all sorts of woo-woo stuff. The lady is totally out to lunch. Grief will do that, but this is one of the worst cases I ever heard of."

Eddie turned and mouthed to me with an exaggerated expression, "Capri."

I had already figured that one out. Just like Capri to walk right into the lion's mouth to get rid of the heat.

Eddie said to Strunk, "Sounds like she's gone off the deep end."

"No kidding, and not in a swimming pool. She's at the deep end of the frigging ocean." Strunk scratched his head. "Lady, I don't know how you got mixed up with this bunch, you almost seem like a regular person. You even have a trailer, for godssakes."

A hot pink corrugated trailer with rusted axles, flamingos, and plaster penguins out front. I must be a regular person, all right.

"I've got to clear out of here before that woman does some real damage. If you get any ideas about Baumann or Wells, give me call."

"You've got two dead people from the same law firm. Start there."

He patted Eddie on the back. "SFPD already has, but you know that, don't you? By the way, that fed up on the hill? Talked to him while I was out there. Those guys are a pain in the neck when you're trying to work—he told me to ask if you've seen anyone named Pinky Marks. He thinks there may be a connection between him and the deaths, and he wants me to start tracking him.

"Can't help you there," I said.

"Hey, no problem. I said I'd ask you about Marks, I did. You can't know every kook these people are mixed up with. I told him, 'If the entire United States government can't find Marks, how am I supposed to? I'm investigating a murder in my own county. I'm assuming you'll stay out of the way.' "

Pinky Marks sat fifteen feet from us, both legs over the arm of my chair. He looked up and smiled at Strunk. I thought he might wave at him. He went back to reading the newspaper. Pinky wore glasses, studied the business section, and used a highlighter pen on the Dow Jones.

Strunk closed his notepad, put it in his pocket, and patted it to make sure it hadn't disappeared. A man prone to losing things.

I said, "Before you leave, could I ask a question?"

"Shoot."

"Why is that agent watching Pinky Marks?"

"Mr. Marks is being investigated for mail fraud, conspiracy, wire fraud, money laundering, RICO, bilking insurance agencies, tax evasion, any scam you can imagine, maybe more."

"Industrious, isn't he?"

"Yeah, but he wouldn't be on my most-wanted list—not for

murder. He enjoys life too much to be a killer. Mr. Marks loves larceny the way some men love babes and gambling."

"What do you do now, Strunk?"

"I got a dead body, I follow the money. I can almost smell that money, and it's coming from downtown San Francisco." He scanned my old comfortable furniture, braided rugs, and worn wood floors. "There sure isn't any money around here. None with that crew of Gypsies, either."

"Can you ask the feds to leave me alone and concentrate on the office that smells like money?"

"Nope. They think Pinky might show up because he has the hots for some broad named Madame Mina."

Mina. The last time I'd seen Mina she was by the limo. I didn't know how, but I'd lost her.

Strunk looked apologetic. "As long as the feds believe that, they're here."

"Which means I'm under surveillance, too."

"Right. You've got a dead body, which may or may not be connected to Pinky, although my gut says no, which means you've got me in your life. If they see or think Madame Mina's around here, you've got the feds."

"I've got you, and I've got the feds."

"Also SFPD," Eddie chimed in.

"There are no words to express my gratitude."

"Ma'am? Sorry we got off on the wrong foot. This is a quiet county. Death shakes me up. I'm not as used to it as you are."

Strunk announced that everyone, including the studious-looking Pinky, should leave numbers where they could be reached and to remain available. He handed me his card, gathered his guys, and they broke the speed limit driving off my territory. His brakes came to a screeching halt in front of the Oldsmobile. He and the federal watchdog barked at each other, each claiming my territory as theirs, and Strunk disappeared over the rise into civilization to deal with the grief-crazed Capri. If she hadn't already given them the slip.

Fifty-One

I searched for Mina, but couldn't find her in the house. I combed my yard and called her name softly.

A ground-level voice answered. "Is the coast clear?"

"All clear."

She rolled out from under the limo and brushed leaves off her clothing, out of her hair. There was a grease stain on her cheek.

"Okay, let's get these papers in the house before someone else shows up."

She mumbled to herself as she plucked dead twigs out of her stockings and sweater. "We got enough law here to give me ten kinds of ulcers. This has got to end."

"The cops aren't after you. You can relax."

"You think it's so easy? You relax."

It wasn't easy. There wasn't much to unload, and we did it fast. I also hauled in my own papers and bags sitting on my backseat. My serene little respite at the Shelter Cove Inn was a lifetime away. Literally. Someday life would return to normal and there'd be articles to write and bills to pay or ignore.

We stacked what we had in the living room. I dumped the stuff from my aborted vacation in my closet. After a few futile attempts

at organization, I gave up and changed my clothes. Capri and
E. B. stood in my doorway.

"Where'd you two come from?"

"E. B. waited with her engine running while I gave the cops
a little entertainment," Capri said. "That station house must get
pretty boring. After I heard their boss was on his way back, I tore
my hair and ran screaming out the door. That pick-up truck of
E. B.'s is as anonymous-looking as it could be. We're heading out
to the trailer."

That was it, and they were gone.

I felt better in fresh clothes, and I plunked down on the arm
of Pinky's chair. He'd moved to the entertainment section of the
paper. The only sound in the room was the rustle of paper as he
turned the pages.

Mina slapped her chair with her hand. "Pinky, I can't stand you
being quiet one more second."

Pinky peered over his reading glasses at her. He put his paper
down and folded it in four parts, slowly.

She said, "You understand what's happened? Your lawyer is
dead, murdered!"

He rubbed his scalp. "Where do you think I've been? I know
damn well that snake Bill bit the dust."

"I can't believe you hired him." Mina said, "He didn't do one
single thing for you."

"You got to be kidding, right? Bill did more than plenty. I got
cops of every kind coming out my ears, and I dropped a cool
seventy grand for that honor. All I wanted was to give you the
divorce I thought you wanted, but I got pushed about it left and
right until I didn't know which way was up."

Pinky propelled himself out of the chair and paced. He ran his
hand through his hair and gestured with his arms like an airplane
trying to get airborne. His skin went from pink to red.

"Jerry says, 'There's tax issues here, let me figure things out.'
He tells me he's made a new will that takes care of you, Mina,

and that Annie's in charge of it if he drops dead. He makes me swear not to mention the details of that will to Bill. No chance of that—I don't understand one word he tells me. What I *do* understand is that it's gonna piss Bill off. Big-time.

"Then Saturday afternoon Bill shows up at my work and offers me a pile of dough to steal that new will from Jerry's private office before it gets set in cement or something."

Saturday. Jerry was dead Saturday.

Pinky picked up his newspaper, unfolded it, rolled it into a ball and threw it in the chair. His face went from red toward pale purple.

"Mina, all the time Jerry keeps saying that we got to un-fix the marriage for you. But he's worried about taxes. Your taxes. What about me? I got a tax rap that, if I wasn't mostly bald, would make me bald."

He bowed his head to show us the spotty evidence of his stress.

"I got to get out of this country," Pinky said, "and I can't even figure out how to get out of this house! Mina, baby, come to Mexico with me. We'll take your limo, we can start over."

She put her hands out to him. He paced in her direction and took both of them in his.

"I got a business to run, I can't just pick up and take off. You got to calm down, or your heart is gonna blow a gasket."

"What a waste of dough. You and me, we understand each other. If you wanted a legal divorce, I should have paid some kid fifty bucks to type up the papers and bought you a big ring with the leftover money."

Mina went soft-eyed and dewy like Vaseline had been wiped over her lens. She rubbed the closest part of his body, his belly.

"We both got caught in something we didn't understand. But, Pinky, look at the amount of government you brought down on us. All because of your greed. You love money like it was a beautiful woman."

"It's a true vice," he said. "A little money leads to a little more, pretty soon you got a lot. It's harmless, but the U.S. Government don't like a regular guy like me to make money. Rat-Infest Bill with his degrees and good clothes, he can get away with being a bigger crook than I ever dreamed of."

"He *used* to be a bigger crook," I corrected.

This didn't comfort him. He gave me a distracted glance, then went back to his life.

"Anyway, a regular guy like me is asking for trouble if he's not rich enough to keep the heat off his back. Now that Bill's got every cop in the U.S. of A. out for my scalp, it's never gonna work for me here again."

Pinky sat on the arm of Mina's chair, she put her hand on his knee. "You should be more concerned about your spiritual life and your family than your pocketbook. You're not gonna live forever, you know."

"The way people are dropping like flies, I'm lucky I haven't checked out already. I got a lot of making up to do with my family. To be honest, I'm probably not up to the job."

"You can act like a father and comfort Capri about her dead husband. Used-to-be husband."

"I'm no good with that stuff."

"You're a coward."

"When it comes to the women in this family, being a coward is the safest way to go."

"You got to be good for something!"

"I been good at making money, but it's gotten me into hot water. I been good at loving you and not stopping. That's about it."

Pinky leaned against Mina's shoulder and closed his eyes. "If there's a chance for me to make a run for it, somebody wake me up. By dark I ought to be able to shake that Oldsmobile."

There was one thing Pinky was sure about. He'd rather face an uncertain future in a foreign country than his wife and his daughter.

Fifty-Two

The Oldsmobile stood its ground, and there wasn't much I could do about it. I understand they've got a job to do. So did I. My job was to make sure they didn't overstep their job into the middle of my life.

E. B. stood beside me at the window. We both watched the cop watch us from the hill. E. B. pulled up her shirt and shimmied. Artists.

"What are you doing? Inviting him in?"

"I'm embarrassing him."

"It is so aggravating when you remind me of myself. And pull your shirt down. Notice he hasn't shifted the binoculars. You're giving him a thrill, not chasing him away."

She pulled down her shirt: he lowered his binoculars. He watched us, now bare-eyed, while he pretended to watch the trees turn colors and the leaves blow off their branches. Watching autumn happen must be a thankless job.

"Mom, when you talked to that cop, Strunk, and he asked you about the trailer . . ."

"Right."

"You didn't mention me, and you didn't tell him Oscar stayed here last night."

"An oversight."

"You didn't even tell them that Jerry's dad was in town."

"Slipped my mind."

She shifted from one foot to the other. "I think Oscar took off."

"Took off?"

"I haven't seen him since last night."

"Probably wanted to give you and Eddie some space. If you wanted it."

I ran back through my head. The last I'd seen Oscar he was weaving his way through the dark toward the trailer. As far as I knew Bill was still alive then.

"E. B.," I said, "there's something else I didn't tell Strunk. The .45 they found? It belonged to Oscar."

She went pale and still. "How do you know?"

"Jerry and I played with that gun when we were kids, cops and robbers. We both wanted to be the robber because the robber got to hold the gun. Oscar caught us with it once. Boy, did we catch it. He scratched a groove in the handle. Oscar told us if we touched it again, our skin would leave traces in the groove, he would know it, and we'd be nine kinds of sorry. We never touched it again."

A flashback of Jerry and me chasing each other across wet grass in bare feet, the soft summer light of Southern California turning us brown, ran like a film clip between my fingers.

"And?"

"And there was a groove on the handle of the gun Lieutenant Strunk had in his Baggie."

"Are we protecting Oscar?"

"You bet."

"Good," she said. "You think he killed Bill?"

"No, but it wouldn't surprise the hell out of me if he did. I won't get into the similarities between Bill and an insect, but if he started arguing with Oscar, pushing him, and Oscar momentarily lost it. . . . Maybe we're all capable of killing someone we think hurt our family. Who knows? I do know that the cops will take into serious consideration a murder weapon connected to a person with a reason to want the victim dead. So, yes, we're protecting Oscar."

"Where do you think he went?"

"Right about now he should be somewhere in the air between San Francisco and Asia. But, Oscar being Oscar, I'd bet he's hiding in the tree house or the old chicken coop, waiting to tell us what happened. If anything."

"Let's go rescue him from whatever hole he's hiding in."

I pointed to Mr. Federal up the road. "He's watching both of us and hoping to catch Pinky. In the off chance that Strunk has or will connect that gun to Oscar, let's not hand them Oscar as a bonus."

"I'm going to go nuts if we hang around the house twiddling our thumbs."

"We're going to get real busy, and we do not mention Oscar to anyone. This means your grandmother. And definitely not Eddie. We have to find a mission for him that'll keep Eddie out of our hair. That's your job. Obviously.

"Then we're going to brush the animals, sweep out the barn, clean the chicken coop—all the usual chores we don't usually do. While we're working, we look for Oscar. If we find him, we ask if he's got any reason to hide out, then we decide what to do with him. The end."

"You take the barn," she said, "I'll take the chicken coop."

"First I take a fifteen-minute nap, next a shower. Then I take the barn."

"How can you possibly sleep?"

"I close my eyes and it happens."

When I woke up, two hours had come and gone. It was dusky, my mouth was cotton. I was groggy and more tired than before

I'd slept. I opened my eyes a crack. Madame Mina was watching me. I closed and opened them again. She was still there.

"What are you doing?"

"I been watching you sleep."

"Mina, that's strange."

"I know, but you do a pretty good job of it. I'm making you an experiment. You wouldn't believe the people I got coming to me wanting sleep. They fill their lives up with complications, then they lie awake and stare at the ceiling because they're scared of the mess they made. I bet Tony and Skiz sleep better than most of those high-tone clients I got."

"Could you leave?"

"You done sleeping?"

"All done."

"Bye."

I stumbled into the bathroom. I pulled back the shower curtain. Oscar sat on the floor with a fifth of Jack Daniel's in his right hand, sound asleep.

I reached down and touched his shoulder. "Oscar?"

It took a while for me to register. He searched my face, bleary-eyed.

"I didn't do it. I wish I had, but I didn't."

"Do what?"

"Kill Bill," he said.

"You know Bill's dead?"

"I saw it. I saw it happen."

"You saw who did it?"

"This morning, early. I wandered in the orchard, taking a walk, sort of thinking, talking to myself, having a snort, giving E. B. and that clean-cut guy some privacy. It was gray and cold. I wanted a jacket."

"Oscar, who did it?"

"I'm sure it wasn't me."

"Oscar, the cops have got your old gun. Is it registered to you?"

"That thing's a million years old. I never thought about registering it."

"Good. What did you see in the orchard?"

"Something that I couldn't have seen."

"WHAT did you see?"

"A giant bird."

"Oscar, have you gone crazy?"

"I think so."

"If the cops come back, you didn't see anything, you weren't in the orchard, you weren't in the trailer, you don't know anything, you don't say anything."

"Okay."

"A giant bird, Oscar?"

"Maybe a bird costume. I don't know. I need a drink."

I picked up the bottle of Jack Daniel's and tossed it in my trash can.

"As of this moment we're dry around here. Oscar, did Capri kill Bill?"

"Capri? No, of course not. Not unless she has a bird costume." He didn't move.

"Oscar, go to sleep. And not in my shower."

Oscar found my sewing room.

I undressed and turned on the water as hot as I could take it. I positioned my shoulders so the jets hit my muscles hard. The shower, my solitude, the place I can think without censure, and cry my tears without someone trying to comfort me. My last bastion of peace. I stayed inside until the water ran cold.

The steam poured into my bedroom.

E. B. sat in wait on the edge of my bed.

I looked at her. "Please don't need anything."

"I just . . ."

"Listen, I am somewhere beyond the outer limits of exhausted. I'm surrounded by cops, one of whom you flashed, another one

you're horsing around with. I'm in the middle of a torrid affair . . ."

"A torrid affair? Jozef is torrid?"

"None of your business. An old friend is welded for all eternity
to German auto parts, hundreds of people ate SpaghettiOs in my
yard, I found a dead body that I'm not sorry about and probably
should be. My high-wire sister-in-law slept in our dog bed, and
her father's reading the financials in my living room. He is wanted
by the feds. I'm flirting with going broke, but I could have rented
my car a hotel room that would have cost less than the parking
fines I've racked up in the past few days. That's just the part I
remember. Oh yes, I almost forgot about the blood at the theater."

I unwrapped the towel around my hair and sat next to her. A
small pool dripped on either side of me. I was tempted to lie
down and cruise back to dreamland for a good long time. Days.

"Mom, let it go. All these people are puzzle pieces, and we've
almost got them connected. You can sleep later."

"I want to forget they exist."

"Pinky talked to you about stealing Jerry's will, a new one.
You do remember that?"

"Pinky's a wreck. Obviously so was Jerry."

I thought a moment.

"Bill sent me a will. I may even know where it is."

She scoped out my bedroom. With elegant eloquence she said,
"I doubt it."

"Get out of here and let me get dressed. If I can find any
clothes."

"That shouldn't be a problem. They are piled on your floor
approximately three feet deep."

E. B. was almost right. The pile was closer to four feet high in
some places. I needed a power color. I threw sweaters and jeans
around in search of my fire engine red cashmere sweater. A snatch
of red peeked out beneath a powder blue skirt, stacks of papers
and notes, bills, and my tape recorder. All items I'd taken with

me or gathered in San Francisco and dumped in my closet until I got around to organization.

When I retrieved the red sweater, a gray binder came tumbling out, as if the arms of the sweater had been hugging it. It was Jerry's will, the one Bill had mailed me, the one that had hummed and buzzed under my bed at the Shelter Cove Inn.

Fifty-Three

*T*he shower had relaxed me some, not much. I reentered the knotty world I'd left during my nap. The back door was open. Capri stood softened by the autumn sun and the screen door. She pulled a pack of cigarettes from her blouse pocket, lit a match on the seat of her pants, sat down on the porch steps, and inhaled deeply. A different color Oldsmobile sat perched above my house. Still, an Oldsmobile is an Oldsmobile.

I didn't know how long we could protect her. She didn't kill Jerry, we were sure of that, at least I was, thanks to Skiz and Tony. She probably didn't kill Bill, but I wasn't as sure of that.

E. B. fussed around the kitchen slicing vegetables, rinsing pans, and digging through the pantry for spices.

"E. B.?"

She dropped her knife on the floor. "Don't sneak up on me."

"I guess we're all jumpy."

"Slightly."

"Did Oscar resurface after he left my sewing room?"

"Yes, and that cop came back while you were getting dressed."

"Strunk?"

"That's the one. I told him you'd gone to the store. He asked Oscar a bunch of questions—'Did you know how much your son was worth?' and, 'Did you know his partner was trying to pull the business out from under him?,' 'How did you feel about Bill Wells . . . ?' "

"Tell me Oscar kept his mouth shut."

"Not even close. He really went off on the guy. 'My only son is gone, and you talk about money?' And my personal favorite, 'Why should I care if Bill Wells is dead? Maybe I even did it!' Oscar started popping pills, and Strunk left him alone."

"Did Strunk talk to anyone else?"

"Everyone except Capri. Grandma slammed her inside the trunk of the limo. Anyway, we all told him the same thing—we all had alibis, and no one minded that Bill was dead."

I cringed. "Did anyone actually say that?"

"No. But that's the impression he got, and he wasn't wrong."

"Imagine being murdered and not one person cares."

"I care. This whole thing is driving me nuts. I have been looking high and low for a joint I stashed around here when I was a teenager."

I opened the windows and sat at my kitchen table. Outside it had gone to dark, and the wind came up in whorls, writhing deep and round, then skittering in a sheet across the yard into the trees. Autumn is a holy mystery, a quiet low-voiced secret whispering in your ear, reminding you to enjoy the last of earth's scents because soon they'll be buried in an odorless wet winter. I put my head on the table, listening to the pounding of my blood against my eardrums, smelling the pine table, smelling the ancient outer world of trees and bushes turning over, ready to take their long sleep. I drifted away.

I dreamed of Jerry and black swooping birds, buying popcorn naked at the movies, and dirt alligators swimming beneath my yard. I awoke to shuffling and clicking. I opened my eyes. I had a stomachache. The floor was crooked. I lifted my head, straightened it, and the floor went back where it was supposed to be. My stomach still didn't feel right.

Jozef sat across the table from me shuffling a deck of cards, an ordinary deck of cards. His long fingers drew them along the edges, folded them under, let them fly in an arch above his palm. He gathered them, hitting them once on the table, then began shuffling again.

"Want to play a game of rummy?"

This was as absurd as asking if I wanted to go roller skating, fly to Rumania, or cruise Santa Rosa Avenue in a souped-up Chevy.

"Rummy?"

"The card game. I thought it might relax you."

"I was asleep. That's about as relaxed as you can get."

"Depends on what you're dreaming."

"True. Rummy 500? My stomach hurts."

"Too much stress, of course it hurts. You have any ginger root or herb teas around here?"

"E. B.'s overflow from her kitchen is just to the right of my stove."

He poked around and didn't seem satisfied. "Forget it. Let's play cards—maybe it'll go away."

He shuffled the cards, he spoke to me. He didn't look at the cards, only at me.

He said, "What have you been doing since this morning?"

"Listening to the sound of my solitude and sanity unravel. That and napping."

He cut the deck. "I've been watching him."

"Him who?"

Hummingbird cut the deck and turned the card to face me. The face card was the King of Spades.

He said, "Do you know who this is?"

"A playing card."

"This is the person you and Mina want to talk to me about. But there hasn't been time."

He shuffled the deck, over and over. At every cut he turned up the King of Spades.

"A playing card, yes. Also the man I've been watching—everyone has a significator."

"I'm The Fool."

"Only temporary. Besides, jokers aren't in this deck."

His hands deftly moved around the cards and between them. The cards glided through his fingers. He was the conductor of a strange and small symphony. He cut the deck.

"The Queen of Diamonds. Your card."

I laid my head back down on the table. "Only if the diamonds are cubic zirconium."

"Diamonds represent the earth, not always material goods, but money's coming your way. I feel it."

"I won't hold my breath."

"Good idea."

He shuffled endlessly, a river of fine flesh and bone running over thin cardboard water.

"This is my card," he said. "The Jack of Spades."

"Any relation to the King?"

"His son, the one waiting to take power. The King of Spades undoes himself because he's cheated time and the rhythm of change."

I sat up straighter. I felt a note of alarm.

"Where is the King now?"

"Returned from the city, and closer than we'd like."

More shuffling. I was mesmerized by the movement, unsure if I was seeing what was really there, or seeing what he wanted me to see. Unsure if there was a difference, but understanding him.

"You cut the deck this time."

I held up the card for him. "The Queen of Spades."

"Mina," he said. "The only one with enough power to watch

him. My mother doesn't know why she's watching him, but I told her it was important. That's all she wants to know. She'll pull out all the stops to keep him in line. Not easy at her age, but she can do it."

He cut the cards again, the ten of spades reversed. "This is the Hanged Man, Jerry. It signifies . . ."

"I can guess what it signifies."

"Duplicity and legal problems."

"How does a dead man have legal problems?"

"Same way living people do. Enemies, mistakes."

He pulled all the cards together.

"Your stomach feeling better?"

"I'll live."

He cracked open a garden variety 7UP for me.

I stood up, he held me. The circle of his arms was starting to feel like home. That did not entirely please me, too many possibilities that could rattle my self-made cage. He put his cheek against mine, one hand against my face.

To hell with the cage. I lifted my face and kissed him, diving into his soul, tropical colors, a vacation of white sand and fruit.

"Sometime, sometime." He stroked my hair. "First we deal with the legal problems—Jerry's trying to tell us about them from the other side."

That was some kiss. I didn't think twice about believing what he'd just said.

"I'll get you the will Bill sent me."

I remembered it falling out of my sweater, just like the sweater was flinging it at me. Then I laughed to myself. Maybe Jerry'd gotten into wearing women's clothes on the other side. I imagine people were pretty accepting over there. The inside of my head sounded like a cross between delirium and Madame Mina. I retrieved the will from my closet.

Jozef and I scrutinized it. Jerry's signature could have been bogus. There were break lines in the ink—the sign of a pen running dry when held upright against a window over an original signature that's being copied.

Berva hadn't notarized it, nor had she signed as witness. A glaring omission. Not one official document left Jerry's office without Berva's signature.

"Let's hit that paperwork Mina and I pulled out of Jerry's office," I said. "With luck we'll find another will, one with a couple of real signatures and a recorder's stamp. Then Jerry can stop talking to us from the other side."

Jozef acted like what I'd just said was normal. Maybe it was. Reality had begun to shape itself on a new skeleton.

Our haul sat in the living room.

The photos were on top. There was Oscar holding Jerry Jr. when he was a baby. Family outings. People I couldn't identify. It occurred to me that going through them would be painful for Oscar, but it might be what he needed. And he'd slept long enough. I told Jozef I was waking Oscar up, and I would get him to help us fish through what we'd found.

Oscar was curled in a little ball, wrapped inside old quilts until they'd almost swallowed him whole. Getting through the layers of batting wasn't easy, but I did it.

"Don't take the jungle seriously," he said. "it's just greener than you're used to."

I shook his shoulders again. "Oscar!"

"What? What?"

"Wake up. I need you."

"Don't."

"We're looking through Jerry's stuff. You should see the photos, Oscar, they're your family. Maybe when the photos and paperwork come together, we'll know what happened to both Jerry and Bill. I need your brain."

He blinked his eyes until I came into view.

"I changed my mind. I killed Bill."

"No, you didn't"

"I really did."

"Oscar, I don't believe you, but if you killed Bill, don't tell me."

He sat up and brushed my cheek with the back of his hand. "I thought if I confessed to killing Bill, you'd let me sleep."

"Sorry."

"You were a smart little kid. You still are."

Oscar said he'd make an appearance when he was up to it. That was the most I could get out of him.

Fifty-Four

*J*ozef thumbed through Jerry's journals. They sat alone in a tidy stack. Many were old and faded, one was new, had barely been used, the last dated entry being several days before he died.

He asked if I would take the journals to Capri. I felt weird about them. She might want one or two as a keepsake, she might consider it a complete invasion of privacy. What's the etiquette regarding journals written by a dead man? I stacked them in my arms and left Jozef searching for a different will, a missing one, a real one. If one existed.

Capri was planted on the front porch. This was a big improvement over the dog bed, but it seemed like she'd stuck to that porch a long time. She was chain-smoking, lighting one cigarette off the next. Her smoke wafted into the house. I was not only getting used to the smell, I was feeling the urge to smoke again.

The dusk was layered waves of blue that pushed light into the purple sky ridging the tree lines covered with pines and orchards. I'd sit on the steps with her, get a few hits of secondhand smoke, and let her decide what she wanted to do with Jerry's private moments.

I didn't say anything, just laid the journals on the old wood tongue-and-groove porch that peeled paint in a rainbow of colors past.

Capri blew smoke toward the North Star. "Those are Jerry's private property. We shouldn't touch them."

"You know they're his journals?"

"I know exactly what they are."

"They may tell us why he died."

"They should have been burned in his *vardo*."

"Do you want to take a look? When you say so, we'd stop reading and burn them right here."

"Right here?"

"The minute you say so."

More smoke to the North Star, and her cigarette snubbed out on my porch rail. "Okay. Let's do it."

She picked up the first one, felt its weight in her hand, ran her palm along the cover.

"I don't know how to say this, so I'll just come out with it. How is your reading?"

She laughed, not ha-ha, but with a sardonic quality.

"Give me a book, I read pretty lousy. Give me Jerry's writing, I'm good. He's the one who taught me to read, and the one who made it worthwhile. He used to write me love letters that would make a toad cry."

I was wading into deep water. We probably should have burned them and not looked back. Jerry was dead. Maybe we didn't need to understand anything else—that was more than enough. And Capri had just survived one entire dry day. I didn't want to push her over any edges.

It seemed important to give Capri a chance to back out. Maybe she was feeling as squeamish as I was.

"We don't have to do this. We can start a fire right here, right now. We know Jerry loved you, something went wrong, and that eventually he turned into a shadow none of us knew, including himself."

She looked at me clearly. "I want to know why he became a shadow. There were too many things I didn't understand. I might not like what I learn, but the reasons will be true. With ghosts of reasons hanging over my head I'll never have peace."

I'd feel the same way.

She scooted as close to me as she could, and I moved toward her. We were shoulder to shoulder. Gnats and moths made a misery of the porch light, one bare bulb, but there was plenty of light to make out Jerry's writing.

The journal she held was old. It was covered with Chinese brocade, one corner of fabric torn. The pages were dog-eared, written in a water-based ink that smeared in places where they'd gotten wet and rounded with coffee-cup rings. The pages had fattened up and yellowed over time.

She flipped to a page somewhere in the middle and began reading Jerry to me.

I watch the baby, he's just learning to crawl. He looks at me, smiles, his first two teeth showing through his bottom gum. He rocks back and forth snorting, sounding like a train racing down the tracks toward Capri. She picks him up, sings in her own language, soft under her breath, rocking, keeping time. I know it's my job to make a safe place where she can keep loving him so strong. Life does not get better, or more clear, than this.

I want to lie down on the floor and bask in the warmth of Capri's love, too. I brush the back of my hand down her neck. She closes her eyes. She loves me for giving him to her. What else I give her's a mystery. She's so strong, completely whole and beautiful. My lover. My wife. A wonderful day.

Capri put the book on her knees. Her face was destroyed. Her eyes red and full.

She said, "It's hard to remember so much love. Hard to remember being strong."

"I remember. *A pulsing tower of light,* that's what I thought the first night I met you."

She glanced far off to the hills flaming burgundy and gold, and blew a puff of cigarette smoke through her nose.

"What happened to me?"

"You lost yourself for a little while."

"Twenty years is not so little."

"You're right, it's not."

"And now what?"

"You're going to be strong again. Maybe you'll even become a tower of light again."

"Too much energy to pulse and beam."

"Then just work on liking yourself."

"I've been a blob, no use to anybody. I don't even know where my son is."

"You'll find each other again. Capri, you have something soft and warm inside you that feels like the most basic color of love. You've done your best to block it out, shut it down, but you can't keep people from feeling it. And you can't keep from looking beautiful."

She perked up. "Yeah?"

"Even passed out with drool running from the corner of your mouth, you're still one of the most gorgeous women I've ever seen."

"That's a good thing."

"Definitely."

I handed her another journal, the one barely touched by time and memories.

"This is his last," I said. "Do you want to see it?"

"This is too hard."

"It's hard for me, too. Should I read the first page out loud or should we start the fire?"

"Read it."

It was dated two days before Jerry's death.

I'm in that dark tunnel, the dark that keeps me working day and night. If I move fast enough I can stay ahead of the dark, but my legs are tired of running. I had a beautiful wife—lots of men wanted her, she wanted only me. Instead of treating it like a miracle, I did everything to push her away. *If you love too hard, they leave.* That's an easy one to remember.

I've always taken care of Mina, but now Bill butts in. Taking care of people I love in quiet ways is the only good I can still do.

Talked to Jerry Junior today. Offered to loan him money, but he wouldn't take it. He's quit his job, traveling around, working different theaters until he makes enough money to move on. I say, *I hope this lifestyle is temporary.* He says, *Me too.*

Has he talked to his mother? I ask. No. He says he doesn't want to disappoint her.

"My one child. This has to be fixed. But I'm glad to know he called his father."

"So am I."

She lit another cigarette. "Is that the end?"

"There's more. Want it?"

"Same as before—yes and no. Go ahead."

This new disease I've chosen, the one to make me forget me, costs a fortune. But it makes me feel that I'm as bad as I suspect I am, and this is a relief. Pain, being tied up, small injuries—I can't be injured by other people. I injure myself. I know it's sick, and that it digs my tunnel darker and deeper.

I have to unload all those toys—I think of them as war toys. I want to see my son. I want to be with Capri. I can't do that until the war is over.

Then Zoltan. He steps into the middle of my nightmare like the black knight. Sends me photos of Capri and Bill, says Bill hired him to mail them to me, to hurt me. Anyone could have asked me about Capri. No point in more lies.

Zoltan says he took the PI job, snapping those photos for Bill, to bring out the truth so we could all heal. What crap.

I wanted to walk a road that was good. Instead I've torn up the pavement behind me as I ran, done it so I couldn't turn back and so no one could follow me.

Mina. She couldn't care less about her money, what little she knows she has. I've just written my will, I'll give it to Annie. No one's seen the will but Berva—thank God for her. She has the only key to the metal box. This will take care of my family—it'll also settle some debts.

Stacks of journals that were filled with his life.

I asked Capri, "What should we do with these? I don't see the value in keeping them."

She looked at me like I'd smacked her.

"Forget I said that. You're right. This was too hard."

"Don't be sorry. We found some truth."

She took the old journal with the picture of their home life on a good day, and tore out the pages she'd read. She stuffed them down her blouse. She took the last dark pages he'd written, folded them and put them in her back pocket.

"We'll keep these and burn the rest," she said.

Capri took her cigarette lighter and began lighting the corners, word by word, book by book, until each year, thought, and feeling became entangled, indistinguishable. She walked like a robot, getting newspapers from the trash bin, collecting dead leaves to keep the fire burning.

"Capri, the words are gone now."

She ignored me and faced the sky. "Jerry, I've saved both sides of your life. Everything that was in the middle you don't have to think about or remember. The good part of our life is right next to my heart. I'm sitting on the bad part."

"Capri," I said, "did you know what Jerry had gotten involved in?"

"Not the details, no," she said, "but I'm no saint, either. Not many heavy drinkers are. Think about it—I even fooled around with Bill."

We shuddered at the same time.

She smiled at me. "You too?"

In my head I took the Fifth, but smiled back at her.

The last of the papers caught fire. There were still a few whole corners left unburned. She turned them over until they glowed, until they'd meet the sky as they should have at Drake's Bay. A pale orange tickled the air just above the ground. The night held a spark of chill.

I sat with my knees curled to my chest. "What's next?"

"I'm going to light another cigarette and watch the sun finish going down. When that's over I'll decide what to do next."

Fifty-Five

My living-room floor was covered with photos, papers, and Pinky.

"How's Capri?" Pinky asked.

At that exact moment, the universe displayed its sublime timing. Capri stood up and leaned in the kitchen doorway. She tossed her cigarette toward the smoldering ashes. She was a painting of perfect vulnerability and primal grace. Framed in that light, it was easy to see who she was. She hid nothing—an exceptionally rare thing in a human animal. She joined us.

I held up one of the pictures of her and Bill. "Capri, why Bill?"

I could have asked myself the same question. My answer was desperation. I assumed Capri's answer was the same. It wasn't.

"Jerry broke my heart, over and over," she said. "He even ran around with women while I went on vacation with Oscar and the baby. He always pretended he had to work. A lie. I knew we loved each other and always would. That made it even worse.

"One day, several years after we'd split up, Bill asked me to go on vacation with him. I thought, 'Why not be Bill's lover? That will hurt Jerry, and it will be so easy.' "

"It doesn't look like it's been easy."

"I was joking with myself. You can't turn love off and on like a faucet. You feel the throb of it day and night. Then you look for something to make you numb, then you forget why you wanted to be numb, but numb is all you know. Anything else feels like too much. Numb starts to feel like the safest place you hid when you were a kid."

"You're too much like your mother," Pinky said. "Mina ruined her life over passion. Me she hated, but I'm her power pole. We couldn't stay together, but we couldn't stay away from each other. Zoltan, I got no gripes over him. The universe threw those two together to make the Hummingbird Wizard. I never been able to do anything about that. But, Honey, I'm sorry your other man had to be Bill."

"Believe me, no one's sorrier about that than me." Capri considered her father. "And, actually, it's none of your business."

Nothing like new sobriety to bring out the truth.

Pinky came to attention and sat up straight. He put his hand out like a traffic cop. "You know what? The feds, the cops, the whole bunch of them, they're all easier to deal with than the women in this family. I'm thinking of swearing off women for good, that's how tired I am of romance. Where is Mina, anyway?"

I said, "Pinky, the man in the Oldsmobile has poor visibility right now. It's headed to pitch-black outside. If you want to make a break for it, now's the time."

"You're helping me get away?"

"You have to swear one thing to me, and swear it in blood."

"What do I got to swear?"

"That you absolutely did not kill Bill."

"I swear. He was a poor excuse for a man, and it's hard to admit, but I didn't do it. I don't have the heart for that kind of thing. No guts."

I looked at Capri. "What do you think?"

"I believe him. If he wanted someone dead, he'd hire someone.

He's too much of a tightwad to lay out that kind of dough, so I think he's clean."

Capri stood up and tucked her shirt into her jeans. "I'm disappearing into the night. I don't have any use for the cops on my own account, and I don't want them asking me questions about Pinky. As you get sober lying gets harder."

She walked to the chair, the one I was beginning to think of as Pinky's chair, and she kissed him on the top of his head. She held his face between her hands. "Good-bye my dad, Pinky Marks. I'm glad you knocked on my mother's door that day in Barstow and sold her croak insurance."

She faded into the dark, Pinky fought back tears. Maybe he didn't have guts, but the guy had heart.

I followed Capri outside and sat alone on the porch.

I'd bummed a cigarette from Capri, and I intended to enjoy it. It was a Lucky Strike, my ex-favorite. I lit up, inhaled, and felt the hairs in my lungs burn fire. I kept smoking, but I didn't inhale. I tried to remember how to make smoke rings, I tried to remember how to clear my mind.

Jozef came out, leaned against the railing.

"Okay if I share your porch?"

I patted the old wood, and he sat next to me.

I tossed my cigarette. I squinted to read Jozef without my glasses.

A stab of guilt sliced me sharp. "I should have been Jerry's reality check, his home base. I was busy obsessing about the world's largest cabbage or a ghostly Madonna seen in a Croatian Laundromat."

"That's your job, your living. Phone lines work both ways. He could have called you if he needed help."

"Maybe."

I told Jozef about my conversation with Tony Tiger and Skiz. We were circling a horrible truth, one that sat heavy waiting to be birthed, one that there was no way around. Not as far as I could see. I held Jozef's hand.

"Jozef, it looks like your father supplied Jerry with the darkness he was looking for, the permanent kind."

"His death. I was afraid of this. When you were with Mamo did you touch anything over by the place Jerry was killed?"

"No."

"Me either. Only with the corner of my shirt."

"You were there?"

"This morning, right after you. But no fingerprint trails. I prefer my invisible life, the life that sees me as dead."

Zoltan couldn't be ignored or laughed away. Action was called for, but I didn't know what or when.

"You have another smoke?"

He handed me a cigarette. I'd enjoyed the last cigarette. This one I needed. It was either that or suck my thumb.

I tore the filter off the cigarette, some horrible brand, a Newport or Salem. Something that smelled like a minty-fresh forest fire. I blew smoke at the sky, I blew smoke to the trees. In the midst of the menthol mist I got a squirmy feeling.

"I think it's possible," I said, "that Zoltan also got rid of Bill."

"I think it's certain. Bill wouldn't go away, and Zoltan was tired of trouble. Too many people were between him and the money Mina would have gladly given him. I think Zoltan killed Bill right after the argument we heard last night in the orchard. Wrapped the gun's muzzle with a cloth, put it right next to Bill's chest. Even without those things, who would have heard a shot in the midst of music and fireworks? I can't prove it, and I don't know if the police can, even with some subtle help."

"Honestly, I didn't care who killed Bill. I thought he'd killed Jerry."

"Everything pointed that way."

Jozef picked up the manila envelope. Turned it over in his hands.

"And I don't believe Bill hired Zoltan to take these pictures of Capri and Bill together. I believe Zoltan is sick, perverse."

"Jozef, Zoltan was shrewd. Can you think of a better way to turn one partner against another than to throw photographs of one man having sex with the other's wife, or ex-wife, into both their laps?

"Lay those pictures on the table between two men already at odds about a vast sum of money. All you'd have to do is stand back and let them destroy each other. Zoltan was ready to pick up the pieces when the carnage was over."

Jozef rubbed his chin.

"What?"

"If the police find these pictures of Bill and Capri, they'll think maybe Bill killed Jerry, a crime of passion they'll call it. Bill wanting Jerry out of the way. That will close Jerry's death."

"Zoltan will be off the hook, at least for that death."

"This is not justice."

"Bill's dead. Jerry's dead. Pinky's on his way out," I said. "Zoltan has no more enemies, nothing to stand in the way of his and Mina's happiness."

"Not true. You're an enemy, so am I. He's afraid of me, but not you. You're in danger as long as you know the truth about him. And as long as Mina loves him, there will never be enough distance between him and any of us.

"He's not aware I know about him."

"Don't count on that for your protection."

Jozef lit one more cigarette, another spearmint forest fire newly ablaze.

He sat in silence a few moments.

He tossed the envelope of photos into the last of Capri's fire.

"We want the police to concentrate on Jerry's murder, we don't want them distracted."

"What about Bill's murder?"

"One death at a time, but it will be taken care of."

I studied the stars. Two weeks past the autumn equinox. The world seemed to be turning more slowly.

"I'll ask Eddie to call Lawless now," I said. "Jerry's death is his territory, a San Francisco murder. We'll hand him everything we got from the office. Tell him to question Skiz and Tony, what to ask. Gently. You keep Zoltan here until Lawless arrives."

"No Lawless yet. I have private family business to conduct with Zoltan. Business comes before the police arrive."

I looked in his eyes, recognized something there, and I knew exactly what wave he was riding.

"Jozef, you're thinking a man who doesn't exist could get away with murder."

"Jerry was lost, Bill was greedy. But the man who killed them was evil. Annie—look at me: A man long-dead could get away with making things right, with restoring balance in the universe."

"Bullshit. Kill your father, and you kill half of yourself. You couldn't live with that. I hope you couldn't."

"You'd be surprised at the things I've had to live with."

"We all have, we all do every day. Don't do this."

He ran his hand along my thigh. "There are things I'd rather do, no doubt about it. But I have an obligation to this family. Jerry gave me the gift of a living death. This is the right time to use it, and Mina will help me."

'Hummingbird brings messages from the gods, becomes a bolt of lightning to carry out their vengeance, blows prophecies in the ears of the soothsayers . . .'

"I'm not going to wait for Eddie," I said. "I'm calling Lawless now."

"Please. Not yet."

Fifty-Six

I dusted off the back of my jeans, Jozef and I separated. I committed to this path with him, wherever it led. I was scared, but I trusted him to do what was right, with or without the approval of the law.

He went in search of Zoltan and Mina. I wanted to clear out the extras around my house before the police arrived. This meant getting rid of E. B. and Eddie. Capri. Also Pinky. He was still under the watchful eye of the government.

"E. B., Eddie, why don't you head out to the trailer for a little while? A long while."

"You trying to get rid of us?"

"I'm sure you can find something to do out there."

"There's all those old games out there, Boggle, Monopoly—all that stuff."

"Playing board games?"

"Mother, people just don't hop in and out of each other's beds anymore. Eddie is a gentleman."

"I'm sorry to hear that."

She got into a minor snit, and they cleared out.

I called after them. "Eddie, no kidding, stay out there. And don't feel compelled to be a gentleman around this place."

Now it was Pinky's turn to escape. He was still sculpted around my chair. Having finished the newspaper, he'd started reading *Moby-Dick*.

"Like that book?"

"Because of the title I thought it'd be hot with babes. It's turning out pretty good anyway. Annie you look like a nervous wreck."

"Too much going down that I don't want to be a part of. And you definitely don't."

"The Witch Woman and her nutty boyfriend."

"Yeah, but worse than you want to know. Pinky, you have any cash stashed?"

"Enough to last if I keep it pretty simple. A place on the beach where I can fish, some place in another country where they don't got that un-American bunch of gangsters called the IRS."

"Another country sounds good." I meant it. Any country other than my living room sounded very good. "But there are probably guys around the airport keeping a lookout for you."

"I've never been in this much hot water before, but I've seen plenty of movies. I know enough to avoid airports. I figure to get a ride from somebody to the Greyhound station, look like any other guy who's visiting poor relations. Maybe even carry an old suitcase held together with brown tape."

"You weren't kidding about the movies."

"I told you, I'm an all-American guy. Anyway, I head to some hogwash town on the Canadian border with tall grass and I just stroll into another country. I lie low for a month or two, then I take off for someplace warm and without women."

"Sounds like a good plan."

"It's Plan B. My mind don't rest easy unless I feel plan B stuffed in my back pocket, walking down the street with me just like my wallet."

"Let's find you a ride to the bus station."

"Maybe Zoltan?"

"Forget it, Pinky."

"I always wanted to ride in Mina's limo."

"Too conspicuous. I'll get E. B. and Eddie to drive you."

"Mina's not going to like seeing me in a junky car."

"Mina's not going to be a problem for you anymore. Either is Zoltan or the rest of us."

"I guess I can get in touch with the family should I want."

"Should you want."

Pinky took both my hands in his. When we stood facing each other, his head reached the bottom of my nose. I controlled an urge to sneeze.

"Listen, you've been great to me," Pinky said. "I'm sorry I believed everything Mina said about you."

"You ready to take off?"

"And how. Let's find me a way out of this cuckoo farm fast."

He'd been sitting in that chair so long that when he stood up, the chair cushion looked like he was still there. Might be time for a new chair.

We couldn't take a flashlight. It would illuminate our shapes for the fed, so we stepped carefully in the dark trying to avoid roots, old bicycles, chaise lounges, chicken wire, and E. B.'s giant sculptures lying on their their backs and stomachs, the moonlight passing through them like a barium enema.

We stumbled upon Mina and Zoltan wrapped around each other like kittens in a hammock between two apple trees. Chinese paper lanterns were strung between the trees and shed a soft light. The dancing glow gave the orchard a 1920s party effect. Shades of green, red, orange, and yellow light were cut into shapes by the crooked branches of the dark trees.

Mina didn't move when she saw me and Pinky. She had no guilt about who she loved or when. Part of me knew I could never be like that, and part of me envied her for it. Felix sat perched on the head of the hammock. With the slightest pitch or sway, Felix lost his balance and caught himself like a sailor on a rolling sea.

Pinky was silent, studying the two of them together. Embarrassment, jealousy, resignation, loss of pride. Maybe all those going on. Somehow he'd come to terms with this. Mina rolled on her side, tried to prop her elbow on her chin and she continued her roll right out of the hammock. She climbed to her knees and straightened her skirts.

Pinky looked at Mina, but he spoke to Zoltan. "Hey, Zoltan, how about a ride to the bus station in Mina's limo."

Pinky had chosen to ignore my advice, and was still shooting for a joyride in the limo.

Zoltan, who'd patted my hand like a father because he was worried about my car; Zoltan, who was the calm in Mina's storm; Zoltan, who'd tried to get away with cheating the woman he loved out of a large sum of money; Zoltan, who'd murdered and felt no need to run from it—that Zoltan sneered at Pinky.

"Why should I do you a favor?"

"If nothing else, it'll get me out of your life, probably forever."

The hammock was on the side of my house that backs up to the barn, the side that was out of Agent Oldsmobile's line of vision.

Zoltan said, "You're nothing. I don't care if a speck of dust is in my life, why should I care if you're in my life?"

"Of course you care. I'm Mina's old man, her only legal marriage."

"What you and Mina had was no real marriage."

"Zoltan, you and me, we both know that ain't true. Jeez, me and her we even had two kids together."

"And she and I have one. She didn't want any more, or we'd have put out ten kids."

Mina watched them with her hands on her hips. Neither of these men who knew her so well noticed that she was about to blow. For one moment she looked to her left. I followed her line of vision and saw Hummingbird crouched behind a sculpture. She was center stage in this small drama, but now Zoltan was Hummingbird's responsibility, not hers.

Zoltan sat up in the hammock. He was a graceful man, and he kept his balance, barely rocking the webbing. When he stood up, Felix the parrot flapped his wings and flew to the ground.

When Zoltan and Mina had been wrapped around each other I didn't notice, couldn't have, what Zoltan was wearing. Now, standing, I saw that he wore his feathered cape—full, dark, shining silk, lined with coal black feathers. There was a pile of feathers under the hammock. They'd apparently been loosened in his and Mina's tumbling and turning.

Ignoring Mina's body language, Zoltan put his foot farther down his throat.

"Pinky, Mina is mine. You can ask her that yourself."

Mina glanced in Jozef's direction. She'd keep his presence hidden by her anger and banter. Safer for all if Jozef was a surprise.

She exploded in indignation. "What is it? Not one brain between you? Listen how you talk about me. I'm with who I want to be, when I want to be. Right now it's neither of you. I've loved you both, but you do not shape my life. Ever."

Zoltan cowered.

Pinky enjoyed her spunk. "You are one beautiful woman, Mina. Sure you don't want to go to Mexico? Zoltan can give us both a ride to the bus station."

Zoltan sputtered. Mina shouted at them. "You're two dogs tearing at the same bone, dried and old. I have nothing for either of you. I leave you the habit of your fighting and hate."

She'd crossed the line. Zoltan was devastated, speechless. First the money flew out the window, now it was bye-bye Mina.

Pinky was puzzled. "I'm out of here, Mina. You don't need to get bent out of shape on my account."

"And don't think I'll be lonely! There are plenty of men out there, I've always had plenty, and this was when I thought I was a poor Gypsy woman. Like just last week! Now I have money, too much, but I got it, and maybe I'll flaunt it. There'll be so many men it'll take ten lifetimes to try them all."

Mina tossed her scarf around her neck, stomped toward my house, her boots covered with mud, carrying more dignity than most queens.

Zoltan and Pinky not only heard what she said, so did my closest neighbor, the shrink, who was gathering firewood at the property line. My place had been quiet for so long, he probably thought I was in the middle of a massive midlife crisis and had dragged a circus along with me. He wasn't far off.

The two men didn't make a move. They'd both lost the woman they alternately loved and disliked. For Zoltan she was breath and blood. What would fill the space that had been her? Money probably didn't seem like such a big deal to him anymore.

A man with nothing to lose is a dangerous man, a man to be watched. A bit of cowboy wisdom I learned from my dad. Zoltan stood in a circle of impenetrable solitude. In one graceful movement the hand inside his cape became the hand outside his cape. It became the hand holding a gun that he brandished wildly, and it happened in one moment, swift and clean. Zoltan wanted to kill us all. The erratic pendulum that was Zoltan's arm stopped swinging. It stopped in front of Pinky.

"Pinky," he said, "you want a ride? Name the place you want to go, and I'll blow you all the way from here to there."

"Jesus, Zoltan, put that thing down. You could do some real damage around here. Like to me." Pinky skittered to the ground and tried to put some old gnarled roots and brush between him and Zoltan.

Pinky's fast dive startled Felix. The parrot burrowed deeper into the safety of the feathers under the hammock, making a brew of eerie sounds that ruptured and overpowered all others. Zoltan stared at Felix, mystified by his actions, forgetting for one moment that he was contemplating another murder.

Felix emerged from under the hammock dancing in chaotic circles. He pecked the fallen raven feathers, pecked their black center. Squawking, crying, screeching, and screaming was the music of his circular dance. He made a nest with insane bird-brain energy. He ruffled his feathers, hopped on one foot, then the other, and offered his familiar phrase—'God Bless You!' Felix was possessed by the danger that surrounded him.

Zoltan had become human flesh hung on the bones of violence. Nothing more. He was spinning inside a whirlpool of rage, of fear and anger, love and loss. And Pinky was his vortex. Zoltan kept the gun trained on his rival.

As always, I felt him before I saw him. Jozef spoke to Zoltan in a quiet voice. I didn't understand the words. I thought fear had made simple language incomprehensible. Then I understood he spoke to him in Romani, strange and powerful. Jozef moved out of that privacy, back into English.

Hummingbird said, "Zoltan, you need to leave what's left of our family whole. You'll do that by putting the gun down."

"Leave the family whole? Pinky is the one who's torn this family apart."

"Pinky is not the one who gifted Jerry with his trip to eternity. Nor did he offer that same ride to Bill."

"You are ridiculous."

Hummingbird touched Zoltan on the shoulder. In the lanterns' soft light, I saw the veins on the back of Hummingbird's hands and the top of his fingers pulse.

"Zoltan, you must put that gun down."

"You've never called me 'Father' or 'Dad.' Why?"

"I have a mother, no father."

Zoltan didn't register surprise or hurt. Nothing. Jozef kept his hands on Zoltan's shoulders, and his hands pulsed their work.

From the litter of chaise lounges scattered around us came a rusty, scraping sound. E. B.'s metal men looked on, bygone sentries of the oracles.

Oscar rose from one of these lounges like a man raised from the dead. The back of his khaki shirt was covered with rust. He held a drink with an umbrella in it.

For one moment the pulsing in Jozef's hand stopped, and his eyes grew wide. He leveled his gaze at Oscar, silently asking him to retreat. No response from Oscar. Jozef refocused his energy to Zoltan.

Oscar strolled into their center with the serenity of a saint lying on nails, a savior walking on water. In front of Oscar stood Zoltan, a man on the verge of murderous mayhem. Oscar met him with the innocence of a child or the fatalistic heart of someone who no longer felt alive or dead. This sight was stranger than the maniac holding a gun or the deranged dancing parrot.

Oscar spoke as if we were having a cocktail party.

"Capri made this drink for me. Just juice. She made me promise."

Oscar stood directly between Zoltan and Pinky.

Oscar took a sip and hoisted his glass in Zoltan's direction. "It's not ridiculous. You're the one who killed Bill."

"What are you talking about?"

"You killing Bill," Oscar said. "I was crazy with grief when I got here. I thought Jerry's mother, when she died, killed my heart. But when Jerry died, I felt it again. It shattered.

"Zoltan, I wandered these apple trees an empty ghost, a man who'd been killed twice. And I saw something weird under that one." Oscar pointed in the direction of the black night.

"I thought I saw the shadow of my madness. A bird man? A bird man with Capri?

"But it wasn't a bird man, just an old man in a weird cape arguing with Capri, trying to scare her."

"Absurd." Zoltan sneered.

"And up comes a regular person. Someone like me who heard

the ruckus, but unlike me he doesn't think he's lost his mind. He tries to calm the other one down, to fix things for Capri. In the middle of my haze I think, *Hey, that normal guy is Bill, and he's trying to be a good guy.*"

"Bill wouldn't know how to do that."

"He can't learn now, Zoltan, because you took a gun, but not that fancy one you're holding now. You fired it at Bill. You blew Bill back into the tree, nailed him there like a crucifixion. He slammed against it with terrible surprise and anguish. You looked at the gun as if you didn't know where it came from, as if it had a life of its own. You cleaned off the handle and tossed it on the ground.

"You walked to the limo, opened the car door, and disappeared into its upholstered womb.

"I stopped hiding and picked up the gun. It was my gun, I remembered giving it to Annie's mom years ago when she had that burglar scare. I never thought about the gun until last night, when I saw it in your hand."

"Bill was a nuisance, a moron besides," Zoltan said. "I told him how to make it all work, how to push Mina into a simple divorce. He was greedy. It kept him from getting Pinky and Mina untangled."

Pinky looked up from where he was lying on the ground. "Hey, that's what I wanted, too—a simple untangled divorce."

Zoltan looked down at him. "You shut up."

Pinky wouldn't. "Zoltan, this is pretty funny when you think about it. You steal my wife, and I'm the one lying on the ground hoping I don't get killed."

Zoltan's eyes took on a fine, brutal edge. "I said shut up."

Pinky did.

Zoltan's attention turned inward once again, a man in a trance. Slowly, Pinky pulled a knife from his boot, hefted it, looked at it as if measuring his life, cocked his arm, and threw it hard at Zoltan. Upon takeoff the knife hit a tree stump, old and rounded, two feet in front of him, a few inches to my side.

A faint sliver of new moon was at our backs, turning us to darkness, and Pinky's effort had been so pitiful that it hadn't disturbed Zoltan's trance. The knife vibrated in the trunk and stopped. I cautiously reached over and pulled it out. A throwing knife, the real thing. Sharp and strong.

When Zoltan was satisfied that Pinky would be quiet, and that he had our full attention, he spoke to all of us, to none of us.

"I just wanted money to take care of the woman I love."

Oscar ignored Zoltan and continued his story. I wished Oscar would shut up. "I wandered," he said, "clutching a bottle of Jack Daniel's like a lifeline."

Zoltan turned the gun on Oscar, squinted, reconsidered, and took aim at Pinky once again.

Oscar played his story out to the end in a monotone key. "It felt like a dream, but it wasn't. This was real—a nasty fact woke me up. The gun I held in my hand was a murder weapon. The lucid part of me realized my prints were all over it.

"I wiped off every square inch of that gun. When I finished, I held it with dried leaves and tossed it under the trailer.

"I drank the Jack Daniel's until it was gone. Until I was gone. I hoped Bill's murder was a bad dream caused by the death of my son. When I woke up, the dream that was real life was worse than any dream my head could invent."

Zoltan's anger rose in his face, and he yelled at the world, a screech that blended with Felix's mad voice. "You shut up, too! Why don't you understand? Bill was a vulture, it was time for the vulture to leave. I opened the sky for him."

Hummingbird took Oscar by the shoulders and pushed him toward me.

"Zoltan," Hummingbird said, "who stays in the world and who flies away—you've lost the ability to make that decision. You have strong magic, not strong enough to deliver death as an invitation to the afterlife."

Zoltan spit on the ground in front of Hummingbird. Several veins in his face looked like they were about to burst.

"You're impudent. I've never handed the power to you. You know nothing of the nature of flight, nothing of the nature of birds, nothing of their power. You see the sky and don't know birds own it. I'll take who I want when I want them. You're not enough to stop me."

Jozef gathered his face in a tight bundle of superb fury, and disappeared—maybe under an old chaise, behind a stand of trees. I didn't see him anymore.

A tempest of wind rushed by my shoulder, a circle of wind licked our feet, kicked up dirt, knocked Oscar's chaise lounge end over end, and stirred the fallen raven feathers into a tempest.

Felix jumped from the raven feathers singing, God Bless You. Standing fierce, he sang it over and over at Zoltan's feet. Felix leapt high, then used his talons to climb the cape's old fabric. In a flurry of feathers and rage, Felix attacked Zoltan's face and eyes. His bright turquoise feathers were splattered with deep red blood.

"God damn bird, get off my face. Get off!" Zoltan flailed his arms, tried to kill the bird, tried to grab it and wring its neck. Zoltan's face was a mass of shredded flesh and shock. The stronger his attempt to rid himself of the bird, the stronger was the bird's attack.

In this blind rage Zoltan squeezed the trigger and screeched Pinky's name.

I rolled over to cover Pinky. The searing heat of pain carved my body. I howled in anger so strong I felt it on an animal level.

This man, this Zoltan, had killed my oldest friend and had injured my family. He wanted to kill us all.

I flung Pinky's knife hard, fast, and true.

The silver blade caught the lanterns' light and glowed orange and green.

It hit its target and shuddered.

This man was dead.

Felix fell exhausted into the pile of raven feathers. His eyes clouded over.

There was quiet so dense as to be diced and eaten. Pain shimmied down my limbs, but my insides were peaceful. I had done the right thing, I would do it again if I had to. Black waltzed toward me and I wanted it.

Fifty-Seven

ozef bending over me, searching my skin, a flashlight in my eyes. I shielded my face.

Jozef said my name in a question. "Annie?"

"Jozef, you entered the bird's body and attacked Zoltan."

"A hallucination. Things like that don't happen."

"Zoltan is your father. I told you to leave this alone. The police would have handled Zoltan."

"You were shot, you're in shock. You killed a man, a man that needed killing."

I closed my eyes. "A woman's work is never done. Please call 911."

He checked my arm. "The bullet tore your skin, but not the bone, it went through the upper fleshy part."

"In one end, out the other. It burns like hell. I'm quite sure I'm dying. Someone call 911."

Jozef asked Oscar to call 911, but to wait five minutes. Oscar ran toward the house. E. B. and Eddie came out of the trailer and helped Pinky up. Not one hair out of place. They honestly must have played Monopoly. What a waste. Pinky wasn't in such great shape. All their faces swam like wavy mirrors above my head.

"Annie," Jozef said, "I need to do something before the authorities get here. You may not want to look."

"I've been shot in the arm, I'm not brain-dead." I struggled to open my eyes. In fact, I did feel brain-dead, and it wasn't half-bad compared to the previous few days.

Jozef looked to Eddie. "Hey," Eddie said, "nothing to worry about. Right now I'm in the house waiting to call Lawless. I can't see anything from there."

Hummingbird walked deliberately to Zoltan. Leaving the knife buried in Zoltan's chest, he took a corner of his own shirt and wiped off my fingerprints, he wiped off Pinky's fingerprints. He placed his hand around the handle of the knife in the position it would have been had he thrown the knife. He left one perfect set of prints. His.

He bent over the man who was his father. Jozef stroked his face, looked at him with sorrow and understanding. He lifted his shoulders and removed the cape. He kissed Zoltan on his forehead.

"Rest easy, old man. The cape is now where it belongs."

Jozef left his father and cradled my head in his arms. I was shivering cold and hot. He was right. Shock. He covered me with the cape.

I kissed his fingertips. "You can't have fingerprints," I said. "You're dead."

"Not anymore."

"They'll think you killed your own father."

"They don't know he's my father. He shot you, I used the knife to protect you. He died. That's the story."

"It works for me."

"You saved my life, I'm certain. Pinky's also. The police can have my fingerprints. I'll deal with them on a case of self-defense. You've been through enough without the police."

"Is Pinky okay?"

"Fine. E. B., will you take Pinky to the bus station? Drive

down the neighbor's property line so Agent Oldsmobile won't see you leave."

E. B. and Pinky said, "Sure" in the same breath.

One more reason for my neighbor the shrink to think I'd lost my mind. Eccentricity was one thing, driving places where there aren't roads was headed straight for psychosis. Maybe he'd offer me discount therapy because we were neighbors. My arm was in some region beyond pain. I imagined a cosmetics counter and smiling women in long blue shirts.

"Annie, where are you?"

"Shopping at Macy's. Estée Lauder. I disappeared because my arm is killing me. Someone call 911."

"We've got that covered."

"Jozef, you saw your own father killed, and I did it, or we did it together. How are you going to handle that?"

"I'm the one who should have taken the bullet. Not you. How do I handle that?"

He ran his fingers across my forehead.

"Zoltan and Pinky both loved my mother. One was as much my father as the other. One's love was twisted, Pinky's was forgiving. That love I understand."

Our old station wagon chugged as close to me as E. B. could manage without laying tire tracks across my chest. What the hell, 911 was already on its way.

Pinky rolled down the passenger window and pointed to the house. "Watch out for the old witch. Mina's not a bad person, just hard to get along with."

"I've noticed that, Pinky."

There was someone in the backseat. Capri.

I was surprised, to say the least. "Pinky?"

"I'm trying to act like a father, a parting gift for Mina. Capri's going to Mexico with me. Maybe I can get her up and running again, good as new. I was always a great bodywork man."

"Pinky, if I could get up, I'd kiss you good-bye."

"No more women." He pointed to the backseat. "This one's going to be a big enough job. Maybe the next kid in this family will be a boy."

Capri waved from the backseat wearing the look of adventure I'd seen on Mina's face earlier.

Pinky lit a small cigar, rolled up the window, and gave E. B. the go-ahead. She must have said something funny. I saw Pinky put his head back and laugh.

A man had just walked away from everything familiar and was headed into the great unknown. My daughter had made him laugh. I must have done something right.

I saw flashing lights. One set belonged to an ambulance, the others were a battalion of cop cars. Saved and thrown to the wolves all at once.

Fifty-Eight

It's hard to imagine that pain so intense doesn't herald on-coming death, but the paramedics cleaned me up, bandaged me, and swore I only had a superficial wound. They offered to take me to the hospital. They also said I could wait until the next day and see my own doctor, who might want to put me on antibiotics.

If I wasn't going to die during the night, I'd just as soon wait until morning and call my doctor. I could die later. They gave me a shot of something that made me loopy. It was great. I forgot about my impending death, and I loved the whole damn world. I even loved Officer Strunk.

Everyone gave him the same story, which was the truth except for who actually threw the knife, but that seemed like a technicality. The real truth was that a man, Zoltan, was killed. A man who would have killed us all, one by one, in an attempt to ease his pain. And then, most likely, he would have turned the gun on himself. I had saved Strunk several body bags.

Eddie confirmed my story, told Strunk about the conversation Jozef and I heard the night before between Bill and Zoltan. Except when Eddie told Strunk he led him to believe he was with me and Jozef—also a witness to the conversation. Another pull on the truth, but considering both parties were dead, it seemed like another technicality. At least to me.

Maybe I was too goofed-up to have an attitude problem, but Strunk liked me that night. "Lady, I don't want one more body at your place unless it's breathing."

I reached over and patted him somewhere or other. "Me either, Lieutenant Detective Alfred Strunk."

"Your neighbor thinks you've gone crazy over here."

"He's a shrink. It's in his best interest to think that."

A look of broad understanding crossed his face. "I didn't know he was a shrink."

He'd pass the gun and the information along to Lawless, who would undoubtedly question me later. I hoped I could keep my story straight.

Strunk closed his notebook and did his routine chest patting to make sure his notebook was really there.

I said, "Would you like to join us for tea?"

Strunk looked puzzled.

Jozef said to him, "The paramedics gave her a painkiller. She's not quite herself."

Strunk stood up and shook his head. "I'm sorry you got hit, but you're real lucky it didn't take you out. We're going to leave you alone now."

"Alfred Strunk?"

"Yes?"

"Can you tell the fed to bug off now? He's getting on my nerves. Obviously, Mr. Marks is not here."

"I'd be glad to tell him to bug off. He may even have inflamed this incident by his constant presence."

Strunk was working himself up for a confrontation. Okay by me. He was out the door, protecting the little lady, and getting rid of the feds. Hooray. Life was looking up. The paramedics shut their bags and prepared to go. I asked them for another shot before they left. They laughed politely and didn't give me one.

Fifty-Nine

I lay on my couch, Jozef's arms wrapped around me large, strong, warm. He brewed me tea that tasted terrible when it first hit my tongue, but it felt good going down. I could feel it to the end of my toes. I closed my eyes and felt a delicious kind of drowsy.

Mina gently touched my knee. I'd forgotten about Mina.

"Are you watching me sleep again?"

"No." She leaned forward with her hands together.

She leaned closer still. "You think Jerry wanted to ruin my life by getting me so much money that I'm going to lie awake worrying about where to hide it all?"

"Is that what you think?"

"For a minute I did. E. B. said he wanted to take care of me, and this was the best way he knew how. She acted all enthusiastic about it, but she's an artist. You now how they blow with any wind that comes along. Also, she'd want to make it easier for me."

"Jerry wanted nothing but good for you. You know that."

"Yeah, you're right. I know that."

"Mina, after you sell the cafe you can retire. No more listening to people's problems."

She looked at me like I was nuts. "You think someone told Picasso. 'Hey, you just sold that *Cock-Eyed Blue Lady* for a pile of dough, also that *Yellow Lady With the Crooked Eyes.* Buddy, you don't have to work one more day!' "

"Of course not."

"Reading people is my art, it's who I am. The day I stop is the day I drop dead."

"Mrs. Liu will be happy you're not retiring."

"Mrs. Liu will have to wait. I'm not quitting, but I need a break. This whole thing has been almost too much, even for me. I'm going to travel."

"Where are you going?"

"Me and Oscar"—I hadn't noticed he was sitting on the other end of the couch two feet away from me—"we're going to look for Jerry Junior. After all, he's our grandkid. He belongs to both of us. Right now he's lost to both of us."

"Oscar?"

"It's true," he said to me, "and I'm pretty sure she didn't talk me into it. We both need peace. We've got to forgive ourselves for pushing Jerry, and we've got to forgive Jerry for being too stubborn to ask for help when he needed it."

Mina's brocade satchel was by her side. "We'll head to San Francisco tonight so I can get some clothes, not much, and we'll get a good early start from the city."

I looked at Oscar. "You're staying at her place in Chinatown?"

"Sure, why not?"

"Nothing."

Mina said, "Besides, I been stuck in one place too long. It's against my blood, I got to look for my roots. They're on the road."

Oscar put his head back and laughed. "You're one hell of a woman, Mina."

"Thanks," she said, "I appreciate that. My self-confidence is at an all-time low. One of my men is wanted by the whole United

States government. Who knew Pinky'd ever get that far? And think of it—the other one is dead, killed by a nutty bird and a Gypsy knife. The road's a good place for me to start over."

Mina wore a small grin, and that grin was pointed in Oscar's direction. It made her look about twenty years old. Oscar was no dummy. He picked up on it right away.

"Don't look at me for a love replacement!"

"I'm not looking at you. I'm not looking at anyone, although I sure liked those Westerns you wrote back in the fifties."

"Yeah?"

Oh boy. Mina'd found the Oscar button.

"You bet I liked them. *Red River Sunset*? That about tore my heart out. All that leaving and country and duty and poverty and wealth. A masterpiece."

Oscar glowed like a new bride. "Not many people understood the depth of that film."

"Imbeciles."

Time to end the love fest. "I hate to be rude, but I've been shot, I want to go to bed, and I don't want to do it while you're in here yakking it up."

Mina said, "Jozef, I think that medicine is wearing off. She's starting to sound like her old self again."

Without one word, Oscar and Mina stood up at the same time. Their rhythms were frighteningly similar.

I said, "Oscar, before you go, do me a favor."

"Anything, sweetheart."

"Check the registration on Mina's limo."

She protested. "That's my car!"

"Oscar, just check the registration in case you get pulled over. If I get a call from Porkswallow, Kansas I'm not bailing you out on a stolen car wrap."

Mina looked at me and patted me on the cheek. "It's good to be careful, but Annie, I could probably buy Porkswallow if I wanted to."

I knew it. That limo was not registered.

She smiled large and sincere. "I'm going to get used to money, I can feel it."

I'd almost gotten rid of them when E. B. ran into the house and gave them both a big hug. She presented Mina with business cards she'd printed on her computer. The card stock was 3-D paper. Electric blue. In black ink the copy read *Madame Mina— Vagabond Mystic of Highways, Laundromats, and Cafes.* There was a large Egyptian eye under the lettering.

Mina took E. B. inside her arms and held her there a good long while. She rocked back and forth with her, she rubbed her back. "Boy, you got your father's art in you, and that's a fact."

E. B. walked Oscar and Mina to the door. Mina told E. B. to stay out of the house tonight.

Mina called to me from the doorway. "Hey, one last piece of advice."

Here we go. "What?"

"When my son stays here with you all night? Lock your door. Nobody's got a right to know your private life. That includes your kids. And please don't kill this son of mine. I'm running out of kids."

An engine turned over and purred.

"Good-bye, Mina. I love you," I whispered to her as she and Oscar sailed away in their all-American Lincoln limo schooner.

Sixty

I did my best getting cleaned up for bed, but movement was a painful thing. I pulled on a clean T-shirt that I'd line-dried. It smelled like home. One foot under the covers, then the other. I fluffed my pillows and lay back. I loved my room, I loved my bed. The spiders had almost completed their artwork in my corners. I even loved them.

Jozef entered, carrying another cup of tea. The steam spiraled its way to the ceiling. The painkiller was wearing off, the first cup of tea was wearing thin. Maybe this would kick in pretty quick. He tossed two gray binders next to me.

"Eureka," he said.

"What's this?"

"One's the will Bill sent you, one is the will Berva gave you."

"Berva didn't give me a will."

"You said when you and Mina waited for the elevator Berva got into a huff and started clearing out her desk. She piled invoices and memos and folders and basic garbage on top of you."

"I was there, I remember."

He waited for it to sink in. Somewhere in the middle of painkiller haze, peace and love for spiders, a dim bulb went on.

"Berva gave us Jerry's new will, it was stashed in that mess," he said. "If the cops had come in, she was covered. So were you. And she doesn't make mistakes—she wanted that will out of the office."

Berva was a wonder. I leafed through the pages. "Have you read these documents?"

"Yes."

"The two wills aren't the same, are they?"

"Not exactly."

"How not exactly?"

He picked the thin one off my lap.

"This is the will Bill sent you. It leaves everything to a so-called charitable organization. Maybe you've heard of it. I never have."

"I'm guessing if it were taken apart, layer by layer, the core would be an organization that funds a charity named Bill Wells."

"That's my guess, too."

I thumbed through the fat one, the one Berva had slipped out of the office by concealing it with paper clips and memo books.

"I'm assuming this does not fund the Bill Wells Foundation."

"It does pretty much the opposite."

"Good for Jerry."

"Annie, here's the bottom line. I think you now have as much money as your movie star friend. So do Mina, Capri, and Jerry Junior."

"Get out of here."

"For starters, Jerry was his own landlord."

"Jerry owned his house, he didn't rent."

"That's what I'm talking about, and his son, if we can find him, owns Jerry's house with Capri. That place is worth about five million, give or take."

"Jesus God."

"No money left to God," he said. He was pretty zippy for a guy who'd just lost his non-identity. "Jerry was also his own land-lord at work."

"Meaning?"

"He owned the building his law offices were in."

"The eighteen-story building on Townsend?"

"The very one."

"No way."

"He owned every floor, and, according to this, the building has a 90 percent occupancy rate. This now belongs to you, Mina, his son, and Capri."

"I'm having a hard time digesting this."

"If Bill were still alive, you'd be his landlord."

"I was about to say I'd evict him, but he's already been evicted in the biggest possible way."

I looked at the will more carefully. What I understood is that we also had a pile of mutual funds and stocks and percentages of businesses that Jerry'd put together. Some of these mutual funds belonged to Oscar now.

"Also, he left Berva enough so she can retire comfortably and hire an attorney on retainer for her son, Rydell, if she wants."

So Berva's actions were not entirely unselfish. By getting that will into the world, Berva was also taking care of herself. I'd need to find an honest lawyer to sort this out. I didn't know where to begin to look.

I closed the cover. "Pretty obvious why Bill wanted to bury this will," I said.

"I can't believe he didn't."

"Bill may have been smart, but he was no match for Berva."

I laughed. I stopped. It hurt to laugh. I smiled as big as I could without letting a guffaw escape.

Forget it, I didn't care if it hurt. I laughed loud and deep. "Jozef, I'm rich!"

"Do you have to lose your mind about it?"

"I guess so!"

Jozef rubbed the bottoms of my feet. "Just think about it. Annie, you can get a new car. An American one. Isn't that great?"

"I like my car."

"You can get new wood for the kitchen floor."

"My feet fit the grooves pretty well."

"What will you do with all that dough?"

"Try to forget I have it. I take that back. I'm getting a new chair to replace Pinky's. I'm sending Tony Tiger and Skiz on a vacation to Hawaii. They won't need as much clothes there. I'm funding The Home for Unknown Street Soldiers in Oregon. And you, you I'm buying a new non-identity. An ironclad one. I like you invisible."

I started laughing all over again, this time keeping it small. Jozef stroked my hair. "Are you still laughing about being rich?"

"No, I'm thinking about Berva and Mina going to the Baptist church. And I'm thinking maybe that was Mina's big rush to get out of town."

My face fell to my chin. "Jesus Christ. She thought the café was bad. Who's going to break the news to Mina about her latest millionaire status?"

Jozef had an *Oh Shit* look on his face.

I said, "She is going to be so pissed off at Jerry it will be unbelievable."

Jozef leaned over and whispered in my ear which turned into a cuddle which turned to a kiss. Jozef and I would sleep together in a bed just like normal people who love the feel of each other.

"Jozef, you and I haven't been alone together. I mean not without a lot of crap going on."

"You think maybe I haven't noticed that?"

"Tonight things change."

"Yes, they do."

I considered his face, his hands, the way his body was strung together. He felt mythic, but there was something else going on. Something close to ordinary.

"Jozef, do you have a life somewhere out there in the world?"

"Many of them."

"I don't want to know about them."

I snuggled into him, smelled him, held the feel of him inside me. Somewhere between painkiller and the tea I felt soft, comfortable, liquid, serene.

"Jozef, what are we going to do with each other?"

"Enjoy each other."

"That's it?"

"Not by a long shot."

We nestled up close under the comforter. Where does one leg begin, the other's leg begin, where do they end? Don't touch my arm. Our skin, a soft and gentle cello's hum.

A voice shouted from the trailer. "Hey! Would you two keep it down! Some people are trying to sleep, or at least not hear you."

E. B. laughed and slammed the trailer window closed.

I looked at Jozef, he'd fallen asleep.

I whisper in his ear, *Death is a lie*.

We curl up side by side and don't wake until first light.

Acknowledgments

FAMILY MATTERS: Thanks to Allegra and Sam, my kids, for teaching me I could love and worry with equal amounts of enthusiasm. You've learned that without craziness, without passion, and without family, life's a pretty flat-line deal. That's a good thing to know. (Pass it on.) I'm glad we chose each other. Also, thanks to beautiful Barbara, my mom, my own personal Madame Mina. Somewhere in that dimension you inhabit, I still see you reading tea leaves and talking to spirits. And I still see men falling all over each other to be near you.

MATTERS OF THE HEART: Thank you, Ann Lasko, dear friend—the woman brave enough to read this book before anyone else, the one who said, "Hooray!" Thanks go to Eric L. Stone, my oldest pal, for teaching me a million words—and also things a lot less useful but more fun and often illegal. Anyway, where else would I have learned words like ferret-warden, humphsnout, and all other words that eschew the dictionary and spark my imagination? Large gratitude to Peter Morin for first dazzling me with the Gypsy music of the open road. So many roads, so much music—all of it good. And thank you, Catherine De Prima, for giving me a place to write and a bed to use when I ran away from my grown-up home. (NOTE: When sleeping in a twin bed with a Rottweiler, do not roll over. They will growl in their sleep, and you will stare at the ceiling until dawn.) Cath, you're a rock. And thanks to Liv Needham MacKay for filling me with stories of her Gypsy heritage, including how many families are shamed by their Gypsy blood. Someday we'll get over this stupidity, right? Your grandma's spirit runs through you fine and rich.

MATTERS OF THE WORLD AND SPIRIT: Thanks to the Gypsy Lore Society for pointing me to books and people; thanks, also, for over a century of good work. To my agent, Susan Gleason, for taking a chance, for being bold enough to laugh big and to think quiet—thank you. And thanks to Bob Gleason, my editor, for getting inside my head and encouraging me to look at the sky, and under the rocks, too. Worlds of appreciation to Tom Doherty at Tor/Forge for his integrity and kind heart. Finally, to Larry and Lucinda Yoder for making me feel like there is a place for me in the world of storytelling—thank you.

Look for Annie Szabo again in

The Vanished Priestess

available October 2004 from Forge Books

$\mathcal{T}$he earth was cool, slightly damp. Spongy-sharp redwood needles squished between my toes, and moonlight spilled down my shoulders. There was a very particular Sonoma full moon that night—perfectly large, deep yellow and round—as if a casaba had made love with a planet and this was their child.

Margo and I sat outside, a bottle of Jack Daniel's between us, deck lights catching the amber and spinning it.

She said, "Annie, you want to split the last corner?"

I said she could finish it off. Margo poured herself a slim line of bourbon while I riffled through the pages of a 140-year-old circus route book detailing the towns and troubles, marriages and affairs of circus artists long gone.

Margo's 21st-century version of the circus was about to open— a phantasm filled with human creatures morphed into beings as primal as uranium punch, with bodies tuned and toned to the max. We talked about her Cirk, both of us busy ignoring my front door lying flat on its back a few feet away.

There was a stretchy silence and then Margo stood, holding onto the edge of the table. She gathered her wobbly dignity. Arms opened wide, she told me to keep the rare route book. Forever if I wanted, she was lightening a life filled with too many possessions. Theatrics. When the Jack wore off, she'd forget the grand gesture.

She leaned across the table, balancing on the edge, nailing me with eyes deep and strange and wise.

"Annie, do you ever think about the big stuff?"

"Not if I can help it."

"You know what I ask myself every day?" The bourbon on her breath blew my skin warm, but her words were a chill. "How much is my life *worth*? How much will I risk to stay alive?"

"Margo, maybe you should sit down."

"Ignore me," Margo smiled, shaking her head. "I've had too much to drink," she said, glancing at the door, freshly decimated by a raving madman in her honor.

Margo laid a sloppy good-bye kiss on my cheek. She wandered up the hill, fumbled with the latch on our mutual gate, and disappeared.

I blew her shadow a kiss, and I blew a soft prayer to the moon, one to ease her bare and beautiful heart.

Detective Lawless pulled into my driveway, his old Suburban packing the moist ground. He parked, thrashed around the back of his truck, tossing junk left and right. He pulled out a dark roll, stuck it under his arm, and found a toolbox.

I searched for a witty hello, but Lawless cut me off. He put his arm around my waist and walked me into the kitchen. My feet were cold. I poured him a cup of coffee, and he went to work filling the empty doorway with visquine and duct tape. I started to protest. He told me to be quiet, and I was.

Madame Mina ambled in and waved a careless hello to Lawless. She was wearing the XXL t-shirt I wear to paint and clean. It had been hanging on a hook near the dryer.

"This is pretty colorful," she said, scrunching her face at the t-shirt. Mina studied my walls, lightly touching the trim, and peered into my living room. "You know something? I've never been dressed like a wall before."

She turned in a circle as if she were standing in front of a mirror at Macy's deciding whether to blow two hundred bucks on a dress.

"Mina," I said, "You're the only woman I know who'd think about clothes when a crazy nut is on the loose."

"Look, you've got a gun, I've got attitude and glamour. Between the two of us, that nut doesn't stand a chance."